MEDDLING KIDS

PAR

A BLYTON SUMMER DETECTIVE CLUB ADVENTURE

MEDDLING KIDS

A Novel by
EDGAR CANTERO

TITAN BOOKS

Print edition ISBN: 9781785658761
E-book edition ISBN: 9781785658778

Published by Titan Books
A division of Titan Publishing Group Ltd
144 Southwark Street, London SE1 0UP

First Titan edition: April 2018
10 9 8 7 6 5 4 3 2

This edition published by arrangement with Doubleday,
a division of Penguin Random House LLC, in 2018.

Additional art by Jordi March

A CIP catalogue record for this title is available from the British Library.

Printed and bound in Great Britain by CPI Group Ltd.

Did you enjoy this book?
We love to hear from our readers. Please email us at
readerfeedback@titanemail.com or write to us at Reader
Feedback at the above address.

To receive advance information, news, competitions, and
exclusive offers online, please sign up for the
Titan newsletter on our website:

TITANBOOKS.COM

the Pennaquick Telegraph

F. 1954 by Stratemeyer Press, Belden   MONDAY, AUGUST 29TH 1977   15¢ Belden and suburbs, 25¢ elsewhere

The weather Cloudy in the afternoon, maximums drop to 60's. Storm system and strong sea winds arrive in the next days.

TEEN SLEUTHS UNMASK SLEEPY LAKE MONSTER

Unofficial Investigation Ends In Dramatic Showdown at Deboën Mansion

---

Blyton Hills Heroes Expose Local Legend, Uncover Criminal Plot

USAF Capt. Al Urich (left) and Deputy Sheriff W. Wilson (right) flank the members of the "Blyton Summer Detective Club:" Peter Manner (13), Kerri Hollis (12), Andrea "Andy" Rodriguez (12), Nate Rogers (11) and dog Sean, guarding their astounding catch: the "Sleepy Lake monster." (Photo by J. March.)

Haunting debunked: Deboën Mansion, built on a small islet on Sleepy Lake in the Gold Rush years, has been shunned by townsfolk since the 1940s.

Nancy Hardy Blyton Hills

The reign of terror of the 'Sleepy Lake Creature' –the elusive figure that has been scaring herdsmen and campers in the upper Zoinx River area– was put to an end last week-end by some unlike-

ly actors, namely, four children and a dog.

Peter Manner (13), Kerri Hollis (12), Andrea 'Andy' Rodriguez (12), and Nate Rogers (11), along with their hunting dog Sean, are credited with the capture of Thomas X. Wickley, from

California, who was recreating the creature legend as part of a convoluted scheme for burglary at the historic Deboën Mansion.

A LEGEND REKINDLED

It is not the first time that the so-called "Blyton Summer Detective Club" delves into a case that has local authorities baffled. As habitual vacationers in Blyton Hills, the kids are so well-known in the neighborhood as is their proclivity to run into crazy adventures—which often culminate in the arrest of evil-doers!

Recent reports of a "monster" prowling around Sleepy Lake were this summer's topic of conversation in town. Tales of lake creatures are as old as they are typical of any large water mass, according to Deputy Sheriff W.

▶ **Wanted drifter Thomas Wickley to be charged with attempted burglary:** "I would have gotten away with it too, if it weren't for you meddling kids!"

FULL STORY ON PAGE 2

t starts when you pull the lamp chain and light doesn't come. Then you know you will never wake up in time, you will not make it to the end of this paragraph alive. Desperate reassuring thoughts try to rise over the panic in your head: it's okay, you don't need lights, you are practically awake already. You are lying on your bed, you can guess the familiar shape of the side lamp in the morning twilight and hear the old radiator clunking in the night; you are safe. It's just that the lamp doesn't work. But you want it to work; you need to dispel the darkness and let certainty outline the room so the things outside know you're awake and won't dare enter, and you pull the chain again and again, and you recall the lamp switch has failed before (has it?), and look, the lightbulb really is trying, though it barely manages to seep a wan glow, and it's not enough to flash the room out of the shadows, but who needs more, the lamp says, you're here, this is your room, I am your lamp, that's your radiator going *clunk* in the night, that's the same old closed door beyond which things might lurk and breathe skinless and eyeless, but you can rest, we promise we don't exist really, lie down. Or are you lying down? Because you think you're up on your elbows, but your arms aren't feeling the weight now that you focus on them; in fact, your eyeballs are not moving, and then you try to say "hey" but your throat isn't responding either, so you cling to the sheets (Do you? Are your fingernails truly scratching the linen?) and you struggle to emit a sound, make your vocal cords vibrate, push some air through your windpipe, just feel your fucking windpipe, for God's sake, shout and wake up the slumbering blob that is you on your bed, sleeping, dreaming, at the mercy of drooling things outside the closed door, and you pull pull pull pull pull the chain and the lamp insists, I can't, it's a technical fault, but I promise you you're awake, look at me, I'm your good old lamp, I've never lied to you, the chain has failed before, you know this, you should install a real switch you can snap on and off, and that's when you realize your bedside lamp never had a chain. Furthermore, there's no radiator in the room that can go *clunk*. It's their footsteps *(clunk),* and the door is already open—try to shout—they're in your room—try to shout—they're creeping up your bed *(clunk),* stretching toward you *(clunk),* squamous ice-cold webbed fingers aiming for your spine—try to SHOUT!

Her own scream woke her up. It probably woke the whole block, really. She could still hear it resonating in the shoebox width of the room while her racing heart geared down from sprint to marathon and senses swept her surroundings, checking up on reality (of course this is your room, you dimwit, look at how cold and smelly and dampened by bureaucratic rain-pattering and faraway sirens it is). It had not been a bad scream, Kerri judged by the echoes of it. Not so much an *eeek, a mouse* kind of shrill as a strong, hard-boiled *holy mother of fuck.*

Tim's grave, silent stare seemed to confirm it: On really bad nights she would wake up to the dog on the bed, barking away the nightmares. Today he was just sitting by, eyes level and fixed on her, an *At ease, soldier* expression on his face.

She sat up in her unheated room, lit by the TV static sky, and touched the ice-cold window glass. Real sensations, all of them. She wondered how dreams managed to deceive her every time; they were so blatantly dreams in retrospect, the fake stimuli so dim and shallow. She caressed Tim's head: his short fur, his wet nose, his whiskers. It was all too complex to be fabricated.

"How do you stay sane, Tim?" she asked him.

Tim whimpered, olivertwisting his pale blue eyes.

Kerri gave him a flirt-acknowledging smirk and allowed him to hop inside the spartan cast-iron-framed bed. She sat against the wall, flipped through the dozen books on the solitary shelf, opened one paperback, and retrieved the newspaper clip.

The teen sleuths grinned back at her across thirteen years, from the sunny grayscale shores of Sleepy Lake, 1977.

* * *

"Do you still see them?" asked the shrink.

Nate, crash-landed on the armchair opposite, threw back a dehydrated stare.

"Your friends, I mean," Dr. Willett clarified. "Are you still in contact with them?"

Nate took a drag of his cigarette clutched between Band-Aid-wrapped fingertips, stalling for the end of the session.

"My cousin Kerri calls from time to time. She went to study biology in New York, and she stayed there. I see her once or twice a year. Her mom still breeds Weimaraners back in Portland.

"Andy just left. At sixteen or so, she threw a backpack over her shoulder, left home, and jumped on a train to . . . I don't know, find herself or whatever. She was always the complex one. I think she calls Kerri sometimes, or sends her postcards.

"Peter was the golden boy. He stayed in California to finish high school; he planned to attend the Air Force Academy, follow Captain Al's steps . . . and then at sixteen he got discovered by a casting agent. He did movies, became a big star."

He snorted, put out the cigarette, and dropped the tone of his voice.

"Then he overdosed on pills and died in a hotel room in L.A."

In another city in another state, Kerri stroked the pulp-quality paper on which the *Pennaquick Telegraph* was printed, its pores, the jagged edges of the page. Real sensations, like this cold room and the coarse army blanket and Tim's ears brushing her thighs. This did happen. This piece of paper says it. "Teen Sleuths Unmask Sleepy Lake Monster." "Uncover Criminal Plot." "Haunting Debunked." We did it.

"Do you miss them?" Dr. Willett prompted.

Nate gazed at the window. It was March, but still winter. That's what the last thirteen years had been: a very long winter.

"Nah," he said. "We were kids. Childhood friends don't last forever. I mean, who holds on to the past for that long?"

Thomas X. Wickley's own thirteen-year-old copy of the *Pennaquick Telegraph*, stained with blood and urine, burned inside his breast pocket during the parole hearing.

"You were charged with fraud, attempted burglary, kidnapping, and child endangerment. And you pleaded guilty to all four. Is that correct?"

"Yes, it is."

Thirteen years.

"Now, you know kidnapping is the most serious of these charges. And yet it's also the one for which you could have more easily pleaded innocence. You were aware that this crime in itself, kidnapping a minor, added ten years to your sentence?"

Thirteen fucking years.

"I was," he answered.

His hands on the table didn't even shudder at the number. They stayed still and gnarled like ancient trees, mumbling in grumpy voices, *Thirteen years, you say, boy? That's nothing!*

It was true. He never had any plans for those thirteen years anyway. Not since things went awry in Blyton Hills.

"Mr. Wickley? I was asking, would you mind retelling for us the circumstances of that charge?"

"Not at all," he said, in the tone both weary and secretly glad to be asked of every old man who has a chance to tell a story, no matter how embarrassing. "My . . . perceived rivals at the time were teenagers. Children. During that night at the house on the lake, they split up to cover more ground. I saw the chance to seize one and I did. She'd accidentally fallen through a trapdoor and I found her in the basement. I gagged her and tied her up. I didn't even consider she was only a little girl. I was blinded by greed. I am no danger to those children anymore. I don't hate children."

He stopped well before being carried away into saying he liked children. Words must be picked carefully in a parole hearing.

"You are aware, of course," the commissioner said, "that those kids are no longer children."

They giggled. The kids in the picture did, with their shiny hair and bucktoothed smiles. He heard them through the breast pocket of his orange jumpsuit.

He scoffed out of the gaffe: "I am sure I am not a danger to them, whatever their age."

It burned him. The newspaper was scorching through his breast pocket.

"They were doing the right thing," he said. "They weren't meddling. They were the good guys."

The commissioner leaned back in his chair just as the quietest, meanest member of the board saw it fit to intervene. "Still, the circumstances are aggravating. Here you are, doing fifteen years on account of being captured by four teenagers."

"And a dog," Wickley added.

"Yes, and a dog. That must have been a blow to your ego. You had problems with other inmates because of it. Some resentment would be altogether reasonable."

Wickley looked down at his hands again, admired them upon finding them perfectly calm. Dry and undaunted, like tree trunks in the gentle breeze that carried the giggles of four teenagers. And a dog.

"What we mean to say is that there was, so to speak, some insult added to injury in the way you were apprehended. Actually, the word in the police report is 'snared,'" the commissioner read. "By means of a contraption involving . . . 'a high-speeding serving cart, two flights of stairs, and a fishing net'?"

Wickley watched him frown, briefly striving to pry an image out of the type, while the giggling in his own breast pocket grew into a television laughtrack.

"So, whatever—what we mean to say," the man resumed, "is that some extra concern about you taking revenge is not unjustified."

The prisoner drove his right hand to his heart. Violently. Slapping the picture silent.

"Gentlemen. I staged a haunting in an old mansion and dressed myself as a giant salamander to scare people away. I was captured by four teenagers and a Weimaraner. And I am sixty. Do you seriously believe I pose a threat to anyone?"

The board members chortled. The commissioner started putting away his papers.

Five days and nineteen hours later, he made parole.

The riveted iron doors opened the following Monday and sun shone on Wickley's arid face, on the sentinel turrets, on a reservoir-sized puddle on the cobblestone road.

He put his box of belongings at his feet, took out the crumpled pack of Raleighs and lit one with the second-to-last match from his Sambo's giveaway matchbook. The first drag tasted rancid, and yet periorgasmically good. The legendary afterjail cigarette.

Smoke curled away in the sun like a flower out of the animated film *Yellow Submarine*.

He unfolded the newspaper page he'd transferred from his orange jumpsuit to his civilian jacket pocket, next to a movie ticket stub for *The Eiger Sanction*. The grinning children in the picture met sunlight again.

The names in the second paragraph were highlighted in faded yellow: Peter Manner, Kerri Hollis, Andrea "Andy" Rodriguez, Nate Rogers, Sean. Peter Manner's name was struck out in pen. That had been a recent addition; he'd overheard the news in the library two years ago. "Peter Manner, the kid in that flick with Lisa Bonet, he OD'd," some convict had said, followed by the usual condescending platitudes on the rough lives of child stars and whatever. If bad fortune had struck out the other three names too, their deaths never made it to the prison grapevine. Not everyone stars in a Christmas blockbuster movie after all. The dog would most likely be a strike-out too, but lacking any official confirmation, Wickley would rather wait.

He further browsed the box for his father's wristwatch and strapped it on. He was due to check in with his parole officer in two hours.

He picked up his box and crossed the street to a nearby pub.

They'd changed the label of his favorite beer. Also that of Coca-Cola bottles, the red background now shattered in the furiously sharp-angled pattern of the new decade. Two men by the window table were talking baseball, and Wickley, sitting at the bar, didn't recognize a single name. He was going to light himself another cigarette when the barman approached and said, "Sir, you can't smoke in here."

He stared at the guy's afterimage for a while before he tipped the cigarette back into the package and continued drinking. At least he'd called him "sir."

The *Pennaquick Telegraph* clip lay unfolded on the counter while he enjoyed his beer. The verb is not an overstatement—he was really enjoying it. Now and then he side-glanced at the picture for no reason in particular. Perhaps because it was one of the few familiar things he could turn to: the panting dog, the smiling children. Even the dead one was smiling. Christ, even the deputy sheriff was smiling. The only one not smiling in that photo was him.

He glanced at the mirror across the counter. The old man there looked remarkably weary for someone who had spent thirteen years shelved in a cold, dry place, but not thirteen years older than the one in the newspaper. He had been blessed with one of those faces that age rapidly through the first three decades, but later remain relatively unchanged throughout adulthood. He continued not to smile now, but he somehow looked better than the detainee in the picture. Having lost the salamander costume helped.

The highlighted names stared up at the ceiling fan. He looked down at his hands and gnarled fingers slumbering on the counter, as unfazed as they were during the interview. They really didn't give a damn.

He stayed on his stool, drinking in little sips, listening to a new but not bad song playing on the radio. One of the men by the window loudly rejected the idea of a player Wickley had never heard of being a better pitcher than one he remembered perfectly well.

Delicately, Wickley grabbed the newspaper clip, held it up, crumpled it into his hand, lit the last match in the book and burned it. The barman grunted at this act of arson not covered by the nonsmoking sign.

Wickley sprinkled the ashes on the floor and left for the restroom.

Life out of prison is full of easily overlooked luxuries, such as using a public urinal without having to check your back. He smiled at that adage as it shaped in his mind, and took pleasure in reading the ageless poetry scribbled on the tiles and trying to aim at the little pink spongey cube near the drain.

Thirteen goddamn years.

He was free.

Without the warning of a toilet flush, the door to the stall behind him slammed open.

"Good morning, Mr. Wickley."

He knew then, by the sudden suspension of all lower bodily functions, that his subconscious mind had recognized the voice. Even thirteen years and a puberty later.

He spun on his feet and corrected his visual line upward and choked at the face of the bully confronting him—the dark-browed figure filling and brimming over the ghostly contour of a smiling memory.

"Andrea 'Andy' Rodriguez!" he blurted out.

The woman blew a bang of black hair off her face. "Andy. My name's Andy."

"I am not allowed to talk to you," he protested. "I just got outta jail."

"Really? Me too," she said, checking her freebie Coca-Cola digital watch. "They must have noticed by now."

He tried to sidestep her; she blocked his way. Wickley quivered, his fortitude crumbling at the sight of his own hands surrendering to shakes.

"I did my time!" he whimpered. "I paid my debt to society!"

"Hell yeah, you paid it, and with interest. Explain that to me. Thirteen years in a high-security prison with no visitors, for what? For putting on a costume and chasing kids around a tumbledown house? Are you kidding me?"

"I kidnapped one of you."

"Please."

"I staged a haunting. I made an elaborate scheme for fraud."

"You are the fraud, Wickley. You're nothing but a careless gold digger. You want me to believe you went to all that trouble just to scare people? The mystic symbols? The dead animals?"

"They were props."

"The hanged corpses? The things in the basement?!"

"All props."

"Steven fucking Spielberg could not have made props like that and you know it! It wasn't you!"

"It was! And I would've gotten away with it too, if it weren't for you med—"

"Liar!" She clutched his neck and shoved him into the wall, shattering some tiles with the back of his head.

One of the baseball talkers entered the restroom at that moment and stopped dead at the sight.

On the left, standing, Andrea "Andy" Rodriguez, 25, in big military boots and a white tank top, turns to camera as she lifts a squirming old man two inches off the floor.

"Fuck off," she growled, and the intruder obediently retreated.

Wickley was gagging, writhing, kicking the air. Andy turned back to him, face slashed by the obstinate bang of hair, a furious and not fully devoid of self-satisfaction smile in her lips.

"I was twelve years old in 'seventy-seven and I beat you; now I'm twenty-five and you're old and weak; just imagine the ways in which I can humiliate you. Tell me, why did you confess?"

"I did it."

"Bullshit. Why did you take the blame?"

"I did it. I made my costume out of a diving suit. It was a good costume."

"No, it wasn't, really."

"I set everything up. I made the lights fade and the house shake."

"No, you fucking didn't!" *(She slams him to the wall.)*

"I did, and you were terrified. *(Sniggering in pain.)* You pissed your pants."

"That was Nate, not me! And it wasn't you! *(Her grip hardens, closing shut his windpipe.)* Why did you take the fall?"

"Ack! G-g-g—"

"Tell me or I swear I'll throw you in my trunk, drive to Blyton Hills, and dump my car into Sleepy Lake!"

"Ng . . . ng . . ."

"Why?"

"Ng'ngah . . . ng'ngah'hai!"

"WHY?!"

"Iä fhtagn Thtaggoa! Iä mwlgn nekrosunai! Ng'ngah'hai, zhro!"

Andy banged him against the wall and released her grip, gaping at the echo of the odious words that had made the hair on her arms stand and the sun dim, shocked by the blasphemy.

Slowly daylight returned, and a silence punctuated by dripping water pipes. The old man slid to the floor, leaving a little smear of blood from the back of his skull along the way.

"I wanted to go to jail," he moaned, panting, clinging to consciousness.

Andy stood, full of hate, fists clenched, adrenaline trickling down her temples.

"I wanted them to lock me away," Wickley sobbed. "I had to get away from that place. I can't go back. I don't want to go to that devil house ever again! Never!"

And he sank his head in his palms and broke into tears. Sitting on the floor in a public restroom, crying grown-up sobs.

Andy snorted back the fury, panting, and flushed the urinal for him.

"You won't. Good-bye, Mr. Wickley."

And she stormed out, feeling not the least sorry for the pathetic old man left crying on the floor. Because he was right: he would never have to go back to that house.

Lucky bastard.

PART ONE

REUNION

She flung the door open to clamorous nonreaction, silhouetted down to a bulky jacket and a baseball cap, the blue wind blowing away the title card. Dramatically opening doors was one of Andy's few natural talents, one she had perfected in the last thirteen years while roaming over the country. She could push or pull or even slide a door open and either go entirely unnoticed or make all heads turn and music stop, at her will. She even succeeded in causing the latter effect in a concert hall, during a Van Halen gig. It's all in the wrist, really.

This time she'd gone for incognito: the country singer continued to wail in the jukebox, the beer-drinkers didn't sense her, a couple of pool players hardly glanced in the direction of the EXIT sign in the second it took her to canvass the place. She had to step forward—*Insert close-up shot of military surplus boots abusing the floorboards*—to locate the person she'd come to fetch behind the counter, blocked by a group of cough-a-chuckling workmen.

In profile, Kerri Hollis, 25, bends over to retrieve two beers from the icebox while mindfully ignoring the appreciative growl the workmen address at her posterior, where the orange lavafall of her hair ends.

And here the country music faded out a little, at least in Andy's ears, triggered only by this: Kerri turning to serve the beers, her curls swinging around and cheering gleefully like kids on a carousel. It was a minor entry in the list of Kerri's innumerable talents. Her hair had this joyful quality about it, in the way it trailed after her as she rode her bike downhill or dove off a rope swing. Andy used to admire it even when they were kids; it had already reached the border between her back and the end of her back back then, though it needn't be too long for that, and it breathed and moved like it had a life of its own, or many. Andy used to imagine each individual strand with tiny cartoon eyes and a perennial *kawaii* smile, happy to participate in Kerri's adventures, to witness every moment in the life of that promising child. When she stood in the rain, her hair welcomed the water. When it was sunny outside, it kited behind her as she ran, sparkling, greedily storing up solar energy like it planned to run a plane factory. When she sat down and read a book, which she did more often than any child and most grown-ups Andy had met, you could see her hair glowing with stored sunlight, humming quietly, shushing strangers. When they last saw each other five years ago at Kerri's university, she had bound her hair in a ponytail while they toured the campus. She released it only briefly in the cafeteria, and Andy could have sworn she heard a collective gasp as she shook it loose. Those must have been four tough years for her hair. Now it was free at last, and Andy heard its happy song even through the depressing country music and the orcish grunts of the ape-men surrounding her.

It took another minute for Andy to notice a second novelty: Kerri wasn't wearing her glasses. That was strange. Merriment and catastrophe ensued whenever Kerri lost her glasses during an adventure. She used to be defenseless without them. Now, however, she looked ready to battle.

She looked like she was halfway through the battle, actually. And losing.

Andy watched her in the mirror behind the bar, talking to the last man in the pack. "And for you?"

"I'll have a beer too."

A silence like a tropical cyclone formed above them, Kerri glaring at the guy with glasses-less, hateful eyes.

She turned and bent back down to the icebox, and the ogling and sneering through munched cigars resumed: "Oh yeah" . . . "There you go" . . . "That's what I'm talking about."

Andy claimed a stool at the other end of the bar, head low, left hand toying with the charm she carried in her pocket. Discreet as her entrances could be, she often had trouble keeping a low profile for too long, especially in crowded places. To counter this, she used this security blanket of sorts.

A second, completely unnoticed bartender materialized from the shadows, slapping Andy's claimed acre of counter with a cloth. "Name your poison."

"Coke."

"Coke?"

"Make it Diet."

The bartender left, an unfocused mustached blur.

"How about something to eat," one of the men croaked at Kerri.

Kerri's reflection stood in the mirror, dirty rag over her shoulder, arms akimbo, orange hair hushing expectantly. "What would you like, Jesse?"

"I don't know," said the alpha male. "Something hot." The pack punctuated the jape with a timely snigger.

Don't engage, Andy attempted to telepath forward.

"Some hot wings?"

"That'd be nice."

"Any sauce?"

"More than you can swallow, honey."

The gang laughed with fat, bearded, smug-faced laughter. Andy risked a side glance at Kerri's face. She was holding her stance, unfazed, hatred steadily growing toward a boiling point.

"You're revolting, Jesse."

Something, probably the nondescript bartender, went *hey.*

Andy squeezed the last drops of magic out of the charm in her pocket. The country singer continued to babble his own notion of romanticism like an idiot.

"I'll check the kitchen," Kerri said, departing for the door. A man leaned over the counter as she retreated.

"Some well-buttered buns would be nice too!" he said, and the comment was celebrated with mirth.

"Good one, Neil."

"You know, because 'buns' as in 'ass,' right?"

"Yeah, gotcha. Clever."

"Excuse me."

The whole pack turned.

Andy had stolen the five yards from her stool and was now standing in front of the gang, her jacket left behind, folded neatly on the bar next to her Diet Coke. She flipped her cap aside to show her face. Mm-hmmed comments of sexual appreciation were quickly mitigated by squinting eyes and rising eyebrows—the usual mixed feelings a five-foot-six brown-skinned woman with boots and an attitude tends to stir.

The alpha male, previously identified as Jesse, took the lead. "Yes, how can we help you, miss?"

"Well, um . . ." Andy's hands moved nervously, her eyes searching for the right words somewhere on the floor. "Uh, God, I'm sorry; this is awkward . . ."

"Not at all," he said with a smile of many-colored teeth.

"The thing is, I am legally obligated to respectfully ask you to stop behaving like inbred dicks before I go on to beat the shit out of you."

Silence. The kind upon which comedians would shoot themselves onstage.

"Are you now?" Alpha calmly said, his surprise concealed behind his Ray-Bans.

"Yes, well, you see, because I've had military training, and lots of experience gathered here and there, I've become so proficient in battle that on one occasion, after a brawl in a bikers' joint in Sturgis, South Dakota, a judge dictated that I should not engage in a fight without giving a fair warning. In particular, my nut kicks are astoundingly accurate." She waited for some feedback from the other side, then chose to continue. "Because, you know, when you get kicked in the balls, as I imagine you know from personal experience, your ballsack just gets squashed into your pelvis. Soft tissue and your clothes absorb most of the impact while the testes themselves are pushed to safety. Because testicles are some slippery little rascals," she said, pulling her left hand out of her pocket and showing her lucky charm to the rest of the class. The men stared blankly at what very unambiguously looked like a plastic penguin.

"See, if you examine your scrotum," Andy went on, "you'll notice you are able to locate the nut, but if you try to pinch it, which is kind of painful ... *(She roughly squeezes the toy, making it squeak, and the lower half of the penguin bloat-pops out of her fist.)* ... it always squirms out of your grip."

"Yes, mine do that," one of the men said, wildly interested.

"Yeah, right? But here's the thing: my nut-cracking kicks are literally nut cracking. The testes cannot escape the impact. At least one of them always bursts open, and sperm pours into your bloodstream and it's a disaster area all over your netherlands. And you'll never get that teste back, so your reproductive ability is lowered fifty percent for life. Not to mention it reportedly hurts like giving birth to a sea urchin through your pee hole. But I wouldn't know that, of course."

Alpha had been rubbing the bridge of his nose for a full minute already. "Sorry, I'm missing the plot; your initial point was ... ?"

"Yeah, my bad, I get carried away. My point was, seeing

how you guys were harassing that waitress and being very vulgar, I wondered if you could stop behaving like . . . well, *being* inbred dicks."

She paused, and then finished with a candid appeal:

"Just give me an excuse to thrash you."

Alpha sighed, faking discontent. She stood still, chest and crossed arms swaying gently with her breath, full lips shut tight, repressing the joyful anticipation while she mentally captioned the whole gang. First row, sitting down, Alpha, six-four, black-and-red leathers, Ray-Ban aviators; second row right, Beta, six-two, jackknife under the belt; left, Gamma, six-foot, broken nose, pool cue; in the back, Delta, five-nine, grabbing a beer bottle.

"You see, sugar," Alpha began, raising a slow, ominous hand toward Andy's cheek. "I would love to fulfill your request."

His fingertips stretched dangerously close to Andy's skin.

"But you forgot to say the magic word."

Atoms away now.

"Which is . . ."

Any passerby to the conversation would have mistakenly concluded that the magic word was "CRUNCH." For that was the incredibly loud sound Alpha's fingers made when Andy pulled them apart by five inches, measured from the ends of the middle and ring, virtually disabling those extremities for any purpose other than effusively greeting Vulcans.

Alpha attempted a hopeless slap in midscream with his left hand that she easily blocked with her forearm, and she was already driving energy to her right leg to launch the much-hyped semicastrating kick when the rest of the thugs forced her to abort.

Beta charged, making her lose her step, and threw a punch at her face. She dodged it, kicked him in the knee, and, as he bent in pain, grabbed him by the parts of the human skull most resembling an ergonomic handle and smashed his head against the counter, making room for Gamma to attack.

Except this one swung a pool cue, which she didn't dare block. Instead she rolled to the floor, waited for the cue to swing back, and dodged it again, letting a chair slow it down, then grabbed it by that end, snatched it out of Gamma's hands, and swung it all the long way around back to him. That gave Gamma time to duck himself. Not Alpha, though: the cue whacked him as he was tending his dislodged fingers, whiplashing head spraying spittle as far as the mirror.

Delta managed to do nothing before Andy stepped forward and bashed his head with the pool cue. Because you can't just wait for every bad guy to come at you.

She moved toward the pool table as Gamma retreated and grabbed a new cue by the midsection. The healthy ratio of broken bones per second fell for a minute while he swung the cue in midair, windmill style like the purple-masked Ninja Turtle. The improvised staff whooshed loudly through the tobaccosphere of the room like a gigantic hornet from outer space.

Andy stood through the demonstration, a skeptical Little John look messing up the angle of her perfect frown.

"That's not how you grab a pool cue."

She grabbed hers properly, point forward, and Gamma wasn't able to block before she jabbed his sternum, pushing him off his stance. A side hit to the temple put him on the ground.

Beta and Delta were ready for battle again when she jammed the cue in one of the table pockets and snapped it in two. She took the resulting clubs and went on to do her own exhibition of audacious stick-wielding.

Delta stayed put, clearly impressed at this point. Beta took avail of his position behind her to whip out a jackknife and charge. Sadly his warcry, inspired by the Hong Kong movie overtones the fight was taking, betrayed his strategic advantage.

Andy spun on one foot: right club straight to hit the blade-carrying arm, left club to the inside of his elbow, right to the torso, left to the temple, right to the face of Delta joining in from behind, left heel to Beta's shin, right to Delta's crotch, and simultaneous strikes with both clubs on two different heads, in time to face the enraged Alpha charging like a mad buffalo and throw both clubs away and at last fling up her left foot.

The music stopped. And conversations ceased. Among dogs. In a two-mile radius. Their ears pricked up at the piercing ultrasonic howl coming from a small bar far away.

Alpha dropped to his knees, then to all fours, finally down into the fetal position, his hands cordoning off the devastated area.

"Andy?"

Andy turned on her feet, fists raised, and that's how Kerri saw her for the first time in five years.

That wasn't the plan. Andy swiftly blew the bang of hair off her face and smoothed her top. "Hey."

Kerri came hopping over the counter to hug her, ignoring the nondescript mustached blur of a bartender (and possible employer) offering his unsolicited opinion about the whole mess.

The last thing Andy ever remembered from that scene was being smothered in happy, cheering orange hair, pouring over her own shoulders like streaming confetti, mind overwhelmed by the mob of excited questions, taut muscles caught in the unexpected embrace. And the red cells inside her body, still drunk with adrenaline, gazed up in awe, dented shields and blood-dripping axes in their little hands, wondering where in the world did all this peace come from.

Then there was some heated dialogue between Kerri and the nondescript bartender, among threats to call the cops and the whimpering of neutered thugs crawling on the floor, and Andy later recalled hearing Kerri say "fuck this job" somewhere in the background and yank off her apron and throw it at her ex-boss's blurry face, but all those bits were blurry themselves.

Next time she checked her surroundings, they were in another, louder bar having shots and peanuts, and Kerri wore a black-sleeved raglan shirt and smiled the loudest girl-smile ever.

"God, you were awesome!" she said. "I've been playing out violent scenarios with Jesse in my mind for months, and you just improvised that? It was so much better than anything I'd come up with!" She finished off a drink, then her grin narrowed into a proud smirk. "Girl, you've grown to your full potential. You're everything I wanted to be."

"Shut up," Andy whispered, trying to hide behind the very tiny glass. It was becoming a night full of experiences she wasn't used to. Alcohol. Praise.

Kerri signaled for another two shots in a gesture that seemed too vague and aimless to be of any consequence, but proved effective in under five seconds.

"So, apart from cleaning up the gene pool one asshole at a time, what are you up to?"

Andy shifted in her seat. "Well, not much. I hitchhiked for a while after I saw you at your alma mater. Took some jobs. What about you? I thought you'd be a biologist by now."

"I am," Kerri said. "We're allowed to take off our lab coats on the Sabbath." She waited for a reaction, then clarified. "Kidding. But I am a biologist; I got my BA two years ago. Not too glossy grades—the place where I did the internship sucked. And I had a falling-out with this guy who was supposed to tutor me during my senior year. You know, we were keeping it professional, but then we met at this crazy afterparty and we slept together, but we agreed it was nothing serious, so I slept with other guys, and he said it was okay, but then it wasn't, and you know . . . Old story, right?"

Andy debated between saying "right" or just shrugging, and did neither.

"So you're not doing any biology work now."

"Well, no, not at the moment. I applied for some PhD programs, but I wasn't lucky, and that bastard would not even give me a fake recommendation. And my GRE wasn't dazzling either because ... well, I can't even remember taking it. So, anyway, I'm taking some time to put my shit together now. You know, 'cause a biologist's got to eat. But soon I'll start applying to colleges again, show my résumé around, get back on track."

She idly inspected the half-full glass in her hand.

"Any time now."

And she gulped down the rest of the drink.

The second place was fuller, dirtier, and louder, but Andy hardly gave any attention to these circumstances, except for the time Kerri tried to pull her onto the dance floor and she refused and stayed on the sofa, pretending to enjoy a rum and Coke while watching Kerri bounce and shake to Zulu electronica, orange hair splashing around like a Hawaiian volcano. And every time a guy approached her and spoke inaudible words at her, Andy would stiff her back up for a second, trying to mentally push the message in his direction: *That's Dr. Kerri to you, and no, she doesn't want anything.*

Then they sat together again and continued talking, and Kerri's white laughter glowed under the UV lights.

"That was Mr. Magnus!" she went. "He was stealing his own boats for insurance fraud! Who would ever suspect him?"

"No, the boats were spring of 'seventy-seven!" Andy insisted. "Captain Al took us scuba diving in Crab Cove! The time we went kayaking it was about the sheep-smuggling case."

Kerri contemplated the memory. "Shit, you're right! The werewolf and his sheep-smuggling network!"

"Can you believe we were scared of that guy?"

"God, the lowlifes we've encountered. Who the fuck smuggles sheep?"

"No one now. They know better since we busted them."

"Seriously, we made the crime rate around Blyton Hills drop like ninety percent. Pity we didn't spend summer here in New York; the Bronx would look like Sesame Street by now."

They waited for laughter to remit, and Andy considered it convenient to force another sip of rum into her body, bite her lip, and bring up another file.

"Deboën Mansion and the Sleepy Lake monster."

"Our last case," Kerri said, after a quasi-unnoticeable pause. "God, someone should compile a casebook with all of these. 'The Archives of the Blyton Summer Detective Club.' Kids might like it."

"You never would've read it," Andy scoffed. "And by the way, what happened to you? Little Miss Not Ready to Confront the Sheep-Smuggling Werewolf Yet, Let's Spend Another Week in the Library? And now you take over a dance floor all by yourself? And what happened to your glasses?"

"Okay, okay," Kerri placated her, resting a brown suede boot on the seat opposite as she leaned back and articulated her defense. "One, contact lenses. And two . . . Well, college changed me."

"But college was supposed to be a bookworm paradise!"

"God, you beautiful naive thing." She drank, with Andy rendered helpless by that line. Then she added, slapping her knee, "What can I say? I changed."

"We all did," Andy agreed.

For a minute, silence somehow nudged itself into the deafening dance beat.

"I should have called you after Peter," Andy said.

Kerri took a very obvious pause this time. Then she raised the bottle. "Fuck it. World's for the living."

And she finished off her drink, while Andy struggled to find meaning in that abstruse carpe diem.

The third place they hit felt even more crammed than the club, not much tidier, and surprisingly quiet. It was Kerri's apartment.

As soon as Kerri unlocked the door, a bluish dash of a dog poured over them like a roomful of Marx Brothers.

"Hey! Look who wants to go to the bathroom!" she greeted. "I was talking about me, actually. Make way!"

She sneaked through a side door while Andy stared at the excited blue-gray hunting dog clambering up her leg.

"This . . . Is this Roger?"

"You've been out of the loop too long," Kerri said offscreen. "That is Roger's son Tim."

Tim, 3 according to the Hollis family's records, reacts to his name by standing down, as alert as his drooping ears manage to indicate, then seems to order himself "at ease" and lets his mouth open and his tongue unfold, panting proudly.

Even to Andy's trained eye, Tim was the spitting image of Roger, the son of George and grandson of Sean. Sean, of Blyton Summer Detective Club fame, had died years ago in Portland, but he had been already a grandfather in the time he used to accompany the children in their adventures—the one grown-up on the team, founder of a lineage. All of them the same shade of blue gray, somewhat undersized for their breed standards, and maddeningly energetic.

"They all come through the male line?"

"Nope. George was a female, remember?"

A toilet flushed, and Tim tracked down his leash, ready to offer it to Kerri as she exited the coffin bathroom.

"My mom spoils them too much. I adopted Tim the last time I was home in Portland to teach him some discipline." She attached the leash to his collar. "Gotta pop downstairs. Make yourself comfortable. There's a bottle of vodka somewhere."

"I'm fine."

"You won't be. That toaster is the only heating you get. Be right back."

Kerri and Tim left, and Andy glanced over Kerri's austere apartment, pondering the thinness of the line between glancing and snooping. Probably opening drawers marked the boundary, but there was only one and it was open already. Kerri's garments lay scattered on the floor, pouring out of a yawning red travel bag. She checked the single bookshelf, unbelievingly: only a dozen books, most of them fiction. Not one pocket encyclopedia, not even a bird spotter's guide. The walls in Kerri's bedroom in Blyton Hills (the most awesome place in the universe) were fully dressed with bookshelves and butterfly display cases and maps of other continents. The cool ones: Africa, Oceania.

Reverently, she pulled down one of the book spines, an illustrated edition of Wyndham's *The Chrysalids*—the same one Andy had read as a child in Blyton Hills, per Kerri's recommendation. She opened it.

A familiar piece of paper fluttered down onto her lap. She picked up the newspaper clipping delicately and smoothed it on the book's cover. It had been almost three years from the last time Andy had read the article, and yet her memory misquoted hardly a couple of words.

TEEN SLEUTHS UNMASK SLEEPY LAKE MONSTER

Nancy Hardy/Blyton Hills.—The reign of terror of the "Sleepy Lake Creature"—the elusive figure that has been scaring herdsmen and campers by the upper Zoinx River—was put to an end last weekend by some unlikely heroes, namely four children and a dog.

Peter Manner (13), Kerri Hollis (12), Andrea "Andy" Rodriguez (12), and Nate Rogers (11), along with their hunting dog, Sean, are credited with the capture of Thomas X. Wickley, from California, who was reenacting an old Indian legend as part of a convoluted scheme for burglary at the historic Deboën Mansion.

A Legend Rekindled

This is not the first time that the so-called Blyton Summer Detective Club has taken on a case that had local authorities baffled. As frequent vacationers in Blyton Hills, the half-and-half Oregonian-Californian bunch is famous in town for its crazy adventures, which often end in the arrest of evildoers!

Recent sightings of a "monster" around Sleepy Lake had been a hot topic in Blyton Hills this summer. "Rumors of lake creatures are as old as they are typical of any large water mass," says Deputy Sheriff W. Wilson, of the Pennaquick County Police. "I myself grew up hearing the old Walla Walla tales of ancient underwater spirits that crawl up the misty shores at night. But when hunters start finding alien tracks in the mud, you know something is amiss."

"We just had to go and see those for ourselves!" young Nate boasts excitedly, a little daredevil who makes up in courage what he lacks in size. However, when they first visited the lake, they found more than tracks: they encountered the creature itself, and it had them fleeing away! "He gave us a heck of a scare!"

Summer Detectives on the Job

For Peter, the oldest of the gang and a natural-born leader, the mystery had just begun. "We found footprints in the forest that seemed to lead straight into the mines upriver. That was odd: What business does a lake creature have in an abandoned gold mine?"

It was at that point when the kids contacted their old

ally, Captain Al Urich, a retired air force veteran living in Blyton Hills.

"I have had the pleasure to work with the Blyton Summer Detective Club before and I do my best to assist them whenever they require a grown-up's point of view, or simply someone with a driver's license," Captain Urich joked.

Together, the children and Captain Urich searched the woods around Sleepy Lake and the abandoned mines. "I hope to become a biologist someday, so I was eager for a closer look at that creature," says Kerri, the brains of the team. But the clues pointed to something bigger than a prowling monster: "We went to the library and learned that the mines were connected to the old Deboën Mansion. All our findings pointed to that house."

The House on the Lake

Built during the Gold Rush years by a merchant-turned-prospector on a tiny islet in Sleepy Lake, Deboën Mansion has been shunned for years by townsfolk who still resent the family's alleged ties with piracy and witchcraft. Rumors of a haunting have persisted since 1949, when a fire destroyed part of the building and forced the bankrupt family to sell the property and relocate in town. Ms. Dunia Deboën, last of her bloodline and the police's main suspect in the case, refused to comment on this story.

Nevertheless, when the teen detectives finally dared investigate the house, they were in deep water. "Weather capsized our boat and we ended up stranded on the isle," recounts Andy, who despite being a girl was never afraid to take refuge in the haunted house. "It looked like we were up for a night of frights!"

However, not only did the four friends overcome the thrills of that eventful night, but they also managed to set an ingenious trap for the fraudster himself. When police reached the isle the next morning, they found the missing children and dog guarding their astounding catch—the Sleepy Lake creature unmasked!

"Wickley had heard rumors about Deboën's lost gold hidden below the mansion, and he took advantage of the creature myth to scare off people while he searched for the riches," Peter explained, recapping a new entry in the exploits of the Blyton Summer Detective Club. Criminals of Blyton Hills beware—the children are coming back for Christmas!

Andy, her mouth filled with a sweet aftertaste, put the clipping back inside the book and the book back on the shelf, reassured. That was all she wanted to find.

Plus Tim. Tim was a welcome extra. Things were all going according to plan.

Tim and Kerri returned soon enough, the former going straight to the toaster Andy had turned on, the latter snatching the bottle of vodka.

"Shit, it's cold," she mumbled, crashing on the bed as gently as the *Hindenburg* in the very narrow gap between Andy and the wall. "Go ahead, take your shoes off. Let's do a pajama party like the old times. We'll build a pillow fort and ask the Magic Eight Ball who will we marry."

"We never did that," Andy complained, undoing her boots. "You wouldn't do it; it's too unscientific. Instead you tried to explain genetics to me to determine who we should marry to spawn superdetectives."

"Hey, it works with dogs. Right, Tim?"

Tim sneezed in a very dignified Sherlock Holmes fashion. Kerri was sitting up against the wall, after she'd toed her suede boots off into oblivion. She took a big gulp of vodka and watched as Andy maneuvered out of her jacket.

"You know," she said, "sometimes it crossed my mind that next time I'd see you, you would be a boy."

Andy gazed at her, not completely off-balance. She replied, seriously, "Sometimes it crossed my mind there'd be no next time."

"Fuck," Kerri countered, Andy's line gone seemingly ignored. "Sorry. That was inappropriate." She would have added, *It's the alcohol speaking,* but she knew better than blaming the voluntary ingestion of bottled faux pas for her mistakes.

"It's okay."

"It's because you always wanted us to call you Andy and hang out with the boys. And you liked it when people took you for a boy."

"I know."

"And now, you know, I've been outside, met people . . . I talked to this guy once, a really handsome boy who had made the change, and I thought . . ." She paused, eyebrows arcing up a little farther in helplessness. "Am I sounding ignorant?"

"No, you never do."

"I'll drop it. I'm drunk."

"It's okay. I saw the world outside my Christian home too. I saw that it's all right to be the way I am. It's fine to be a girl and prefer jeans over dresses and mountain bikes over dollhouses."

Kerri listened, hugging her knees. "Did we make it hard for you?"

"No," said Andy seriously. "You were great."

A memory seemed to cross before Andy's eyes, and she dispelled it together with the bang of hair in front of her face.

"Though I could have killed Joey Krantz on more than one occasion."

Kerri laughed. "Joey. What a dick. He picked on all of us. You know he was actually jealous, right? He called you butch because he would've loved to hang with us."

"No, he called me butch because I was butch. Some people are like that, they need to state the obvious."

"Whatever, fuck him." Kerri leaped over Andy to claim the outer side of the bed as good hosts do and slithered under the blanket, waving Andy to do the same. "Pull over that quilt. You can take your pants off, but do it at your own risk; it's like Alaska in the mornings." They locked eyes for a second. "You've been to Alaska, right?"

"Yeah."

"Yeah, I remember now. I keep your postcard somewhere. Okay, maybe it's not like Alaska," she said, reaching out to throw her coat over Tim, who lay curled on his cardboard-carpeted corner. "We slept in worse places, right?"

Andy looked at the narrow iron bed, the coarse wool

blanket, the sinusoidal wave of Kerri's body in the raglan shirt. "I have."

"You still have to tell me what you've been up to these years—don't think I forgot," Kerri said, tidying her hair up for the night. "How long are you staying, anyway?"

Andy hadn't lain down yet. She was leaning on one elbow while her other hand had been forced to relocate on top of Kerri's hip. It was now wailing for the rest of Andy's attention like a child calling for Mom from a diving springboard.

"I'm not staying," Andy said. "I mean, we're not staying."

"Really? Where are we going?"

"Blyton Hills."

Kerri chuckled. "Blyton? Are you going to kick-sterilize Joey Krantz too?"

She waited for Andy to laugh, in vain.

"Are you serious?" she insisted. "Andy, I haven't been there in years. Uncle Emmet died; Aunt Margo moved to Portland. Why are we going there?"

Andy didn't answer right away. In the lapse, she grew aware that the night had become incredibly silent, like big cities hardly ever do. Like there was no big city outside those black windows, and the room, the only piece of universe left, was floating in the void. Only the colorless walls, the piles of clothes, a toaster, a bottle of vodka, an astronaut dog, and Kerri and herself all dressed in bed, cruising through space.

Whispering seemed only proper.

"Kerri, don't you feel like . . . we left something unfinished up there?"

The layer of alcohol on Kerri's eyes blocked any

reaction from surfacing. "What do you mean?"

Andy tried to shift on the narrow bed.

"Ever since Peter died," she said, "I've been thinking about the last time we were all together up there, all five of us. And . . . I think I want to go back. I want to go to Deboën Mansion again."

"What for?"

"You know," Andy said, as if Kerri did know. "Look into the Sleepy Lake case."

"But we solved that case," Kerri said. "It was Mr. Wickley trying to scare off people while he searched for Deboën's gold."

"Actually, no, I talked to him—"

"*What?*" The italics just flew out past the alcohol's guard. "You talked to Wickley? You went to see him in prison?"

"Yes—I mean—no, I just waited for him to come out, but—"

"You met with Wickley? Are you insane? He's a criminal!"

"Please!" Andy scoffed. For a moment she considered relating the actual meeting, until it dawned on her that no part of that episode would cast her in a good light. "Look, I had to talk to him. I had to talk to someone. We never talk about that case."

"What's there to talk about?" Kerri asked. "We caught the creature, it was a guy in a mask."

"No, it wasn't," Andy reacted, almost painfully. It had become that obvious in her head. "I mean, there happened to be a guy in a mask there, and we captured him. But there was something else going on in that house, Kerri. Come on, you know it."

"Andy, we solved that case! It was in the papers!"

"I know, I learned the story by heart too! 'Tracks in the mud'? 'Sightings of a monster'? What about the slaughtered deer?"

Kerri faltered, then offered without attempting a smile: "Grizzly?"

"There are no grizzlies in Blyton Hills! Do you think if they had fucking grizzlies to worry about they'd have time to invent stories about lake creatures? And what about the hanged corpse?!"

"Gosh, it's a local paper, Andy; I guess it was too macabre for the *Pennaquick Telegraph*!"

"What about the house? The pentacle? The empty coffins? The symbols written in blood?!"

"Those were props! Wickley staged the haunting of Deboën Mansion to direct blame at Miss Deboën!"

"Kerri, come on, stop pretending you forgot about that night!" Andy begged. "Don't you remember when I found you in the basement? When we locked ourselves in the dungeon? The things outside scratching the walls, all of them? We were in each other's arms, sweating pinballs, shivering, Jesus Christ, choking on pure terror! Do you want me to believe that Mr. fucking Wickley did that? That a guy in a mask made us cry?"

"Is that what this is about?" Kerri regretted and then finished saying, in that order, but her mouth wouldn't stop now. "Andy, I'm sorry your self-imposed tough guy persona got shattered that night, but I'm not going back to Blyton Hills because some creep got your ego hurt!"

"That's bullshit!" Whispers had slowly given way to

shouts. "It was not a creep! And they weren't props! I know what I saw! We all saw it!"

"We were scared!"

"We are scared!" Andy countered. "We've been scared ever since! We never went back to Blyton Hills after that. The next year, we found an excuse to stay at your house in Portland and we didn't even dare to look each other in the eye. And Sean, your Sean, Tim's great-grandfather, was standing there, trying to bark us to life again, like 'What the fuck are you doing here? Why aren't we back in that house solving the real mystery?'"

"Because we grew up!"

It went downhill from there, Tim noticed, watching the girls on the bed (not in the bed: blankets had receded long ago), a moody *Mom and Dad are fighting* look on his Byronian face.

Kerri caught her breath, tired and sad. "We grew up, Andy. We grew apart. That's life. You move on, make new friends, lose the old ones. We can't spend our whole lives in Blyton Hills, chasing sheep smugglers and lake creatures."

She brushed some orange hair aside, and she seemed exhausted.

"I'm sorry, Andy. I'm not going back."

She lay down and switched the light off. The coils in the toaster glinted yellow in the dark, a poor but well-intended impersonation of a fireplace.

Andy met Tim's eyes, the dog's profile outlined in the warm glow. They held a silent exchange for a minute or two, until Tim deemed it courteous to lay his head down, close his eyes, and pretend to sleep.

Kerri murmured in the brown dark, "Can you please take your arm off me? I feel smothered."

Andy's right hand radioed a message: *We've been spotted.* And it fell back.

She changed positions and tried to lie down faceup in the narrow space between Kerri and the wall, making sure to touch neither. She tried to swallow something in her throat, careful not to make a single noise, and kept her eyes open.

The tiny room went on flying through space, wrapped in zero Kelvin silence.

Several hours or light-years later Kerri felt her again, a peach-fuzz brush against her back that didn't wake her up so much as give her a gentle reminder of the world beyond her body.

She felt her own left arm, crushed under a bad posture but too numb to complain anyway, and her right one, hanging off the bed. She felt the almost excessive heat on the toaster-lit side of her wrist and the cold on the dark half. She felt the twilight zone along her forearm like the Greenwich parallel of Eternia. She guessed the yellow aura of the toaster behind her closed eyelids, and Tim lying by it.

The bitter memories of their argument were beginning to rush in when something unexpected happened: a second caress. This time it was deliberate, Andy's hand brushing her side like a petal stroke. She focused on the body behind her, the microearthquakes it caused on the mattress. And she smiled, internally, for her lips were too deeply asleep to be bothered, but she did acknowledge Andy's touch as it clumsily tripped on every little wrinkle of the tight shirt around her torso, descending toward the waist where the shirt ended.

And that's where she noticed it. Cold.

She suddenly found herself wondering whether Andy would have cold hands from being far from the toaster, or if they could be that cold, while the hand sped up slightly across her skin and then hesitated by the edge of her jeans, and it didn't resume its path over the clothes, but burrowed beneath, and Kerri's thoughts hurried up too, deliberating how she should react, because the hand was hovering south over her belly and sending a scouting fingertip, cold and smooth, surfing between her thigh and her abdomen, scurrying easily under her panties. And a long fingernail was brushing through her pubic hair, and another finger and another and another followed, too quickly, over her labia and bending around her legs, cold and skinless and clawed, closing in a burning icy clutch ready to grab her groin and rip her womb apart *shout now!*

The scream woke every single cell in every body in the room. Hers, and Tim's, and Andy's, who immediately grabbed Kerri by the shoulders and shook the dream off her.

"Kerri! Kerri, wake up!"

She fought to break loose, blinded by panic.

"It's me!" Andy insisted. "Kerri, I'm real! I know how it is; feel me; I'm real! You're okay!"

She was.

Kerri noticed the hands clutching her whiter wrists.

They were strong and warm, a landscape of veins and knuckle valleys, untiringly detailed like every millimetric hair on Tim's paws on the bed and the voices of both—Tim barking in a pathetically sweet attempt to soothe her, Andy's words slowly succeeding. She recognized the room in twilight, the yellow glow of the toaster, every piece of junk on the floor, Tim's compassionate eyes and Andy's dark, resolute ones, inches from her.

And in the next breath, the dam broke. Massive, physically painful sobs burst out of her chest.

Andy released her wrists and tried to hold her head, but she recoiled, hiding under the sheets.

Andy sat still. She had not seen Kerri cry since they were kids. She used to feel awkward back then too. So did Tim, apparently. She settled with resting a hand on her, over the blanket.

"Kerri, we have to end this. You can't go on like this. It broke us."

The gesture of her hand encompassed everything in Kerri's room, in Kerri's life.

"You were going to be a scientist. By this time you were supposed to be in the Amazon rain forest, naming a new species of butterfly after each one of us. We won't find peace until we fix this."

Kerri had cowered into a corner, hiding behind her knees, her orange hair so inconsolably distressed.

Andy saw Kerri Hollis, age twelve, in the way she swiped her eyes and nose and tried to woman up.

"I don't want to go back," she said with a quiver.

"Kerri, the fact that you don't want to go back is proof

that we must go back," Andy sotto voce'd, recognizing a softness in her voice that she had not used in the last thirteen years. "Would you be scared to go to the place where you had the greatest times in your life if we had really caught the bad guy?"

Kerri shied away. "I prefer to think it ended happily."

"But it didn't!" Andy exploded, softness lost to a passionate monologue. "Look at us! Look at what we are! I wish it had ended happily and that we'd gone on to solve more cases, and that somehow our teenage adventures had morphed into a happy sitcom of our adult life with all of us turning to face the camera smiling and every scene beginning with a long shot of a great house with a garden and a big-ass pool while a stupid fucking sax went *dibiddydawahwawah*, but it didn't happen! Peter's dead and Nate's in a loony bin and you live in this hole and I'm going psychotic and even the dog knows there's still something out there!"

Out the window, New York had slid back into view, blowing steam and pining for coffee.

Kerri and Tim both watched Andy panting after the climax. The darkness of the immediate future trickled in like saltpeter down the walls.

"Okay, I get it," Kerri whispered. "There's something out there. I can't ignore it. But why do we have to take care of it? Why us?"

Andy sat back down, a rogue hand holding one of Kerri's. Softness took over again: "Because we're the Blyton Summer Detective Club. BSDC forever, right? It's what we do. We help people, catch the bad guys, fix problems.

It's the last thing I remember being good at. You want to know what I've been up to the last five years? I've been a cook, a cabbie, a welder, a train operator, an air force cadet, and I sucked phenomenally at every single one of those things. So I'm going back to what I was good at, and you and Tim are coming with me."

Tim stood on all fours again, panting at the prospect of action.

Kerri murmured, "Can I sleep some more before we go?"

"Okay," Andy said, lying down again and pulling the sheets back up. "But not too long. We gotta fetch your cousin Nate in Arkham."

" They were onto us," said Xira, swiping the wharg blood from her ax blade. "We must get to Actheon's citadel before them."

"We'll cut through the woods," Adam suggested.

"We'll cut through the woods," said Princess Irya, Xira's faithful companion.

"You know they make wharg blood with maple syrup and purple dye?" Ethan triviaed, but no one listened. "It's actually delicious."

"Go! The sun is setting," Xira bid, hopping over the gurgling carcasses toward the Bierstadt sunset that shone red upon Adam's acned face, inches away from the screen.

"This show is stupid," Craig grumbled from his armchair.

All seats in the living room had been tacitly assigned among the inmates long ago, mostly through ancient pacts among the elders, with the occasional revision of terms by means of an amicable skirmish. The twin armchairs with autumn motifs were for people no one really liked; Craig was one of them. Old Acker was granted the rocking chair. The corner chaise longue was for catatonics. The sofa was a sort of UN demilitarized zone, an upholstered Jerusalem that members of different creeds reluctantly shared during interbellum periods. Anyone actually caring for the TV broadcast had to relinquish his seat and take the first row on the linoleum floor.

"Adam," said Nurse Angela, beginning the four o'clock roll call for medicines. She approached the unresponsive fat kid in front of the TV, put a red-and-white pill in his open mouth, prodded his chin shut, and moved on. Adam knew every word of dialogue of *Xira the Princess Warrior* by heart. He liked to read Irya's lines.

"Kimrean."

"Meeeee!" cheered the schizophrenic hermaphrodite lying on the sofa.

"You know, this was one of Linda Hamilton's ten least favorite episodes," said Ethan, bearing Kimrean's mantis legs on his lap. "The filming was so taxing."

"How do you know?" Kimrean asked, childishly interested.

"She told me."

"Oh, come on!" went Craig, snapping off his chair and getting an automatic first warning from the head nurse— barely a nasal caveat in a sitcom housewife tone. "I'm so sick of this! So Linda Hamilton told you. Was that when you chaperoned her to the Golden Globes?"

"Before that," Ethan replied matter-of-factly. "We weren't officially dating yet."

"You dated her?" wowed the hermaphrodite, staring

with mismatched eyes, brown and green.

"Bullshit!" cried Craig, just short of loud enough to merit the second warning. "Christ, it's infuriating! They don't want us to make any progress—they're just locking us away! How do you expect patients to recover when you put the pathological liars next to the only guys dumb enough to believe their shit? *(Aside, to the nurse offering him a cup.)* No, Dr. Willett put me off that yesterday; Belle knows— tell her, Belle. *(He goes on, undisturbed.)* All day I have to listen to your collective fantasies! This asshole dated Linda Hamilton, that one met Peter Manner, you screwed Patty Hearst—everyone in this place is so well-connected and full of shit!"

ADAM: A storm is brewing, Xira.

CRAIG: Shut up!

"I screwed Hearst?" Kimrean wondered, and then recalled, "Oh, yeah, I did."

"Rogers."

The nurse neared the second armchair, where Nate sat, or lay, a cigarette between two Band-Aided bony fingers. He took the Dixie cup, swallowed his pills, opened his mouth in a hippo display for the nurse to see, and continued smoking, all this using a record low number of muscles.

The nurse, a young woman right out of school, leaned closer to him. "Did you really meet Peter Manner?"

"Yeah, I did," Nate groaned. "He was my best friend."

"Really?" she whispered excitedly. "I loved him in that movie with Shannen Doherty—I used to have such a crush on him! You went to school with him?"

"No, he was from California; I grew up in Oregon," he

retold, tired of his own story, words dropping off his dry, flaky lips. "We met in summer camp and afterward spent all holidays together at my aunt Margo's house in Blyton Hills: my cousin Kerri and her friend Andy and Peter and me. And we went camping, and climbing, and fishing, and we got into trouble every school break."

He was speaking in a low voice to spare those who'd heard the story already, but for some reason everyone was listening. Craig stood in tension, a skeptical eyebrow arched up.

"He was so talented," the nurse said. "So did you continue to see him after that?"

Nate locked eyes with her.

"I still do."

The room dismissed him with a scoff as *Xira* went to commercials.

Tim had been gnawing the armrest into submission for the last ten miles. In the front seat, Kerri sat with her head against her window like a broken robot, hazy eyes surfing the flowing tarmac.

"I need to go to the bathroom," she beeped.

"Now?" Andy checked her for a split second. "You went only an hour ago."

"I need to go again."

"Can you go there in the woods?"

"No. It's number two."

"But it was number two last time."

"Yes! Well spotted, Inspector Craphound from the Rectal Police, you caught me!"

"Okay, okay. Jesus."

Andy was uneasy too. Not so much about the destination as the journey itself, to put it in Confucian terms. Bad becomes unbearable only when contrasted to expectation; Andy had learned through her life on the road to bear little or no expectations, which enabled her to weather most scenarios without visible wearing. But a car trip with Kerri was one of the few premises she had often allowed herself to fantasize about. Of course, in her daydreams the radio worked, the car was certainly something better than a 1978 Chevrolet Vega Kammback wagon, and the destination, albeit undefined, was definitely not a psychiatric asylum in Arkham, Massachusetts. Nor Massachusetts, period.

Also, horror and apocalypse did not lurk in the near future.

Ever since they crossed into Connecticut, the mood inside the car had begun to mimic the concrete-and-evergreen landscape along the interstate: murky and unrepairable. Their rare exchanges escalated into Kerri's anger in shorter and shorter times. Andy had tried to mitigate the gloom with snacks and candy when they first stopped for gas, only to realize once back in the car that neither of them was hungry. A carnival of plastic wrappers sat now self-consciously on the dashboard, like guests to a garden party after somebody drowned in the pool. Tim had been the only beneficiary of that purchase, which explained why he was now bouncing between the backseat and the trunk and going Baskervilles on the upholstery like a sugar-powered dingo.

"Can you tell him to stop?" Andy begged.

Kerri looked into the front mirror. "Tim!"

The dog swiftly sat down, stiff like an Egyptian jackal god, throwing a Terminatorish *I'll be back* glance at the armrest.

"Thank you," said Kerri.

Andy smiled as the dog in the mirror nervously sniffed for more chewable car parts.

"You're great with him."

Kerri bit a fingernail, eyes back on the curb line. Her hair had been dozing off since morning.

"Kerri. I'm scared too, all right?"

"So you keep saying, but I'm the only one longing for adult pull-ups."

"Listen, it's not gonna be like before. It's gonna be you, me, Nate, and Tim. Together. All the time. None of that 'let's split up' bullshit Peter always came up with." She resented criticizing Peter's field strategies so early into her leadership, but whatever. "And we're grown-ups, right? Look at us. We're better prepared; we got a car. We're not riding bikes anymore; if things get ugly, we just drive away." She hadn't really thought about this before, but she believed it now. She patted the steering wheel, though not too hard, for fear the Chevy Vega would disassemble. "Hell, the whole town is gonna look different. And a lot smaller. You'll see; remember how huge Deboën Mansion seemed? I bet you we'll get there and we'll wonder how could we be scared of that tiny little cottage. Shit, I bet you even the lake will look like a pond."

"I doubt that. It's the second-deepest lake in the

Americas after O'Higgins in southern Chile."

"Really? That's as deep as . . . what, Lake Superior?"

"Twice as deep." Kerri shifted on her seat, eyes fixed on the blurry asphalt. "It was a sort of collapsed volcano that the Zoinx River flowed into. The rest of the river disappeared for centuries before the gap was filled."

"See, that's the Kerri Hollis we need!" Andy cheered, laughing at her automatic shyness. "Kerri the Encyclopedia. 'The brains of the team'!"

"Shit. You remember that."

"Course I do. I'm sorry, I snooped around your place a little last night. I saw you keep the *Telegraph* too. My copy is somewhere in Tulsa, I think. Hey, at least you got a cool nickname."

"She kind of gave you one too," Kerri recalled. "You were not afraid, 'despite being a girl'!" They delivered the quote together.

"Thanks for reminding me," said Andy. "Can you believe a woman wrote that?"

Kerri gave her a tender look—the first one this side of the Harlem River. "It was meant to be a compliment, you know?"

Andy innerstruggled to keep her focus on the road.

"So, why was Nate put in Arkham? Why so far from home? His mother doesn't like him?"

"He committed himself; he's all grown up too," said Kerri. "And he doesn't live with his mother anymore. He doesn't like her."

A trailer truck roared past them.

"You ever visit him?"

"Not in Arkham, no. I saw him when he was in this other place upstate last year, McLean Hospital or something."

"Why does he do it? Commit himself?"

"He thinks it's good for him. He says it's like a vacation. He spends the rest of his time buried in fantasy books and computers."

"Why doesn't he just go outside?"

"You know. He doesn't like people." She paused. "He always had issues."

Andy waited for a development, then inquired, "What kind of issues?"

"You know." Kerri was looking away again. "Broken home. Father left, mother drank. That's why Aunt Margo took him in every school break. He had bouts of depression. He was bullied at school. All that."

"Really? He seemed fine when he was with us."

"Yeah. We were that awesome."

Andy registered a rest area after the next exit. "Do you still want to go?"

Kerri consulted with her digestive system. "No. I'm fine. But I could use some cigarettes."

Andy decided the nicotine would help her relax, so she pulled over.

They parked close to the highway, only a ten-feet-wide strip of incredibly resilient plant life away from the flow of eighteen-wheeled trucks. The world was wide and flat and smelled like oil. And it was mostly gray and damp and ugly. But for the last few minutes the cloudscape was shattering in patches of blue and the sun peeped through in funny angles, creating cool chiaroscuro effects, sparkling off the drizzle-washed amber bodywork of the Chevy Vega and infusing it with supporting character charisma.

Andy stepped out and touched the asphalt with her fingers. She always liked the feel of transit places. They're thankful for the attention. Sunlight painted the scene with unsolicited detail: the plainest blade of spartan grass, the skin on Andy's hand.

Tim escaped the car right after Kerri and ran off into the wild like a wolf released to repopulate New England. She called after him in vain.

"Christ, if only that energy could be harnessed," she grunted, and turned to Andy. "Try and make sure he doesn't, you know, go feral, eat children, and listen to satanic music."

She headed to the minimarket, leaving Andy to try to imitate Kerri's martial tone to call after the dog. Tim had hardly gotten used to Andy, but so far he seemed to respect her. In the old days, Sean was obedient to everyone in the group as well, but he performed his best with Kerri. Andy would have to win Tim over.

The Weimaraner reappeared in his own time, ever running, ears flapping in the wind, his crazed expression far from the "awaiting command" range.

Andy knelt down and put her hand forward. Tim approached to smell it, realized she had nothing important to tell him, and roamed off again.

"Hey, Tim! Come back! Come!"

He trotted back describing a wide arc, every pebble on

the way deserving his hummingbird attention. Andy was checking her pockets for a treat when her fingers touched something better.

She did a quick mental self-inspection: despite all the tempers and the impending doom, she felt fine since she had reunited with Kerri. Maybe it was time to pass her security blanket on.

"Come here, boy. Come here."

She knelt to make the dog understand this was specifically for him, waited until Tim came close, and tossed the plastic penguin at his feet. Sunrays quickly spotlighted it in high definition.

Tim simply smelled the novelty, considering its edibility. Then Andy stretched forward and squeezed it gently. It squeaked.

Tim stepped back, the countenance of eighteenth-century gentlemen first meeting a time-traveler in his face.

For the next two minutes he continued to sniff the penguin from every conceivable angle, learned how to make it squeak by pounding it with his paw, learned how to stand on three legs to pound it, and finally took it in his mouth and hopped back into the car.

Kerri returned a little later, a cigarette between her teeth, marigold hair rejoicing under the new light.

"You know, in frontal view, it can almost pass for a sports car from far enough away," she commented. She stopped a couple yards before the station wagon and tilted her head. "Not in profile, though; then it's like a hearse for dwarves. It'd look cool with a black racing stripe."

Then she glanced inside. Tim, lying on the narrow

backseat, made the penguin between his forelegs squeak for her, an intense *Can we keep it, Mom?* look in his Dickensian orphan eyes.

"You gave him a squeaky toy?" she asked Andy.

"Yeah, it's my, like, you know . . . a stress-relief thing. I thought it would help him focus."

They read each other, then Andy dodged Kerri's look and sneaked into the car.

"You suffer from stress," Kerri said, getting in. It wasn't so much a question as a line of questioning.

"Not stress, just—" Andy buckled up, pressed cancel on that sentence and started a new one. "They think I have aggression issues."

"Oh. I hope you launched their gonads into orbit for their diagnosis."

"I couldn't," said Andy, impervious to sarcasm. "It was the military doctors."

"The military said you have aggression issues," Kerri recapped. "Good. Not meaningful at all."

Xira the Princess Warrior returned just in time to Actheon's citadel during the commercial break and Adam shushed Craig, who had just initiated a tirade over Kimrean's implausible sexual exploits. Nate did not share Adam's passion for *Xira*, but found it an entertaining format. And Adam's zealotry in itself was comforting, when compared with Nate's hardly unhealthy penchant for the sword and wizardry genre. That was about the sum of the benefits of being institutionalized: living with crazier people helped put things into perspective.

"So, Blyton Hills," said Old Acker.

The man had just sat down in the armchair next to Nate's, his raspy voice entangled in the threads of his white beard. Nate checked him out, his astonishment only surfacing as a mere frown, as required by his veteran inmate persona. This was clearly in violation of the Geneva seating conventions.

"Uh-huh," he replied.

"That's in the Pacific Northwest, in the Cascades," said Acker, glimpses of his old academic life poking through. "Near Sleepy Lake, is that right?"

"Indeed," Nate pinged back, taking another drag.

"In the area the Walla Walla Indians called Land of Deadly Shadows."

"I think even they agree to call it Oregon now."

"Mentioned by Simón de Urribia in his *Book of the Last World*, whose American translator was burned during the Salem witch trials."

"Christ, why does every single horror story have to make a connection with Salem?" Nate ranted. "It's like, I don't know, are you implying something actually demonic happened there? Because I'm sorry to tell you it was only a bunch of Christian fanatics burning women and being massive fuckheads; stop giving credit to their actions."

Acker didn't seem sidetracked. Instead, he added: "Named the Sea of Yottha in the Necronomicon."

The last puff of smoke out of Nate's mouth hurried away from the awkward silence.

"That book doesn't exist."

Acker did not reply. Instead, always at grandfather speed, he produced from his breast pocket a crayon stolen from the art room and a newspaper from the rack, and he started drawing in a margin. It began with two basic strokes, combined into a five-pointed star. Nate watched with badly faked disinterest as the little figure grew long, angry-angled branches, and tortured spirals, and arrowheads stabbing the original figure, nudging the sound of the TV into the background and causing sunlight to dim, and time to slow down, and Nate's heart to suddenly adjourn the next beat.

Old Acker put away the crayon. Nate commanded his throat to swallow.

"That's a fake," he argued. "It's from Clint Sorhein's short story 'The Secret Gate to Kathom,' 1959."

"That's not where I got it from," Acker teased, a wrinkled hand alluding to his beard and the yellow uniform that distinguished patients at Arkham. "I can tell you reading science fiction is not what landed me here."

He peered over his spectacles and into Nate's eyes.

"You've seen symbols like this before. You've been there. Things live at the bottom of that lake and under the hills. Ancient, corrupt things that are not granted the gift of death by their cruel gods."

Nate breathed deeply, striving to pull his *God, I'm surrounded by crazy people* mask over his true fear.

"You've seen them, as the Indians did, stealing out into the world they once claimed. You felt, deep below the water, the heaving slumber of the quiescent monstrosity they call Father, whispering your name."

"Rogers."

Nate popped back into the asylum's living room, unprecedentedly quiet. All the inmates' attention was funneled into the hallway behind Nurse Angela.

"You have visitors," the nurse announced.

"Ooh, women!" Kimrean pointed out.

Kerri peeked into the bleached living room.

Sitting in a grandmother armchair, clad in yellow, Nate Rogers, 24, caffeinated blue eyes and blond hair cropped to half an inch, stares back, holding the trembling ash ghost of a cigarette between his fingers.

"Hey, Nate."

Every single crazy person in the room turned to Nate. He rose to his feet.

"Hey."

Kerri took a breath, orange hair gathering strength, strode into the room, and hugged her cousin. Andy thought she heard Kerri's curls sighing for real, objectively loud, until she realized it had been the other patients.

"Hi, Andy," Nate greeted over Kerri's shoulder, arms around her parka. "Long time."

Kerri wished she had come to visit him sooner.

They switched to the nonsmoking parlor, where they could smoke and be alone. It was literally four papered walls around a table and three chairs. Nate had never stepped in it before, but he automatically knew how to use it; he took the solo chair at the far side of the table and let the girls sit across from him.

Andy had not seen Nate since he was fifteen. He didn't

look that different: pale, blue-eyed, more worn but still fragile. His body looked like it still had a growth spurt left to hit.

"So how've you been?" Kerri started.

"Groovy." He dragged on one of her cigarettes and ashed it in a flowerpot. "Place is nice. Good people. Apart from those claiming a mental disorder that compels them to steal my socks."

"Kleptomania?"

"Oh, it's a thing? Shit. I owe someone an apology." His right hand played with Kerri's lighter. Such devices were discouraged in the ward. "Anyway, how are you? How's . . . Tim, was it?"

"Fine! Fine, he's three already. A bit unruly, but honoring his ancestors. He's in the car right now."

"Oh, good. The whole family's here," he said, just the teensiest bit overacted. Enough for Andy to hold her frown for a little longer. "So what's the occasion?"

"Well . . ." tiptoed Andy. "We came for you. We're putting the band back together."

"Oh, really?" he said in interested-mom pitch. "What's come up? A damsel in distress? Sheep smugglers?"

"No, we . . . we're reopening the Sleepy Lake monster case."

A thrush on the lakeshore looked up toward the horizon spiked with fir trees and took flight with an agitated wingbeat.

* * *

Nate continued to smoke, the ghost of a smile on his face. His eyes pinged Kerri just once, enough to be persuaded she was into it too, and returned to Andy.

"All right. Let's do it."

He squished the cigarette in the flowerpot and sat up, avid for orders.

Andy and Kerri didn't move for another minute.

"So ..." Andy began, and resumed, much later, "You okay with this?"

"Hell yeah. About damn time, if you ask me."

The girls sidechecked each other in a brief reaction shot.

"In fact, I don't know what kept me from taking the initiative myself," Nate elaborated. "I mean, how much longer could we go on ignoring the elephant in the lake?"

"So, you're willing to come?" Kerri asked. "To Blyton Hills?"

"Yeah."

"Cool." Andy checked Kerri again. "So ... We're good to go?"

"I guess."

No one stood up.

"Okay, let's go then," said Andy, willing herself onto her feet.

"Let's," said Nate, following suit.

"On our way! Gonna solve the shit out of that mystery!" said Andy, leading them out into the corridor. "Sleepy Lake won't know what fucking hit it."

"Hell yeah!"

"Where do you think you're going?" said the head nurse.

They stopped at the end of the corridor, two inches from the stairway.

"Oh, right," said Nate, noticing his yellow uniform. "That's what kept me."

The girls confronted the armfolded nurse behind the counter, an overacted frown on her face, like this was the weirdest thing she had ever witnessed in that building.

"But you committed yourself," Kerri told Nate. "Can't you just uncommit?"

"Mr. Rogers chose to put himself into our care until the doctors see it fit to discharge him," the nurse intoned in her wild attempt for a sweet, diplomatic voice.

"Can't he take a leave of absence or something?" Kerri wondered.

"You've been fucking with us," Andy accused Nate.

"Partly," Nate said. "I didn't want to rain on your parade. I loved the *we're on a mission from God* pose and everything. But I was serious about Blyton Hills." He shrugged innocuously. "We should go."

"Really?" Kerri still had trouble believing that.

"Sure. I've done a lot of thinking too. Shit, if there's something we do in this place it's thinking. It's not all bouncing in padded cell rooms and riding wheelchairs to Waterloo," he said with a flourish. "That's Tuesdays."

"But how are you gonna get out?"

"He needs a straitjacket," Andy said, and repeated for the nurse on her way out, "Put him in a straitjacket."

"Loved seeing you too," Nate grumbled.

"I'm serious," she told him. "And get a helmet. Tomorrow, high noon. We're doing a reverse werewolf trap."

And she grabbed Kerri by the wrist and left through the stairwell, leaving Nate standing on the limits of his privilege area.

"A reverse— Andy, wait! There is no skylight in here!"

Twenty-four hours later, Nate was sitting on his armchair, being bound.

"What are we doing?" Kimrean wondered.

"It's a game. Buckle this up," Nate said, wiggling his left shoulder. "Tighter."

"I get it's a game, but why aren't we using Chuck the Plant as usual?"

"Because the orderlies said it's wrong to play with the catatonics," Craig grumbled. "Pull that strap! You're doing it wrong."

It takes two madmen to put a straitjacket on a third— the answer to an old philosophical question. The jacket itself had not been difficult to obtain; since Kimrean had been transferred to that floor, the orderlies always kept one on hand at the nurses' station, just in case of a particularly heated argument with his inside voices. Safety devices are usually easy to borrow in psychiatric hospitals because of the staff's mistaken assumption that patients won't possibly find a way to use them to harm themselves or others. It takes a while in the yellow uniform to grasp the reach of a patient's imagination for mischief. The helmet had been trickier to procure: Nate had had to steal it from the locker of the head nurse, who rode a scooter to work. It offered no jaw protection, just the skull, but it would have to do.

A bloodcurdling roar came through the TV's low-fi speaker. It was *Xira* time again.

"The hounds of Tindalos have been released!" Adam and Princess Irya warned in unison.

"Back off!" Xira ordered, brandishing her ax.

Kimrean suddenly let go of the straps and gave Nate an asymmetric, squinting gaze. "Is that true? You're leaving?"

Nate tried his best to stare back at either the green eye or the brown one. "Who told you that?"

"You are, aren't you?" If anything, Kimrean sounded saddened to lose a playground friend.

Old Acker was slouching toward the armchairs. Nate, sitting with his knees up, acknowledged him with a nod. The straitjacket didn't allow for much loquacious body language.

"Land of Deadly Shadows, eh?" Nate said casually.

"I wouldn't dare go within a hundred miles of that lake" was heard from the thickness of Acker's beard. "You must have your reasons."

"I've got unfinished business to attend to."

Acker nodded, then sat down in Craig's armchair, since Craig was too engaged in an argument to notice. Nate closed in as well as he could, trying to conceal their conversation from daylight.

"The symbol you drew," he said. "I've seen it before. Not in a fantasy paperback. It was a large, ancient book inside an abandoned house, on an isle in Sleepy Lake, thirteen years ago."

Just a few volts of excitement tautened Acker's spine.

"You read it?" he whispered, frowning as he guessed

Nate's age and did the math in his head. "But you couldn't possibly." Then a flimsy, Gothic smile warped his lips. "Oh, but it leaves an impression, doesn't it? I know, I know. It's been only a year since I leafed over the copy at Miskatonic University while it was being transferred. I used to teach anthropology there. I can only imagine what it could do to a child's mind."

"We exposed everything; county police saw it and they didn't care," said Nate, pushing back the chance for self-pity. "They said it was a prop in a staged haunting."

Acker nodded, understandingly. "I would have been inclined to agree once. But not today. Not in Sleepy Lake. Whoever owned that book had an agenda. And I am staggered they left it behind."

He paused, lost in his grave thoughts. When he spoke again, he seemed to be quoting someone else.

"No book is dangerous in and of itself, you know. But historically, reading a book in the wrong way has led to terrible consequences. I can only think of one person more dangerous than a man who reads the Necronomicon and knows what he's doing. And that is someone who reads the damned book with no idea of what he's doing at all."

Nate's reaction shot was ruined by the voices of Craig and Kimrean, who were having a Pythonesque discussion over the window.

"You nutjob, penguins can't fly!"

"But this one just flew in!" Kimrean wailed, putting the bird in question under Craig's nose. "Look! And it brings a message! It's a carrier penguin!"

"Hey, Kim," called Nate. "Can I see that penguin, please?"

Kimrean capered back to him, carrying the plastic toy. Two words had been penciled on the penguin's white breast. "Keep squeaking."

"Put the penguin between my knees, please," Nate requested. "And use that leash to tie my ankles together."

"Ooh, Patty Hearst liked that too," Kimrean commented.

Nate pressed his knees, extracting a wheeze from the plushy toy between his legs. He then tried a quick, sudden press; the penguin squeaked.

"What are we doing?" Craig grunted.

"I don't know. But stay silent."

He kept twitching his knees, making the penguin sing every few seconds, all while Craig and Old Acker observed him with taxing solemnity, Kimrean finished tying him up, Xira and Princess Irya ran for tactical advantage, and Adam sat hypnotized by the screen, watching out for the denouement of that episode.

It arrived, two minutes later, in the form of padded footsteps on the linoleum floor. Not from the TV.

The head nurse in her station screamed, "Hey! Who let that mutt in?"

Tim trotted by happily, already way past the counter before being noticed, glancing back cheerfully at the head nurse like he meant to tip his boater and bid her good morning. He followed the squeaks into the living room, where the circle around the armchair opened to welcome him, flabbergasted.

"Look!" Kimrean pointed, his split brain about to explode with all the unfiltered awesomeness the day was providing. "It's a towing dog!"

The Weimaraner ignored the audience, having already caught sight of the penguin between the knees of the straitjacketed Nate, and dropped at his feet the heavy iron hook and rope he had been carrying in his mouth. The rope extended all the way down the corridor, through the inward-opening escape-proof door to the stairwell. Inches behind the hook, secured between two knots in the rope, a funnel-shaped piece of steel was supposed to play the role of a locomotive's fender. Nate did his best to underreact once he'd fully comprehended the parameters of the escape plan.

"And you must be Tim," he said to the Weimaraner.

Tim sat down at the sound of his name, tail wagging with delight now that he had replaced the boring hook in his mouth with the talking penguin.

Nurse Angela and the head nurse and a security guard arrived next. It was time to go.

"Kim, hook me," ordered Nate. "Craig. Helmet. Quick!"

"What's happening here?" asked the head nurse.

"Werewolf!" Nate shouted toward the open window.

Outside the building, and across the garden, on the other side of the wall, Andy, hanging from a low branch of the big chestnut tree, echoed, "Werewolf!" and banged the roof of the car.

Kerri stepped on the gas and gunned the Chevy forward.

In the living room, the guard pulled out his truncheon and gave the most useless command in his career as an order enforcer in a mental hospital.

"Don't move!"

In the next heartbeat, Nate was quite literally fired off

his armchair and through the human barricade of wards and nurses, scattering them like rubber bowling pins. By the time his backside touched the linoleum again he was already halfway down the corridor, zigzagging off the walls like a pinball, zooming toward the stairwell door, scurrying through the gap opened by the fender, and flying off the first landing.

He touched about six steps in three floors. With his head.

The two guards on the first floor inspecting the rope stretched across the foyer heard the loud bumping in the staircase several seconds before the screams accompanying the noise augmented suddenly in volume and the 150-pound projectile bashed through them, bolting toward the exit.

The guard in reception didn't see it go past his booth. He only grimaced at the shouts, turned the volume up on *Xira the Princess Warrior,* and resumed his lunch.

Ethan, sitting on a bench in the garden reading *Mad,* hardly noticed the running rope under the bench and between his feet, and simply waved at Nate after he'd dashed by, peeling off the lawn and an inch-thick layer of dirt like a derailed dining car.

"Yeah, bye, Nate."

He even saw him colliding with the outer wall and being hoisted over it, hanging upside-down from the top of the chestnut tree like a caterpillar in a pupa.

At that point Kerri, sighting the wriggling package fly over the wall in her side mirror, stopped the car and got out, prepared to untie the rope from the front bumper as soon as Andy cut Nate loose from the other end.

"You can stop yelling now, Nate," Andy suggested, shimmying toward him along a branch and reaching out to unhook him.

"No wait bitch don't it's too high no no no fuck!"

The helmet and the grass of the park surrounding Arkham Asylum absorbed the best part of the fall damage.

Andy jumped to the ground and helped him up while Kerri swerved the Chevy around and rushed back to them, already flipping the right seat and stretching to open the door. She brought the car skidding to a stop two feet short of running over them and Andy shoved the guy in the straitjacket onto the backseat and jumped in.

"Go!"

Kerri pressed the clutch, shifted to second, and drove off north along the asylum wall.

By the time they turned around the corner, every single guard from the maximum-security ward was rushing out through the gate ahead. Three of them dared to step in the car's trajectory and order it to stop.

Kerri made a point of shifting again really loud, engine revving in an unequivocal statement.

The ephemeral determination in the guards' eyes segued to panic in the tenth of a second before they jumped aside, dodging the stampeding vehicle.

None of the other Arkham employees coughing at the dust trail noticed the Weimaraner with a penguin in his mouth running through the open gate and bolting behind the station wagon. And they didn't even start running themselves until several patients from Nate's ward had poured out too, chasing the dog, with Kimrean in the lead, crying, "I saw the whole thing! A dog and a penguin helped him escape!"

At the head of the chase, the Vega slowed down, with Kerri and Andy both leaning out and waving.

"Tim, hurry up! Run!"

The dog sprinted down the gravel path, ears flapping in the wind, penguin squeaking between his teeth to the frantic beat of his footsteps, catching up to the car where Kerri was forgoing all of the driver's duties to wave him over. They were reaching the end of the park by the time Tim jumped into Kerri's arms, Andy holding the wheel and steering them all onto the main road, out of the path of a honking eighteen-wheeler. The driver's side door banged shut right behind the dog.

In the rearview mirror, the pointy roofs of Arkham Asylum dipped back behind the maple trees.

"Go, get in the back! I'll drive!" ordered Andy, maneuvering to swap seats with Kerri at 70 mph.

"You dumb fuck!" Nate shouted at the dog, tied up, rolling upside down on the backseat. "Next time you go around the furniture, not under it!"

"Don't scold him! He did great!" Kerri protested, wrestling Tim and rubbing noses with him. "Didn't you? You did a great job! Good boy! Very good boy!"

I know, Tim panted, overjoyed. *I rescued the penguin!*

n his hand he held a pink safety razor, the last item in his welcome gift pack. His old bandaged fingers ached under fresh contusions. Bruises sprawled throughout his slender chest and arms like industrial developments in nineteenth-century Britain.

He caressed his chin. A semitransparent fluff under his lower lip was pretty much the total of his facial hair two weeks after he had last been allowed a Gillette in Arkham.

One of the toilets behind him flushed. Nate quickly put on a T-shirt, one of the two he had taken the precaution to wear that morning. It had been the easy workaround to the impossibility of carry-on luggage, and the extra padding had also been welcome.

A stall door flung open and Peter came to the sink, tucking his striped polo shirt.

"All right! Seems like the club's back in action."

Nate remained silent, watching the new guy in the mirror.

Peter Manner, theoretically 26, fixes his wavy hair with Nate's comb, then pockets it in his jeans, a glistening smile of approval toward his reflection.

"Just like the old times," he sighed. Right then he noticed the razor in Nate's hand. "Why did they give you that? Is Kerri still expecting you to hit puberty or something? You never had body hair."

"I know." Nate chuckled.

"Look at me, though." Peter checked his clean-shaven square jaw. "Some days I grow a full five o'clock shadow by a quarter past nine. I even grow hair after death."

"That's actually a myth," Nate said. "The rest of your body shrivels and shrinks, which makes your hair look longer."

"Oh," said Peter, giving himself a closer inspection to make sure he showed no aging or decaying signs. "Well, I look fresh enough. And hey," he added, nudging Nate, "the girls don't look bad either, huh?"

"I guess."

"Oh, come on! Kerri was already hot in high school; no surprise there. But have you seen Andy?" He did something that cowboys probably do when communicating with other cowboys across long distances. "For someone who used to hate being recognized as a girl, she's turned into the kind of woman you can see from a mile away!"

"You wanna go out there and tell her that?" Nate challenged him, addressing the ghost beside him, not the reflection.

Peter scoffed. "Nah, you know me. I always went for Kerri. You don't have a problem with that, right? You two are family, so it's the logical pairing."

A biker walked into the restrooms. Peter said hi, cheerfully. Without stopping, the newcomer registered the open bag by the sink with toothbrush, razor, and shower gel spread out, and continued into the stall, respectful of a traveler's toilette. Or maybe he'd caught a glimpse of the yellow uniform sleeve sticking out of the trash can, Nate thought.

Peter fixed his letter jacket.

Kerri and Andy sat at a window booth overlooking the truck parking, a vast road map spread on the table.

KERRI: Look, I can just phone my mom and have her transfer the money; we can be in Portland tonight. She'll love to have us.

ANDY: I know, I'd love to see her too, but I'd rather go by road.

KERRI: But why? With the amount of fuel that piece of junk must need it won't make a difference. And it's only six hours by plane.

ANDY: I know, I . . . *(Tired, she leans closer, as in confidence.)* Look. I can't ride a plane.

KERRI: *(Concerned.)* What do you mean you can't ride a plane?

ANDY: I mean, I can ride a plane, I just can't go to an airport.

KERRI: Why?

ANDY: Because . . . *(She checks the bikers by the bar and the couple with children at a faraway table.)* Okay, remember the topic of what I've been doing for the last five years? Well,

I didn't mention everything. For a month recently I was also . . . doing time.

(Pause.)

KERRI: Time for what?

ANDY: *(Pauses, disarmed. Sighs patiently.)* Jail time, Kerri.

KERRI: You've been in jail?! What for?

ANDY: Nothing serious. A street fight. Collateral damage. We were . . . arguing at the door of a Spago, and I accidentally damaged what turned out to be a congressman's car. *(Beat.)* With the congressman inside. *(Beat.)* By throwing the congressman's son through the windshield.

KERRI: *(Digesting that, laboriously.)* Okay, so . . . you're not allowed to fly for that? You served your time.

ANDY: Uh . . . well, let's say after the first weeks I decided I'd learned my lesson already, so I cut my time short.

KERRI: You broke out of jail?!

ANDY: Shh! *(Checks their audience again.)* Look, it's no biggie; it happened in Texas, so I'm safe here. But airport security use federal databases and my name would light up, so I can't go to Texas and I can't go to airports.

KERRI: So instead we have to drive through twelve fucking states?!

ANDY: Uh . . . thirteen. I'd better stay clear of Ohio too.

(Nate, wearing clean clothes, joins them.)

NATE: The pants fit, Kay. Thanks for those. *(He sits down next to Kerri and across from Andy, and waits for dialogue to resume. It doesn't.)* What's up?

KERRI: Andy was in jail!

NATE: *(To Andy.)* Wow. *(To Kerri.)* Well, you have that in common.

ANDY: What?!

KERRI: It's completely different.

ANDY: You were in jail?

KERRI: I spent a couple nights in the pokey. Friends bailed me out.

ANDY: What did you do?

KERRI: Nothing. Drunk driving.

NATE: A concrete mixer truck.

KERRI: Around an abandoned mall.

NATE: Through the mall.

KERRI: It was nothing, okay? A couple nights grounded.

ANDY: Then what's the big deal? I just did forty-three more nights!

KERRI: Only because you fucking broke out!

ANDY: Yeah, a little louder, please.

KERRI: *(To Nate.)* We're gonna have to drive to Blyton Hills because Ms. T here punched a guy through a car and then broke out of prison.

NATE: Okay. *(Tries a sip of coffee, then notices the others' bafflement with his placidity. He looks at both alternately.)* Was that supposed to impress me? 'Cause I broke out from a mental asylum like forty-five minutes ago.

ANDY: Okay, I think we have established we have all led intense lives so far; can we please move the fuck on?

KERRI: Whoa, I'm nothing like you two jailbirds, okay? I didn't break out from anywhere. When I was put in jail I stayed there until they let me out, like a good girl.

ANDY: Wow. Your mom would be so proud.

NATE: I once spent five weeks digging a tunnel out of a clinic where I'd been admitted for two weeks.

ANDY: *(After rereading the line above.)* Why didn't you walk out after the two weeks?

NATE: I'd started already; I hate leaving stuff unfinished. On a completely different subject, do either of you happen to carry any anti-hallucination drugs?

(Kerri and Andy look at each other, then back at him.)

KERRI: You're hallucinating?

NATE: Well, it's a funny story. I've had a few odd episodes before Arkham, so they put me on this drug to get rid of them, and now whenever I don't take the drug they come back.

KERRI: So you are seeing things.

NATE: Seeing, hearing . . . sharing combs . . .

ANDY: *(Serious.)* Is this gonna be a problem?

NATE: *(Stares.)* Shit, I don't know, Andy; tell me: Are you really here right now? *(Continues despite her eyeroll.)* Is Kerri sitting right beside me? Is there a dog next to you lapping your coffee while you're not looking?

(Kerri reaches over to slap Tim, drags the cup away from him.)

KERRI: Little fucker, you've had enough sugar for three lifetimes.

ANDY: Okay, look, it's a forty-five-hour drive to Blyton Hills. Do you guys think we'll have time to go through all our criminal and psychiatric records during the trip? 'Cause if you do, I suggest we grab some sandwiches and leave now.

(They consider the proposal for a second.)

NATE: *(Slaps the table.)* All right. Let's do it.

ANDY: Good. *(To Kerri.)* Make yours a root beer; you're driving soon.

* * *

Kerri took the wheel about a hundred miles later, and Andy dozed off in minutes. When she opened her eyes again, the sun ahead was sinking into a trippy pool of purple liquid clouds, and the Chevy Vega and the cast were dyed deep pink. Kerri looked like she did under the UV club lights two nights ago, only bored.

"We need a new radio," she said, not needing a side glance to confirm Andy was awake.

"The car drives better than it looks," Nate added, looking up from the crossword puzzle, with Tim resting his head on his lap trying to read the *Peanuts* strip on the same page. "Did you restore it yourself?"

"Shit yeah, Nate, I did," Andy said. "Like a good old butch girl; I put on my overalls, grabbed my tool belt, and torqued the shit out of the engine!"

"Jesus, girl, chill out. Just asking."

"Right, sorry." She rubbed her face, trying to inhale some of the soothing magic purple air. "Sorry I jumped at you, Nate. No, I didn't restore it; I just painted it and had the transmission changed. I bought it off an impound auction. And yes, we could use a radio."

"We can buy one tomorrow before we set off," Kerri said.

"I just slept, actually; I can drive during the night."

"No, Andy, I want to sleep in a real bed. Sleepy Lake's waited for us thirteen years; it can hold on for a couple more days."

Andy did not object. Her hand, however, palpated the

thin lump of a wallet inside her pocket.

"I can still ask my mom for that transfer," Kerri guessed, again without even glancing in her direction.

"No, it's okay. I have some money saved."

NATE: Is that from the time you robbed that bank in Albuquerque?

ANDY: No, Nate, it's from the time I ass-modeled for your favorite magazine, *Amazons in Skimpy Armor.*

Nate scoffed, Kerri smiled. Andy felt a little proud of that.

"Hey, anyway," Nate started, "I was thinking we could save money if we stopped in Portland to see Aunt Margo and borrowed the keys to her place in Blyton Hills."

"It's okay, I have the keys," Kerri said.

Andy nodded approvingly at the plan. Then she thought. Then she noticed this pause was growing awkwardly long. Nate was staring at Kerri in the front mirror, who was just now becoming aware of her slip.

"Why do you have the keys to the house in Blyton Hills?"

"Uh, Aunt Margo gave them to me. I mean, to us."

"Us? When did this happen?"

"I don't know, like last Christmas? No, two Christmases ago."

"I didn't come home for Christmas two years ago."

"I know." Kerri was putting clear effort into playing it down. "Whatever. Aunt Margo had been trying to sell the house for a year and couldn't find a buyer, so she just gave me the keys. Thought we might like to crash there sometime."

"You never told me this," Nate complained.

"I . . . I just came back, threw the keys in a drawer, and didn't think about it again."

"Wait a minute," Andy requested. "You have the house in Blyton Hills at your disposal and you and Tim were living in that shithole?"

"Okay," Kerri said, laying out her defense, "first: ouch, feelings. And second, I could not just switch coasts overnight; I had stuff going on in New York!"

ANDY: Working as a waitress?!

NATE: And you told me nothing? Do you know the kind of places I've been living in between clinics? My last two roommates were Chechen terrorists and *I* was the shady one in the house!

KERRI: Right, like you would have considered moving to Blyton Hills just for the free lodging!

NATE: Maybe I fucking would have!

ANDY: Okay, okay, everybody shut up!

Tim curled up in a corner of the backseat, sheltering his penguin from the storm, all tensed up in "scandalized Maggie Smith" pose.

The Chevy hummed its best attempt at elevator music while the passengers cooled down, pined for cigarettes, and mentally calculated the miles to Blyton Hills.

"You're right, Nate," Kerri said. "I'm sorry. I should have told you."

"It's fine. I wouldn't have gone anyway," he said.

Andy inspected Kerri. The sun visor cast a crisp border across her face between shadow and light; the lower half of her face was purple and soft, the upper half dark and red-eyed.

"I never thought it'd be like this," Kerri told the road.

"I know what you mean," Andy replied.

"No, you don't. I mean—" She sighed, impatient at her own impatience. "I'm sorry. It's that to us Blyton Hills wasn't just a summerhouse. Aunt Margo and Uncle Emmet didn't have any kids, but they built rooms for Nate and me. It felt like home. I never thought I'd be reluctant . . . not reluctant, unwilling to go there," she said, pointing at the dying sun.

Andy allowed a respectful silence.

"I know. It wasn't home to me. It was paradise."

She checked the others to make sure that didn't sound like an exaggeration.

"Blyton Hills was better than home," she resumed. "Home was where I fought my parents and couldn't be myself. Your aunt and uncle were family to me. Uncle Emmet taught me how to drive when I was eleven. Your aunt Margo gave me my first tampon. What do you think used to keep me alive in Catholic schools where I was forced to wear skirts and put up with rednecks laughing at my short hair? All the time I was just waiting for the next vacation so I could pack my bags and jump on the bus to Blyton Hills. Even my parents resented all the time I spent with your family, but I guess they were glad I had friends somewhere. If you made me choose between tickets to Disneyland and Disney World with anybody else or Blyton Hills with you guys, I would have chosen you in a heartbeat."

"Same here," Nate voted. Then, pushing the newspaper aside, he added, "Although, implying that Blyton Hills was a redneck-free zone . . . Joey Krantz, anyone?"

The gravitas dissolved into laughter.

"God, everyone remembers that prick!" said Kerri. "Can we please focus on the good people of Blyton Hills?"

"Nah, just kidding," Nate said. "We had great times."

Everyone used the honesty moment to sigh, sniff, shift in their seats.

"Shit, I wish Peter was here."

Kerri said that.

"I always thought if one of us were to take the initiative, it'd be him," she expanded.

"Well, he took one initiative," mumbled Nate into the newspaper.

"What do you mean?"

"You know. Offing himself."

"What? What are you saying? The police ruled it an accidental overdose."

"Come on!" cried Andy and Nate ensemble. "Kerri, he killed himself."

"But why? Why would he kill himself? He was the most successful of us—he was the only successful one! While you were trainhopping and you were institutionalized, Peter had a penthouse in Hollywood and was on the cover of *Rolling Stone*! Why would he want to die?"

"The same reason I was trainhopping or Nate was in the loony bin! Because of what we went through!"

"No way! Peter was . . . he was okay," Kerri protested. "He was the one who made it out without scars."

"He just hid them better than we did," Andy said bitterly, returning to the violet landscape, biting her knuckles. Mountains and woods were steadily flowing toward nowhere.

"He called," Kerri said. Her eyes stayed fixed on the lava lamp effect of dusk.

"What?"

"Peter. Before he died, he phoned me."

Andy and Nate shared a new exclamation.

"When? What did he say?"

"I don't know. It was late at night and there was a party in my dorm and it was loud and I couldn't really hear him, so I told him I would call back later, but I drank a lot and I kinda forgot. Then two days later I read his obituary in the paper."

Everybody fell silent after that.

A scything moon had appeared in Andy's window.

They checked into a motel not uglier than the rest, which is remarkable, road motels being relentlessly competitive when it comes to creating the most depressing atmosphere out of blank walls and PVC. The country-style rooms, furnished in light wood and tasseled curtains and quilts, featured so few amenities that even Tim became bored fifteen seconds after arrival—and this was the same dog that had, on one occasion, spent eight hours straight fascinated by an egg.

Kerri poured some kibble into his tin bowl from his very own travel bag, which fit inside hers, and sat on the bed farthest from the door with a bottle of beer. The motel slept in silence, all the guests probably busy counting stolen money or chopping up corpses in the bathtub.

"Beer?" She offered the bottle across the space between the beds.

"No, thanks," Andy said.

"Your body is a temple."

The line "Not one adhering to the moral codes of any major religion I know" took way too long to find its wording in Andy's mind, so she just smirked.

"You're enjoying this," Kerri noticed, dimly amused.

"Enjoying what?"

"This. What we're doing."

Andy surveyed the carpet for a good answer, then shrugged. "At least we're doing something."

Kerri nodded, glanced over at her. "You don't seem very scared yourself."

"I'm fine when I'm with you," Andy said, shrugging again.

Kerri grinned at the line and left the bottle next to her sleeping pills and Andy's wallet. The room was cold. She slithered into bed and tucked herself in.

Andy stayed in place, vigilant. "Why did your aunt leave Blyton Hills?" she asked, her voice too shy to dispel the quiet.

"She moved after my uncle died, in 'eighty-five. Business wasn't going well anyway, because of the depression."

Andy frowned, embarrassed of her history knowledge. "There was a depression?"

"In Blyton Hills there was. The wool trade went down; most of the town economy resented it."

The only sound between lines was Tim munching from his bowl, filling the blank seconds Andy spent just staring at the figure drawn by the single bedside lamp, and making her feel self-conscious about it.

"Why did the wool business sink?" she tried, just to extend the moment. "Sheep smugglers?"

"No. The sheep died."

"Shit. All of them?"

"Most. In spring they used to graze them in the valley downriver. One morning the shepherds just found them all dead. Remember the chemical plant south of town?"

"Yeah."

"They think it was water poisoning. There's a big class-action lawsuit." She turned over. "Fuck, what I wouldn't do for a warm night."

Andy responded swiftly by laying Kerri's parka on top of her. Hundreds of orange curls oohed and aahed under the wool lining.

She sat down next to her on the mattress. Her gaze strayed over the fake wood paneling and the halfhearted attempt at rustic.

"Do you know what this place reminds me of? Chippanuck Camp."

A scoff came from under the covers. "Shit, what a miserable place that was."

"Hey, only until we exposed the owner's scheme for forging Indian craftwork."

"I bet it's better now that the children aren't stitching 'fair trade' labels onto hand-sewn Cherokee purses," Kerri sniffed.

Andy felt warmed up by the mere memory.

"Our very first case, remember? At the end of that camp you invited me and Peter to Blyton Hills."

Somewhere under her right hand, through the parka

and a blanket and the bedsheets, she could feel Kerri's shoulder breathing. Andy's eyes had lost themselves in a flame of orange hair, in the way eyes are attracted only by lit fireplaces.

"Do you know what I remember most about that summer?" she said. "I mean, apart from the child labor thingy?"

"Heh. No, what?"

"When I met you. Do you remember it?"

"Uh-uh."

"There was that dumb counselor with big tits who introduced us."

"Right, the one who was sleeping with the head supervisor."

"Shit. She was?"

"Yep, I'm pretty sure."

"Okay, so she dragged me toward a bunch of girls because I wasn't making any friends. She put her hand on my shoulder, and said, 'Kerri, this is Andrea.' And I said, 'Andy.'"

"You grumbled, 'Andy.'"

"I did?"

"You were mad at somebody, probably at everybody, and very, very sulky. You looked like one of those evil kids in horror movies. *Children of the Corn,* Latina version."

"Yeah. *Children of the Coca Fields.*"

Kerri laughed into her pillow. "That's so racist!"

"I know; it's my race, I'm allowed. So anyway, I grumbled, 'Andy.' And you stuck your hand forward, smiling, and said, 'Hi, Andy.' That was it. Never questioned it. Never looked at me funny. And then we bumped into Nate and you said, 'This is my friend Andy.'"

Tim had finished his supper and lay down at the foot of Kerri's bed.

"I remember," Kerri whispered.

"You probably don't know—you surely didn't know then—but that is rare. Meeting someone who not only respects it, but believes it."

Kerri's eyes were closed now, a peaceful expression declared in her lips.

"That's what you and Blyton Hills represent to me," Andy resumed, sotto voce. "And I want to win it back. For all of us."

Leaves cracked under the tread of a furtive smile. "Joey too?"

"Yes, him too. I bet he never got out anyway; he'll be an unemployed slacker. Worse than all of us."

"Combined?" Kerri said dreamily. "Ex-con, mental, and alcoholic? That's a lot of boxes ticked."

In the next room, Nate sat alone on the left-side bed, hearing the merry humming tune that came from the bathroom.

Peter spat in the sink, rinsed his toothbrush (Nate's toothbrush), and returned to the bedroom.

"Ah, the boys' room again." He slumped onto the other bed. "Should we draw a treasure map before it's lights-out? Perhaps brush up on our sign language?"

"Get off my bed," Nate said, without moving.

"Says who?"

"What did you tell Kerri on the phone?"

"Why? Jealous I said good-bye to her and not you?"

"I'm serious. What did you talk about?"

"It was private."

"You have no idea."

"I have no idea what I told Kerri on the phone?"

"You have no idea because Kerri didn't talk to you on the phone," Nate concluded, and he treated himself to a pill out of a prescription bottle and a sip of Orange Crush.

Peter kept observing him closely, slightly off-balance.

"What are those for?" he asked.

"Hallucinations."

"Really? What are you seeing?"

"Right now? A moron who still wears bell-bottoms."

"Do you think a pill is going to just make me puff away? Because I'm warning you, it took like thirty pillf laft time to make me paff away."

Nate couldn't help a sportive laugh. "Good one," he acknowledged, capping the bottle. "But that's the point. Peter passed away. You're not Peter."

"Come on! We're the Blyton Summer Detective Club," Peter protested. "When have you ever caught a bad guy without me? You are going to need my help."

"I'm afraid we'll have to get by without it. Get up."

Nate had stood up and now he was taking over the bed opposite. Peter sprang swiftly on his feet, the remote possibility of someone walking in and finding him sharing a bed with another man being clearly inadmissible. No matter who hallucinated whom.

He peered down at Nate kicking off his sneakers. "Of course you're the expert here, having lived among delusional people far longer than me, but don't I sound pretty consistent to you for a hallucination?"

"Not really," Nate answered. "You'd be surprised by the consistency of people's delusions. If they were easily dismantled, they wouldn't believe them."

"But I look like me. Sound like me. Know what I know."

"No, you don't know what you know. You know what I know you know." He faced Peter again. "Tell me what you told Kerri on the phone."

Peter sat on the left bed, an unusual angle in his lips.

"That I loved her."

"That's what I think you told her," Nate replied. "Because I am fabricating you. I am feeding you your lines. You're just a figment of my subconscious, trying to tell me . . . something."

"Tell you what?"

"I don't know; do you need to ask me?"

He reached for the lamp switch and turned it off, lying still dressed on the bed.

"It's irrelevant what you have to tell me," he continued, "because I know consciously, without any doubt, that we are doing the right thing here. Andy is right. We must go to Blyton Hills, solve this case, and find peace. And that begins by ignoring our minds' tricks. So I'm sorry but no, we will not be needing your help."

Peter remained sitting, a wide-shouldered silhouette against the window.

"Okay," Peter started, in the exact voice Nate recalled

him using when laying out an attack plan. "So I'm just a hallucination, a subjective experience that—what?"

Nate had started laughing.

"The real Peter would never use the word 'subjective.' I mean, sorry, man, you were just a leader; Kerri was the brains."

He gave time for his laughter to remit, then fell silent, a smile on his face. When he noticed a minute had passed, he wondered. He risked a glance toward the other bed.

The silhouette was still there.

"Okay," it said. "I see it. You don't need me. You guys got a new leader. And I'm a figment of your subconscious, so what can I possibly know? About Peter's life. About Peter's death. About what waits for you back in Sleepy Lake. About what he saw when you were too chicken-scared to look. About the massive, heart-withering evil you and your friends hardly brushed over while fighting a stupid yokel in a costume. The evil that will catch up with you as it caught up with me, Nate."

"Shut up."

"What can I know about the cold, like your body naked and buried in the snow, the infinite cold gripping you, burning you, numbing you, seeping through your pores, frostbiting your muscles, killing the marrow in your bones? About dirt being shoveled over your lips and nostrils, about centipedes scuttling into your ears and gnawing the inside?"

"Stay there."

"About maggots living in your body, growing fat, eating their way out? About gigantic god worms sleeping in the center of the earth, curled up, miles and miles of a single primordial thing that will devour your house with you in it, and let you sink into the unspeakable sickness of its gut, Nate? You and Andy and your beautiful cousin burning alive in hell?"

Nate reached the light switch before Peter's slithering hand reached him. It still was Peter, eyeless, rotten, worms pouring out of his mouth.

"It will kill you all."

"Nate!"

Nate opened his eyes back to the ugly motel. Andy banged the wall between their rooms once more.

"Nate? Are you okay?" she said.

Nate sat up on his bed, clothes soaked in sweat.

"Yeah," he said to the wall. "Bad dream. No problem."

It took him another minute to notice he was back in the left bed.

Lying fully dressed on the right one, Peter crossed his legs and fixed his perfect hair.

"Yup. All together then. This is going to be great."

PART TWO

RELAPSE

They bought a new car radio with a tape player and no CD tray the next morning in an unmanned hardware store in Winter River, Connecticut. The next day they had the oil replaced in a gas station near Brahams, West Virginia. They had a flat tire that afternoon, so on the morrow they bought a new spare at a retail shop outside Dark Falls, Illinois. On the fourth evening, the front brake cylinder broke in the middle of the interstate, almost causing them to sodomize a VW Camper, and Andy had to persuade a gang of road racers to take the Chevy into their garage for new hydraulics twenty miles north of Raccoon City. By that time, the question of whether the car that would eventually reach Oregon would be the same that left the East Coast was beginning to acquire philosophical relevance.

* * *

On the fifth morning, Kerri emerged from a motel room late in the morning, about 9:30, to find Andy in stained overalls and a breathing mask, removing strips of two-inch vinyl tape from the car. Two fresh racing stripes in metallic black flowed down the hood of the fish-eyed Chevrolet Vega, glittering under the blazing morning sun like diamond dust.

"The racers let me borrow their paint gun," Andy explained, removing her mask. "Like it?"

"Yeah. I mean . . . I think it likes it," she replied.

"You said it would look more like a sports car."

"I know. I was kinda joking, but . . . whatever. It looks good."

The two-door station wagon sat like any other twelve-year-old while two of grandma's lady friends complimented his haircut.

The restaurant door banged shut behind Nate and Tim walking out into the dusty parking lot. Tim hurried to kiss Kerri good morning while Nate offered a tray of coffee cups to Andy first.

"Buy you lunch if you drive my turn." A hand fended the front-charging sunlight off his reddened eyes.

"Okay," Andy agreed.

Nate distributed breakfast and crawled onto the backseat.

"You had a rough night again?" Kerri asked him, but he had slammed the door behind him already. Tim studied the fresh, sweetly intoxicating paint on the hood.

"Do you think he's gonna be all right?"

"He's rationing the drugs he bought in Lexington. They

ought to last him for a couple weeks," Andy guessed. She then read Kerri. "What about you, did you sleep well?"

"Not bad," she said, thinking of it for the first time. She was wearing yesterday's shirt under her violet T-shirt from two days ago, Andy recalled. "Pretty well, actually. I don't know. Maybe it's helping. Not being alone."

Andy nodded, began putting away the paint gun.

"How about you?" Kerri followed up. "You never talk about how you coped. Don't you have nightmares? Did you used to think of us at nights?"

Andy tossed a can of spray paint into the box and paused to examine the question. Kerri stood by, gold-haloed.

"Yeah. Quite often," Andy answered.

During that day they crossed another three state lines: Colorado, Wyoming, and Idaho. By late evening, Tim was riding shotgun, leaning out the window and panting at the wind, his head about to be turned completely inside out. Every now and then he popped in to spit the dead insects and then stuck his head back out for another five minutes. Kerri and Nate were playing Scattergories in the backseat. The radio blasted "Funky Cold Medina," the remixed version. Andy was driving and nodding to the beat.

Her Coca-Cola watch on the dashboard *beep-beep*ed.

ANDY: Time's up.

KERRI: *(Lightspeed scribbling.)* Waitwaitwaitwait done! Okay, people you've been compared to: Vanessa Paradis.

NATE: Poe. Because of the gloom.

KERRI: Cartoons you like: *Pink Panther,* double score!

NATE: *Pole Position,* double score too.

KERRI: Fuck. Places you've been to: prison.

NATE: Uh, Portland? As in, where we used to live?

KERRI: Okay, should've thought of that. Places you dream about going: Port-au-Prince.

NATE: Pluto. Port-au-Prince, not Paris?

KERRI: Port-au-Prince scores double, loser. Things you're very good at: psychology.

NATE: *Prince of Persia,* double score.

KERRI: Damn. Things in this car: a penguin!

NATE: Nothing.

PETER: *(Offended.)* Thanks a fucking bunch.

Kerri raised her arms in the greatest V sign the car roof allowed. "I win!"

"I'm cold; close the window, will you?" Nate asked.

Kerri scurried to the front seat, pulled the dog inside, and cranked the window up. Tim snorted smugly and moved on to explore the carpet for leftover Cheetos.

Andy groaned at the third full motel they drove by.

"Can't find a place for the night."

"I heard it's 'teen detectives going back to confront their ghosts' season," Kerri said.

"I'll take their ghosts over ours any day of the week," Nate added.

Kerri checked the map. "We've driven a lot today; we could be there in another ... eight hours? We'd get to Blyton Hills by three a.m."

"I'd rather stop and continue in the morning," Andy said. "I want us to see Blyton Hills in the light of day."

Kerri lingered on that answer for a moment, then

chuckled. "You want us? Why?"

"So we all realize there's nothing to be scared of. I don't know. It'll change our perspective."

"Okay." She polled the backseat. "Nate?"

"Okay by me. Tim?"

Tim coughed up Kerri's winning Scattergories sheet and tail-nodded.

They stopped for a late dinner, then continued driving into the dusk past another three neon NO VACANCY signs.

Night closed in on them. For a while they stayed on I-84, flowing along with other blurry sets of white and red lights, carrying other silent wraithlike people in their tiny warm sepia-lit cubicles pretending to have their own places to go and lives to live, and Andy gazed at them while Kerri drove and silently challenged them to have a better story to tell.

Later on, even these extras became sparse. At that point Kerri left the interstate for a state route, then moved onto an empty single-lane road, and finally swerved into the first dirt track, rolled a few yards off-road, and pulled over. They would sleep in the car. Nate had long ago called dibs on the backseat. Tim lay curled up in the minimal footspace there. Kerri keyed off the engine and dialed mute the radio.

"Last night on the road," she said, pushing her seat back. "We should do this again in better circumstances, huh?"

Something about the beige upholstery inside the car made it look like a very small and cozy hobbit living room. Kerri shifted over to face Andy, smiled good night, and closed her eyes.

Andy stargazed at her skin for a couple minutes and then switched the roof light off and followed suit.

She actually enjoyed sleeping like that—she often preferred her car to beds. In motels or cities there are always faraway noises and blinking lights beyond one's eyelids, distracting the conscience, but inside a car in the middle of nowhere there is nothing to hold on to, nothing to see or hear. Which means, in a way, being able to see and hear everything. During her nights alone on the road she liked to sink into that void. She could dive in the all-enveloping silence and swim toward any signal-emitting system she wanted. She could navigate toward a highway, or a small town, or a big city. She could zoom across state lines toward the lights, fly over the red-and-white traffic and through concrete and neon signs until she spotted Kerri in a crowded club, and watch her for a while before whispering into her ear to call it a night.

Though she didn't need to do that tonight. Kerri slept right by her side, sharing that metal eggshell with her, her curly contour clearly defined against the driver's side window. Andy could close her eyes and easily tune her mind to the breathing of Kerri's hair, the warmth of Kerri's blood, all inches close. Tonight she was physically sitting right where she wanted to be on Earth, next to the source of the signal she always longed for.

The rest didn't matter. Not Nate, not Tim, nothing else in the sleepscape. She could hear the grumblings of the mountains and valleys, and the legions of trees crowding the Pacific Northwest. She could perceive the gentle snoring of a wooden church and the window blinds of the restaurant in Blyton Hills, the roads north under the starry night, and the aloofness of firs. She could feel the icy quietness of the moonlit mirror that was Sleepy Lake. She could eavesdrop on the whispering conspiracy of trees on the solitary island, and the neutral, unassuming walls of the haunted house. She could peek through the battered windows and spy between the dusty floorboards. She could sink into the basement and even see the dungeon where she and Kerri locked themselves up. She could near the walls and still hear the things outside. Their squelching footsteps, the sandpaper breathing. Their needle fingernails tapping the bricks, scratching the glass, smelling the warmth of Kerri and Andy sleeping inside the car.

Andy opened her eyes and the creature banged the windshield and screamed.

She jolted awake and the seat belt around her arm prevented her from crashing her fist through the windshield just as the creature flew away in terror. Probably an owl. Andy had to cover her mouth with both hands to exhale the adrenaline without waking up everyone in the car.

She checked on Nate enjoying the whole of the backseat, Tim on the floor, and Kerri, still asleep like a beautiful charm, her power to repel bad dreams yet unchallenged. It had been the owl's fault. Anyone would have jumped because of that owl, she rationalized. Almost anyone would have tried to one-punch it dead through a car glass.

After a while she considered it safe to sneak out without disturbing anyone. She miscalculated, though: as soon as the door latch clacked open, Tim scurried out from under the seat and ran into the wild.

Andy left him to reconnoiter the area and stayed close to the car. Condensation had fogged up the windows and locked the landscape out of sight from inside the car, but Andy was glad to notice the outside world had not deserted them. It was a busy night; not clear, but shared by enough clouds and stars and a half-crescent moon to keep owls and cicadas and rodents entertained and the scene as alive and thrilling as a never-sleeping metropolis. The dirt track they'd been driving on veered a few meters shy of the top of a hill, and Andy found the top and the opposite slope sparkling with early flowers in the blue night.

She sat down, feeling the damp dirt under her jeans, and thought.

Tim came back from reconnaissance some minutes later and sat down comfortably close to her. He seemed to scan the horizon with a seed of astronomer's curiosity.

"Tomorrow, Tim, we'll be in Blyton Hills. You know what that is?"

She scratched his head, their eyes locked and perfectly level, and Tim listened closely.

"You've never been there, but your great-grandfather Sean had. It's the best place in the world," she told him. "A very little town in a valley filled with summerhouses, not like those shitty plastic suburbs, but with cute gardens and really old trees, where not yuppies, nor rednecks, but real nice people live. And all around it, in every direction, under the green mantle of woods, miles and miles of . . . adventure."

Her sight, and Tim's, had strayed into the stars.

"Mountains to climb, and creeks to cross, and treasures in every spot. Swamps where you can build rafts, and caves to take shelter in when it rains, and old mills and barns where hand-wringing bad guys think of their evil plots, and lakes with monsters, and haunted houses where pirates used to live."

She paused. Tim nose-prodded her like she was a music box that had stopped playing.

"It's actually a little scary," she warned him. "We're going to need you at your best, soldier. We rely on you."

Tim held her stare.

"But if it ever gets too bad, you don't worry. Because Kerri has this place in Blyton Hills, her bedroom in Aunt Margo's house, and it's the safest place on earth. Like a sanctuary where we heal our wounds, lay out our strategies, and laugh away fear. And nothing can happen there; no monsters, bullies, or harm can reach you, because it's the place where Kerri lives. It's where she sleeps and reads and it's the core of Blyton Hills' warmth, the source from where everything soft and sweet and orange sprays onto the world. And that's where we're going. You'll see. It's going to be fine."

"What is?"

Kerri wandered by, hands deep in her pockets, a trail of steam and a flame of hair carrying her words away.

"Hey."

Tim rose to greet her, his tail causing cyclones as near as California. Kerri stroked his snout.

"Am I interrupting a moment? I can leave."

"No, stay. We're done."

"Can't sleep?"

"I needed to stretch my legs," Andy said. "But no, not really."

Kerri lotused down by her side, careful not to squash any dandelion. The nightscape teemed with guessable constellations.

Andy stayed silent, but the train of her thoughts had derailed already.

KERRI: *(Amused.)* Scattergories?

ANDY: No. Please, no, I suck at that.

KERRI: Oh, come on. Okay—word bluff! It's like a simplified version.

ANDY: *(Embarrassed.)* No! I'm so bad with words!

KERRI: Come on, it's not about words. You play the other guy's mind.

ANDY: I'm no challenge.

KERRI: Just let me explain how you play it.

ANDY: Okay, go.

KERRI: Normally we'd use paper and pencil, but you and I can play on an honor code. You think of a word. And you just say one letter in it. Any letter, got it? Then I think of a word that has that letter, and I say another letter in it. Follow me?

ANDY: Uh-huh.

KERRI: Now, your word needs to have both letters in it. So if it doesn't, you must think of a new one. And then you say a third letter. And I think of a word with all three and say a fourth letter.

ANDY: Uh-huh.

KERRI: And that's it. All you can do is keep adding letters, even if you can't think of a word anymore. Or you can call my bluff, and if I can't produce a word, you win. Or you can guess the word I'm thinking, and if I can't produce a different one, you win. Get it?

ANDY: Okay, so I either bluff, call your bluff, or read your mind.

KERRI: Exactly. Wanna try?

ANDY: Okay.

KERRI: Okay, I think of a word and say a letter. *X*.

ANDY: Oh, come on! *X*?

KERRI: It doesn't mean it begins with *X*; it just has an *X* in it.

ANDY: Right. Okay. Uh . . . *E*.

KERRI: *F*.

ANDY: *X* and *F* in the same word?

KERRI: Yup. And *E*.

ANDY: *(Thinks lengthily.)* Okay, *D*.

KERRI: *T*.

ANDY: No way. There's no such word.

KERRI: *(Smiling proudly.)* "Exfoliated."

ANDY: Oh, come on!

KERRI: What? It was easy. I was thinking "exfoliate"; you gave me *D*; it was easy to adapt.

ANDY: But you're a biologist and I don't even know what that means!

KERRI: Who cares? You know "exfoliation" is a word, right? That's all that matters; you gotta think big. And by the way, it means a tree losing its leaves.

ANDY: Oh. *(Confused.)* I thought it was something in cosmetics.

KERRI: Yeah, that too, but you don't use makeup and you like nature, so stick with the bit that concerns you. Try again?

ANDY: Okay. You start.

KERRI: All right. *V.*

ANDY: *V. (Thinks.)* Can I say *V* again?

KERRI: Two *V*s?

ANDY: Uh-huh.

KERRI: Okay, we're playing high stakes. *(Thinks, front teeth biting her lower lip in a frozen labiodental fricative.)* Oh, right . . . Gotcha. *L.*

ANDY: *A.*

KERRI: You're thinking "valve"!

ANDY: No. "Vulva."

KERRI: *(Dropping backward onto the grass).* Aw, fuck! You sly, sly dog.

Andy repressed a smug grin, making sure to capture the moment for later wallowing.

Kerri sat up again when Tim tried to lick her face. "Well played. See, it wasn't difficult."

Andy looked down, hiding her smile.

"I'm glad we're doing this," Kerri commented. She waited for visual contact. "What moved you? Why come fetch us now?"

Andy plucked a blade of grass, indulged her fingers to play with it.

"I've been thinking about it since Peter died. But I needed to talk to Wickley first. Or maybe I didn't; he only said what I expected to hear."

"I wish you'd come for us long ago," Kerri said. "We had to do this."

* * *

Inside the car, Nate slept despite Peter clambering over him, spying through the window.

"Check it out. The girls are just sitting there, having a laugh. What do you think is going on?"

Nate rolled around, burying his face in the fake leather upholstery.

"I'll tell you what I think is going on," Peter responded rhetorically. "I'm picking up some strong signals here, Nate. Just look at them. The smiles. The body language. That shared intimacy. It doesn't take a detective; you just need to have been around, know the female mind, know the game. Now I realize, it's been going on all week! Even in this car! *(Accusing, at the empty front seats.)* Haven't you noticed? The jokes, the chemistry in the air . . . You can almost breathe the hormones! *(Gloating.)* I'm telling you, Nate, this smells like something I am pretty familiar with."

NATE: *(Sleepily.)* Embalming fluid?

(Pause.)

PETER: That was fucking rude, Nate.

On the sixth day, they set off even before Nate was fully awake. They crossed into Oregon some two hours later. After another four hours neglecting the federal speed limit they came into sight of the Cascades. In another forty-five minutes they'd crossed into Pennaquick County.

Time declined any relevance beyond that point.

The route became a hair-thin asphalt line amid black-wooded dunes, slithering uphill and westward with bewildering faith for longer than anyone would try. A wavy ocean of fir trees spread for miles and miles in every direction.

All three people in the car had begun to wonder whether they'd taken the right detour when they suddenly crossed the truss bridge over the Zoinx River—a cobalt-blue, rust-bleeding structure dangling over the busy rapids. All human eyes glimmered with acquiescence.

At the next turn left, a blue wooden sign welcomed them to BLYTON ILLS. Rot had eaten through the letter *H*.

It had begun to drizzle.

Without an introductory long shot, the town just happened on the sides of the road—a few wire fences first, then suddenly a building rising from the growth, and then the elementary school, and then a crossing and houses and stores. Andy had to check her watch to confirm it was a weekday. Most shops on East Street had their shutters down—had for a long time, by the look of it.

The first business of any kind they saw was an old man pushing a cartful of scrap metal in front of a vacant lot that Kerri was sure had once held a sporting goods store.

A few cars turtled by the Main and East junction, unwilling to reach their destinations, quarter-spirited like unpaid extras. In the southwest corner of that junction, the church's parking lot lay deserted.

Two women and one man and a dog stared out their windows, the taste of copper oxide on their lips.

The sun had forsaken them after all.

* * *

Kerri turned left on Main, offering the first panorama of town, a composition of blue shingles and crestfallen puffs of smoke out of chimneys. Ben's Corner Diner was open and serving. So were the pharmacy and Mr. Maxence's grocery store. The flag on the city hall yard waved on top of the pole, though the image would have hardly inspired a decimated army back into battle.

A pickup truck drove past them and the driver tipped his cap at the girls. It was an irrelevant gesture, but for some reason Andy and Kerri and Nate clung to it.

Andy asked, "Is this the depression you mentioned?"

"Which depression?" Nate counterasked.

"I don't know," Kerri said. She pointed at the blue, red, and white frame of the barbershop's front window. "My uncle used to take me there first day of summer to cut my split ends."

The barber sat outside his shop, as he often did in the past, though this time there was no one to talk to. That didn't seem to bother him, though; he was still talking.

The movie theater was closed, but that was to be expected. A video rental store had appeared a few doors farther down the street.

"Do you . . . I mean, does it look that different to you?" Kerri tried.

Two workmen loading a truck stopped for a breather at that exact second, and sulkily watched the Vega wheel by at 20 mph.

"Yes!" Andy complained. "Fuck, where are the kids?"

"We only used to come during holidays, remember?" Kerri said. "They must be in school."

"What about young people?"

"Probably around the school," Nate suggested. "Selling crack to the kids."

The west side of town, a four-block residential area off the end of Main Street, didn't look very different. Wooden FOR SALE signs sheltered under the trees from the gentle rain, but the houses they referred to stood old and solemn on desolate gardens.

The Chevy Vega crawled the few final meters to a stop before a low stone wall and a brittle wooden gate, pink paint peeling off. Kerri switched off the engine. Herewith ended a weeklong journey.

Andy got out of the car and, even before caressing the asphalt skin of the street, she looked up at the house.

It didn't look back. It stood grave and stiff-upper-lipped like Mount Hood, window pots of wildflowers and weeds as shoulder patches indicating rank. It barely caught the striped station wagon with the corner of its left dorm window and mumbled, *Punks.*

The punks stood outside the fence, bags at their feet, glancing up at the gray-and-pink stone-and-wood cottage. Pink flakes snowed off the shutters, the front door, the swinging chair, the meek gate quivering on its hinges under a Japanese breeze. Andy mouthed the word "exfoliation."

Kerri strode over the aimlessly low gate because she couldn't waste time searching for the right key. Pacific rain forests had grown between the irregular slabs that made the narrow walkway.

Andy stopped halfway along that path and gazed back at the street. This was how every adventure had ever started. In Andy's mental dictionary, the entry for "adventure" featured this exact picture: the walkway across the little garden, the pink gate, and the uncharted wilderness beyond.

Kerri located the front door key and rattled the lock awake.

Aunt Margo had told her that she still drove her VW Beetle up from Portland once or twice a year to check on the place. As soon as the door swung open, though, Kerri knew they were the first ones to step inside in at least two years, since she was given the keys—just like one can tell that their space has been violated in the five minutes they've been gone. The house was a cave, clean of campfires and energy bar wrappers. A Roman temple minus the guided tour posts. A catacomb for shrouded sofas.

Even Tim walked in slowly.

Kerri and Andy and Nate ventured in, holding on to their scant luggage, guessing the shapes of furniture under wraps and noting the silent airstrike of dust particles in the broken sunrays. Floorboards creaked exaggerated cries of pain under their suede boots and rubber shoes.

What annoyed Andy the most was the utter silence. Worse than reminiscent piano music, worse than a panicking violin. Nothing.

There was something more that bothered her, but she couldn't grasp it. Everything was like she expected it to be: every framed photograph, every book on the shelves that she still felt too young to read, the wallpaper, the fireplace, the prehistoric TV set. Everything was okay; it just didn't . . . sing.

"Let's go upstairs," she said, trailblazing ahead.

The steps agonized like B-movie actors.

"You take your room as usual, Nate?" Kerri said upon reaching the landing.

"Yeah, I guess," he replied, peering down that side of the hallway like he expected dart traps to shoot from the walls.

Kerri followed him from a safe distance as he walked up to the dark end and pushed open the door. A somehow cozy blue crypt welcomed him.

Then Nate took a leap of faith, crossed the darkness, and unbolted the shutters.

The rest of the colors splashed in, defibrillating the boys' room back to life: two berths, a desk, a dartboard hanging on the door. Despite his frequent visits as a kid, Nate's shier nature had never left a deep imprint in the room; the walls were poster-free and the books on the shelf weren't his.

"It always felt like a really, really nice hotel," he said.

Kerri nodded from the threshold, understanding. "I hope it beats the loony houses."

Andy's voice came from across the hallway like a fire alarm.

"Kerri! What the fuck happened to your room?"

Kerri sprinted back down the corridor, startling the porcelain dishes, and stormed through the door at the other end.

She saw the sloped ceiling and the sun cat-scratching the shutters. Her butterflies pinned inside their showcases.

Her maps. Her books. Her Lego models. Her desk with her colored pencils in a clay vase.

"What? What happened?"

Andy stood wide-eyed in the middle of the carpet: "It shrank!"

Kerri checked the distance between her head and the sloped roof. She had to duck to look through the dorm window now.

"No, it didn't. This is what you said was going to happen when we saw the lake again, remember?"

Andy made a slow, Mars-speed orbit on her feet, inspecting around. She stopped on Kerri, her lips beginning to sketch a smile.

"It was always like this?"

She caressed the 1960s-flavored paisley quilt, glance-queried Kerri for permission, and sat down on it. The mattress sighed gently under her bum.

A full smile settled on her face and bit her lower lip, a silent wow in her eyes.

Nate wandered in, coatless, hands pocketed.

"So what now?"

Andy sprung to her feet, shaking off the tipsiness of bliss. "Okay, uh . . . We got a case to solve."

The other two agreed voicelessly.

"So, um . . . We should have a club meeting. Uh, five minutes . . . At Ben's Corner. You okay with that?"

"Yeah, I guess."

"No, I mean it, because . . . You know, it's not like I want to take command or anything; I think we should be a team, make all the decisions together, you know. Reach consent."

"You mean consensus."

"Yeah, that. So, you agree on meeting at Ben's in five?"

"Yeah."

"Okay, then . . . I don't know, unpack, go to the bathroom, whatever."

"I'm fine," Nate said. "I never unpack; I just take my clothes from the bag as I use them."

"Yeah, me too."

"Okay. How long is it to Ben's Corner on foot?"

"Five minutes."

"Let's go then."

Ben's Corner had changed little, in the way of other humble establishments that wager that if they don't try to chase trends, trends will eventually run all the way round and embrace them back. Short of a nuclear attack throwing America twenty years back in technology, Ben's Corner would not live to see the day it would become fashionable again.

The restaurant was busy enough with lunching workmen and beer-drinkers so that the staff didn't notice the three hikers arriving, or the dog shaking the rain off on the blue-tiled floor. The jukebox had gone. The radio played "Groove Is in the Heart," which is a radio's way of saying it couldn't care less about the mood of a scene.

They claimed a booth by the window, Andy and Tim sitting next to the tearful glass. Nate grabbed a menu, checked that it was just the same old Michael Jackson—new face-lift—and dropped it.

"Okay, so." Andy laid her hands on the table. "The Sleepy Lake case."

Kerri and Nate leaned forward, looking executively interested. Tim suddenly noticed some of his body parts did not look shiny enough and set about to correct that. Andy wished they had a file, or even a cardboard box full of evidence like cops do when they're revisiting an old case, but all she had at hand to shuffle with was sugar and a bottle of Heinz ketchup.

"Well, we thought we solved it, but we didn't. Because . . ."

"Because the least effed up of us is Tim, and he's licking his testicles right now," Nate assisted.

"Tim," Kerri called. "Not at the table."

"Yes, that's it," Andy replied to Nate's statement. "So, what went wrong?"

No one spoke.

"I think we should try to retrace our steps," Andy continued. "Let's think about what we did in 'seventy-seven and figure out what we missed. Kerri?"

Kerri cleared her throat and spoke like a confident sixth grader. "Okay. So, summer nineteen seventy-seven. Uh, I'd been in town for a couple weeks already; Peter and Nate came next, I think; then you. And . . . we had heard about these sightings of a creature wandering around Sleepy Lake, and we told you about it when you arrived, and then Peter urged us to bike to the lake the following day and, you know, do some fishing and investigate a little. The fishing was kind of an excuse for Aunt Margo."

"Good. So we packed our fishing gear and a tent and lunch and we went to the lake. Then what happened?"

"Well, it was morning when we got there, and it was a rainy day, like this, with very thick mist. So we set camp, and we probed around, but we found nothing. Then later in the day, we heard something in the woods. We went to check it out . . . and we encountered the creature."

"Okay. Was it really the creature, though?"

"We found the slaughtered deer earlier," Nate intervened.

"Isn't that just an anecdote?" Kerri said.

"Tell that to the fucking deer."

"Look, there's a billion things that could've happened to that deer."

"But all at once?"

"Okay, okay, I take note of the deer," Andy umpired. "We'll get back to that. But when we first saw the creature in the woods—"

"It was Mr. Wickley in a costume," Kerri finished.

"Really? Are we sure it was him?"

The question levitated for a moment over the table.

Nate said, sounding surprisingly calm, "I think it was Mr. Wickley. Because . . . I don't know, I mean, I was scared at the moment, but later . . . it felt worse when we saw the others. Right?"

The girls eyed each other, mutely, without seeing, lost in their own recollections. A solid, monolithic silence sat on the table.

"I mean," he went on, "did the other ones even have eyes?"

A waiter sailed in, icebreaking through the gloom.

"Hi, welcome to Ben's; our special today is beef and carrot

stew." He looked up from his notepad at the fourth customer at the table. "Uh, the dog shouldn't be sitting there."

Tim scoffed aristocratically at him and returned to the black-and-white Americana view outside the window. The kids tuned out of their flashbacks.

"I'll have coffee, please. Black," Nate ordered.

"Same," Kerri said.

"I'll have a milkshake. Peach."

"Kerri?"

They looked up at the waiter.

"Kerri Hollis?" He checked the others. "Nate. And Andrea!" He took his hat off, long blond hair exposed like a very lame TV quiz prize. "Joey Krantz!"

"Hey," Kerri said, smiling before her brain had even told the mouth to do anything. "Joey. Hi."

"What are you guys doing here?" he asked, loud enough to turn some heads along the bar. "How's your aunt Margo doing?"

"Fine, she's fine. She's in Portland. We just, uh . . . came for a long weekend. You know. Reminiscing the good old days."

"Cool! I expect you'll find a lot has changed, eh? Seen the water tower? It's white now. Hey, you still solving mysteries, or are you keeping out of trouble?" His pen wiggled at Andy and Nate, who looked at the table and then at each other and then at pretty much everything in creation minus Joey.

"So what about you? What're you doing?" Kerri deflected.

"Well, you know. I traveled around . . . Had a girlfriend in Belden—we just . . . we broke up recently. And since my old man hurt his back, you see, I'm helping out with the family business."

"Cool. Cool."

"I also volunteer for the sheriff's office from time to time, so who knows? Maybe I'll get to be a law enforcer like you guys. Anyway. Uh, two blacks and a milkshake, was it? Coming right up."

He scribbled some dots and basic shapes onto his pad and moved along.

Kerri and Nate checked each other, facial muscles still tense.

"Okay. So," Andy said, "we saw the lake creature, and then—"

"Peach, was it?" someone cried from the bar.

"Yes, please," Andy shouted back. "Right. So we saw the lake creature, and then what did we do?"

Kerri and Nate were still fighting a smile each.

KERRI: We ran away.

NATE: Sorry, was that "ran" away then, or "run," as in now? Are you telling or suggesting?

ANDY: Guys, c'mon.

KERRI: Yeah, sorry. I mean . . . *(Chuckle.)* You gotta admit that was . . . strange.

ANDY: Kind of, but—

KERRI: I mean, "How's Aunt Margo doing?" Like, you know . . .

NATE: Like he's channeling the town's housewives suddenly.

ANDY: Okay, it was awkward.

NATE: It was funny. I mean, he's a waiter.

KERRI: Yeah! Well, I was a waitress until last week, so that bit's not funny, but still, something there was funny. I can't quite put a pin on it, but . . .

NATE: Maybe the part where he didn't treat you as a beaver-toothed nerd, or me as a piece of shit, or Andy as a wetback.

ANDY: Okay, I see it was funny. But really, I mean . . . fuck him.

NATE: Said the girlfriend in Belden.

KERRI: Yeah, shit, "I traveled around . . ." I think you can walk to Belden.

Nate chortled as Kerri endeavored to pick up the thread again.

"Okay, anyway, what did we do after the thing in the lake? We ran away."

"Yes, we bravely retreated like Sir Robin."

"Right," Andy continued. "What next?"

"We went to see Captain Al."

The name dropped flat on the chrome-rimmed table, with no one able to follow from there.

"Two black coffees," the timely waiter said, landing the order off his tray. "And a peach milkshake."

"Hey, Joey," Kerri said. "Is Captain Al still around here?"

"Who?"

"Al. Captain Al."

Joey frowned at the name.

"Oh, wait, you mean Crazy Al?"

"Uh . . . maybe."

"Yeah, he's still around. Have you seen the old man pushing around scrap metal on East Street?"

Andy, Nate, and Kerri stared at the waiter in horror.

"Oh, no, no, it's not him," Joey quickly mended. "Don't worry. Not him. Anyway, you seen the guy? Just follow him. It's Crazy Al who buys the metal."

Some form of unremarkable weather, profoundly commonplace for meteorologists but somehow relevant to the overall color of the scene, was taking place. Let us say soft rain and sunshine; let us say lightningless, borborygmic thunder.

The amber Vega roared through dirt roads, spraying waves of high-definition gravel.

It wasn't necessary to follow any scrap metal harvester; Kerri knew where to go. After the Blyton Hills gold mine was abandoned in the early 1960s, following a brief grace period during which tin had become the main product, the same California company that owned the mines converted the smelting furnace south of town into a chemical plant. This new works extended the life span of the town's industrial economy and gave rise to a small residential neighborhood for qualified employees, about a mile southeast of the town proper. In the 1980s the plant was shut down too, and the residential area around it was quickly abandoned, its population of retired workers yielding their housing to the increasing demand of shelter for the homeless and privacy for the troubled youth.

South of this area, the bad neighborhood began.

To get rid of the vast amount of toxic waste and scrap metal the plant had generated, a junkyard had to be laid and a new furnace set up to burn the residue. The incinerator had worked at full capacity for two years—enough to dye the sky the color of iron rust—and then it was shut down as well. The junkyard was still open, its business merely consisting in hoping for all the incombustible trash to just evaporate so that planetary exploitation could resume. A long-retired employee was posted in a watchtower atop four steel columns, waiting for that to happen.

That is where Kerri parked: a few yards short of the watchtower, at the foot of which, basking in a flimsy shaft of winter sun in a frayed hammock, wrapped in a wool blanket with a baseball cap over his eyes and an unlabeled bottle of twelve-year-old battery acid by his side, lay the old man they were looking for.

Two pairs of sneakers and some suede boots trod the yellow dirt, car doors clacking behind.

The man's dusty lips quivered to produce a sentence.

"Fuck off."

No more steps were heard.

Except for paw pads, and some panting, and the brush of a wet snout against the man's fingertips, which finally made him look. A microquake shook a fly off his cap as he faced the Weimaraner licking the dirt off his knuckles.

"I know this dog."

The man sat up, removed his cap and his blanket, and stared at the color festival—swirling orange and amber and black. The slits of his eyes squinted further to identify the long-legged woman before him.

"Kerri."

A smile dawned like a postwar sun.

"Holy shit, Nate! And Andy! Oh, shit!" he chuckled, then pulled up some seriousness and asked, "It's okay to swear in front of you now, right?"

"Fuck yeah," Kerri assured him, still insecure herself.

They hugged. Kerri was startled to feel the minimal body under the Salvation Army clothes.

"Come upstairs!" he said after hugging everyone, waving at the dog. "I'm out of lemonade, but I'll find you something."

They followed him up a long flight of rotten iron stairs that threatened to infect them with tetanus by skin contact, Kerri watching Al's back all the way up. There were very few things he had not lost in thirteen years; his wide frame was one.

The single room on top of the tower was warm, by virtue of a single gas heater in a corner near a mattress on the floor. A table turned workbench sat in the middle of the room; an airplane engine lay where other people would have chosen to place a bowl of wax fruit. Tim, smelling the mattress on the floor, decided it was some other animal's bed and left it alone. Al searched a cabinet in the area that had inexplicably landed the role of a kitchen.

"What can I offer you? I have instant coffee . . . Damn, but no milk."

"We're fine," Kerri said.

"No, wait, I just remembered, you're twenty-one already, right?" He produced and laid on the table a bottle of whiskey and four glasses that had definitely never seen one another before. "Sit down, sit down, put that anywhere and take that chair. Shit, look at that. The Blyton Summer Detective Club knocking on my door!" The kids could feel his eyes feeding off their youth. "And where's Peter? Don't tell me that big jock has let you come all the way here without him watching your back; where is he?"

And there, of all places, he actually stopped for an answer.

In a matter of seconds, Kerri's brain had produced a thousand plausible stories. Some of them were even good. Peter got married and he's tied up with the twins. He's shooting in Paris with Juliette Binoche. He's on his last year in the Air Force Academy in Colorado Springs. But no sooner had the fiction department in her head spread out all these stories for her to choose from than she discarded them all. She would have to tell Al the truth. For one reason, she argued to her flustered imagination: because the Captain Al we need right now is one who can take the truth, not one who must be fed lies.

"Cap, I'm sorry," she said. "Peter's dead."

Andy and Nate watched the smile on Captain Al transition to incomprehension, then to incredulity, then to sadness. As smoothly as flowers closing up at night, almost too slow for the naked eye, Captain Al's smile withered and died.

"No." His voice quivered. "No no no no no. Why did he die?"

"Don't tell him the truth," Peter begged, startling Nate by his side. "Please. Nate. Don't tell him the truth."

Nate didn't even flinch. He stood still, barely registering Peter through the corner of his eye, measuring the opportunity window before him. He spoke before anyone else could phrase an answer.

"Car crash." He noted the girls' stare, but neither disagreed. "Wasn't his fault. I'm sorry, Al."

Al took a seat. He was the first to sit down, after all.

Distant mountains of metal against a yellow sky mourned behind the dirty windows.

"Man, it's wrong," he stammered from the ruins. "It's all so wrong."

"Captain," Andy called, "we need your help."

Al refocused on her like he stood far, far away. His hand poured some whiskey into one of the glasses and he drank it up.

"What can I do for you?" he asked. It was not a courtesy formula; it was actually a baffled question.

"We're on a case, Al."

"Are you now?" he tragichuckled. The guests waited as he poured himself another glass and gulped it down. "Villains of Blyton Hills beware, the Blyton Summer Detective Club is back in business. What is it this time? Ghost train on the old railway? Stolen goods from the history museum?" Each new example came to him with more difficulty. "A . . . ciphered message dropped by a dark-coated man on the run?"

"Al, what happened to you?" Kerri begged. "What . . . I mean, your house?"

"They took my house, Kerri," he said, a couple decibels too loud. "Couldn't keep it on my vet pension. The money I put on the sheep at the co-op, I lost. They killed them."

"But . . ." Kerri searched for a grown-up's word to dispel disaster. "What about insurance?"

"No insurance; the co-op went bankrupt. What little we had left, we spent fighting the corporation lawyers."

He drowned the building momentum in the rest of the drink, and the pathos ceased.

When he spoke again, the words were slower, darker. "Blyton Hills needs your help, kids. *(Looking up, two-thirds joking.)* Shit, we're beyond salvation. It all went sideways after you left."

The girls fell silent. Tim lay down, feeling the depression in the atmosphere. The curtains at the end of the conversation were about to fall.

Nate lingered onstage: "What corporation?"

"RH, from California," Al said. "The one that used to own the chemical plant."

"And the gold mines," Kerri recalled.

Andy spotted the last chance to wedge in and seized it: "Al, we're reopening the Sleepy Lake case. Remember it? You took us to the mines."

Al nodded, or his head wobbled. His eyes weren't closed, but not manifestly open either.

"Remember we came to you after we encountered a monster in the woods? And then you came with us the next day, and we didn't see the creature, but we found its tracks leading into the abandoned gold mine?"

"Remember the slaughtered deer?" tried Nate.

"I remember a dead deer, yes," the old man mumbled from under his cap.

"Not just dead, Captain; it was torn open. And the birds had stopped singing."

An eye glistened audibly. Al raised his head.

"Had they?"

"Yes." Nate checked Kerri and Andy. "Don't you remember? When we returned to the lake with him, we tried to find the deer again. I remember Peter saying, 'Listen,' and we listened, and then you said"—he pointed at Kerri—"'Where are the birds?'"

Al rose up and reached for the cabinet. He retrieved a cookie tin. Kerri was about to refuse politely when she realized there were no cookies inside. The first item she recognized was a page from the *Pennaquick Telegraph*.

Al picked up his reading glasses from the sink and scanned through the page.

"Jesus, Al, you keep all this?" Andy had approached the tin box and picked up another item: a hundred-dollar bill. "This is the counterfeit money from the missing accountant case. And . . . shit, are these the werewolf's teeth?"

"There's no mention of the deer here," Al said, reading.

"Al, they never let us have any of this. The sheriff said it was evidence!"

"I still have some friends," he answered briefly.

"They never mentioned it 'cause the deer had nothing to do with it," Kerri said. "How would Wickley hunt it and cut it open?"

"They never mentioned it 'cause it doesn't fit their version; doesn't mean it's not related," Nate argued.

"It probably isn't," Al commented. "For starters, it's happened again since."

Andy's attention snapped back from the tin box. "More slaughtered deer? Near Sleepy Lake?"

"Yes," Al said, not giving it much importance. "A few years ago. I didn't see it, but I remember a couple of campers freaking out. Anyway, it's not the slaughtered ones I worry about."

Andy, Kerri, and Nate eyed one another, deciding who was going to inquire further.

"Most often, the animals are found dead," Al expanded. "On the lakeshore, just like that. Not eaten or mauled, just dead."

"Poisoned," Andy assumed.

"Not from the chemical plant; it's way downriver," Kerri said. "Maybe ... I don't know, toxic gas leaks from the mine vents? Tunnels run beneath that area. It could also explain the birds fleeing."

"Yeah," Nate added, "like when miners carry a caged canary into the tunnels to ensure the air is breathable."

PETER: Hey, I was thinking the same thing.

NATE: *(Whispering.)* Shut up.

"The vents are sealed now," Al pointed out. "So is the entrance near the lake. The only access left is a drainage ditch opening onto the river, out of Sentinel Hill."

"Where we found the footprints," cued Andy.

"I'm pretty sure those were Wickley's too," said Nate.

"Who owned the mines back then?" asked Kerri. "RH Corporation?"

"Yes," Al answered from the newspaper. "Says here they

bought them from the Deboëns in nineteen forty-nine. More like got them for the loose change in their pockets, really. The family was broke."

"How come no one suspected RH back in 'seventy-seven?" Kerri wondered. "They seem to be everywhere."

"People in town weren't prejudiced against big faceless corporations back then. They hated the Deboëns best. When rumors of the Sleepy Lake creature rekindled in the sixties and seventies, people blamed it on them. Legend was the lake creature was haunting Deboën Isle, so somehow it was all the Deboëns' fault. I'm sorry to say the official inquiry didn't do much better."

"Maybe we should check that," Andy said, distracted from the box of mementos. "The official inquiry. Deputy Wilson might let us look into the case files."

"Wilson died in 'eighty-six," Al commented. "Lung cancer. Copperseed is the new deputy sheriff of Blyton Hills."

"Wait, Officer Copperseed?" Nate said. "The one who never listened to us?"

"The very same. Police presence in town has been stripped down to him and a couple part-time volunteers. Your old pal Joey Krantz is one of them. Anyway, the case file was nothing more than a collection of creature sighting reports. Most were later connected to Wickley."

"Most," Nate underscored.

"Well, the rumors clearly were there before Wickley arrived; they're what gave him the idea of the costume. Deputy Wilson at least had the good sense not to believe in hocus-pocus, but when it came down to finding a real suspect, he got the wrong one."

"Dunia Deboën," Andy quoted from memory. "The last in the family. Is she alive?"

"Oh yeah. She still lives alone in the same house on Owl Hill. A resilient woman. She's taken a lot of shit from people around here."

"We could go see her," Kerri suggested. "Ask her about RH, how they gained control of the mines. They sound pretty reckless."

"If you go to Copperseed with that, you're bound to find an ally," Al commented. "He hates RH. Been pressing for sealing the mines and dismantling the plant for years."

"Are you guys sure about this?" Nate polled. "This whole 'evil corporation polluting the lake' theme, it's like we've gone from Blyton Summer Detective Club to *Captain Planet and the Planeteers*."

"I hate that show," said Andy.

"It's not that bad."

"Yes, it is. The Latin American kid's got the shittiest ring. I mean, since when is 'heart' an element?"

"But that's the point, they wanted a Latin American Planeteer so bad, they had to create a fifth element for him."

"Then why did they put two Caucasians, an American and a European? Where do you think white Americans come from—Saturn?"

"Anyway," Kerri said, steering the conversation off pop reference territory, "it's a plausible villain. You can't expect it to be another Wickley. Because . . . we're grown-ups now; four of us against one petty criminal wouldn't be fair. A shady company with an army of lawyers sounds like a worthy opponent."

Andy considered the argument. "Yeah, well, it's a start."

"Yes, but . . ."

They turned to Captain Al. He was back in his chair, blank stare drifting off again, idle fingers holding on to an empty glass.

"It's not right," he reprised. "The . . . the whole case, the way it ended."

A couple more phrases eluded him. Then his mind seemed to track back to what it knew for certain.

"The night you went missing," he started. "The final night, when you went back to the lake by yourselves . . . We were searching for you, Deputy Wilson and I, and . . . *(A crooked smirk.)* Your aunt Margo was frantic; she always was; she hated these adventures of yours. But I was . . ." A word fluttered before his eyes, one he hesitated to clasp. "Scared. Wilson and I, we were riding the police motorboat and we were scared. I can't . . . And when we found your boat capsized I . . . for a second, I feared the worst. I knew you all could swim, but it was so dark . . . not night dark, but veiled dark, and . . . damn, so quiet. The world is not supposed to be that quiet. Not the deserts, not the bottom of the ocean.

"And then, hours later, against my gut feeling . . . morning came. And there you were, waving at us from the pier on Deboën Isle. So we drove there, and we found you outside the big mansion at sunrise, and birds singing, and wind blowing your hair, and there was Wickley tied up in a fishnet on the pier, wriggling in that ridiculous costume, and . . . *(Al looked up at them.)* You were smiling. And then while Wilson was cuffing the guy, I took you aside and asked, 'What happened in there?' And none of you said anything at first, and then Peter said, 'We solved the mystery.' And . . . that was it."

The audience remained silent.

Andy checked Kerri. Nate checked Peter.

Tim listened to the captain, compassionately.

"When Wilson fell ill," the captain resumed, "I went to visit him often. Talk about the old times. And you were . . . Hell, you were brought up so often. He was so fond of you. And one of the last days, I was in his room, he was bedridden, and he said, 'Remember, Al, when the children got lost in the lake and we spent the night searching for them? Remember when we found them? How frightened the poor things were?'"

Al looked up again. Water wavered across his eyes.

"But you weren't frightened. You were smiling."

Thirteen years later the children stayed still, not breathing.

And then the moment passed.

Al rubbed the bridge of his nose.

"You okay?" Kerri asked.

"Yes. You must excuse me. I'm an old man and . . . I've usually drunk myself unconscious by this time of day."

Tim was already aiming for the exit, having picked up the signs that the scene was over.

"Okay," Kerri said. "Take a nap, Captain. We'll take it from here. Thank you."

Al nodded, eyes closed, and didn't walk them to the door.

Tim and Nate and Kerri had already started down the stairs when Al called, "Andy."

She turned around. The captain put the lid on the

cookie tin and pushed it across the table.

"No way," Andy said. "These are yours. Your memories."

"They were always for you kids," he explained, with a melancholic look that had taken decades to forge itself. "I was planning to give them to you when you came back the next holiday. But you didn't come. And I just ... forgot about it." He raised his head and smiled the sorrow away. "But it's yours. You're gonna need it. Remember all the good work you did."

Andy retraced her steps and took the box. It was heavy. Treasure rattled inside.

"Thank you, Captain," she said.

She was back at the door when he called again. "You still wanna be called Andy, don't you?"

She smiled. "Yeah. Thanks for asking."

She clacked her heels, saluted, and left Captain Al's house.

As she hurried down the stairs she noticed nobody had gotten inside the car yet. The rain had ceased and the sun channeled a shaft onto their striped station wagon as if Heaven were appointing a quest to it.

"What's wrong?"

Kerri handed her a white envelope.

"This was inside the car," she said.

"I left the window open a slit," Nate explained. "It was beginning to smell."

Andy flipped the envelope in her hands. The front side bore the letters *BSDC*.

"Someone followed us here?" she said, surveying the junkscape. Andes of car parts and rusted metal rose against the yellow afternoon.

"They may have left it while we were parked in town," Nate conjectured. "It was between the seat and the door; I just didn't notice it until now."

Andy opened the envelope. It contained a single sheet of paper with a short message written in caps: "STOP PROCRASTINATING. GO TO THE LAKE."

"So what now?" Kerri asked.

"We go to the lake," Nate answered.

"Why, because an anonymous note told us to?"

"We were planning to go anyway, weren't we?"

"We could also go see Dunia Deboën, or talk to the deputy. There's only a few hours of daylight left; we should put off the lake till tomorrow."

"We could go today and camp for the night," Andy suggested.

"Whoa!" Kerri checked the other two, then backtracked to make sure she hadn't put an exclamation point too many there. "That's quite a crash therapy, isn't it? We were supposed to be taking it easy; now we're talking about spending our first night at the lake?"

"What's there to fear?" Nate said. "You think we're fighting a big evil corporation. Worst that can happen is a CEO in a chupacabra costume."

Kerri turned to Andy. "Okay, you decide; what do we do?"

"I decide? No, I don't. I told you, I'm not the leader; we do things together."

"I'm for going to the lake, Kerri isn't; you're the tiebreaker," Nate recounted. "So, what do we do?"

Suddenly Andy found herself between Kerri and Nate, both with their arms crossed, expecting leadership from her.

She queried the dog. "Tim?"

The Weimaraner sat down obediently, awaiting command, a kerosene breeze blowing at his ears.

Andy checked the handwritten message in her hands again.

"STOP PROCRASTINATING." Those two words did it, actually. She took offense that easily.

"Let's go back to HQ and get our camping gear. We're going to the lake."

The road to Sleepy Lake sprouted northwest of Kerri's neighborhood in Blyton Hills as a paved parkway crossing through ranks of semiordered cedars. Old people used to promenade along this part, as far as the wooden bridge if they felt adventurous, but the road went on farther than most locals cared to remember. It turned north soon after the bridge and tunneled through groves of older, less civilized trees; it crossed two ravines, or the same ravine twice, and finally reached the junction where once trucks filled with machinery and clean-faced mineworkers used to leave the lakebound path, taking the better branch to the shaft on Sentinel Hill. The worse branch continued northwest, slaloming the hills as it climbed upriver, burrowing its way through the forest, and along fifteen miles it managed to lose most of the features that defined it: road signs and milestones first, then asphalt, then gutters, then the respect of varmints, then a good five or six feet in width. And by the time it was but a shrunk, fickle snake of a dirt track serpentining among the massive, twisted roots of gigantic firs, the woods ended and a sunblast came crashing through the last line of trees.

Andy floored the brakes, bringing the amber cannonball to an earth-grinding stop ten feet from the water, a tail of dust and scared insects surrounding it. She had been driving too fast and had misjudged the breadth of the lake bank.

A bright sun glimmered off the surface of two hundred square miles of water.

"Okay," Andy admitted. "It wasn't a pond."

Tim jumped out of the racing-striped caravel and ran to conquer the New World.

Andy's sneakers felt the soft, grassy shore. In all her experience on the road, she could remember few places, including tundra deserts and national parks, where man had left as shallow a print as in Sleepy Lake. She could not tell precisely why. It was possible that pioneers first scouting the Pacific Northwest had once reached that spot, registered the lake in their notebooks, and moved on, anxious to finish charting out Oregon before dinner. But it was also likely that the place itself conspired to erase what little trace people had left throughout history. There were signs of human presence—a dock not far on the east bank, and the timorous shape of the house crouched under the firs on the faraway isle, but somehow the lake had taken them over, successfully convincing the visitors that the dock and the house were original features of the world, waiting to be found.

The three humans wandered around the car, timidly nearing the water, and took in the immensity of the lake that memory had surprisingly not exaggerated. It was in fact hard to size up: its edges broke into gulfs and capes, with heavily wooded peninsulas blocking a complete view. The opposite shore was far enough away to appear grayed out, even against the rainwashed sky.

At what might well be the geometric center of the lake, or not by a long shot, the tiny elongated isle lay low under the weight of colossal trees, whose original seeds had long ago flown from the mainland and landed with uncanny precision there to colonize it. A few pointy dormer windows spied from among the treetops.

"So here we are," Kerri stated.

Andy scrutinized her profile, sunlight on her freckles and her orange hair glowing. She smelled the trees and the petrichor off the grass; listened to the Shanghai of birds; checked the summits of the firs rocking gently in the cold, damp air, looking like what the top of every tree is, no matter the size: a willful, sun-hungry bud.

"It doesn't look that bad," she judged.

Kerri just went "Hmm" and studied the landscape with a biologist's eyes. An iridescent dung beetle caught her attention.

Nate was apparently covering the shore to the right of the car, therefore Andy wandered to the left, toward the edge of the bay where a pile of white polished rocks forming a rough cliff jutted into the water. She remembered this pile as being big enough to build a fortress, but it rose only three feet. She leaped to the top, small crayfish scuttling from under her feet and splishing into the water.

The lake bank had narrowed down to just a few yards there, and a natural path poked into the woods. She peeped inside, from the forest mud that the sun had lost all hope of reaching, up the umber pillars of the living cathedral, toward the vault of embracing branches of yellow leaves.

No slaughtered animals. No hanging bodies.

Something crashed into the lake behind her, splashing stinging cold water. Tim waded back to shore around the cliff, overly amused, giving Andy a transient look that said, *You were right—this is the best. Place. Ever!*

Then he ran away, zooming through the shallows and spraying water and mud like a herd of buffaloes all along the shore and eventually over Kerri, who was squatting for a close-up on the insects farther up, and who resignedly stood up and shouted after him: "If you so much as whimper next time I put you in a bathtub, I'll kill you!"

The bank was widest on the right side and drier, so that was where they made camp, and as they unloaded the gear from the Chevy and pulled up the tent, the virgin land grew slightly hostile, like a general frown from the earth and the trees at the visitors' insolence of coming uninvited. But it stopped bothering Andy once she'd started hammering the poles, like a boisterous announcement of their intention to stay. And the ominous sentiment she had anticipated from the lake never fully manifested that evening. Instead, what little uneasiness the motion of the firs and the burbling of the miniature waves breaking on the shallows had cast upon her mind was gradually nudged aside by the clanging of stacking cooking pots, the texture of her canvas rucksack, the bright colors of the gear they had exhumed from Kerri's closet just an hour ago. And all this sensory feed was growing a new sensation inside her: something alien and unexpected tingling under her touch that, far-stretching though it felt, had all the characteristics of what people call bliss. Because she was just starting to realize, Nate and Kerri and herself, they were camping in Blyton again.

They had settled near the right end of the bay, not far from the old dock sticking out of the rocky horn, and that whiny structure was the only thing objecting to her complete happiness. For at the dock there was a rowboat, and oars inside.

The three gathered on the platform, staring alternately at the boat and the lonely isle ahead.

"Is this a clue?" Nate finally asked.

"Maybe," Andy said. "You said no one came fishing here."

"No one but us, that I know of," Kerri argued.

The boat knocked gently on the dock's pole, self-consciously, bound by a piece of rotting rope.

"Okay, so shall we go take a look at the isle?" Andy said, taking the hint.

"May I remind you," Nate started, "that we're here because an anonymous note told us to come, and now here's an anonymous boat inviting us to go even farther?"

Andy couldn't think of a counterargument.

"It's okay, I'm just saying," Nate excused her. "I'm in."

"If we're trying to retrace our steps," Kerri argued, "let

me point out that we never rowed to the isle until the very last day of the case."

"We didn't find a boat until the last day," Andy said.

"Which in retrospect should've been a big red flag," Nate added.

Tim trotted by, nosing the warped boards, finding the humans in silent deliberation.

"Isn't it a little late already?" Kerri argued. "It's like a ten-minute row. And there's an hour of sunlight left, possibly less. I'd rather pass," she decided. "It's okay, you two go. I'll stay."

"No, no way," said Andy. "I'm not leaving you alone."

"I've got Tim."

"I don't like splitting up the team," Andy insisted. "And we can't afford it anymore. We'd need a fourth man."

KERRI: Better a fourth woman.

ANDY: Why?

KERRI: Because if it were a fourth man, he and Nate would go, and you'd be all, "Ugh, why do the boys get to explore the isle? I can do anything boys do," and you'd want to go with them and leave me.

ANDY: I never did that.

KERRI & NATE: Yeah, you did.

Andy tried to think of a comeback and desisted after a second.

"Also," Peter inserted during the subsequent pause, "what's with the no-splitting-up policy? It's a sound strategy; it covers more ground."

NATE: *(Aloud, for the girls.)* I agree with Andy, though. We shouldn't split up.

"Fuck off, Nate," Peter said. "And by the way," he

continued, stepping into the circle and thumb-pointing Andy, "how is she calling the shots?"

The party had fallen silent.

"Nate? Don't pretend you can't hear me; it hurts enough that not even the dog notices me," Peter complained. "Answer me this: Who died and made her—right, wait, no, let me rephrase that: How are we going to solve this shit if—"

"We are not going to solve it!"

Nate paused, then noticed the furrowed brows on the girls, the eyebrow-raising dog, the startled birds.

"Sorry. That came out wrong. I mean . . . we are not going to solve this by watching from a distance. It's no longer about the case; this is about us. Kerri, it won't help to send anyone ahead. You won't fix this unless you personally see it through."

All eyes now fell on Kerri, and she noticed. She felt her pockets, longing for a cigarette to hold on to, then hugged her waist and peeked through the boards under her boots at the gently dancing waters below.

Tim yawned, not at all intending to put pressure on anyone.

"Okay, right. Fuck it," she capitulated. "Let's do it."

Kerri had brought along her binoculars. They were the same ones she used to carry as a child for bird spotting, but they were good binoculars that she'd treated with care, and they befitted a grown-up. Same went for her magnifying glass and her compass, both artifacts of beautiful craftsmanship that she had owned since childhood and still suited long-fingered hands. Andy was sure there was a company in England, possibly founded by a society of African explorers in the Victorian era, a bunch of Colonel Mustards with pith helmets and friendly mutton chops, who manufactured this high-tier field equipment especially for kids, aware that young explorers like Kerri must not be patronized with cheap plastic toys, but be offered the best durable tools to encourage their vocation, because those curious children shall be the great discoverers of tomorrow.

Andy, in charge of both oars after having found it too difficult to synchronize with Nate, checked her own freebie Coca-Cola watch and made a mental note to replace it as soon as she could afford it.

The boat's path had hardly sundered the lake's surface. Sunshine drew sparkling racing stripes across it. Kerri put down the binoculars, her hair bathed in tangerine solar wind. Her right hand comforted Tim at her feet, who was not as fond of the lake now that he wasn't a leap from the surface anymore.

"At least the weather's good," she granted.

Nate, backlit and squatting on the bow, dipped a finger into the water.

"Maybe it's not the best time to bring it up, but we didn't have very bad weather last time." He allowed a beat for reactions. "I know what the *Telegraph* said. I'm just saying what I remember. The weather did not knock us over."

Andy glanced over the bulwark. Nothing could be made out below the surface. "Second-deepest lake after O'Higgins in southern Chile," she recited.

"Actually, the deep end must be over there," Kerri said,

pointing west, where the lake seemed to expand vastly beyond a cape. "After all, mine tunnels connect the isle and the mainland."

Andy reckoned the cruise would still take them five minutes. She took a deep breath and went all out to make it four.

"So, what's the story of the house?" she requested in the meantime.

"You know it as well as I do," Kerri said.

"Humor me. A fresh briefing before we land."

Kerri sighed, and her hair shushed and hushed, listening to the very important story to come.

"The house was built by Damian Deboën, a prospector who came to Blyton Hills during the Gold Rush in the eighteen forties. He had a lucky strike, made a fortune, built the mines, pretty much refounded the town, which was but a small parish at the time. The Deboëns lived here for a century, until a fire destroyed part of the mansion in nineteen forty-nine."

"Oh, come on," Nate protested. "You're skipping all the juicy bits."

"Like the bit about him being a pirate?" Andy recalled.

"That one might be true," Kerri conceded. "There are records of a Captain Deboën who escaped the gallows in Florida and sailed for the Pacific."

"Also the part about him being a sorcerer who lived for a hundred and fifty years," Nate pointed out.

"A sorcerer?" Andy checked both.

"At least, he learned a handful of voodoo tricks while sailing the Caribbean."

"Funny how only *your* books mention that part, Nate," Kerri mocked him.

"Rumors in town said his house used to be filled with mysterious artifacts and potions."

"Guy was a mining engineer and the townspeople had not seen a chemistry set in their lives."

"Lived on his secluded island, seldom showed up in town, never went to church."

"Right, because you never fail to come out of your den for Sunday service."

"Lived alone, never married or wooed anyone."

"Nate, stop giving me arguments so easy to fling back at you; I might hurt you."

"And he didn't age one bit while he lived here."

"Which didn't add up to a hundred and fifty years."

Andy listened carefully under the path of flying arguments between both of them—the keen fantasy addict and the scientific skeptic. "Aren't there any records?" she asked.

"No," Nate answered, in a *Glad you asked* pitch. "But let's do the math: he came in the eighteen forties, as you said, looking about, what? Forty years old? Remember he'd been scallywaggin' previous to that. Anyway, let's say he was thirty. So, he digs the mines ... Let me remark that you actually need a lot of gold to build a gold mine. This guy wasn't your average fortune hunter who came west with an empty sack and a shovel; he must have carried along some booty from his sailing days. In my opinion, this gold mine thing was a money-laundering op. Anyway, business booms, the town prospers, and suddenly people start noticing old Deboën has hardly aged since he arrived. This is just a funny anecdote in the first decade, an oddity after two decades, fucking astounding after five. And that's when the guy, at the age of eighty by our account, but looking not one day older than forty, moves back east, saying he has business to attend, and leaves everything in the hands of a trusted employee named Allen. Nothing is heard of Damian Deboën for years, then sometime in the nineteen twenties a young man arrives in town claiming to be Daniel Deboën, son of Damian, who recently died in Massachusetts."

"So he lives to a hundred, being generous," Kerri said.

"After begetting a child at eighty," Nate countered. "And if you believe it was his child. Because according to the old people in town, Daniel happened to be the spitting image of Damian, only younger."

"So they haven't seen Damian in twenty years, they hardly caught a glimpse of him while he lived here, but they all remember him perfectly."

"Did he age?" Andy inquired. "The new one?"

"He didn't have much of a chance," Kerri said, "because in nineteen forty-nine that happened."

She pointed to bow, and Andy turned her head again to the looming isle and the backlit, mutilated shape of Deboën Mansion.

The boat and the shadow of the isle had finally met, and under its shelter the colors of the landmass could be told apart, trees from buildings. Andy soon realized that the house, much like the lake, was immune to rediscovery shrinkage. It was grand. Disturbingly big, as overgrown fungi and beetles are—the size something growing by itself in the woods should never reach.

In the area where Kerri was pointing, the top section of the east wing was bitten off, wooden beams torn like blades of grass, the gaping hole covered by brambles like blood platelets containing a hemorrhage.

Kerri again looked through her binoculars. "Did we bring a rope? There isn't one on the dock."

"It's okay, I'll pull us into the shore," Andy said.

"I'll help."

"No, you can't." Andy chin-pointed at her suede boots. "You always did overdress for camping."

Andy jumped a few yards out and sank only to her knees. Tim followed and swiftly paddled to the surface, again becoming the first of the party to land on a new setting.

Andy was still dragging the boat to land when she noticed tracks in the mud under her feet. She checked her soles.

"These footprints are fresh."

Kerri and Nate disembarked and checked the area. There were deep, fresh prints of a large-sized shoe.

"Funny how they lead away from the water," Nate said.

Everyone looked up at the mansion after that remark. In front of them, beyond depressed willows and hunchbacked oaks, the house rose, vast and overdetailed with windows and balustrades and balconies and towers and chimneys, unfolding in odd symmetries, jagged by dormer windows, crawling with salamanders of stone and live ones too. Ivy crept all over it, from the mold-scarred foundations to the shingles, covering up the riot of ruins in the east wing, peering through the glass, exploring the columned porch. Weeds brimmed over the stone chalices. Rotting acorns carpeted the stairs. Firs stood like sentinels far above the tallest roof, guarding it, hailing the darkness.

Tim's human entourage followed the dog into the growth, striding over some fallen boughs and onto the disregarded clearing in front of the porch. He nose-scanned the mold on the right pillar as the other three squinted at the high-reaching crown of the building.

"Just the way we left it," Andy said almost through a resigned sigh. "I kinda hoped someone would've knocked it down."

"Yeah. And put a 7-Eleven in its place," Nate seconded.

"Never too late," Kerri thirded.

Andy breathed in and stepped forward before anyone could stop her. The dog's obliviousness to dramatic shots had inspired her. The sudden bravado took her up the stairs, acorns popping under her soles, and up to the front door.

"We aren't going in, right?" she heard Kerri ask.

"No," she whispered, staring at the chain and padlock around the double door's handles. Cruised by snails, the half-digested remnants of an irreverently yellow sticker babbled something about a safety hazard. "The place's been locked," she informed the others. "For many years, I think."

"Maybe they didn't want any more kids fooling around," Kerri said.

"But the footprints. Someone's been here recently. Maybe still is."

Kerri gave it a thought and found no rational argument against yelling out: "Hello! Is anyone there?"

A crow fluttered away, its complaints fading quickly into a not-so-great distance. Then a hush fell over like a deflating balloon. Tim sneezed somewhere.

"If they were still here, there'd be a boat," Nate reasoned.

"Or there were two people, and someone rowed back."

Andy hurried downstairs again, feeling the porch frown behind her back.

Tim sneezed again, then puffed twice, shaking his head vigorously.

"Tim? Please don't tell me you inhaled a slug again." Kerri knelt beside him, but Tim didn't linger about, busy trying to clear his nasal conduct. Instead, Kerri noticed something on the ground. The dirt was humid and black, difficult to find under several autumnfuls of leaves, but a few scattered spots of neon yellow stood out.

Kerri took a pinch of dust, smelled it, wiped her fingers and nose. "Sulfur."

"So . . . Satan's been here?" Andy wondered.

"No. Elemental sulfur is used as a fungicide in gardening."

Nate glanced around. He could almost feel the mildew inside his nostrils. "Not doing a very good job."

"This has been here awhile," Kerri said. "It seems to follow a line."

The trail, not so much a dotted line as a vague row of spots of less enthusiastic undergrowth, led them away from the house, as away as the isle allowed: the westernmost tip stretched only some sixty yards from the building. Some feet short of the water they faced one monumental tree.

It was a fir. The trunk, too thick to embrace, exhibited a large, oozing ulcer in front, slightly above their line of sight, exposing a large cavity in the wood.

This distracted them at first from the symbol painted over the wound. It appeared to be a monogram of sorts, more complex than a letter, somewhat simpler than an advanced Chinese character, though it resembled the latter in the way it had been drawn, a convoluted glyph broken down to simple strokes. In red.

"Is that . . . ?"

"Paint," Kerri assured Andy.

Nate swallowed what felt like a tennis ball in his throat. "I've seen this symbol before."

Andy turned to find him iceberg white, eyes fixed on the red mark. "You mean here, thirteen years ago?" she prompted.

"No. Maybe. I don't know."

"Man, you all right?"

Nate blinked out of the trance, seemingly surprised to be welcomed by Andy on the other side. "Yeah. Fine."

"Fine," she echoed. "Let's follow the sulfur trail the other way. Kerri?"

Kerri was standing in front of the tree watching the tiny maggots feeding on the edges of the gash.

"Kerri, what's up?"

It took her a little time to gather the grit to raise her arm and reach into the hole. Her fingers dipped in a pool of sticky resin. Then something grassy. A plump black beetle came scuttling down her arm.

"Ew," Andy contributed.

Kerri grasped something, then retracted her hand, shaking the bugs off, and looked at the tiny bundle of straws and twigs in her palm—a sort of spherical bird nest.

Gently, she unwrapped it. At last her face surrendered to a grimace.

"Fuck."

"Oh, God," Andy groaned. "Is it human?"

They all leaned over the small treasure in Kerri's hands. It was a tooth—a little too small for a human molar, Kerri considered, but too big for a burrowing animal or anything a bird would prey on.

"What does it mean?" Andy asked.

"I don't know." Kerri returned the tooth to the nest and tossed it into the tree hole.

"You're putting it back?"

"Why not?"

"It's a clue."

"I don't wanna carry a tooth around, and I have no way of telling where it comes from. If we happen to need it again, we know where we left it, right?"

"Yeah. I guess," Andy slowly assented. "There's more of that sulfur that way and that way. Let's follow the trails."

They tried, but the lines proved too blurry to follow, and in both cases they seemed to lead straight to the water. However, upon following the first trail in the opposite direction, they found another two monograms in red.

One was painted on a tree stump on the south side, facing inland, lurking over a parapet of bony shrubs. It was as inextricable as the first, but definitely different.

From there, they made out another line leading to the

east, past the beach where they had landed. A decrepit willow, veiled by a curtain of its own drooping branches, slouched there, leaning suicidally over the water. Andy pushed the curtain aside and stepped into the vault. Inside it, a smooth marble slab, once white, now marred with mud and weeds, lay forever sheltered from sunlight.

"Daniel Deboën's grave," Kerri captioned. "Killed in the fire in 'forty-nine and buried here on his isle according to his will."

"I remember this," Andy said.

"I don't think we saw this, though," Nate said, pointing at the third monogram painted on the trunk. Again, in red.

"These marks look old," Kerri observed. "Maybe they were here last time, but it was too dark to find them?" She was addressing Nate now. "Where else could you have seen them?"

"A book," he said, a fingernail scratching the paint. And then, focusing on Kerri, he added: "My kind of book. Not yours."

Andy tried to dispel the gloom and let the curtain of branches fall. They drifted away from the willow like they would from an old man offering candy.

Kerri stayed near the shore, making sure the boat didn't move until Andy decided it was time to go. Nate spent some time copying down the monograms on a piece of paper.

Andy borrowed Kerri's binoculars for a last tour around the house. With the doors padlocked and the first-story windows barred and shuttered, there was not much left to explore. Still, the isle had its own exclaves. A row of small, sharp rocks lay scattered beyond the contour of the mainland. A solitary shape swam stranded some sixty yards off the northern shore. Night was falling too quickly, but with the help of the binoculars Andy made out a buoy.

"Hey, Nate. Check this out."

Nate stood facing the house, seemingly studying the rear façade. More specifically, the round window atop the house.

"Nate. You okay?"

What made her queasy was not that he didn't stop looking. It was that Tim was right next to him, looking up too.

"Nate!"

"Yeah," the boy said as he clicked back. "Sorry. I remember that room."

"Me too," she joined in, reminiscing. "It's where we set the booby trap with the serving cart and the fishing net. The 'Lake Creature Phony Express,' wasn't it?"

"That was a good trap," Peter rated, standing between them. "Simple mechanics, flashy results. Instant classic. Also, catchy name."

"Too bad it caught the wrong guy," Nate said to Peter's face, but instead he found himself confronting Andy.

She gave him the kind of concerned, furrowed squint that mental patients often complain about getting from strangers in group therapy.

Tim had lost interest in the house and padded off to join Kerri by the pier.

"Hey, check out that thing on the water," Andy said. She walked Nate to the shore and gave him the binoculars.

"Yeah, it's a buoy," he quickly concluded. "Maybe it signals a reef or something that can be a danger to boats."

He didn't try to make it sound convincing, but Andy didn't come up with anything better.

"It's called Necronomicon."

"Nec-what?" Andy frowned. "What is?"

"The book. The one the symbols come from. It's a grimoire." He caught her second frown, rephrased: "A book of spells, a witchcraft manual, written a thousand years ago; almost all copies were burned; most people don't even think it's real, but it is. There was a copy in the house, in the attic."

Andy made sure to process all the information, rogered it with a nod.

"Don't tell Kerri about this," Nate added.

"What? Why? I don't want to complimentalize information."

"Compartmentalize."

"Yeah, that. It's important we don't keep things from each other; we should all be on the same page."

"Look, Kerri is on the ecovillain page now. She's not ready to accept something unnatural is going on here, but there is. There always was. The . . . creature. The hanged corpses. Whatever capsized our boat that night."

"Nate, how many times did we think we were chasing, or being chased by, ghouls and monsters? And every time it was a guy in a mask."

"Yes, I know, we were kids. But Damian Deboën was real. That book was real. And the symbols and the sulfur and the tooth are not props meant to scare children away.

They are signs of a very old science. Not the kind Kerri took in college."

Andy gazed back at the round attic window on top of the mansion. The dark, resilient glass returned her tough, jail-inmate glare.

"Okay," she said, appeasing him. "Point taken. Let's go back; it's getting late."

A couple of raccoons had approached the tent in their absence and were keenly admiring the product of human craftsmanship when the detectives returned. Tim took no small pleasure in shooing them away. It was still twilight, but the sun had taken all the warmth with it. Priorities such as finding kindling for the fire and preparing dinner kept them busy.

The night was cold but gentle like an X-rated metaphor. It was crowded too—with owls and fireflies and distant galaxies. Except for the latter, all of those things kept Tim alert for most of the meal, until he decided there were too many living things to chase and settled for not letting any of them steal his food, the same way the humans ate their baked beans in silence. Andy, who had lived on nonperishables for longer periods than some apocalypse survivors in Nate's sci-fi novels, was amazed to corroborate that beans never tasted better than when cooked in Kerri's portable aluminum pots. Those Colonel Mustards in England sure knew their shit.

"So," she chose as the first word in almost an hour, still chomping through the last of her meal. "Not bad for day one. We have some clues to follow."

Kerri and Nate munched a little slower and said nothing.

"Maybe it was a little late in the day to go to the isle, but I think it was a good move anyway, to prove to ourselves there is no imminent threat. We can go back tomorrow when it's light and keep searching. Or the owner of the boat might appear and he may have some info to share."

Kerri side-glanced at her, mouth full, and nodded.

"So what do you think?" Andy invited. "What's the best piece of intelligence we gathered today?"

Nate put down his plate and fork, wiped his mouth, and carefully considered the question. "That Joey Krantz had a girlfriend?"

Kerri made sure to swallow first, then laughed gently. Nate popped a last bit of bacon in his mouth. "I mean, it's not a shock, but it kinda hurts. Makes you lose faith in humanity, doesn't it?"

Andy smiled and mentally dismissed the meeting. It had been a good first day.

A malicious wind rose from the lake soon after dinner and the party chose to relinquish the fire and move to shelter. The tent was bound to be warm enough, especially considering it was designed to fit two kids and now had to lodge three adults and a Weimaraner. In the old days, Peter used to bring his own tent to Blyton Hills, thus providing separate housing for the boys. Fortunately, Aunt Margo had kept the extra sleeping bags and Sean's old blanket. Tim lay on it now, nursing his plastic penguin and whispering into its ear what a dangerous world there was outside the kerosene-lit tent.

KERRI: Come on, you start.

ANDY: Okay. Uh . . . *F.*

NATE: *(Quickly.) F.*

KERRI: *F.*

ANDY: *(Stares at her.)* Three *F*s? Fuck off!

NATE: *(Processing that.)* Hey, very good.

(Andy smiles, realizing.)

KERRI: It was actually "fluffy," but whatever, that deserves winning. *(Slipping into her bag and removing her sweater.)* Nate, your turn.

NATE: Okay. *B.*

ANDY: "Boobs."

(Hush.)

NATE: *(Staring, mind blown.)* How the hell . . . That was uncanny!

KERRI: *(To Andy.)* It wasn't even your turn! *(To Nate.)* Why are you thinking boobs, you perv? We're family!

NATE: Look, I was in the boys' ward at Arkham until just a week ago, okay? I'm rediscovering the amenities of coed, what can I say? It's cozy, it smells good, I'm all positive thoughts. I don't know why you'd ever want to sleep in the boys' tent.

ANDY: I never wanted to sleep in the boys' tent!

KERRI: Okay, whatever; lights off before Nate decides to start a royal dynasty with me.

NATE: *(Slipping into his bag as well.)* Yeah, yeah. Don't come rubbing on to me for body heat later.

KERRI: If you feel that happening, that would be Tim.

(She turns down the Coleman lantern; the dark takes over.)
Good night.

NATE: Night.

Andy mouthed good night, zipped her bag up, and closed her eyes.

She was only halfway to sleep when she felt the rustling in Kerri's bag. The clarity surprised her: she was able to discern the silhouettes of everybody in the tent against the blue canvas—all smooth, streamlined shapes, except for the infinitely complex fractal pattern of Kerri's hair.

"Hey," Andy whispered. Her head and Kerri's were very close. "Can't sleep?"

She heard a smile.

"I'll never have a warm night again," Kerri said.

A zipper slid a few teeth back. Andy couldn't really see it in the dark, but somehow she felt one of Kerri's hands moving into her line of sight. It stopped there, lying on the tent mat, inches short of her face. Andy stuck out her own hand to meet hers. Fingers clasped gently like plants coiling around each other.

Andy closed her eyes. Kerri's hand was warm and white and so rarely soft like one of the only three species of flowers native to Antarctica.

"It's all gonna be okay," she murmured. And the sound wave from her rosé lips flew like a leaf in the wind across an ocean twelve inches wide, over the island of clasped trees, right into Kerri's ear, with no one else in the whole universe noticing.

* * *

The next time Andy opened her eyes, she knew within a second that things were not okay.

If her hand had still been holding Kerri's up to that point, she failed to notice; she was already sitting up by the time she thought about it. The light outside the tent was white, though it was not exactly light. Light shines; this just hung there like stagnant water. The thought occurred to Andy that the whole tent had been dropped into the lake, which would also explain the solid silence. Tim was up, and so were his ears, to the best of their ability, radaring for insects, birds, wind. In vain.

Kerri was in deep slumber. Alarmingly deep.

Nate's sleeping bag was empty.

Andy put on a sweater and started shaking Kerri. Tim was already considering digging his way out of the tent.

"Kerri. Wake up. Wake up!"

"What . . ." Kerri muttered languidly, opening her eyes, then trying to rub the waking world off them. "What's happening?"

"Put on your clothes, quick." She didn't know what was happening. Only that it was happening again.

She zipped the door open.

The lake, the mountains, the sky were gone.

A white mist had drowned the camping site. The colorful plastic equipment and the tent itself could hardly fight it. Tim slipped out, and Andy lost him just three yards ahead. The grass, the dirt, the microscopic pebbles just faded out past that distance, erased from reality.

She squiggled her feet into her sneakers, pulverizing the dirt. Kerri crawled out, now fully awake and fully distressed.

"Where's Nate?"

"I don't know."

"Andy, what the fuck?!"

"Calm down! It's just fog, right?"

Somewhere out there, Tim burst into a riotous bark.

"Tim! Come here!"

Andy surveyed their environs, breathing hard, assessing the situation. On the bright side, maybe their island of visibility wasn't that narrow; she could make out the first line of trees behind the tent, some ten yards ahead. For the first time, she heard a familiar sound: the hollow knock of the rowboat against the dock pole.

On the not so bright side, Tim's barking had turned to growling. The threatening kind.

"Tim!" Kerri called, stepping forward. Andy grabbed her by the shoulder and pulled her back.

"Go to the car."

Kerri spun 360 degrees, her hair too agitated to swing gracefully. "Which way is the car?!"

A new sound was slowly rising over Tim's growls, taking shape like an underground train or the murmurings of an angry mob. A hateful, familiar sound. Although "familiar" could hardly refer to something so alien. It resembled breathing, but it was distorted, tortured, broken. It had qualities that should not be associated with breathing. It was viscous, and jagged, and swarming.

Tim recoiled into view, resolute to defend the girls, snarling in a portentous pretension of viciousness. Andy read the confirmation in Kerri's eyes: they both knew that breathing. They'd heard it before.

She scanned the camp for a potential weapon. A pool cue. Any kind of stick. A medium-sized stone. Only the frying pan was red enough to call her attention. She crouched to grab it, and both her knees gave out and hit the ground. She had to sarge them up, gritting her teeth: *Get up, ladies.*

And then came the most unexpected roar. Mostly because, she was sure, it had come from Tim.

The dog leaped forward into the fog again, and they heard a crunch, and Tim's unbelievable snarling, and the sound of flesh being torn, and the wheezing breath segued into the sound of a radial saw cleaving through metal. It took a long while for the mind to accept that that must have been a scream of pain.

More loud, ill-boding barks were heard. And steps that sounded too close together, and something plumping into the water.

Kerri managed to push words out of her throat. "Tim! Come!"

The answer was the wheezing again, only different. Raspier, hollower, astoundingly clear. Perhaps because, as the girls understood in a synchronized, heart-stopping realization, it was only about six feet away. Behind them.

It staggered out of the mist onto their island of visibility; they saw it instantly. But they didn't react at once. It took some time for the human brain to comprehend. A few things could be established without ambiguity. It stood, or slouched, on two legs. And the upper limbs, overjointed as they were, might have been called arms. The limbs in between were harder to classify. It wheezed—a gurgling, cackling kind of respiration—but it was difficult to ascertain through which of the slit-holes in its emaciated torso, all below a ribcage that was gaping open, ribs jutting out through the skin. And it had a face of a sort. Most of its head, wobbling sickly at the end of a twisty-tendoned neck, was blank, all smooth gray salamander skin; but a single feature, a deep barbwire impression from absent ear to absent ear, smeared with black blood, seemed to mark where the mouth was supposed to be.

Andy became aware she would have to react way before her reflexes did. Or her heart. Her whole body was literally paralyzed. The literal literally.

"It's a dream," Kerri piccoloed next to her.

"No, it's not."

"It's a dream!"

"Kerri, open your fucking eyes!"

The thing responded at her outburst with its own roar, debunking Andy's sketchy perception of its face by proving that the moving jaw was the one on top. Nothing out of its throat, not even the chord-gashing furnace scream, could have impressed Andy more than the sight of the hundred long, needle-thin teeth dirty with the creature's own blood.

At least three of those teeth broke when Andy's right arm finally reacted and whacked the frying pan across its face.

Tim rushed onto scene, barking, trying his best to scare

the thing away. Andy pushed Kerri back, remembering later she had not checked to ensure it was clear behind them. She couldn't tell where the tent was anymore. She was lost.

The thing stepped forward, a sort of webbed two-fingered foot finally making Tim cower, and it thrust a clawed hand at Andy's face. She jolted back, her legs about to give way again, but she managed to push off with all her strength and launch a kick. It connected; the monster screeched and stared eyelessly at Andy in incredulity. Then its jaws opened once more in a scream to show the actual mouth within.

And then its head exploded.

Black matter and pieces of cartilage splashed onto Andy's sweater and face.

The headless thing wavered and collapsed on the ground, its medial limbs still twitching.

Nate lowered the smoking shotgun, gaping at the corpse. Then he polled the girls: "We were all seeing that, right?"

Andy tried to remember how to breathe. She turned to Kerri for help: she was standing right behind her, next to the tent (there it was!), catatonic.

Tim sniffed thoroughly the wreck on the ground, then jumped over it and ran to Nate, erect tail signaling extreme concern. *About effing time,* he strongly communicated. *We could have died here—we were lucky the thing's head exploded!*

"Where the fuck did you get that gun from?" Andy asked.

"It's Uncle Emmet's; I put it in the trunk. I just went to the car for my pills."

"I'm gonna faint," Kerri announced.

"No, don't," Andy bade, holding her. "Kerri, take deep breaths. Deep breaths." She tried to demonstrate and failed miserably. Even her lungs were rebelling. "Okay, okay, look, everyone's fine, right? So the next step is . . ."

She looked for the next step. Her eyes couldn't pan past the gray limb-tangle of a corpse on the ground, its three-dimensional volume, the space it stole from the natural world.

"Holy shit," she concluded, and fell on her knees.

Nate pulled his shirt up to his mouth and spoke through it. "Next step is, we get the fuck out of here."

"Okay," Andy answered. Some wind was blowing; visibility was improving. She started to make out the amber blur of the Chevy Vega. It had been ridiculously close the entire time. "Take care of Kerri and pack up. But don't bother taking anything that won't fit with you in the backseat."

"Why? Wait," he asked and self-answered. "We're gonna . . . We're carrying this?!"

Andy looked up, the adrenaline she'd failed to use bleeding through her eyes. "This is the thing that has almost driven us mad for thirteen years. God help me if I'm not putting it on the *Pennaquick Telegraph* front page."

It had been only early morning when the attack occurred; the fog had deceivingly enhanced the twilight. The sun was just beginning to rise between karsts of scrap metal when the racing-striped station wagon made a quick stop by the junkyard. Nate jumped out of the car and climbed the shivery stairs of the watchtower, three steps at a time, and banged the door on top.

Andy, staying at the wheel with the engine running, saw him a minute later returning downstairs, with Captain Al hurrying behind—the latter only wearing what seemed like a bathrobe, and hopefully underpants beneath, and striding barefooted through the aluminum-littered grounds.

"See, here he comes," she reported to Kerri. "Captain's in charge now, like he used to be."

Kerri had not uttered a single sound since they'd propped her on the front seat. Tim just didn't know what to do to earn her attention.

Andy watched the rearview mirror as Nate opened

the trunk, where they had dumped the skull-torn corpse of the wheezer after wrapping it in a tarpaulin. When he slammed the trunk closed, Captain Al was transfigured, his hangover banished from existence.

"Police station," he ordered, going for the door to get in the backseat.

"We never got the cops involved so soon before," Nate said.

"You never blew anyone's head off before."

Rumors abounded on the life of Blyton Hills' deputy sheriff, Sam Copperseed, before he joined the Pennaquick County Police in 1964. He was known to be a Walla Walla Indian, raised in a traditional community in northeastern Oregon, and his first uniform had been the black-and-green one of the forest rangers, until the realization that human carelessness was the biggest threat to the environment compelled him to switch to an outfit that allowed him to arrest idiots. This motivation behind his enrollment determined the type of policeman he'd become. As assistant to Deputy Sheriff Wilson, and in contrast with the latter's warm, cordial, first-name-basis approach to law enforcement, Copperseed cultivated the persona of the cooler, stricter cop whose zeal for law abidance could not be placated by an appeal to old friendship or the memory of a shared childhood. It was even historically plausible that Wilson and he had consciously assigned themselves these roles, and Copperseed was fine with his, certain that never being the public's favorite was no hindrance to becoming its finest. Copperseed had been, in fact, one of the reasons the Blyton Summer Detective Club, back in its heyday, always hesitated to bring their cases to the attention of the police, for fear that the friendly Deputy Wilson would be out on patrol and they would have to share their childish suspicions with then officer Copperseed, whom they never managed to impress.

But this time Andy was confident in their success. The minute she and Captain Al and Tim climbed up the steps of the humble police station, crossed the empty reception room, barged into the new deputy's office, and unrolled the tarpaulin wrap on the floor, exposing the decapitated nightmare within, she knew she had hit a new milestone in her career of jaw-dropping walk-ins.

Copperseed, albeit on guard, stayed behind his desk through the whole performance, only leaning over to decipher the abomination on the floor once unveiled, a hand sheltering his nose from the insulting smell. Andy could read in his grimace how hard it was to, first, make heads or tails of the whole mess and guess where the head in particular would have been, and then, at a later stage, to reconcile oneself with the notion of such a monstrosity ever existing on God's green earth.

Once he looked up at the fully dressed woman and the half-naked man and the blue-gray Weimaraner, however, he seemed to have sketched out a considerably accurate picture of the situation.

He sat back on his chair and proclaimed: "See? This is why I never drink tap water."

Andy smiled: she was able to identify with his tough-guy underreaction.

Copperseed picked up his phone and dialed. "Morning. Deputy Sheriff Copperseed, Blyton Hills. I've got a four-one-nine-Charlie. We will need a forensics team and possibly a consulting biologist."

Andy jumped in: "Hey, I have a biologist right out—"

Al just needed to touch her arm.

"Yes," Copperseed continued on the phone. "Yes, from State. Possibly. Thank you."

He hung up and faced the captain.

"Al. Good to see you."

"Deputy," Al replied, smoothing his bathrobe.

Copperseed addressed Andy. "Tell me exactly what happened."

It took her two minutes and forty-seven seconds to retell the events. She never faltered once. She was good at reporting to authorities; the fact that this time she was sure to be innocent of any charge just made it easier. As did the fact that Copperseed was starting to look like the kind of cop she would have chosen to handle this situation. Copperseed had always struck her as a sort of sulky patrolman who couldn't find his place in always-friendly Blyton Hills. But in thirteen years, Blyton Hills had degenerated into a town that needed less of a Carl Winslow police type and more of a Dirty Harry. And 1990 Deputy Copperseed's weathered skin and dry smirk could more than pass for Clint Eastwood grit.

After he finished up his notes, Copperseed asked, "Are you still staying at Mrs. Shannon's house?"

That caught Andy by surprise. She hadn't even thought that the deputy would have recognized her after thirteen years, linked her with Kerri, or remembered Aunt Margo's married name.

"Yes."

"How is Mrs. Shannon?"

"Fine," Andy answered. "I'll send her your best."

Copperseed nodded, then returned his attention to the blatant profanity on the floor.

"Will you please help me carry this to the freezer?"

About ten minutes later, Andy and Captain Al stepped out onto the porch of the redbrick police building. Rain ran down the dirty sign with the county coat of arms.

"What are you kids gonna do now?" Al asked.

"We'll go home," Andy said, and sighed. The idea that she would have to try to sleep again at some point in her life stressed her out.

She glanced over at Al. White chest hair rippled under his bathrobe.

"Do you need a lift?"

"No, I'm gonna go back in, talk to Copperseed. I'm sure he'll give me a ride later."

Andy gazed at the Chevy Vega parked down the stairs. It did not look at all like a sports car, she was realizing now.

"I think I broke Kerri," she said.

"Go fix her," Al commanded, unfazed. "We've got enough broken parts."

* * *

Kerri did not utter a word on the ride home. Nor did she seem to notice anything around her, although they drove by several corners of Blyton Hills whose transformation deserved commentary. Andy was so focused on her, she almost hit two pedestrians in a five-minute trip.

As she stopped at the last light before Kerri's street, she turned to her and spoke the first words since the police station.

"Kerri. I just want you to tell me you're okay."

"I'm okay," Kerri obeyed, lost in the dashboard. Her fingers idly rubbed Tim's head. Nate sat behind, gnawing at his nails.

When they pulled over in front of Aunt Margo's house, they had to help Kerri out of the car. The keys jingled in her hand.

"Let me," Andy said.

She noticed Kerri pressing harder on her biceps as she unlocked the front door.

"It's nothing. We're safe."

Tim proved so by stepping in, relieved to be at headquarters again. He needed to think.

Nate carried the bags from the trunk and headed upstairs.

"I'm gonna try and sleep for a while," he said, not offering much of a chance for objections. "You girls will be okay?"

Andy nodded for both. Kerri had not let go of her arm yet.

She kept holding her as they went upstairs. The house, floorboards excepting, remained silent. The common sympathy of some tender music could have been expected.

Kerri jolted a little when Andy pushed open the door to her room.

"Okay, see? We made it." Andy pulled her inside. "There's nothing to worry about here."

Kerri still refused to let go. Andy monitored her as her eyes swept the tiny flowery room: the bed, the miniature desk, the wardrobe.

"Kerri. Look. There's nothing here."

"No, no . . ."

"I'm just showing you." She opened the wardrobe, a pinkblast of small T-shirts and pullovers and shorts yelling hello inside. She pulled the chair from under the desk, silent on the thick terry cloth carpet. She made a point to kneel down and check under the bed. "See? Nothing here, except for the guest bed. Come on. Sit down."

Kerri carefully sat on a corner of the Darjeeling-colored paisley quilt. From there she closed the door and locked it. Then her attention turned to the opposite wall.

"Can you block the window?"

Andy was on her knees, pulling out the guest bed.

"Kerri, nothing's gonna come through the window."

"I know. But can you please do it?"

"Kerri . . ."

"Please!"

It did sound more like a command than a plea, but the effort nonetheless pushed a tear down her cheek.

Andy went to the window and pushed the wardrobe in front of it. The colors inside the room went *oh* and became very sad.

"Right," Andy panted. "Let's get some sleep now, okay?"

"No, please—"

"I meant you, Kerri. Okay? I'll keep watch. Nothing's going to happen. But you need to get in bed."

"No!"

"Kerri, come on, please!" She was holding Kerri's arm with one hand while she opened the bed with the other. "Just lie down."

"Don't leave me alone!"

"I'm not leaving you alone, I'm staying here with you. Just lie down." She tried to let her go, but it was Kerri holding on to her body now. "Kerri, you're having an anxiety attack. I need you to relax and get into bed."

"Don't leave me!"

She had almost laid her down now, but Kerri was clinging to her so firmly she was practically cliffhanging from her shoulders. Andy had to hold her arms to restrain the spasms.

"Kay! Please look at me. Look into my eyes!"

Kerri's terrified irises suddenly discovered Andy's, three inches away. Andy tried to sound as soothing as chemically possible.

"We are going to be fine. I promise. Okay? This is your room. Nothing bad can ever happen in your room."

Kerri swallowed a bezoar rising in her throat. The tremor was receding. "Promise you won't go."

"I'm not going anywhere. But you're hurting my back a little."

With their eyes locked, Andy noticed the grip around her loosening up some, like Kerri's fingers were admitting circulation again, trying a gentler clasp around Andy's neck. Andy let her alight on the bed, as though she were holding a wounded sparrow on her palm.

"Can you pull the sheets over?" Kerri asked in her flimsiest voice.

Andy's eyes wandered for a second to evaluate. She was leaning inches above Kerri, one knee sunk in the mattress, one foot still touching the floor as a mere concession to appearances.

"I have my own bed."

"No, don't leave me!"

"Okay, okay," she conceded, alarmed by the returning exclamation points. "I'm not leaving. Just let me—"

"Don't move!"

"Kerri, I can't stay like this, you'll suffocate under my weight."

"Don't—I don't mind! Pull the sheets over us!"

"Right, here!" She did as commanded, slithering under the bedclothes and pulling them over her back. She stretched her legs, toeing the south end of the mattress, cozying up to their tight rabbit hole under the paisleyfield.

"See? I got you covered. Nothing's going to happen. Now I need you to take deep breaths and chill, okay?"

Kerri eased the pressure around Andy's neck a notch and forced her lungs to fill. Andy did what she could to shift her weight without triggering a panic response; she managed to stand on her elbows and feet, in plank position, her torso merely brushing Kerri.

"You know, the last time I held this position for so long I was doing push-ups in military training, and I wondered what possible use it would have in real life," she joked.

Kerri didn't seem to appreciate it, busy trying to control her respiration.

"Just breathe from your abdomen," Andy advised. "Take a deep one. Like that. Now out. Good."

The next breath was just as deep, and slower, and a little quieter. Shortly, under Andy's strict watch, the rhythm fell from frantic to vivace, and then to piano, and every minute it would become softer, gradually merging into the candleflame silence.

They were lying in a soundless house, in a soundless room, in a soundless burrow of wool and cotton and butterflies. And that was when Andy started to pay attention to the many excited sensations that were calling for her awareness. A thousand orange curls of hair falling asleep. Kerri's breath on her neck. Her own breasts, through her clothes and Kerri's clothes, cozily nestling up against the ones below.

Her biceps had started giving way long ago.

"This is . . . kinda awkward," she underwhispered.

"I just saw you wrestle a Sleepy Lake creature; whatever you're talking about, I doubt it beats that."

"Okay." She tried to accommodate her left hand around Kerri's head, burrowing among her curls without awaking them.

"That thing could have killed us," Kerri said.

"It didn't."

"It could have killed Nate, or Tim. There was more than one."

"Yeah, there was." Her head was touching Kerri's now, cheek by rose-petal cheek.

"What if you hadn't woken up, what if they had surrounded us? They could have killed us all in our sleep."

Andy rounded on her and kissed her mouth.

The universe skipped a heartbeat.

Then she jolted back to see the aftermath, the taste of sun after bathing and raspberry ink and August in her joydrunk lips.

"They could have killed us and dragged us to the water and that would have been the end," Kerri said, her eyes hardly afloat over her fantasies.

Then, slowly, her pupils drifted to meet Andy's hovering over her like a first sight after a coma.

"Did you just kiss me?"

"Uh . . . yeah."

Neither moved. Kerri's tongue discreetly reconned the inside of her lips.

"Why?"

"It . . . seemed the right moment," Andy stuttered. "But maybe it wasn't. I've been known to get it wrong before."

"I see."

"Do you want me to move off?"

"No," Kerri said quickly.

"Okay."

A blank-meaning time-lapse paragraph fireflew by.

"So . . . you like girls?" Kerri said.

"Yeah. Well, no. I mean . . . mostly you, really."

"Oh. *(Pause.)* It's . . . maybe 'cause we've been so close this week . . . ?"

"No, I've . . . I've been feeling like this awhile."

"How long?"

"I don't know, since I was . . . twelve? Is twelve too early?"

"No, I think it's the normal age."

"Maybe eleven."

"Wow."

It was the quietest "wow" in history.

"Does it . . . shock you?" Andy asked.

"No," Kerri said firmly. "No, it's just that . . . I didn't know you were . . ."

"*L*?"

"Yeah . . . *E* . . ."

"*V* . . ."

"Uh, wait, you lost me there."

"In *love* with you."

All around them, Kerri's hair was awake and eavesdropping.

Kerri mentally checked her constants. Her heartbeat was slowing down. Her breathing was tranquil. Her breasts felt the marshmallow pressure of Andy's, but there were no complaints there. Nothing had come as a shock indeed.

"Andy, I . . . I mean, it's very sweet, but . . . I'm not into girls, I think."

"Have you tried?"

"No. But I haven't tried skydiving either and I'm pretty sure it's not my cup of tea," she said. "I mean, no, wait, that wasn't—" She sighed. "That was harsh. Andy, I'm sorry; I was freaking out a minute ago."

"I know."

"Maybe it wasn't the right time."

"I know," Andy said, realizing, but the bitterness of that realization could not possibly spoil the sweet smell surrounding her. "It's just that . . . you were like . . . hugging me, facing me, and I thought it wasn't fair to you because you didn't know how I felt."

"Do you want to move off?"

"No."

"Okay."

Kerri shifted a little, her hands clasped around Andy a little more gently, pulling her closer. Andy noticed: her own pulse was now beginning to pace up. She made a conscious effort to bridle it.

"I just thought that . . . if I kissed you it'd be less awkward." She took a second to evaluate. "Fuck, that worked out great."

"Hey."

Andy's own hair gasped as Kerri caressed her cheek.

"Never punish yourself for this. You hear me?"

They were too close to see the other's whole face, but Andy noticed Kerri's eyes smiling.

"I'm glad you told me. Plus, you succeeded in calming me down."

"Yeah. I'm not sure I was aiming for that, but whatever."

"Andy, listen to me," she began, carefully. "I don't think I like girls. But I do like you too. A lot. And I really, really need you to be here right now. Can you do that?"

The soldier in Andy took over. "Yes. Of course."

"You can?"

"On top of you."

"Yes, on top of me. Will that be a problem?"

"No, I can handle it."

"Good."

"Can I move my hand? It hurts a little."

"Make yourself comfortable."

They both maneuvered a little, full-cycling a mutual hug, Kerri's arms resting surely on Andy's back, Andy's hands sunken in pure orange euphoria, legs intertwined, breasts still clothed but formally acquainted.

When Andy looked again, Kerri had closed her eyes. A peaceful cub smile dozed on her face.

"Kerri."

"Yup."

"Would you rather I was a boy?"

"No. You wouldn't be in this room if you were."

"I like this room a lot," Andy said. Butterflies and paisley dozed around their burrow. "I was afraid if I told you, you wouldn't want me in here anymore."

"Don't ever worry about that," Kerri whispered, fingers caressing the back of Andy's neck. "Nothing bad will ever happen in this room."

Andy closed her eyes and rested her head next to Kerri's, face sunken into welcoming sugar-candy orange hair.

"Well, that was an interesting development," Peter told the ceiling of the next room, lying on the upper berth. "No man in a mask this time. I hope."

"Shut up," Nate groaned below him.

Peter jumped off the berth, ghost sneakers landing lightly on the carpet.

"Come on, man, I'm honestly congratulating you on a good job. Packing Uncle Emmet's gun—that was a smart move." From the pencil pot on the desk he grabbed a fistful of darts and faced the target on the door.

"You told me to pack the gun," Nate reminded him.

"Oh, yeah, I did. Good old me."

He threw a dart; Nate covered his ears with his pillow.

"Anyway, it was a long shot," Peter went on. "Not literally; I mean my telling you to pack the gun. Because those lake creatures turning up was ... *(A dart hits the board.)* Well, not totally unexpected, but still a good twist. There was a chance they'd be there, but they were supposed to be asleep, right?"

Nate dropped the pillow and confronted Peter, who was standing right in front of him, his smug grin and perfect hair impervious to post-traumatic stress.

"We didn't wake them up," Nate said.

"I know we didn't, Nate. I'm saying you did," he said, waving a dart at him. "That night in 'seventy-seven, when Kerri was kidnapped in the basement, and Andy went to search for her downstairs, and I had to rescue them both; what were you doing in the attic all that time?"

"Like you don't know!" Nate shouted. "You are in my head!"

The next thing in his head was very nearly the steel tip of a dart. It missed his skull by a centimeter and stopped with a thud right above him, nailed into the upper berth.

"I *do* know!" Peter gloated. "I mean, whoa, Nate, telling Kerri about the Necronomicon is gonna be tough enough, but what do you think the girls will say when they find out that you not only saw the book in Deboën Mansion, but you also *read* it? Aloud? You fucking twit?!"

PART THREE

COLLAPSE

The bunker was reached some minutes past ten a.m. Andy woke up, found herself face-sunk in orange curls filling her eyes, ears, nose, and lips. She was joyfully drowning in Kerri's hair, its fragrance and softness pounding on her senses like a cheerful Mongol army banging on the gates of Baghdad. And the truthfulness of that sensation, the physical reality of it, was beyond philosophical doubt. She even recognized it from the last time she'd felt it, that night thirteen years ago when she was hugging Kerri, twenty feet underground, in a dungeon, in smothering darkness, too busy sobbing in terror and listening to the lake creatures scratching the walls to notice the bliss back then. But she was paying attention to it now, in Kerri's bed, their top-bottom position changed during sleep into a sort of overprotective spooning, her face drowned in real, 100 percent pure rainbow-powered ecstasy.

A certainty that in all its glory could not mitigate another truth: what had just awoken her was the sound of scratching on the walls.

She laser-eyed the wallpaper right next to the bed, trying to make out a clue in the dim light of the bedroom, shushing Kerri's hair down. Nothing happened.

Until a minute later, when something scratched the door.

Andy got up, for some reason careful not to wake Kerri, and scanned the bedroom for a weapon. She knew only too well there would be nothing. Weapons were not known in Kerri's bedroom; it was a war-free territory; it was a utopian civilization oblivious to the greedy, fanatic, barbaric things living outside.

The door quivered on its hinge, flinching under the graze of claws on the other side.

Andy felt her heart defect to chaos. The scratching was becoming deafening. She couldn't believe Kerri didn't hear it. She couldn't believe the creature outside had not heard her galloping pulse. Desperately she ordered her brain to slow down and go through her options. The window was blocked; she would make less noise by ransacking the wardrobe for Kerri's old baseball bat. She needed to lay out a strategy. She needed to rein in her heart and think—the skill she sucked at most in the world.

She went for the wardrobe, gripped the bat, swung it with her right hand as she pulled the door open.

Tim padded in with a *Thank you, Jeeves* nod at Andy, went to smell Kerri's hand.

Andy stumbled out into the hallway for a second, a hand to her mouth to block a vomit jet of pure rage, and closed the door behind her. She leaned on the wall, panting, internally yelling at her body to put itself together. The house was as quiet as it had been in years, a time capsule of closed blinds and shrouded furniture.

After a minute, still soaked in sweat, she popped in the bedroom again.

"Tim. A word, please."

Tim followed her into the hallway as if summoned out of a meeting, and Andy knelt down to him.

"Never fucking do that again," she admonished. "Do you understand? You don't go scratching walls or doors. Ever. If you're shut out, you bark. You hear me?"

Tim did his best impression of comprehension.

"Try it now. Bark," Andy ordered. "Come on. Bark."

Kerri opened the door and ordered, "Speak!"

Tim woofed unquestioningly.

"The command to make him bark is 'speak.' 'Bark' is too close to 'park,'" she explained, kneeling to snuggle the dog. "Right, Tim? You're a very smart boy when we use the right words, aren't you?"

She stopped the petting for a second to take in Andy's pose.

"What's with the bat?"

Andy was going to blurt a ridiculous excuse when they were interrupted by the analog ring of the telephone in the living room. She ran downstairs to pick it up.

"Hello?"

"Did you say you know a biologist?"

It took her a while to tell Copperseed's voice apart from the static, and a little longer to pick up the thread from their last conversation.

"Yeah. Why?"

"State can't send a forensics expert until tomorrow. I fear we don't have that long."

"We don't?" she said, self-consciously puzzled.

"I just checked on the body; it's decomposing fast. I don't think our freezer is cold enough. If you know someone, we need to examine it now."

Andy glanced at Kerri on the landing upstairs.

"I'm not sure she's ready," Andy whispered into the phone.

"Ready for what?" Kerri asked.

Andy covered the mouthpiece. "Something's wrong with the wheezer's body. Copperseed says we need to check it before—"

"I can do it."

"You sure?"

"Yeah." She folded her arms, lips pressed, conjuring strength all the way up from her newly found Huckleberry Hound socks. "I'm a biologist."

"But, you know, it's performing an autopsy on—"

"Dissection. It's a lake creature. Local fauna," Kerri said. "All that is required is a scientific description. Like a new species of butterfly. Might even name it after one of you guys."

"I'd rather wait for the butterfly," Andy said, and returned to the phone. "Deputy? Okay. She'll do it."

They were back at the police station within half an hour, the time to shower and gather some instruments from the kitchen cupboard and Kerri's old Polaroid camera.

Copperseed nodded them good morning, thus ending the formalities, and led them down a ramp and into the morgue. In a station with no forensics lab, it was no more than a bare pantry-sized cubicle with a sink and two cold chambers where bodies could be stored, often for convenience, since Blyton Hills had no funeral home. The kids were still adjusting to the dismal room when Copperseed opened one of the chambers and pulled the slab out.

Tim complained vigorously about the smell, and everybody else turned away, sleeves under their noses, mentioning several biblical characters by first name.

The thing lay facedown, minus the face: the medial limbs that sprouted from under its shoulder blades made it difficult to rest on its back. Kerri, who had avoided the body while Andy and Nate were packing it up, immediately captured some details she had not registered before: the webbed toes, the squamous skin, the growths reminiscent of anemone sticking out of the holes under its ribs.

Copperseed took a pen and pinched one of the upper arms. The flesh gave way like lukewarm wax.

"No way," Andy complained. "It was a lot tougher a few hours ago."

Nate shot a photograph of it, started waving the Polaroid. Tim was still yapping, unable to accept that everyone else had gotten over the smell already.

"Tim can't be here," Kerri said, forcing last night's dinner back where it belonged and stepping forward to the specimen. "Take him out."

"Nate, can you look after him?" Andy said.

"Both of you," she firmed up. "This is a lab now."

"But I don't want to leave you alone with this," Andy protested.

"I won't be alone; the deputy will assist me," she said, nodding toward Copperseed and pulling some cuticle scissors out of her kit. "Go, I'll meet you at Ben's in two hours."

Copperseed handed her a mask, put one on himself, and prepared to work for a day as the toughest lab assistant this side of the Mississippi.

Nate, Andy, and Tim found themselves back on the police station porch the next minute, basking in uncontaminated air.

Nate sat down on a step, rubbing his mouth. Andy noticed the somber circles around his eyes.

"You okay?" she asked.

"Yeah." He inspected Andy. "You okay?"

"Yeah."

"Cool, everyone's okay!" Peter said, kicking litter along the sidewalk. "Fuck the signs, we're all systems go! Locked and loaded! Five by five! I don't even know what that one means."

Nate popped a pill into his mouth and pocketed the bottle. Assuming Andy was waiting for the right time to ask what now, he suggested, "We could go see Dunia Deboën."

"Why?" Andy asked. "We've got the lake creature in there. What could she possibly have to do with it?"

"I don't know. We never met her last time; since we're

reopening the case, might as well check every angle this time around."

"And say what? 'Hi, we just caught one of the Sleepy Lake creatures; as the granddaughter of a pirate who practiced black magic, can we have your input?'"

"If we were still kids, what would we be more likely to do?" Nate said. "Sit here and wait, or go visit the witch's house?"

Tim was already halfway down the block, calling over his shoulder like, *Yo! Where did the witch live again?*

The witch lived on the northeast side of town, on a winding street that followed the creek at the foot of Owl Hill. All the backyards on that street looked out onto unabated wilderness, which started, with astounding impetus, just ten feet away from the fences, normally on the inside. Frontyards, demoted to the storage of junk and sale ads, had long lost all appearance of tameness. Houses stood in the middle, half digested by the forest.

Deboën's house, which Andy and Nate still remembered from hushed pointing and rumoring when they used to cycle by, stood slightly prouder than the rest, having apparently agreed on a fragile nonaggression treaty with the invading rain forest. The front garden could almost have been described as beautiful, until on a closer look the observer noticed that most of the blossoming whites and pale blues were actually wild species in their early-spring exuberance, unassisted by gardeners. Junipers and blackberry bushes coexisted peacefully with cast-iron lamps, a bird fountain, and a moss-ridden set of garden furniture, and the brownstone building tried its best not to cramp the hill's Gothic sense of style.

Crows perched on a fig tree announced the arrival of visitors. A squirrel fled the rough path of sandstone slabs at the sight of Tim. As they pushed open the gate, Nate pointed out that the name on the mailbox was Morris.

They resolved to knock anyway and ask for directions.

Andy rubbed the verdigris off her fingers as they waited by the front door.

"So this is a witch's house?" she said. She checked the spiraling ornaments of the porch lamps and the handrail, the silent wooden wind chime, the withered Christmas wreath on the door. "Looks like the place of an old lady who never got married."

"That's Puritan for 'witch,'" Nate said, and he knocked again.

Tim finished wreaking havoc among the abnormally dense animal population of the tiny garden and climbed up to the porch, the trip having already been well worth his time. Andy and Nate deliberated wordlessly.

They were coming back down the stoop when a figure under a wide tornado of a coat and a flower-bearing hat shuffled through the entrance gate, towing her shopping bags, negotiating the sketchy garden path in her high-heeled boots. A black-eyed face looked up from under the hat.

"Can I help you?" she said, with the exact tone of someone whose next line is going to be *Yes, I heard of this Jesus Christ guy, but I'm not voting for him.*

"Are you Ms. Deboën?" Nate asked.

"It's Morris now," the woman said, hurrying up the steps past them to drop the bags on dry land. She examined the visitors while producing a jingling tangle of keys. "Who are you?"

She had a flimsy, high-pitched voice, kind but tired. Andy poked herself out of confusion.

"Uh, my name's Andy Rodriguez; this is Nate Rogers. We are ... uh, doing some research on the history of Blyton Hills. We wonder if you could spare some minutes to answer a few questions?"

"About what?"

"Your ... I mean, the Deboën family."

The woman managed to find a key that agreed to fit the lock and opened the front door. An unsubtle aroma of thyme and tobacco rushed out.

"I'm not sure I'm the best person to tell you. Why don't you ask, I don't know, every other man or woman in town?"

"We did," Nate lied, softly blocking the door after her. "We heard some unflattering gossip; we were hoping to get the facts from you."

"Okay," she said. "My father was such a creep that just for carrying his name I've been getting the worst cut at the butcher's and having to cut my own hair for thirty years. How's that for a fact?"

She held looks with Andy, Nate spying his favorite brand of canned mac and cheese inside the woman's shopping bags. Then they all checked on Tim. He had half his body inside the house and was carefully inspecting the umbrellas by the door.

"What kind of researchers are you?" the woman inquired. She had manga-sized eyes, emboldened by mascara.

"History."

"Folklore," Nate began to say just a little before Andy. Then he continued. "We're interested in the legends of Sleepy Lake."

The woman examined them again, squinting now. The realization triggered the most volatile, ghostly memory of a smirk.

"You're the kids," she said. "The teen sleuths who caught the Sleepy Lake monster."

"Yes," Andy said, kind of embarrassed. Being recognized like this would be the closest to flashing a badge she would ever do. "Can we ask you a few questions about the house up there?"

Tim was already inside the hall and ready to make himself some toast as soon as he found the kitchen.

"All right, come in," the woman said, yielding the lead.

The house was smaller than Kerri's, but way more cluttered. The tiny entrance hall alone held so many pieces of furniture—all dark wood and aged cloth—but with each piece having a seemingly good reason to be there, that Andy felt she was in the rare presence of a hoarder with a sense of taste. It did look like a witch's house—one that would be featured in the fall '68 issue of *Country Homeowners*.

"Sit wherever, I'll be with you in a second," the witch said while she hatched from her scruffy overcoat and hat, emerging at least two sizes tinier, her miniature hourglass body clad in a tight sweater and leather pants, perfectly adjusted to gracefully navigate through the crammed space. The word "voluptuous" came to Andy's mind, mainly because she thought of it as a word for sexy that was used decades ago, while she watched the little woman drag her groceries into the kitchen.

An iron lattice separated the hall from the living room, where the stuffiness expanded in the shape of megafauna-skin cushions and junglesome indoor plants. Andy called the dog away from the many objects she felt like sniffing herself. Nate orbited toward the books on the shelves—old dusty leather-bound volumes flanked by Tiki book stoppers and luxurious plants. On a closer inspection, they were just jacketless editions of fantasy romance.

"Can I offer you something?" the woman called. "Coffee? Tea? A toad's eye in syrup?"

"No, thank—" Andy stopped short, an eyebrow triggered to stand alert.

Their hostess appeared in the doorframe. "Just kidding. Gotta live up to my reputation, you know."

She closed the fridge and stepped out to join them.

"Please, sit down. Where are the other two?"

The guests exchanged puzzled looks.

"You used to be five, didn't you?" she said, settling on a beanbag sofa and opening a tin cigarette box. "Three boys, a girl, and a dog?"

Andy smiled, thinking how flattered that would have made her teenager self.

"Only one came; she's pursuing a different lead," Nate answered.

"That's cute," said the woman, blowing out the inaugural

puff of smoke. She dragged a table resembling a slice of sequoia and a brass ashtray near her, and crossed her maroon-leather-boot-clad legs. "What can I do for you?"

Andy looked away from the underside of her thighs and queried Nate. He seemed to relinquish the lead.

"Mrs. Deboën—"

"Morris. Or just call me Dunia."

"Dunia. You must be familiar with the Sleepy Lake area."

"Not really, I'm not very outdoorsy."

"But you used to live in Deboën Mansion once."

"Only my first five years. You know, a house on top of a mine, and a lake ten yards off the door: not a very child-friendly place."

"Not to mention your father's experiments," Nate inserted, trying to throw her off.

"No, I'd rather not," she deflected gracefully. "He sent me to boarding school as soon as he could and then bought this place for my mother. I think he was happy to get rid of us."

"Why?" Andy followed up.

"Well, according to popular belief, my father only married my mother and had me to avoid being tagged as a hermit, like his father was," she explained matter-of-factly. "It was what you'd call a PR matter."

"Do you believe that?"

"Maybe. I myself married a man I didn't really love just to borrow his name, so I guess it's possible." As if in confidence to Andy, she added, "It never works out."

"Why didn't you just leave town?" Nate pursued.

"All I own is this house. And I can't find a buyer. I guess

I should've left anyway and hit the road when I was still young and careless. Only I was never careless. I am now, but too old to be a stripper."

The words "Never too late!" were blocked and severely frowned upon by a head-shaking bouncer right before leaving Andy's mouth. Instead, she asked, "What do you do?"

"I write erotica," she answered, pointing at a little workplace set near a window, computer included. Then she added through an impish smile: "Yes, it's people like me."

Tim sneezed as a reaction to all the fluttering hormones.

"But your family must have had tons of money," Nate complained. "They owned a gold mine; it was a big company once; they must have made a fortune."

"I saw nothing after my parents died. I mean after my father died in the fire; I wasn't expecting anything when my mother decided to pass out in the car with the engine running. That was . . . three years after my father?"

"'Fifty-two?" Nate offered. "The mansion caught fire in 'forty-nine."

"Yes, about that. I was seven when he died. Anyway, the lawyers who handled his legacy took a bad offer for the mine and used the money to keep me in a school in Eugene. So after I graduated I had this house in this beautiful neighborhood that loves me so much, and nothing else." She paused, scratched the Weimaraner's head en passant, then continued. "If I know my father, I think he kept his fortune hidden in the house; he wasn't the investing type. It probably burned in the fire. There was some searching, back in the day."

"Of course. That's the gold Wickley hoped to find."

"Who?"

"Uh, Thomas X. Wickley," Andy repeated. "The Sleepy Lake creature."

"Oh, yeah." The woman sighed, as if recalling a minor character from a TV series.

"Apropos of which," Nate detoured, searching his coat pockets, "you may be aware of rumors that lake creatures have been sighted again."

"No, but that was to be expected," Dunia said. "Rumors about lake creatures had been going on for decades; the arrest of a guy in costume had no right to spoil the fun."

"Well, we went creature hunting last night, and we came across this," he said, pulling out a Polaroid and sliding it across the table to Dunia. "We're . . . ninety percent sure it was not a guy in a costume."

The pulpy underheaded, overlimbed corpse lay oxidizing on a thickening film of its own juices, its chest sliced open. Kerri tried not to glance at it as she scribbled on an official Pennaquick County Police notepad. A fetid odor assailed the walls of the dust masks she and Deputy Copperseed were wearing.

"Respiration is most likely carried out through the orifices on each side, though the function of the cilia inside them is unclear," she dictated to herself as she wrote in her nervous, spiky handwriting that had forgone any attempt at legibility pages ago. "What I once called lungs more likely serve as swim bladders. However, it did roar through its mouth." She clarified for the deputy: "Amphibians are born with gills and later develop lungs. This thing seems to have both, and still it breathed with great difficulty when it faced us. Maybe the bladders act as air reserves when it crawls out of the water."

Copperseed stayed vigilant, the mask allowing him to grimace freely at the stench without denting his poise.

"There's no chance these things are the product of toxic dump, is there?" he inserted with a pinch of resentment.

"It's not a mutation, if that's what you're asking," Kerri answered, taking a knife and rasping softly one of the open ribs protruding out of the chest. She could easily peel some bone off it; the skeleton was melting. "This is different at every level. The chemical composition . . . Nothing carbon based could possibly oxidize this fast."

She stepped back a little, trying to zoom out for the whole picture. The stench was insulting. The sight of it, even as a still life, challenged reason.

Pen and paper waited self-consciously on the side table, wondering if they should be doing something for themselves.

After a couple of deep breaths, Kerri pulled off one kitchen glove and neared her bare index finger half an inch above the shoulder of the upper limb. Her finger hovered along the arm dangling off the slab, down to the wrist and the webbed hand and the long, black-caked claws. And then she touched it.

That was the final insult: the solid, cold touch; the alien organic chemistry; the microscopic complexity of it, impossible to fake. Her nightmare, smuggled into the real world.

The deputy grabbed her by the shoulders, signaling time for a recess, while she continued to speak into a nonexisting dictaphone: "It is not supposed to exist. The body is decomposing at an alarming rate; it cannot live for long in air. By tomorrow, there will be nothing solid left!"

By the end of that sentence Copperseed had dragged her into the courtyard. Sunlight and bird language washed on her face.

She snatched her mask off, quenching on pure air.

"It makes some sense," she droned on. "The accelerated decay would explain why we never saw these things before. Otherwise, even if they avoided humans, we were bound to come across a carcass. And yet, some of its features are stuff I only read about in paleobiology. These things must have existed for . . . longer than us, longer than chordates!"

She peered out of her ramblings for a second and found herself sitting on a curb, leaning back on an iron fence. The sky above was a solid blue. Her defiled fingers rejoiced in the cozy caress of the pavement and the interstitial grass. The rumor of Blyton Hills traffic hardly bothered the pigeons fighting over some crumbs by the dumpster.

Copperseed stood at a comfortable distance, unmasked, hands in his uniform pockets.

"The first dwellers," he seemingly quoted.

Kerri looked up at him, hand shielding her eyes from the sun. The deputy spoke as if he read off a prompter in the clouds.

"Back in the days of the Second Sky Battle, when the Walla Walla first settled on the smoking hills, they discovered an elusive people lurking in the misty slopes and the shadowy gorges near the source of the Zoinx River. These folk shunned the sun and the moon, lived only near the water or in it, inside caves where underground rivers flow, and they worshipped Thtaggoa, the undergod in the Mount of Thunder. The Walla Walla knew better than to disturb the first dwellers, for those who ventured too far upriver fell mad with horror at the sight of the brutal, disfigured beings, and those who dared to camp in the deeper valleys were killed and their bodies hanged from trees as a warning to others. For many years the Walla Walla respected their boundaries and never neared the Mount of Thunder or entered the valleys below. But then Thtaggoa grew hungry for power, and the earth rumbled, and the mist from the lake spread, killing the forests and the animals, drowning the villages. And under cover of the mist, the first dwellers marched forth, slaughtering our people. The Walla Walla fought bravely with spears and shields, but the first dwellers were resilient and their numbers never dwindled. Thus, as the undergod in the Mount of Thunder roared, the Walla Walla gathered their clans and sang together, asking the Fathers for help. And in response, from the Warm Snows was sent down a powerful shaman named Ashen Fox. And Ashen Fox walked to the foot of the Mount of Thunder with four brave warriors, and there in a circle of fire he chanted the incantation, and the mount collapsed, and Thtaggoa and its spawn were cast down the pit, and the river filled the pit with water. But Thtaggoa is immortal and still sleeps at the bottom of the lake, waiting to be released and reign again."

Pigeons cooed and fluttered away. Kerri took some

time to settle back onto the white courtyard under her fingernails, the sun on her cheeks, the flat blue sky above.

"Okay. As far as I can tell," she began, "you're retelling the Walla Walla interpretation of the cataclysm that formed Sleepy Lake. What is the time of the Second Sky Battle? Fifteen hundred, two thousand years ago?"

Copperseed shrugged in a way that could pass for agreement.

"Right," Kerri resumed. "There's geological evidence that Sleepy Lake is the collapsed caldera of a volcano that blew up around that time. The volcano was your Mount of Thunder. And the Warm Snows from which the shaman came must be the Cascades. The shaman and that Thookatoo thing are likely personifications of natural forces. Probably the first dwellers too." She paused, allowed the counterargument to catch up. "But then there's the thing in your morgue."

She took a minute to highlight her mental notes, then resumed.

"Okay, let's just say that it is one of these first dwellers, but according to your mythology, the things disappeared. Now this one wasn't exactly avoiding us. Where have they been hiding until now?"

"They haven't," Copperseed refuted. "We've been getting reports of footprints and sightings since the fifties."

"That's still only forty years; why did no one see them before?"

They locked eyes, and said together, "We weren't digging mines before."

"I got there before you, don't pin on any medals," she

warned. "Do you have a freezer? A kitchen freezer; we don't need to keep the whole thing. I'll extract some tissue samples to deep-freeze them; the rest will probably be lost tomorrow, but that and the pictures will be enough to bring scientific attention." She stood up, breathed in the last chestful of clean air before going back to work. "Whether these are legendary hellspawn or a gross error on nature's side, they need to be dealt with."

Dunia slid the Polaroid back across the sequoia table.

"Horrifying," she pronounced, before reading the room. "Are you gonna ask me if I ever saw one of these rummaging our trash cans in Deboën Mansion?"

"No," Andy said apologetically. She had not foreseen that Nate would be flashing the picture around. "I mean, you didn't, did you?"

"No," Dunia said. "My father would've been interested, though. It's a real pity they didn't meet."

"What do you mean?" Nate prompted.

Dunia tapped her cigarette in the vicinity of the ashtray, took another drag, and leaned back in her seat.

"Daniel Deboën was convinced that mysterious beings hid under the hills," she said. "Old, forgotten beasts unknown to modern science. He actually looked for them."

"How do you think he got that idea?"

"His books," she short-answered. "The family owned a large collection of works by ancient scientists and philosophers—so ancient that most of the knowledge in them is myth. But my father used to think there is always some stratum of fact beneath any legend; that the remote lands described by Persian alchemists and Andalusi theologists were actual regions of this continent, glimpsed or intuited by pre-Columbian explorers. The Deboëns were fond of ancient wisdom like that."

"Do you still own those books?" Nate asked.

"No. They might still be in the house, in the attic. That's where he had his alchemy lab; he practically lived there."

"Just to clarify," Andy probed, "when you say 'alchemy,' you mean . . . ?"

"Primitive chemistry," Dunia thesaurusized. "Physics tinted with magic. Science that still considered incantations and the current phase of the moon as part of the equation. Pretty much what any menopausal New Age nut would happily embrace now, but when it's done by men who also live alone in the woods, it looks weird," Dunia said, flicking the joke off the tip of her cigarette. "My father was convinced that there was some overlooked, revolutionary knowledge in the arts of the first philosophers. He kept all sorts of chemical products and samples and astronomical charts, and tried to re-create the experiments."

"Could it have been one of his experiments that caused the fire in nineteen forty-nine?"

"Perhaps." She shrugged. "But the attic was mostly undamaged, I heard. Police said a freak accident caused the oil tank to blow up, taking the east wing and my father with it. He was buried on the isle, as per his instructions. You may have seen his grave," she said, acknowledging Andy's nod.

"There is a rumor," Nate began, in a way that passed

as tactful for somebody accustomed to the bluntness of Arkham patients, "that your father's father, Damian Deboën, was a sorcerer."

"I've heard that one. And he was a pirate too." Dunia smirked. "Oh, and do you know why he set sail in the first place? He was running away after his witch mother was trialed and burned in Salem."

"Fuck shit goddamn testicles, always fucking Salem," Nate ranted.

"There is also a theory," Andy argued, "that Damian and Daniel Deboën were the same person."

"That's not very original," Dunia retorted. "I mean, it's kind of a vampire trope, isn't it? Leaving the country and returning as your own son? It's been done before." She put out the idea along with the cigarette, then recrossed her legs and added, "Anyway, he didn't look a hundred and fifty to me. I wonder where those agelessness genes went."

"Mrs. Morris," Nate started, "back during our investigation of Sleepy Lake thirteen years ago, we spent a night in your house."

"Not my house."

"Deboën Mansion. That was the night when we caught Wickley, who had been pretending to be a lake creature while he searched your—the mansion for your father's gold."

"Yes, I read the story."

"Right. Anyway, despite what the papers said, we're pretty sure we saw . . . some strange things."

Dunia held a chilling Hollywood-producer kind of stare.

"Things like that in your picture?" she prompted.

"No," Nate answered, realizing that Andy had said yes at the same time. It took him several seconds to reformulate. "I spent some time in the attic that night. I saw your father's lab. His books. I even . . . well, I was eleven, but I used to call myself a detective, so I did what I believed to be my job. I went through that stuff. And . . . I found things that wouldn't sit well with even the most liberal conceptions of chemistry or alchemy."

Dunia nonchalantly held his look across the sequoia table, smoking like the Great Sphinx of Giza.

"I mean, the biological samples I saw . . ." he continued. "I would be amazed if they had been all obtained legally. The figures and symbols drawn on the floor had nothing to do with astronomy; they were pentacles, sort of . . . metaphysical phone booths designed to communicate with other existential planes. And the books I saw around weren't normal philosophical treatises; half of them are so ancient no one alive today can read them. They are rumored to explore the sublimation of life and the suspension of death."

A clock on the mantelpiece metronomed the pause that followed.

Curled up on her seat, Dunia gazed alternately at both visitors, Nate tensely holding his ground, Andy too conscious of the taut leather on the underside of the hostess's pants.

At last she unfolded her legs and leaned forward. "Well, you kids already know he was a sorcerer, right? The whole town knows that."

Tim marched past between them, ignorant of the tension.

Andy began good-copping: "We didn't mean to—"

"The whole town doesn't know shit," Dunia snapped. "If they did, they would've burned the house themselves with Deboën in it, and we'd all be better off. I wasn't allowed in his lab, I never opened his books. I only peeked into his lidded flasks one time, but even I know his alchemy had nothing to do with searching for the philosopher's stone or turning lead to gold. He was raising the dead. He wasn't a sorcerer; he was a necromancer."

Even Tim lifted a skeptical eyebrow at that. Andy and Nate checked with each other. She tried some follow-up.

"You mean . . . 'raising' as in he actually did—"

"He talked to them," Dunia said, her voice almost unhinged. "He kept urns of human ashes, stuff I don't know how he obtained, and at night I heard him chanting his spells, words in dead languages whose mere sounds made my skin crawl, and then I listened to him talking. And I was on the floor below, lying in my bed, terrified, because whatever went bump in my room could not be worse than what was happening above me, what my father was talking to, what my father was *shouting* at. What I sometimes heard replying. What I heard replying *in fear*."

Andy inserted the first syllable of an apology.

"You should've asked my mother!" Dunia shouted. "Ask her how a miner's widow could be blackmailed into marrying Deboën because he was in possession of compromising secrets that only her dead husband would know. How do you think he learned to read books that no one alive today can read?"

She turned to Andy, forcing her to stare into her vertigo-deep eyes.

"You think he lived a hundred and fifty years? I'm not sure he's dead today! I grew tired of lawyers and solicitors telling me how sad it was that my father had failed to arrange things before his death; I'm sure he arranged things, but not for me! If he arranged anything, it was for his own return!"

"How?" Nate asked, aware it'd be the last question he would fit in. "How would he return? Who would bring him back willingly?"

"Do you think the ones he brought back for questioning submitted willingly? Willingness is overrated!"

Andy stood up, signaling they would be leaving. Tim took the clue even before Nate, running for the door.

"Mrs. Morris, I hate to ask you this, but . . . if we could have the key to your house—"

Dunia cut him short for the third time: "It's not my house and I don't have a key. No way I'm going back there. If he's dead, good riddance; if he isn't, we're all better off not finding out."

Before they could notice the ellipsis, they were out on the porch again, frowned upon by the somber, wrecked garden. The wooden wind chime above them clopped gently right on cue.

Andy zipped up her jacket.

"Was everybody in Blyton Hills this messed up when we were young?" she wondered.

Nate said nothing. Tim was already at the gate, waiting for a butler to open it and hand him his coat and hat. They followed him, and Andy stopped by the rusty mailbox.

"Mrs. Morris got mail. No, wait. It's not for her."

The white envelope in her hand had the initials *BSDC* written on front.

She spun on her heels, scanning the empty street and widowed gardens. She tore the envelope open and pulled out a single sheet of paper, handwritten, all caps, in a single line.

"DO NOT LISTEN TO HER—GO TO THE HOUSE."

"Who the fuck?" Andy swore, shoving the message into Nate's hands. "I don't know who this is, but I'm not following his orders again. No way. He almost got us killed at the lake. We're not stupid enough to fall for this again, right?"

Nate looked up from the sheet. Color had ebbed from his face.

"Actually, glad you bring that up."

A breeze carrying the distant rumor of old sky battles made the wind chime clop again and brushed his hair.

"Remember that night thirteen years ago? I think I fucked up astonishingly bad."

Nate chucked two more quarters into the pay phone and tried to mute the restaurant noise by squatting behind a flock of roadworkers lunching at the counter while he argued with the operator.

"No, madam; Arkham is the city. Ark-ham, Massachusetts; that's where the clinic is," he said into the phone. "The patient's name is Acker."

Joey Krantz appeared on the other side of the counter to unload some dirty glasses and trickle a fistful of coins for him. Nate thanked him with a nod, put off by the grin on Joey's face, and continued into the phone: "No, Acker. I don't remember the first name. Wilmarth or something ridiculous like that."

Joey marched away with a tray, left a couple of beers along the way, and went on to drop the lunch special and the straight whiskey at the detectives' table by the window, where their Weimaraner sat tall on the seat, scouting other people's plates with the loftiness of a Zagat critic.

"Here we are—rice and beans," Joey announced, serving the lunch special for Kerri while she helped herself to the whiskey from his tray. "Anything else?"

"Thanks," she said, vaguely sketching a smile. "We're fine."

Andy, sitting across from Kerri, waited until Joey had drifted away before resuming the pep talk.

"So, anyway, I think we're doing fine," she said, while Kerri gulped down the whiskey with barely a chance for it to graze her tongue. "I mean, we got here twenty-four hours ago and look where we are now."

"Nearing a nervous breakdown?"

"Yeah, that too, but . . . with what we gathered from Dunia, and Copperseed, and the dissection, we made some progress."

"No, we didn't. All we did was obey an anonymous message, almost get killed by a lake creature, and then poke at its carcass with a stick." She held the empty glass. "I need another one. And a cigarette."

Andy chose to adjourn the motivational talk and stayed silent, watching Kerri sit curled up in the booth nibbling at her nails, ignoring the steaming food Andy had ordered for her, much to Tim's wide-eyed indignation.

Nate rejoined after five minutes. He addressed Kerri: "How do you spell Thtaggoa? *T-h-t*?"

"I don't know, Nate; it was Copperseed speaking; there were no cheerleaders to spell it."

"Right. Look, I just talked to Professor Acker in Arkham."

"Is he your shrink?" Andy asked.

"No, he's not staff, he's one of the nutjobs." He spread out the notes he'd scribbled on napkins over the table. "He used to teach anthropology; he's familiar with all this stuff, and he knows the name. This thing, Thtaggoa, and the lake creatures; they exist. I mean, they exist in literature."

"Flying monkeys exist in literature, Nate," Kerri said. "Horror writers who get laid exist in literature."

"Just fucking listen for a second, okay?!" he shouted, bringing this and two conversations in other booths to a stop.

Tim raised an eyebrow disapprovingly. Nate went on, this time below the background of Top 40 pop hits.

"We just killed something none of us, possibly no one outside mental hospitals, believed to be real. You just spent an hour examining its corpse; is it such a damn stretch to accept there might be other things out there?"

"Okay, Nate," Andy soothed him. "Go on. We're listening."

Nate swallowed, leaned closer, and lowered his voice a little more, down to Italian job planning volume.

"Okay. There is a sort of literature cycle, a loose collection of texts written in different countries and eras, going as far back as Gilgamesh times, that recounts events that supposedly took place before recorded history began, about races that roamed the world and calamities that occurred before the dawn of men. That's not uncommon; all civilizations have their genesis myths; what's uncanny is that many of these works mention the same fallen gods and sacred places by name, both the ancient sources from the Fertile Crescent and the modern ones written by rogue alchemists, accused sorcerers, demon worshippers, and plain madmen. And in these sources, something called Thtaggoa exists. And a race of amphibian monsters called the spawn of Thtaggoa exists."

He exhaled, amazed to have made it this far without an interruption. The frown on the girls' faces could pass for belief.

"Have you read these texts?" Kerri asked.

"No. I tried, but the older ones require fluency in Koine Greek or Uto-Aztecan languages, and others only exist in a few private collections. Too much of it was destroyed for being 'too disturbing,'" he fingerquoted. "But at the turn of the century, when the occult fad was in vogue, several high fantasy and horror authors in America and Europe discovered this material while searching for obscure mythological references they could use. They borrowed the names and some fragments, either verbatim or wildly distorted. Then others came along and built upon those foundations, and thus tidbits of mythical history ended up in pulp paperbacks."

"But that's exactly what you used to read," Andy said. A second later she noticed the loose ends she was supposed to tie.

"That's why you read *Cannibal Nymphs from Pluto* and *Conan in the Desert of Shub-Niggurath*?" Kerri asked.

"Indirectly, yes," Nate answered. "In Deboën Mansion I saw a lot of those books. I didn't know back then, but they were extremely rare, practically mythical, all blacklisted: owning such a collection would have put you in a bonfire not two hundred years ago. So while I was there

I read names, memorized words. Later, when I returned home after that summer, and we'd caught Wickley and everything was supposed to be right, but it wasn't, I hit the library. Because that's what you would have done," he said to Kerri. "And you're the smart one. So research led me to Victorian occultists who mentioned this material, and Gothic authors who quoted it for the sake of verisimilitude, and pulp writers who quoted the Gothics, and comics based on the pulp stories, and video games based on the comics, and so on. There is quite a subculture around the whole thing—many aficionados trying to piece it all together. Also, in the end I developed a taste for the stuff," he admitted, glancing away.

Tim yawned and laid his head on the table, wishing someone would remember him, or the lunch special, or ideally both.

"God." Kerri squinted at her cousin like she would at a door in her house she had never noticed. "I always thought you just . . . shut yourself in your Dungeons and Dragons world because that was your way to cope."

"It was," he said. "Kerri, all we do is try to cope. I coped by studying it. Like when you were six and didn't like bugs, so you read everything there was about bugs and now you're a biologist. I did the same."

"I didn't cope with Sleepy Lake that way," Kerri said. "I just ran away."

"I ran away too," he tried to comfort her. "It's one thing to study it; it's another thing to be on the same coast with it. Look, I'm just trying to apply reason here: according to Copperseed, the Walla Walla have a story about the things in Sleepy Lake featuring Thtaggoa. And I am telling you that Thtaggoa also appears in short stories by Bob Howard, in a forbidden book by a Swiss monk from the seventeenth century, and in a Mayan crypt in Palenque."

"But what is Thtaggoa?" Andy asked, careful not to trip on the name.

"Who knows," Nate said, shrugging it off. "A deposed god. A fallen alien. According to horror authors, one of several primordial chaos entities that used to rule the earth and now lives underground, cast away by rival spirits, in the nightmare city that its hideous slave race built below a location that was once revealed to a possessed Arab as the Sea of Yottha: what we call Sleepy Lake. And there Thtaggoa lies sleeping, bound by magic, waiting for the day it will be summoned back and set loose on to the world, and when that happens . . ." He abandoned the sentence.

"What?" Kerri prompted. "What comes next?"

Nate shrugged again, showing his empty hands. "I guess apocalypse."

An anticoda of background conversations and Cyndi Lauper underscored the word.

"Apocalypse," Kerri parroted, scratching an imaginary itch on her forearm. "That's a big leap from sheep smuggling."

"Wait," Andy tracked back. "You said 'it will be summoned back.' By who?"

"Whom. Well . . ." Nate puffed, searching for inspiration. "Shit, I don't know. Demonic cults, deranged wizards, Nazis . . . the Illuminati . . . If it's specific names you want, Damian Deboën comes to mind."

"Because he owned some books?"

"Let's say if he wanted to summon a primeval leviathan from its millennial slumber, he's got the right bibliography."

"But you said earlier no one alive today can read the books," Andy argued, shepherding the gang out of the gloom. "Right? And maybe Deboën could, but he's dead."

"Yeah, well, about that," Nate said, stiffening back up. "Uh . . . I might have brought him back."

"Good. Well broken," Peter judged, leaning back on his seat, a single-stroke grin inked on his square face.

The girls took a minute to chomp through Nate's line.

"Oh-kay," Kerri spelled. "Uh, care to elaborate?"

"Sure," he said with a sigh. "Look, one of the books I saw in that attic thirteen years ago was the Necronomicon. It's—"

"I've heard about it," Kerri stated icily.

"Good." He explained to Andy instead: "It was written by an Arab who had visions of . . . the world as it once was and the beings that ruled it. According to Old Acker, this book is supposed to contain instructions to communicate with entities beyond our existential plane. It tells how to raise a spirit out of salts distilled from human remains: textbook necromancy. In Deboën's lab there was a pentacle—"

"Painted in blood!" Andy jumped in, recalling.

"No," Nate said disappointingly. "Pentacles only need what's called a 'blood signature'—that's like . . . a caller ID, a piece of yourself you put forward to claim control over the pentacle; you don't need to draw the whole thing in blood; that's a myth."

"Good thing we established that," Kerri commented,

legs stretched on her seat. "I hate it when people mix superstition into strict demonology."

"Look, I'm just saying how it's supposed to work. Dunia said her father used to talk to people in his lab, that she heard him questioning them. That makes sense: to learn everything he needed to raise Thtaggoa, Deboën had to consult many before him, and I think this is how he did it: by finding their remains, distilling their salts, and summoning their spirits; as long as they were trapped in the pentacle, he could coerce them, he could torture them. I saw the urns and the pentacle myself. But the main point is, if he was able to bring the dead back to life on a regular basis, what stops him from making arrangements for bringing himself back in case of an accident? He could have prepared the essential salts from his own body and left everything ready to be raised again. Think of it as a backup copy. A safety net."

"He'd still need someone to summon him back," Andy pointed out.

"Right. Well, remember the last night of the Wickley case, when we were in the mansion, searching for clues?"

"Yes," Andy picked up. "We'd split up in pairs; I was with you and Sean, and Peter was with Kerri . . . *(She points at Kerri.)* But then Peter lost you."

"I fell through a secret trapdoor," Kerri recalled. "And I landed in the coal room, where the lake creature—I mean, Wickley in his fucking costume—grabbed me and tied me up."

"Peter came running upstairs saying he'd lost you, and we all split up again to look for you. His idea. And I found you, but a lake creature—"

"Wickley."

"No," Andy objected. "A lake creature was coming after me, so I took you into the dungeon, and we shut ourselves in." She swallowed, her mouth dried up like she'd just climbed a mountain. "And there wasn't one lake creature. There was a horde."

Kerri lowered her eyes, her left hand instinctively pining for Tim. The dog noticed and gently kissed her palm.

"Right, well," Nate resumed, impressed with their progress, "while all that was happening downstairs, I had discovered the attic and Deboën's lab. And there was a workbench full of pots with powders in them, and a pentacle on the floor, and the Necronomicon opened on a lectern in the middle of the room. And the Necronomicon was written in Arabic, I think, with handwritten notations in English around it, like a pronunciation guide, and I started to read it . . . and I might have read it aloud."

The girls clicked out of the spell, and for a second just gaped at the implications of that line.

"Way to fucking go, Nate," Andy evaluated.

"Okay, wait," Kerri started, "Nate, now you're speculating."

"No, listen, I swear something happened. There was like this dark green smoke coming out of one of the urns, and I felt a presence around me."

"Nate, that's crazy!"

"How can you—you just dissected a monster, for fuck's sake!"

"The monster is real; you're talking magic!"

"Yo, the what is real?!"

The whole table, canine included, turned to Joey Krantz, who had uttered the last line. This was immediately followed by a second realization—that they had been talking way too loud again.

Conversations around them started to rekindle.

"Sorry I interrupted," Joey said. "I've been meaning to ask you all day: Is it true about the thing you found at the lake?"

What puzzled Andy the most was not the excited half of the tone, but rather the concerned half.

"Who told you that?" Kerri asked him.

"Oh, it's all around. Copperseed told Mr. Quinn, who told Irene, who told Deaf Anne, who told Will Martin, who told Mr. Moretto, I think."

Kerri stopped to wonder how the information continued to flow past someone called "Deaf Anne" while Nate took over. "Yeah, we caught the lake creature."

"Shut up!" Joey whisper-cried. "So it's true! There's something up there!" He couldn't stop going from one to another. "Are you all okay? Copper said it was nasty."

"We're fine," Kerri said. "Nate shot it."

"Really?" Joey bro-fisted Nate's shoulder. "That's awesome. Mystery always has a way of finding you, eh?"

The compliment floated unclaimed over the table.

"So, hey, listen, I meant to tell you guys this earlier, but . . ." Joey breathed in, stiffed up, moved the tray out of view. "Uh, it's clear that the Blyton Summer Detective Club is back. This is not just a reunion; you guys are here on business."

Kerri and Nate and Tim looked away, two in modesty, one in genuine indifference.

"And I just wanted to say that . . . I mean, I know you guys are a man down. I read about Peter Manner. Real shame."

"Didn't know my obituary made it into *Tractor Drivers Weekly*," Peter quipped, rolling his eyes.

"And, well," Joey went on, "all I wanted to say is, if you guys need an extra hand, you can count on me. I don't have your experience, but . . . I have wheels. And a boat!" he remembered. "My dad sometimes goes fishing downriver; we can truck it to the lake. So . . . there's that."

Kerri and Nate eyed each other, deciding who would go this time.

"Uh . . . we already have a car," Kerri said.

"I know, I know, it's just . . . Look, I know you guys and I weren't best pals. I mean, fuck, I know I was a pain in the ass. But . . . I respect what you used to do here. Shit, without you patrolling the streets Blyton Hills's gone to hell. So, anything you need, okay?"

He was looking at Kerri now. And Kerri was looking back. For more than two seconds straight. More than four.

"Gee. Thanks, Joey."

"NO!" Andy capslocked.

All heads turned toward her, and Andy stared back at them as the only speaker for sanity at the table usually does.

"No way! What the fuck, man, you think you can come thirteen years later and brush it all aside with 'I know we weren't best pals'? You abused us! You went for any low blow you could! You picked on Kerri for being a nerd, on Nate for being a wimp, on me for being butch and dark-skinned and a girl—you were an obstacle to every single case we worked! And now you think everything's cool because you got over it? You're over it because you were on fucking top in the first place!"

Kerri and Nate sat through this speech, neglecting the state of their mouths. Tim ducked under the table.

Joey stuttered, defenseless, before fighting back with surprising strength. "Shit . . . Andy, I'm sorry! I really am, but . . . I wasn't on top! You were the good guys, I wasn't! I envied you; I handled it badly! Jesus, I was a kid!"

"How is that an excuse?!" Andy howled. "Why do all bullies think they can get away with 'I was a kid'? Guess what: I was a kid too, and I didn't make other people feel like shit! You were not a kid, you were a cunt!"

Peter hollered, covering his mouth as if someone who mattered could hear him.

JOEY: Okay, I was! I was a cunt, I'm not anymore! I grew up! Have you grown up too, or do you want us to fight like kids all our lives?

(Andy grabs Joey's apron, pulls him down, sinking his face into the lunch special.)

The others got up at that point, Nate to dodge the splashing beans, Tim to eat what had landed on the floor, Kerri to spare her parka and stop Joey from retaliating if he tried, which he didn't.

"Right, time to go," Kerri said. "Joey? We appreciate the offer, okay? Don't call us, we'll call you. *(To the others.)* Let's go."

She put a ten on the table and they left, pulling Tim away from the free meal.

"Okay," Joey called, rice snowing off his nose, under the restaurant's unsympathetic stare. "Any time."

They were pulling over at Kerri's five minutes later. Tim jumped for land like the silence inside the station wagon was too thick to breathe. Andy came out right after him, and didn't feel any better. The same static filled the air around them, not so much a storm brewing as a nuclear airstrike waiting to happen. It felt cold and yet she was sweating; air was still and yet it spoke in her ear. She could sense the firs and pines eyeballing them warily as they walked up to the little house.

The inside had barely grown accustomed to human presence. Kerri dropped the keys and headed upstairs.

"Hey, guys," Nate said, "we gotta talk about—"

"Give us five minutes," Andy cut him off, tailing her.

"But—"

"Nate!" she threatened/implored. "Five minutes, please!"

She ran upstairs, where the door to Kerri's room had just slammed.

Peter plopped down on the sofa.

"Sure, take all the time you want," he called after her. "Whatever. I mean, we were just talking about Nate bringing a warlock back to life, but please, go deal with your girly business; make sure we move that subplot forward. Do your girl things, talk through it, hug it out, try on each other's bras."

(He and Nate stay there, eyes fixed on the upstairs balcony.)
PETER: Do you think they're actually doing that?
NATE: Shut up!

Tim stood to attention, wondering, *Sorry, was I speaking?*

Andy knocked softly on Kerri's door and pushed it a couple inches.

"Hey."

Kerri was sitting on her bed, orange hair humming brightly in the twilit room. The wardrobe was still blocking the window.

Andy didn't dare to walk in uninvited. "Are we okay?" she asked.

Kerri looked up, caught off guard, and gave a yes just as automatic and hollow as such a question always engenders. Then she took some time to think, searched her heart, and gave the second answer.

"Yeah, we're okay. Come in."

"You want me to move the wardrobe back?"

"No, it's fine there."

Andy sat down beside Kerri. The sight of the paisley quilt alone comforted Andy more than anything else. That room worked miracles.

"You shouldn't have been so quick to smite Joey," Kerri said.

"We don't need him."

"We're a man down. Joey's got a boat. And he can shoot. His father used to take him hunting. He's familiar with guns."

"That . . . that is the last quality you'd look for in anybody!" Andy protested. "You hate guns!"

"Yes, I do. There's a one in a million chance I'd want to hang out with a gun freak. And this is that one situation."

Andy considered the point, and in the meanwhile said something else. "I don't want to replace Peter."

"Me neither," Kerri said. "But you know one thing Peter could do that none of us can? Shoot."

"I can shoot."

Kerri drew a blank.

"I can," Andy insisted. "I did air force basic training, remember? I learned how to shoot."

"Why didn't you tell me before?"

"Because you don't like guns."

Tim wandered in, sniffed the carpet, the foot of the bed, the magic in the air, and chose to lie down.

Kerri had frozen at the childish, self-evident straightness of that last answer. She scoffed, looked down, all while Andy stared like a six-year-old.

"Do you always drop lines on women like that, or am I just silly for walking under them?"

Andy doubted for a second, then quickly stated, "You're not silly."

"Right," Kerri said. "If I start to retrace our conversations this week, will I find many moments like this?"

"Please don't," Andy begged. "Please, please don't."

"Okay." She smiled. "I won't. Just for truth's sake, you're smoother than Peter."

"I'm . . . what?"

"At dropping lines," Kerri explained, bringing her legs

on the bed. "Peter asked me out."

"What?" Andy repeated. "He . . . when?"

"That last summer. He was thirteen, you know. Puberty kicking in. It's all biology."

"You rejected him?"

"Hmm, no . . . not explicitly. We never really talked about it. I didn't think of him that way; I didn't think of anyone that way yet. And he was nice enough not to push it. Then . . ." Her hands tried to communicate something very emphatically. "You know, the Sleepy Lake case happened, and we never really talked about that summer at all, ever. But he was interested. He wrote me letters. Look."

She sprang off the bed and switched on the orange-shaded lamp on the diminutive desk, where her neatly ordered compass and magnifying lens and pocket dictionaries waited eagerly to assist in the case. She opened the first drawer, filled with postcards and colored envelopes and lined sheets of her own round junior-high handwriting shrieking for attention, and retrieved an envelope with a U.S. Bicentennial stamp.

"After spring break he mailed me a few notes to Portland, and then when I got here in June I found this waiting for me."

She held it out to Andy, who didn't take it. "I . . . I guess it's private."

"It's nothing scandalous. He was a very sweet kid."

"I know. I'd just . . . rather not," Andy declined. As much as she wanted to escape the subject, she suddenly remembered: "The call. You said he phoned you the day before he . . ."

"Yeah." Kerri's eyes, weighed down by the memory, lowered to the carpet. "He probably needed to . . . talk."

Andy swallowed, noticed a bad taste in her mouth. Even for this bedroom, that was a moment a little too bitter to help it go down.

Tim approached the ajar door, anticipating the next character entrance. Nate knocked.

"Sorry," he said. "Club meeting, please?"

Kerri seized the chance: "Yeah, okay. Club meeting."

She slid the letter in the back of her jeans and they sat cross-legged on the carpet. The low-key orange lighting in the bunker infused the scene with an extra air of secrecy. Andy felt solace in it. She made sure to take it in before inaugurating the session.

"Okay. So. New development in the Sleepy Lake case: turns out there was a Sleepy Lake creature."

"There were many Sleepy Lake creatures," Kerri acknowledged darkly.

"Not to mention a former pirate, mining tycoon, and part-time necromancer back in Deboën Mansion," Nate added.

"We don't know that," said Kerri.

"Well, we should consider the possibility."

"Yeah, and let's also factor in the chance the sky's made of jelly!"

"Why do you always—" Nate started but scrapped, too angry. "Christ, do I look like a scared kid to you now?! I was in the attic, with a book on a lectern, in a pentacle in the middle of the room—"

"It was staged!"

"It was a trap!" Nate cried. "I felt it when I read the

words; I saw smoke coming from an urn! I did that!"

"Nate, we can't trust what we saw thirteen years ago; that's why we came back!" Kerri raised her hands, stopping an objection from Nate before it came out. "Tell me, with your hand on your heart, that you can absolutely trust everything you see or hear."

"Ha!" went Peter, standing up. "What a ridiculous question! Of course he can trust anything he sees—tell her, Nate."

Nate sat still, painfully struggling to avoid eye contact with him.

"Nate? Come on. Of course you can— *(To Kerri.)* Course he can trust everything he sees and hears! Nate! C'mon, tell her!"

Tim laid his head down again after a brief access of interest.

Peter, unanimously ignored, dropped his arms.

"Okay, fuck you all. *(Going for the door.)* I'll be in the actual men's dorm."

Nate sighed, nodded, surrendered the point, and lay back, exhausted, Tim promptly coming to lick his face.

Kerri went on: "And Dunia, by her own admission, was a scared child. We can't trust her testimony. Shit, we don't need to—there's enough on our plate."

"The wheezers," Andy interpreted.

"Yes. Those," Kerri said, not really fond of the new name. "But you don't need a sorcerer to unearth those things; Copperseed and I discussed this. If they come from caverns under the hills, and they have been there for thousands of years . . . which is saying a lot, but I may accept it because

I haven't found evidence that they actually need any food or air . . . they weren't set loose through magic. We've been mining these hills for a century; we just dug too deep."

"And whose idea was it to dig here in the first place?" Nate pointed out, jumping back in. "Come on, a guy comes west during the California Gold Rush, stumbles into Oregon, finds a lake, finds a one-acre isle on the lake, and starts digging for gold there? Isn't it possible he was looking for something else?"

"But he did find gold," Andy intervened.

"Did he? Or was he just carrying the gold from his swashbuckling days?" He paused, then switched to Kerri. "Consider this: How long have the sightings been going on?"

"According to Copperseed, since the early fifties."

"Go one year further back: What happened in nineteen forty-nine?"

The date came to their minds in the heavy slab print of the *Pennaquick Telegraph*.

"The fire in Deboën Mansion," Andy stated.

"'A freak accident,'" Nate quoted from Dunia. "I think the accident was old Deboën waking up the wrong guys."

The room, dark enough, went a little darker with the picture those words suggested: a vague sketch of eyeless creatures stumbling upstairs in the dark, and screams; a fight, and an explosion; a puff over the quiet lake.

"Okay, let's say it's true," Kerri said, shaking her hair awake. "What are we supposed to do?"

"Well, if we know the wheezers live underground, and that they came out through the mines . . . then we need to do exactly what we were doing," he concluded, pointing at an off-guard Andy. "Retrace our steps. When we returned to the lake with Al, we found the footprints leading into the abandoned mines, and a few days later Al took us to the mines. That's what we should do now."

"The mines?" Kerri said in high pitch. "We go right to the wheezers?"

"Technically, we could've stumbled upon them last time, but we didn't. We found more footprints, but those could've been Wickley as well. We'd be able to tell now. If the wheezers are using the mines to come to the surface, all we'd have to do is blow up the tunnels."

"It's way too dangerous!" Kerri complained. "Guys, come on, can't we just . . . call the police?"

"Wejustdid.Bythetimetheygetherealltheevidenceleftwill be some Polaroids and a pool of slime in Copperseed's basement." He appealed to Andy again. "Put it this way—as far as these creatures go, we're the experts. Who else has faced one and lived to tell the tale? We go below Sentinel Hill again, but this time around we go armed. Al has guns. One thing we know about those creatures—they can die."

"Christ, that line came straight out of a B-movie," Kerri moaned, sinking her head into her palms. "Might as well put on a shredded slutty dress and start practicing my screaming."

Nate ignored her, focused on the tiebreaker: "All we need to do is find evidence they're down there. That's it."

Andy felt the physical weight on her shoulders. She consulted Nate, then Kerri, still sunk in her hands, then Tim.

She went through the plan in her head: climbing down a mineshaft, fighting, perhaps blowing up stuff. As strategies go, this one actually seemed tailored to her limited skills.

Plus, Kerri had just said something about a slutty dress.

"Okay, we're going," she said. "Tomorrow morning. We're solving this case once and for all."

An actual canary perched in its cage, oblivious to the giant luck-dragon snout puffing against the bars. Tim couldn't care less about any of the other stuff Captain Al was still unloading from his pickup.

"Glowsticks . . . flares . . . phosphorus markers . . ."

"Cap, where do you even keep all this stuff?" Andy wondered, already alarmed at the size of the impedimenta parked on the anecdotic sidewalk.

"I live in a junkyard, Andy," Al said, with as much pride as any mentally sound person could convey through those words. "The one advantage is that there's seldom a tool or instrument you don't have within a hand's reach. Provided you don't mind tetanus, that is." He finished unwrapping a new piece of equipment. "Two-way radios. I doubt they'll do any good underground; if they don't, just chuck them into a shaft; there's more in the pile these came from."

Nate stepped back to catch in midair one of the transceivers as the captain tossed it to him, inadvertently kicking the bird's cage; the canary tweeted in protest like a fenderbent driver. Tim leaned even closer, English microbiologist eyes fixed on the compact featherball inside, tail producing enough aeolic power to feed a small city.

The plastic penguin between his jaws squeaked.

The bird, in turn, emitted a single new chirp.

Tim stepped back in shock, searched for the approval of the audience who had just witnessed that milestone in animal communication.

"Try not to get too attached, Tim," Kerri advised. "He's gonna be the first to go."

"Not really; it won't just drop dead," Al said. "If you encounter gas, it will start chirping and fluttering first. At that point, either turn back or, if you must, put on your masks and set the bird free. It will instinctively go for higher ground."

"Are these masks really gonna help?" Nate asked, banjoing the string of a simple respirator.

"No, those you wear all the time to prevent inhaling silica dust. If the air goes bad, you switch to these."

Al opened one of the rucksacks and showed them the large, insect-eyed breathing mask inside, a long, flexible proboscis connecting it to a tank the size of a bike water bottle. Andy had had one chance to try one on in the academy; Kerri and Nate had seen them worn only by Tom Cruise in *Top Gun*.

"Don't worry, these ain't from the junkyard," Al comforted them. "I drove to Umatilla Airbase yesterday to borrow them. This one's a different story—I had to call in some real favors for this baby."

He pulled out a cone-shaped, khaki-colored leather bag with stenciled letters: E12R8. He unlatched the cover and extracted a fourth respirator. Andy squinted at the distance between the air filter and the two visors, until she figured out the shape of the face that would fit in that mask.

Everyone turned to Tim, way too engrossed with interspecies talks with the canary to care about their travel preparations.

"They stopped making these after World War II, *but,*" Al italicized for attention, "it comes with no oxygen, so the dog will have to stay with the bird. And your bottles only last twenty minutes each, so if you end up needing these, do not linger."

Kerri flipped the dog mask in her hands, figuring out the straps, while Al went on to unbag the last but not least pieces of equipment.

"Shells." He threw a box of twelve-gauge ammunition at Nate, who was already carrying Uncle Emmet's shotgun. Nate appreciated the package, adorned with a terrifyingly realistic drawing of a charging Kodiak bear.

The captain turned to Andy: "I trust you know how to use this."

He flipped the M1911 pistol in the air, grabbed it by the barrel, and handed it properly to her.

Andy could feel Kerri's queasiness like a bright orange siren glowing out of the corner of her eye. She looked up at the captain for a solacing smirk. There was none coming.

She pocketed the gun and some mags in the back of her jeans, saying, "We used the M9 Beretta; it's the new standard. But I prefer the single-action myself."

The captain produced a final piece of leatherware and handed it to Kerri.

"I know you will refuse a firearm, so at least take this until Andy convinces you to trade it for the pistol."

He held a sheathed combat knife on his open hand, stretched out, not pushing or pressuring her in any way, but not retreating either.

Kerri took it and pulled the sleeve off an inch. The steel blade gleamed boastfully at her for a second before she sheathed it back.

Al kicked some empty bags and planted a foot on the side of his truck. It was the same vehicle that had driven them to the mines thirteen years ago.

"So. What else can I do for you?"

"One thing," Andy said. "Put all this back on the truck and drive us to the mines; I don't want to climb Sentinel Hill in a station wagon."

"Thought you'd never ask." He smiled for the first time.

Nate rode shotgun and Andy and Kerri and Tim sat in the truck bed, jolting as the pickup climbed up the rutted lake road fork that led to the mine entrance on Sentinel Hill. Kerri was still carrying the knife in her right hand, grasping it lightly like she would hold a scorpion.

Andy sat watching her, calculating whether she should put a hand on her shoulder. They had not touched the previous night, a remarkable feat given the size of the bed they shared. Kerri's anxiety attack had not repeated; in her words, she was too anxious to afford one. They had spent all evening preparing the trip, frisking the town library for information on the gold mines and exhuming gear from seldom-queried chests in Aunt Margo's house. Andy had failed to give the team a pep talk before they withdrew to their rooms at night. Kerri took a late shower and got into bed after Andy; Andy offered to pull out the guest bed but Kerri refused. Their only contact was a gentle whiplash of dryer-warmed hair as Kerri leaped over her to take the inside of the bed. From that moment, a 38th parallel had been drawn across the mattress. Andy had not dared cross it.

She found her courage now and rested a hand on Kerri's shoulder—right on the one square inch her parka and her shirt failed to cover. Her fingertips quivered with joy.

"You can hang it on your pants. See, this goes through your belt loop. No, not like that; the other way around, so you can draw fast. *(Guides her, white wrists burning in her hands, without unsheathing the weapon.)* Like this, edge up. Never like the killer from *Halloween;* you thrust upward. Okay? You don't want to stab them in the back; that's hard. You want to hit them in the abdomen, hopefully puncture an organ. Also, you may want to twist it as you pull it back. But make sure to pull it back; otherwise, you just gave them a free knife."

"I don't think the wheezers can handle tools."

"I wasn't talking about the present situation only. It's a life tip."

She bent down to fasten the weapon on Kerri's belt and spied her lips through the orange curls.

"Kerri," she called softly, a hand conquering the other's leg. "Everything's going to be okay."

"You keep saying that."

"So far I keep being right."

"And you keep pushing me a lot," Kerri accused, looking up.

"Because you can take it!" Andy argued, surrendering to a chuckle. "Kerri, two nights ago I told you I've been in love with you since I was twelve, and you didn't even flinch. Do you know what that is? It's you being in my thoughts, in my fantasies, all through puberty; it's everything I've held in and been choking on for thirteen years, and you just took it with a smile. After that, you can handle anything."

A flimsy smile in the corner of Kerri's mouth ruined her perfect misery while she sat reading Andy. She was wearing her most transparent, honest, unconcealing face. She had always been inept at masquerading.

"You never mentioned the fantasies before," Kerri said.

"Yeah, well. It was implied."

She gazed away now at the balding hills, but Kerri didn't take her eyes off her.

"Andy, when you came back into my life and said that we had unfinished business to attend to ... exactly what business were *you* talking about?"

Andy gave that some thought, then concluded, "Everything."

Kerri's face saddened up a tiny bit. "Andy, I may not be able to fix *everything*."

Andy nodded tranquilly. "It's okay. Let's deal with the subterranean monsters first and we'll get to the rest later, all right?"

* * *

No one had bothered to replace the old chain and padlock that Captain Al had bolt-cut thirteen years before. Rust and dry mud were all that held the wire gate shut and probably up. After creeping forward for another two minutes, the road crested Sentinel Hill and expanded into a dissolute cul-de-sac, its edges littered with yellow black-bruised machinery and forgotten robots like very sad girls waiting for someone to offer a hand and lead them to the dance floor. Al stopped the truck and the detectives jumped into the arena. A Manhattan of battered signs sporting their warning colors dutifully greeted them, shouting their caveats about self-evident, prosaic dangers, like landslides or moving vehicles: the last of the kids' concerns.

A few things had changed since their last visit: the tunnel where the lake creature's footprints led them and which they used last time to enter the mines had been walled up; the shaft had been sealed; and the timber headframe had crumbled on itself. Nothing they had not anticipated.

"Okay, listen up," Andy called, spreading the xeroxed blueprints over the truck's hood. "This is us, on Sentinel Hill. *(Fingerstabs a point on the map.)* This is the level station, a hundred feet below. We're getting through here. *(Index follows a flimsy horizontal line.)* This is an adit—it's a gutter and waste disposal tunnel that opens above the Zoinx River; the opening should be that way."

She pointed off the map, at the panorama of mourning dark hills surrounding them, all spotted with treeless patches—the scars of human industry.

"Now, once we're underground," she resumed, waving them back to the blueprints, "the whole mine complex is huge, but we've done our homework. Everything south of this line was dug by the RH Corporation after 'forty-nine. And much of what's on this side was abandoned well before that. The only shaft in use at the time was this one: Allen shaft. That's one-point-six miles in that direction. *(Vaguely, over the hills in the east.)* Once there, we go down the Allen shaft to this plateau and inspect these galleries. *(Changing to another, larger-scaled map.)* N-3 is the deepest; then N-4, N-5, and E-6."

"What are these?" Nate asked, pointing at dark geometrical shapes lurking dangerously close to those tunnels.

"Water. Probably underground rivers connected to the lake."

Captain Al took the baton: "A word of caution. The mine was wired for electricity; I'll stay up here and try to get the generator running. The deeper you go, though, the worse conditions you'll find; no lights, no indicators, no steps, and cave-ins are a likely possibility. Also, we'll probably lose communication once you're in the drift. Provided I don't hear otherwise from you, you have exactly six hours before I give you up for lost and call rescue. Roger?"

Andy checked her Coca-Cola watch. "Roger."

"That path there will lead you to the adit. Good luck."

They geared up, carrying backpacks and a caged bird, and started the trek down over a rain-abated stretch of rotting wire fence through which dandelion heads poked and cheered at the sun.

* * *

The path was more properly a track of frequent landslides that faded away just a few yards from the hilltop. Tim led the party for most of the way, finding the more convenient route through low vegetation that thickened and grew up as they descended, slowly drifting toward the east face of the hill into a steep, shadowy valley.

After ten minutes, the harrumphing Zoinx River came into view. It looked like it usually did north of Sleepy Lake: cold and irate.

Not far ahead, a conspicuous slope of gray pulverized rock poured down the hillside and into the roaring waters from the adit mouth. It was less ceremonious than mine entrances were in westerns: an open hole on the hillside, supported by three massive slabs of concrete. No theatrical soul had etched an agonizing KEEP OUT on an ineptly crafted wooden sign; no vultures or forgotten human skulls livened the place. But by the time the detectives stood on the landing before it, they were convinced that no such details could have made it any more ominous. A simple framed square of no-light that the sun could not penetrate and darkness could not escape. A service tunnel leading into the earth's center.

Andy faced the team, and even Tim sat down, tutting the caged canary to pay attention.

"All right, listen: we're not doing anything we didn't do thirteen years ago. Remember that. We were twelve years old and we dared to go inside the mountain to follow clues. And all that time we were convinced there was a lake creature prowling around."

"Actually, that was Wickley, so we were being stupid," Nate pointed out.

"Exactly. And we were stupid. So we're even better prepared this time. Let's go."

They marched in, flashlights beaming the ground, spying wires along the walls and rails on the floor and Tim's hindquarters as he scouted ahead.

A full minute inside the tunnel, Kerri glanced behind at the surface world. She saw nothing but a tiny square of distant, howling light.

The electric lamps on the left wall magically blinked on a space break later, marking Al's victory over the generator and pulling out of the canary a single chirp of ephemeral joy, between seeing the darkness repelled and assessing how little its situation had improved. The line of lights ended ahead, where the tunnel opened into a wider, brighter cavern.

The radio cracked, cuing Al to speak. "You're welcome, over."

"Thank you, Captain." Andy smiled. "We're below Sentinel Hill already. We'll be at the drift in no time. Over and out."

The party marched forward, out of the adit and into the shaft station. Their claustrophobia yielded a little at the wide, level room directly beneath the mine's shafthead frame, and Andy even reexperienced some of the fascination of their first visit. Ancient yellow lighting painted the stopes, loading docks, catwalks, crates, and mine carts.

"We are definitely riding a mine cart this time around," she said.

"I think I've got my quota of video game clichés

fulfilled," Nate commented, examining the rusted wheels on one of the wagons, seemingly as inclined to move as the mountain itself. It had been forty years since those carts had last carried the materials that were still lying around: rocks, tools, hydraulic machinery, gas tanks.

He lingered by that last item: gas tanks.

"Oxygen?" he said, kneeling to read the stenciled letters on the side of one of the industrial-sized bottles. "Should this really be here?"

The rest of the team approached as Tim came by to sniff the objects and formulate his expert opinion.

"Maybe it's not that strange," Andy offered. "We're carrying oxygen."

"Portable bottles. These could feed a space shuttle."

"Maybe they were used to refill the smaller ones."

"It's funny," Kerri commented darkly. "I'm not sure miners used oxygen forty years ago. In fact, I'm not sure they use it now."

Tim puffed at the tank, completing his evaluation— *Yup, it's a big metal thing*—while Andy and Nate waited for Kerri to come to a conclusion. Instead, she just shrugged.

"I guess I'll have to hit the library."

Andy checked the different galleries opening at the other end.

"That's our door. One-point-six miles to the Allen shaft. About twenty minutes."

Those twenty minutes turned out to be some of the longest twenty minutes in the history of minutes. The drift was wired and lit enough to store away the flashlights, but there was very little sighting to do. The novelty of bare rock walls instead of concrete had become old at the speed of *SNL* material. Rails were laid on the floor as well; Kerri tripped twice on them, mind numbed by the dull, everlasting stonescape.

"Why did they even dig this?" Nate heard himself ask out of boredom. "I mean, do they just start mining in a random direction and hope to strike gold?"

"They follow a quartz reef," Kerri explained. "This quartz reef." She fingertapped a dark red vein on the wall across the lights.

"This is quartz? In a gold mine?"

"Yeah. In the nineteenth century, gold was either found along water streams or inside quartz veins. The latter discovery was one of the triggers of the Gold Rush."

"So you think there is gold down here."

"Well, I'm not sure Deboën could keep a company running for a hundred years by planting the gold himself. Plus, quartz reefs happen when the rock cracks and the gap is filled up by crystal growth." She paused, if only to appreciate the fact that she was lecturing again. She went on anyway, because it felt good. "High volcanic activity means tremors; tremors mean cracks. So these hills are not a bad place to prospect."

"If we find gold, Kerri, first thing I'm buying you are some proper hiking boots," Andy joked, glancing at Kerri's suede boots dragging on the dusty ground.

The idea merrily walked along with them for a few seconds, before the rancid air and ichorous lights weighed it down and dissolved it.

One-point-six miles, twenty minutes, 880 lamps, and 1,763 rails later, Kerri thought they were stopping at a random milestone of tedium until she noticed the iron grille under her feet, the steel beams, the handrail before her. They had reached another smaller station.

She leaned over the handrail. Hopeless, brainless pitch-black shadow coagulated below.

"Cap?" Andy radioed. A burst of static responded. "Cap, do you copy, over?" With her free hand, she pulled Kerri away from the chasm. "Captain, we can't hear you. We're at the Allen shaft. Got a little problem. Over."

"What's the problem?" Kerri whispered.

Nate punched two big fat buttons on a yellow control panel: "We were hoping to find an elevator here."

"Al? I'm not copying; we're going downstairs anyway. We stick to the plan. Repeat, we stick to the plan."

"What stairs?" Kerri asked.

Nate directed his light to the opposite wall of the shaft. A flimsy iron catwalk led to a set of metal rungs jutting out of the rock, torn spiderwebs flapping off them.

"How far down?"

"Five hundred feet."

"Jesus Ichabod Christ," Kerri muttered, smoothing her hair down. "How's Tim going to climb down those?"

"He can't," Nate said. "He'll have to stay behind."

"No," Andy objected. "We don't split up. I will carry him."

"You will?"

"Yeah." She paused to reckon the Weimaraner's size. "It's okay; he's what? Forty-five pounds? I've carried that weight in air force training."

"More like sixty-two," Kerri winced to say.

"Right," Andy acknowledged. "Fine. That's what males used to carry." She smirked, irony-punched. "I can do anything boys can do, right?"

Tim did not complain once while they pouched him inside an emptied backpack like an oversized puppy, snugly padded with Andy's jacket, with no footing and all straps on the bag fastened up to keep him safe. His default air of resignation hardly intensified when Andy lifted him and strapped the package around her shoulders, as though he understood there was a valid reason for undergoing all that. Perhaps his biggest letdown had been to learn that the canary would have to stay up with most of the former contents of Andy's backpack. Even as Andy grabbed the first burning-cold iron rung and started the long climb down, he remained perfectly silent, head sticking out of the half-zipped top lid, as grave and determined not to look down as an officer on board the sinking *Titanic*.

Andy did not falter either. They were all tethered together by a rope, with Andy in the rear behind Kerri and Nate in the lead. They had bivouacked for only ten minutes before the descent, eating cereal bars and drinking water. Even Andy had had trouble grasping some joy out of that picnic, by the light of 1940s wiring, beneath two hundred feet of rock.

"There's another platform here if you want to take a rest," Nate announced. They had encountered catwalks every few minutes.

"I'm fine," Kerri moaned. "I'd rather rest with my feet on solid ground."

Andy wondered how much farther down that would be. She had lost track of time. Her arms had begun to smart a long while ago. Tim was small-framed for a Weimaraner, but sixty-two pounds was destined to pep up any challenge. On the other hand, she knew Kerri and Nate had to be putting on brave faces; even with the gear they had left at the top, their backpacks were not light.

"I get more tired thinking we'll have to climb back up," Kerri tried to joke.

"That's food for thought, right?" Nate said.

"What is?"

"Well, if the elevator's somewhere down there, and the cable seems to be fine . . . Either the last person down came back up on this ladder, or they're still down there."

Kerri tried to think of a sarcastic dismissal for that and failed.

"Watch out, there's another rung missing here," Nate warned. "Shit, wait. Two in a row are gone."

Andy stopped, waiting for instructions, struggling to ignore her shoulders.

"Nate?" Kerri queried.

"Wait, I think I see the floor already. I can—fuck!"

"Nate!"

Andy automatically fastened an arm around a rung and clenched for the yank of the rope. It never came. Instead, she heard a loud crash.

"Nate?!" Kerri shouted into the dark, holding on with one arm as she tried to point the flashlight in the right direction. "Nate, are you all right?!"

She was able to see the floor (wooden boards and a cloud of dust) and a hole right through it.

"Nate! Say something!"

"Fuck," Nate whined from below.

"Right," Kerri sighed. "Good boy."

She reached the final rung and dropped to a beam on top of the elevator. Nate had crashed through its roof. She untied the line and slid through the hole into the box to find him sitting on the floor, staring past her, pointing upward.

"Uh . . . I think I found out who took the last ride down."

Kerri turned and flashed her light at the ceiling. Andy was following her, slipping into the wooden structure at that moment, and as she was hanging off the edge, under Kerri's spotlight, she saw the person. Eye to eye. Had his or her eyes not rotted long ago.

The alarming feature about the body was not its nearly bare skull, jutting loosely out of the clothes that had once fitted the body. Nor was the absence of some limbs particularly unsettling. Broken skeletons could be almost expected to lie deep inside the earth's crust, like dinosaur bones. But they should be lying asprawl on the floor. Instead, this one was hanging. From a hook on the ceiling of the elevator. By the base of its skull.

"Holy shit," Andy greeted upon being introduced.

Tim struggled out of her bag and dropped onto the floor, eager for some appreciation of his good behavior before he noticed what everyone was staring at. He quickly caught up with their fascination.

"Does it look like a miner to you?" Andy asked. "How long you think it's been down here?"

"At least ten years," Kerri said. "No more than twenty." She read Andy's bewilderment, then pointed at the cadaver's exposed wrist. "Digital watch."

"Oh."

"This looks exactly like the one we found in the woods," Nate pointed out.

His remark met an awkwardly cold reception.

"Near Sleepy Lake," he expanded. "It was just like this. I always told myself it was a prop. Peter said it was too. It was too high up to verify."

"It's a warning," Kerri acknowledged. "A message to trespassers. 'Intruders be warned.'"

"But who could it have been?" Nate wondered. "No deaths or missing people were ever blamed on the lake creature."

"A lonely camper? Perhaps just a bum," Kerri tried.

"And this guy?"

Andy swallowed, if only to get some time and make sure she'd read the cue correctly, then stepped forward and checked the skeleton's clothes.

His leather jacket was dry and stiff; not so much the corduroy shirt below, stained with what once had been internal fluids. She omitted those pockets and tried the pants first—the leg that was still attached. A wallet came easily out of the pocket around the loose femur. She flipped through the contents.

"Oregon driver's license. Expired 1980. Name: Simon Jaffa. Born 6-1-1943."

Inside the wallet, seven dollars and sixty-four cents, chewing gum, a company ID card.

Expedited by RH Corp.

"RH," Nate usefully reminded. "The ecovillains."

"Maybe he was sent to inspect the mines for them," Kerri suggested. "Tim. Stop that."

At this point Tim was jumping and poking at the sack of bones as if it were a Halloween-themed piñata. His last effort caused another bundle of papers to drop from the skeleton's jacket.

Andy picked them up and unfolded them carefully, wary of the chance they would crumble rather than spread open. It looked like a hand-copied map of the mine. A few flocks of words had been chickenscratched in the blank areas. Not many made any sense: "Blyton Hills," "Allen," "Isle shaft," "Where," "Dead end." The rest was a jumble of letters and numbers, possibly directions. "From W, S-5, E-2, bottom."

Andy queried the back of the page, to no avail. She was sure there was no S-5 gallery in her blueprint. But as she compared this map with her own copies, something else had begun to bug her.

"We have a problem," she announced. "This looks more up to date than what we have. I think I miscalculated the length of the tunnels we're supposed to inspect."

"By how much?" Kerri asked, clenching for the answer.

"Searching one carefully would take two hours. And . . . we've got four hours and need two to get back to Al."

All three rotated their spotlights away from the skeleton and lighthoused the plateau where they had landed. They illuminated more signs of human presence than they had dared hope for: sacks, simple tools, wagons loaded with rubble. Several passageway openings blinked awake at the battery-powered lights.

"Okay, let's think rationally here," Nate suggested. "I think Deboën was digging to find Thtaggoa. *(Facing Kerri.)* You claim all he wanted was gold."

"Look around—they've been following the quartz reefs all along," Kerri argued, lightpointing at the red open wound in the rock right next to her.

"Okay, but this shaft is named after Allen. Allen's the guy who Deboën put in charge when he left for the East Coast—when he left as Damian and came back as Daniel."

"Right. So the people he left in charge were really looking for gold. Therefore, the tunnel that does not follow a quartz reef . . ."

"Is the one we follow."

Andy drew her flashlight across the station, tracking down a crimson scar that snaked vertically across the north wall. Three tunnels, labeled N-3, N-4, and N-5, opened on that same wall. All three were marked with rusted signs and wired, even though the lights were not working.

She then turned east: the gallery seemed to expand casually in that direction, carved by natural forces rather than industry, sloping downward into pitch dark.

"There," she concluded bitterly. "The unpopular tunnel."

From the mining equipment buried in that station like implausible goodies found inside pyramids and hellgates for the use of video game characters, Andy picked up a few items she deemed useful. Two kerosene lamps seemed to be in good order; she lit both and left one by the elevator. The packing of a few sticks of dynamite sparked a new controversy: Nate argued that, if they found the entry to the wheezers' hideout, they would require explosives to seal it; Kerri opposed the idea of detonating dynamite underground without any notion of safety. Andy became the tiebreaker once again, Tim having lost any interest in the discussion once it had been stated that he wasn't allowed to carry the sticks in his mouth. In the end, she settled the argument by allowing Nate to pack the dynamite and forbidding him to carry the lamp at the same time. Then, regretting yet another lost chance to align with Kerri, she marched the party toward E-6.

The kerosene lamp proved somewhat better than flashlights; though it did not shine nearly as bright, the halo was wider, allowing them to see both where they trod and where they headed. It also granted Tim more freedom of movement to scout ahead. There were no rails; the galleries seemed freshly dug, or not dug at all, like natural, conveniently sized caverns. Except for some passages densely flanked with pillars and boarded-up walls, marks of human craftsmanship were dwindling; warning signs had gone extinct; derelict mining gear was infrequent. And that was long before the gallery funneled into a lower, narrower tunnel that sloped steeply downward, a brief inscription crudely chalked on the rock above reading E-6.

Nate scowled at the unceremonious sign. Miner slang for "Abandon all hope, ye who enter here."

Steps had been roughly carved or occurred naturally, too tall and irregular to let travelers forgo the use of their hands. The detectives had to sit and slip in single file down onto the next ledge, each one narrower than the preceding one. At some point Andy stood up and noticed that the ceiling was remarkably close.

Kerri noticed the ceiling too, but she had already decided she would not complain before Tim did. And he didn't. The brave motherfucker kept hopping down from landing to landing without a whimper.

About the depth line of 5,200 feet, as chalked on an exposed slate of basalt, the weight of the ten thousand tons of rock above finally sank in. Kerri glanced behind and could not make out anything six feet back. The light they had left by the elevator was a distant memory. Sunshine was a dream. She tried to stretch her arms: both her hands met walls she knew to be miles thick. She realized that their kerosene lamp was the first thing to have lit that nook of the planet in fifty years, a single bubble of light and air in a one-mile radius of three-dimensional solid matter. And the darkness kept pouring in.

"What is that sound?" Nate asked.

"Running water, maybe," Andy said.

"Maybe?"

"I'm guessing. We may be close to a subterranean river."

"Andy, I can't breathe," Kerri said.

Andy raised the lamp at her. She barely made out some distressed orange hair. "Yeah, you can."

"No, I'm telling you, I can't go on."

"You're just anxious. Look, we all are—"

"This cave isn't safe; there's water on the other side of this wall! It could collapse on us."

"It won't, Kerri; it's held this long."

"We could be buried alive. We are buried alive!"

"No, we're not—we came that way, we'll leave that way!"

"There is no way!"

"Kerri!"

"What's happening to the light?" Nate pointed out mellowly.

The girls stared straight into the kerosene flame. They could. It burned bluish and shy, its halo receding, crawling back from Andy's face.

And then it went out.

Blackness—a million tons of heavy, stone-hard, Neptune-cold blackness took over.

Life, light in the universe, ceased to exist.

Nate switched on his flashlight, a hysterical white beam drawing the image of primordial panic in the new Age of Light. Andy searched her pockets for a box of matches, tried to scratch one and dropped it. She gritted her teeth, commanding her hands to pull themselves together, and tried another one.

Kerri saw the phosphorus flash with a short-lived burst of glee before the flame quickly ebbed down to a helium-voiced, meek, lukewarm drop of blue.

And then it died.

KERRI: Masks! Put on your masks now! There's no oxygen!

They immediately dropped their bags to the floor, frantically scattering most of the contents as they searched for the aviator masks and oxygen bottles. Kerri had hardly taken the first puff of O_2 before fitting the dog mask around Tim's head.

"How did you know?" Andy asked while assisting Nate with the valves, her voice muffled behind the mouthpiece. "Is this firedamp, like in coal mines?"

"No, firedamp would have exploded on contact with the flame," Kerri said. She could notice strength coming back to her arms and legs, the oppression receding. "The most likely gas to displace oxygen without us noticing or Tim smelling it would be ..." Her mind cogs stopped to an audible click. "CO_2. Carbon dioxide." She drove a hand to her chest. "How's your heart rate?"

Andy queried her wrist. "High."

"You sweating?"

"Yeah."

"Vision?"

"Better than a minute ago."

"And your hands were trembling just now. They're all symptoms of hypercapnia—CO_2 poisoning. Your body doesn't react because CO_2 is always in the air; it's what you breathe out. But in very high concentrations it can make you lose consciousness before you notice it."

"That's what I felt yesterday," Andy contributed. "At the lake, when we faced the creature in the fog. My legs were failing; I couldn't focus. Same thing was happening just now."

"It must come from fissures in the walls," Kerri said, the dull rockscape suddenly interesting. "After all, we're on volcanic ... I mean, we're inside volcanic rock; this is what ..."

She sank for a second in the ellipsis, then reemerged.

"Fuck me," she said, running out of expletives. "That's it. They breathe CO_2. The wheezers do. It makes sense! I mean, it doesn't make sense; no known animal inhales CO_2, but . . . that's how they live underground, that's how they're able to come up. The Walla Walla myth says so: the fog carried the first dwellers. It's not fog; it's CO_2 leaking from underground that allows them to emerge."

Nate fathomed the blackness ahead. "So we're on the right track. We have to go on."

"No, we have to go back up," Kerri dissented.

"Now?!"

"Al said if we needed the masks, we'd better turn back!"

"We're carrying oxygen for a reason!" *(Shakes the air bottle connected to his mouthpiece.)*

"Tim has no oxygen! *(Points at the dog's mask.)* This is only helping him not to get poisoned, but he still needs to breathe!"

The Weimaraner had chosen to lie down on a ledge, clearly unhappy with his new accessory.

NATE: Shit. Okay, you're right. You take him up, we'll go on.

ANDY: No. We don't split up.

KERRI: Then we all go back!

NATE: We haven't found anything yet, nothing we didn't know! *(He snatches the blueprints out of Andy's pocket.)* Look, the last depth mark we passed was 5,200, and the tunnel ends at . . . *(Reading the map.)* Oh.

He put the map down, switched back to normal prose.

"We're exactly at the end. This is uncharted territory."

He turned to the girls. "We need to split up."

The fly-face mask amplified Kerri's already deep, dramatic sigh. "Okay, you take Tim up; Andy and I will go."

"No, you take Tim; we will go," Nate countered.

No eyes explicitly set on Andy this time (the masks prevented it), but she knew the decision was on her once again.

"This is uncharted territory," she reasoned. "So . . . this is the loony's playground, not the scientist's."

She pulled out her pistol and offered it to Kerri, along with the extra magazines.

"Take this; we'll keep the shotgun. You click the safety off . . . Hey!" She had noticed the mask in front of her was fixed on her, not on the gun. "Listen to this, it's important. Click the safety off like this, aim, shoot. To reload, you press here to release the mag, shove in the new one, pull here, aim, shoot. Okay?"

"Okay."

Andy turned to Nate. "Ten minutes and we come back, no matter what. Go."

She hardly heard Kerri's voice behind her saying, "C'mon, Tim," but even sifted through the breathing device, Andy could tell she was mad.

The depth marks chalked on the rock ceased after 5,400 feet. After another while, Andy noticed the absence of any supporting beams. The ceiling often forced them to crouch; the passageway never got wide enough to extend their arms. Condensation on the walls had not been extraordinary before, but now small puddles of water on the floor were becoming a frequent sight. The notion that they had long ago abandoned a man-made tunnel for a random rift in the earth's crust was slowly growing into an evident, choking fact.

Andy lifted her mask for a second, just to feel something resembling air on her skin. She didn't. The reflex to breathe overruled her will, the one that sometimes manages to wake sleepers in a gas-filled room before they pass out and die. She put her mask back on and enjoyed the canned oxygen.

Neither spoke a word until they reached the antechamber.

Nate had to scan the minimal room to make sure the opening continued. It narrowed into a bottleneck, or a drain hole, just high enough to crawl through.

Without comment, Nate shrugged off his backpack and his jacket. The resulting boy in a Conan T-shirt and an aviator mask faced Andy with unperceived poise.

"I'm ready."

Andy took off her bag, almost empty now, and crawled in first.

She did not bother to fear for spiderwebs or critters—unless Kerri taught her different, she was sure nothing resembling animal life could survive down there. Her light found and bounced off the opposite end unexpectedly near, blinding her. The bottleneck was only four or five feet long, opening into a small, final chamber.

This was where their journey ended: a room the size of a phone booth in the entrails of the world.

The one remarkable feature was the writing.

Someone had literally covered the walls with script, all

over the chamber, spiraling down, creeping up, orbiting around one single drawing directly facing the entrance: a circle with geometric lines or constellations inscribed in it and some disturbed child's stick figures with their arms raised around it. This was the secret that lay hidden at the end of the wormhole.

Nate stood up in the white-lit egg-cavern, took a pencil and started scribbling on the reverse of the blueprints.

"Holy shit," Andy commented. "Is this . . . prehistoric?"

"No, it isn't."

"How do you know?"

"Well, for starters, the Latin alphabet didn't come to the Americas until Columbus," he said. "And these symbols"—he pointed at the monograms around the circle—"they're from the Necronomicon."

"So, this side of Columbus . . . Is it Deboën?"

"I think so."

Andy touched the drawing, only then noticing how smooth the rock was.

"How come this wall is so flat?"

"I don't think it's a wall," he said, peeking up from his notes. "I think it's a door."

The danger, or the need for perspective, made her step back as far as the egg-cavern allowed. The wall looked a little too perfect to be natural; it must have been carved. And then there were the corners. Right angles were to be expected in a man-made slab, but on close inspection there weren't any; all angles missed exact orthogonality by a few degrees, enough so that it gave the uncomfortable feeling of being both wrong and designed.

"What's on the other side?" she asked.

"Something big," Nate said in a significant whisper. "A city. A god. Nothing that's supposed to see the light of day."

"How does one open it?"

"I don't think you're supposed to open it. You knock."

"Is that what Deboën did? In 'forty-nine? *(Thinking.)* And the wheezers answered."

"Yes, he probably didn't expect that." His pencil pointed at the drawing in front of them. "I think this schematic is the instructions. See, that's a pentacle."

"Looks like a circle to me."

"That's what a pentacle is, in essence—a circular field and a few symbols around it; the power comes from the sorcerer. See the five stick figures? They form the pentacle—five priests to summon the monster." He let the light tour the whole room. "And these spells must be the equivalent of a doorbell," he said, beginning to write them down. "I think that's where it starts; 'Ngaïah Metraton . . .' Is that a *G*?"

"I think's it's a *Z*."

"'Zariat . . .'"

"'Zariatnatmik,'" Andy tried.

"'Zariatnatmik, Thtaggoa kchak'ui . . .'" he wrote down. "And then 'Mflughua Mr, mflughua Ling, khtar mglofk'ui, nokt nrzuguk'ui . . .'"

"Nate?"

"'Ia Thtaggoa gnasha uikzhrak'ui htag zhro . . .'"

"Nate!"

Nate froze, suddenly noticing the trickles of pebbles rattling off the ceiling.

"You're reading spells aloud!" Andy shouted at him, mask to mask, over the crescendo of rocks stirring below them and above. "A-fucking-gain!"

The best of the quake clapped right then, just like thunder. Only it sounded right inside their ear canals. The cave had become a cocktail shaker.

"Out!" she yelled, kicking him into the bottleneck. "Run! Get the fuck out now!"

They crawled up a two-feet-tall gap between miles of vertical rock to find the antechamber leaking. Trickles of water were pouring from once-dry fissures. And new fissures were opening, slithering from under Nate's palms as he toddled up.

Peter sat on the ledge where they had left their bags, swinging gracefully along with the bedrock.

"Nice going, Nate."

"Shut up!"

"It's okay. We all kinda expected it'd be one of your mistakes that would kill the club off."

The next second Nate was flying above the sitting hallucination, ass-kicked forth by Andy as she grabbed both their bags.

"Go! Climb up, go go go!"

A new angry clash of tectonic plates made her lose her balance. She didn't mind; she'd need to climb on all fours anyway.

"Kerri!" she shouted ahead above the castrophony. "Go up! As high as you can!"

She wasn't sure they were within shouting distance of Kerri, especially with the world collapsing around them, but at her speed they would be in a matter of seconds. Nate felt that if they had been tumbling down the hole like Alice and the white rabbit, they wouldn't have fallen as fast as they were climbing up. That was mostly thanks to Andy, who was practically dragging him by the hand, making him feel like his part should be extremely easy. And yet, once they had risen back to the level where supporting beams and carved steps were common sights, his arms and legs were whimpering in exhaustion. An ankle-deep river of water was now cascading down the passage.

At the first bundle of abandoned equipment they came across, Andy stopped to grab a pickax and swung it at a boarded wall that was sputtering water at them.

"What the fuck are you doing?!"

Andy kept striking the wall, twice, thrice, until the hole vomited a loud gush of water and earth, followed by a boulder the size of Utah that slid into the opposite wall with a titanic boom, inches from her face.

She turned to Nate, visage slashed by dark hair, spitting mud between her teeth: "Now it's sealed!"

She pushed Nate forward, and he had to tell his limbs to stop whining and move again. On what seemed like his next breath, they came nose to nose with Tim and Kerri, peeking down into the tunnel.

"What just happened?!" Kerri asked, pulling Nate up. "What was that?!"

"Up!" Andy ordered as she crawled out the mouth of E-6. "Back to the surface, AFSAP!"

She was in the middle of the sentence when she noticed there was no need to shout.

She removed her mask. The quake had ceased. She didn't know how long ago. They'd been running too fast to notice when the earth had stopped moving.

"What did you see?" Kerri said. She was as frantic as they were. "Was that a cave-in?"

"Some of it," Andy said. "Put on your mask again. You're about to do the climb of your life; you can use the oxygen."

They had already started back up the Allen shaft ladder before Andy could notice they had skipped a few safety measures in their haste. They had forgotten to tether themselves together. They had freed Tim from his respirator, but they had not padded him tightly enough into Andy's backpack; she could feel him dangling every time she hoisted their combined weight up a new metal vertebra inside the long vertical tract. Nate was leading the way again, though he could have done a better job at securing the flashlight to his belt. If he lost his grip and fell, he'd drop on Kerri, and both would land on Andy. Andy ground her teeth and made sure to grab each and every rung as tight as the steel could bear.

All she could hear were her muscles plotting their painful revenge on her the next morning. Which was okay by Andy. She was eager to live to the morning.

Her fingers were meeting Kerri's heels more and more often.

"You okay there, Kay?"

"I think I'm gonna puke."

"Okay," Andy acknowledged calmly. "Please lean over to your right."

"I can see the lights," Nate announced from above.

Andy puffed out. She had expected those lights to be visible long ago.

"How's Tim?" Kerri asked.

Tim shuffled inside his papoose and barked loudly, happy to be remembered.

"Good boy."

Static cracked.

"Shit." Andy stopped, her arm curled around a rung, and picked up the radio. "Al, can you hear me, over?"

White noise was the only response.

"Al, we can't hear you, but we're on our way up. I repeat, we're fine and on our way up. Over and out."

She hooked the transmitter back on her belt, ignoring the static that followed.

"Go on, Kay. Just a little more."

"We're close," Nate shouted, farther ahead of them than she expected. "Like five or six floors."

"See, we're almost there," Andy said. "We're starting to pick up Al's signal; that's good."

"Why is it cutting in and out like that?" Kerri wondered.

"It's not me; it's Al. We'll see him in no time."

"No, I mean, why doesn't he just keep the speak button pressed?"

Andy frowned, then gave the matter ten seconds' worth of thought. For five of them, the transmitter on her hip buzzed continuously. For another five, it crackled in short bursts.

"Morse code," she said.

"What?"

"He's speaking to us with the power button. That's *S. . .A. . . F . . . E.*" The signal flatlined to a continuous buzz again. She picked up the radio. "Al, come again, over."

"He just said it's safe," Kerri reasoned.

"He wouldn't need to tell us it's safe. I think he was saying 'unsafe.'"

The static broke down to sparkles of dots and dashes again.

"I'm almost there!" Nate's voice came from up above.

"Nate, wait!" Kerri called.

"I'm nearly at the platform, it's fine! I can hear the bird."

"Nate, wait for . . ." Kerri stopped, glanced down at the darkness where she guessed Andy would be. "Did he say the bird?"

Andy was un-spelling the Morse code. Most of the message had been lost to real interference, but she was now sure that the word preceding "safe" had been "not."

"Nate, the bird's not supposed to sing unless we're fucked!" Kerri yelled.

"Up!" Andy ordered, replacing the radio with the pistol and pushing Kerri; she could almost make her silhouette out against the feverish glow of the lights above. "Sprint up, up, up!"

Kerri sunk her teeth into her lip and ruthlessly squeezed the last out of her muscles, ordering them not to give up.

And they didn't.

A rung did. The rock cracked and gave way just a couple of inches, enough for Kerri to lose balance and fall.

Andy was too close to see her come, but not too slow to try to grab her when she landed on her; in that split second she lost her grip on the pistol, releasing it to gravity. And then Kerri followed.

Andy's hand caught Kerri's forearm, automatically allowing a strap of her backpack to slip off her shoulder. The bag tipped over, Tim facing the whole depth of the chasm for the first time, yelping in panic at the sight of Kerri hanging in the void, digging his front paws into Andy's back.

"Ah, shit!" Andy screamed, her left arm now holding the weight of two people and a dog, her muscle fibers tearing apart. "Kerri! Get a foothold!"

KERRI: Tim, don't fall!

ANDY: Kerri, get a foothold, please!

Andy swung her against the shaft wall, Kerri's feet and hands finally finding and curling around the rungs again. Andy held on with both hands and righted the backpack onto her shoulders, while Tim shouted into her ears.

"Calm down! Tim, calm down!" She looked down at Kerri, below her now. "Follow me closely!"

Kerri nodded, fear restricted to the inside of her mask, and tried to keep up with Andy as she ran up the last of the ladder.

Andy landed onto the catwalk, on her torso, and Tim immediately kicked his way out of the bag and ran away from the hole, his mind made up never to even be in the same state with a pet carrier ever again. Andy hurried to help Kerri up before even allowing herself to take a breath.

As soon as Kerri put a foot on the catwalk, she lifted up her mask and asked, "What the fuck is Nate doing?"

Andy noticed the scene into which they had just

climbed. Nate was a few yards farther down, facing the drift, squatting, searching his bag.

Slightly closer, the bird in the cage was having a seizure.

"Nate?" Andy called, walking in his direction while removing her mask. "Nate, what's up?"

She could see what he was doing now—loading shells into his uncle's break-action shotgun, his hands trembling like an old eremite's defending his cabin from an alien raid. Tim was by his side, yapping into the drift they had traversed earlier.

A howling, chuckling, myriaphonic clangor was approaching from the distant end of the 1.6-mile-long tunnel.

"I've got twelve rounds," Nate stammered, closing the action. "How many you got?"

Andy's fingers ran to her empty back pocket. She wondered whether the pistol would have actually hit the bottom of the shaft by now.

Nate noticed: "You lost the gun?!"

"I ran out of hands!"

Peter stood on Nate's right, arms crossed, contemplating the incoming horde. "That's funny, I wonder who could've summoned those guys."

"We need another way out," Andy realized.

"I mean, it's almost like someone read a spell or something and they were attracted to it, isn't it?"

"Shut up," Nate whispered.

"The vent!" Andy ordered, grabbing the birdcage on her way to where Kerri was finishing throwing up. "There was a utility tunnel here with a vent; maybe we can climb it!"

PETER: Yeah, good idea, try that door over there.

NATE: *(Looking in that direction.)* What? NO! Andy, not that door!

The call arrived just a tenth of a second after Andy had already executed a triumphant door-opening on the steel gate in the rock wall, covered in black-and-yellow cave-in warning signs.

And every twisted amphibian inside the service tunnel, every four-armed and zero-eyed and reverse-skulled wheezer, shrieked in bloodlusty joy.

Andy bought the next second of her own life by sticking an arm forward in a reflex gesture to block the wave of razor claws and needle teeth with the one thing she happened to be carrying: the birdcage. It turned out to be just big enough to get stuck in the narrow tunnel, and for a whole second it held as the creatures thrashed at it, and the bird literally screamed in terror like birds had never been witnessed to do, and Andy spied through the bars to count the enemies on the other side. Alpha, Beta, Gamma, Delta, Whatever the Fifth Letter in the Greek Alphabet Is, all quickly maneuvering over and beneath the obstacle, slashing Andy's aura.

The next second of life she earned at the cost of using whatever hung from her belt as a weapon. The first thing was the two-way radio, which proved a terrible choice; it bounced off a wheezer's head before another crushed it between its teeth. The second item was the pickax she'd used to seal E-6. It proved useful to stab a couple of heads and hold the barricade for a second longer, while Tim, stripped of his stupid breathing mask and ready to bite, arrived just in time to intercept Beta scuttling under the cage.

Andy pulled the cage out of the way, buried the pickax in Alpha's temple and kicked its body away, heeled Beta's skull, and blocked Gamma with the cage again.

"Nate, gun!"

"I don't have a clear shot!"

Gamma slashed through Alpha's corpse blocking the way, all four arms somehow managing to dodge the pickax's thrusts.

ANDY: Nate! Gun!

NATE: You're in the way!

ANDY: Hand me. The fucking. GUN!

Nate threw the shotgun to Kerri, Kerri to Andy; Andy aimed and tried to prioritize the targets.

And she shot at the ceiling.

The loud, echoing bang managed to appease the wheezers for a moment, the shallow depressions on their faces where eyes should gleam staring at the ghost of the explosion fading off, until they in return shrieked a ten-times-louder, twenty-clawed, million-teethed, cord-ripping warcry of psychotic bloodlust and carnage-announcing hyperadjectivated rage.

And then the tunnel caved on their heads.

All that Kerri saw was a birdcage, and a pickax, and Tim, and Andy fly out of the tunnel like shrapnel expelled out of the booming thundercloud, and the sound had not even been demoted to echo before Andy had barely landed on the ground and rolled back onto her feet, not obliging her body a solitary second of respite before the next move. She stumbled toward Nate and snatched the blueprints from him while his attention returned to the wheezer wave coming through the drift, slowly devouring yellow lamps like a nightmare Pac-Man.

"There's gotta be a way out!" she shouted at the map. "One of these galleries must lead to the surface!"

Kerri joined her, compass in hand: "We go northwest! Just find me the tunnel labeled 'Deboën Isle.'"

Andy began speed-reading the prints before fully processing the sentence.

"The isle?" Nate cried. "No way!"

"That's the route we know to be open; Wickley used it in 'seventy-seven!"

NATE: To get to the haunted mansion!

ANDY: On an island, Kerri, we'll be trapped!

KERRI: *(Desperate.)* Just—fuck, trust me once! Okay?!

Andy looked around. Again, she'd managed to stand between the two cousins, physically stand between them. She wondered at how the stage movements betrayed her every time.

NATE: Andy, look at me: there is something in that house. I am not fucking hallucinating.

PETER: No, you fucking aren't!

KERRI: Andy. *(Grabs Andy by her collar, effectively freezing time.)* I can get us out.

And her orange hair gazed up in awe at its commander.

Andy swallowed. "Right. Help me find the way on the map and I'll—"

And that was when the power went out.

For a brief, seconds-long dark age, only the bird's ongoing hysteria eased up the absolute absence of sight or sound. That, and the approaching cacophony of rabid amphibians coming up along the drift.

Suddenly the lamps flashed on for an instant, too brief for the light to even bounce off the walls, and went off again.

Then again, a tad longer, enough to carry a germ of false relief before they went out.

"Did anyone say, 'Things could be worse'?" Nate polled.

The lights kept hiccuping on and off, Kerri and Andy reading in each other's eyes the same revelation.

"Morse!"

"What's he saying?"

"Uh . . . 'Andy' . . ." she deciphered. "Then $E . . . Z . . .$"

"Z?"

"No, X, shit, why am I so bad at this?! $E . . . X . . . I . . . T . . .$"

"Hurry up!" Nate begged, aiming the shotgun at the blinking drift. In the next burst of light, Peter was standing right in front of the double barrel.

PETER: Hey, Nate, I was just thinking about those pills you're taking, ironically, to not see me—

NATE: Shut up!

PETER: *(Closer.)* Didn't the label mention something about epileptic seizures?

NATE: Shut the fuck up!

PETER: *(Closer, dribbling worms.)* Didn't it, Nate?

"$N, W, 2!$"

"There!" Kerri solved, pointing at an unlit tunnel. "Northwest, second opening; go! Tim, come!"

Tim ran toward Kerri and Andy grabbed Nate by the jacket, and during that split second before she pushed him into the tunnel she was able to see the enemy. It filled up the drift like boiling water up a geyser—a swarm of gray fiends crawling on all fours, or sixes, teeth snapping, claws slashing, stampeding, rolling on top of one another.

She scarpered away, snatching the canary cage on her way, and dove into the tunnel to Deboën Isle.

"We're almost there!" Kerri tried to shout, but barely puffed, holding a flashlight in one hand and the prints in the other, all while sprinting downhill through a roughly carved tunnel barely high enough to stand in. "After that turn, the gallery goes back up through something called 'Deboën stairs'!"

"Stairs?" Nate panted. "Please tell me it's not another ladder!"

It wasn't.

The down-sloping tunnel piped them for a quarter of a mile up to a natural cave split by a large crevice, some fifteen feet wide and unfathomably deep. As a reminder of the force of nature that had created it, magma glared red below. The far ledge was some twelve feet higher than the one they'd landed on. A rotten iron structure, corroded into every color iron is not supposed to be, bridged the gap. It consisted of two beams bolted into the rock on either side, with about twenty ascending steps laid across and a single handrail on the left. The right side handrail had probably taken a dip into the lava a century ago.

Before Kerri even had time to screech to a halt and swear at the view, Tim ran past her and climbed up the stairs, and only at the top did he remember to turn and peek down into the chasm.

"Ooh," Nate judged, as he and Andy stopped two steps short of the fall. "Handrail and everything. Luxury!"

"It will hold," Kerri vouched, placing a foot on the first step, keeping her weight on the support beams. She capered up as gracefully as she could, trying to make it quick for the sake of steps that complained more than living small mammals would, ignoring the searing red veins of the planet below. Safe on the other end, her suede boots almost kissed the dusty rock again.

"See? No problem," she said, patting the handrail, which gave way after two taps. Andy and Nate and Tim joined in a perfectly synchronized heartbeatskip as Kerri regained her balance, then they watched the iron bar tumbling down the cliff, clanging painfully all the long way down.

"Okay," Andy evaluated, shaking off Nate's backpack, which she'd been carrying. "Throw the backpack first, then the bird, then you go," she said, standing guard by the tunnel mouth.

Still panting from the previous run, or from the current vertigo, Nate leaned one foot on the first step, then the other foot on the second, took the backpack from Andy and flung it across the chasm. It landed on the tenth step, from which Kerri swiftly retrieved it.

Then Nate halted to check on the caged bird. It was hiding under its water tank as if to stop from bouncing around; Nate could see its little feathered chest heaving at terminal speed, its pea-sized heart about to explode. The whole cage couldn't be more than ten pounds. He decided to spare the bird another jolt and carry it upstairs.

The penultimate step considered that a poor decision and penalized it by snapping under Nate's foot.

He fell facefirst on the ground, half his body dangling off the cliff; the cage flew out of his hands and rolled straight into Tim's care while Kerri dove to grab Nate's arm.

Andy's first gunshot reverberated all over the cavern. She abandoned her post and galloped up the stairs, skipping two of every three rotten plates, grabbing Nate and yanking him up on the way, then turning at the top to face the wheezing ovation.

A staggering swarm of misshapen silhouettes clogged up the mouth of the tunnel. Twisted necks and overelbowed arms bashed at one another before receding at the second gunshot, while Tim viciously dared the wheezers to cross. Nate crawled to his bag and grabbed a stick of dynamite and a lighter.

ANDY: Nate, shells!

NATE: Fuck that! *(Throwing the lit dynamite across the cliff.)*

KERRI: NO!

A rock-shattering explosion flashed the cavern for a split second, pounding at their eardrums, blowing up pieces of stone and broken bodies.

Then, after the eternity it took for the sound to fade, there was silence.

And then the ovation returned, twice as loud, twice as angry, from the smoking cave mouth.

KERRI: TNT explosions create enormous volumes of CO_2.

NATE: Shit.

ANDY: Run.

NATE: I didn't know that!

ANDY: RUN!

A tumult grew inside the cloud of smoke and a second wave of creatures emerged, almost in an orderly fashion, and leaped up the bridgeway while Andy beat her own record time for reloading. She butted the jaw off the first wheezer and fired at the second, blowing its ribcage open in midair, while a third one skipped the stairs and super-jumped across the chasm and grabbed the opposite ledge and managed to bore its two-inch claws into the rock. Its eyeless face lurked above the ledge just long enough to see Kerri slicing a knife through its arm, severing every connective thread within, and then it fell into the abyss.

"Go!" Andy cried, aiming for the exit tunnel. "Any way that leads up!"

The final sprint took place in almost pitch darkness, flashlight beams too nervous to linger anywhere, and when they found the roots of a spiral staircase, they climbed up at maximum speed, quelling any attempt of rebellion from their muscles, and as they did, their frantic heartbeats and burning lungs overshadowed everything else: the exhaustion, the fear, the blindness, the survival instinct. They did not even stop to assess how far the wheezers had fallen back when they reached a landing, and they kept running up a new, shorter set of stairs and burst through a hatch and into a room—an actual room, a basement—and then slammed the hatch closed behind them and Andy pulled down two bookcases to block it.

Nate was in the middle of falling to his knees when

Kerri grabbed his arm and headed for the exit.

"Upstairs! We need to find a window!"

The darkness was somehow comforting, Kerri thought; it didn't allow them to process that they were inside Deboën Mansion, where reminders of a terrifying night lay in wait to trigger bad memories. She focused on keeping those at bay while finding the stairs, kicking a door open, and discovering a hint of natural light, the first in what felt like the duration of the Dark Ages. She didn't pause and led the way up the main stairs, U-turning onto the second floor, focusing on Andy's and Nate's footsteps right behind her as they sped on autopilot along the second-floor hallway—blocking out the furniture and blurry wallpaper and watchful paintings that stared at them, murmuring, *What's the hurry, kids?*—up to the final twelve steps to the door to the attic, and right up until the moment her hand wrenched that ultimate doorknob, she could claim that she had not, in thirteen years, touched Deboën Mansion.

The boisterous, uncensored daylight in the attic surprised them all. Kerri ran to one of the big round windows, opened it, pulled out the flare gun from her backpack, and fired a round outside.

The old, narcissist firs around the mirror waters of Sleepy Lake heard a soft bang, saw the trail of smoke rising from the house and then a bright, painfully off-palette strontium-red burst of sparks.

* * *

Kerri slid down the wall, her legs finally taking the grandstand of her brain's congress and planning a lengthy filibuster to protest the barbaric conditions they'd suffered for the last six hours.

A soothing breeze from the lake caressed her face. Her fingers scratched the floorboards, dirty with dust and leaves and twigs from outside—healthy, sunlit dirt.

"Catch your breath. We'll climb out in a few minutes."

"We don't have a boat," Andy complained, sitting or falling down next to her. "Are you planning for us to swim back?"

"Let's take five. Nate?"

Nate was standing at center stage, taking in the scene. Daylight, and a silence of a good kind, made of mountains and insects, filled the attic.

He waited for his skin to react. It didn't. Sun-riding dust motes floated around him, dodging his movements, outlining the bookshelves and the workbench, sculpting the books and the myriad bottles and jars and flasks in the laboratory. Everything as innocuous as wood and clay and glass.

The place didn't feel haunted, or ominous, or spooky. Not after the mines, not after the bowels of the earth. It looked diaphanous in comparison.

He could have attributed this change of perception to rediscovery shrinkage. But something else, some elusive aesthetic tinge, kept this abandoned alchemy lab from uncanniness.

And then he realized: the attic didn't feel abandoned at all.

Tim, who had inspected the room upon arrival as though he felt he had fallen unforgivably behind in his sniffing duties, was now standing by the door they'd closed behind them, staring up, his right front paw raised like a private detective's pipe-holding hand.

Nate approached the workbench, floorboards acknowledging his weight, and checked a dust-covered open book on the table.

"Nate," Andy said, "if you read aloud a single word, I swear to you I will staple your lips shut."

"Doesn't this room feel . . . oddly fresh to you?" he asked.

A breeze whistled audibly this time, carrying the smell of fir wood and a gentle marimba cue.

"What's that?" Andy wondered.

Kerri opened her eyes. Workbench, books, vases. Then she pointed her flashlight at the ceiling.

"Oh, God."

Birdcages. Every size, every metal—dozens of birdcages hanging from the high roof beams.

Andy didn't have to see all the birds. She spotted the first skeletal wing poking out from one of the cages and extrapolated. Kerri looked back at the floorboards and saw what she'd first mistaken for twigs were bird bones.

Her eyes and Andy's turned at laser speed toward the cage they had been carrying all this way.

The canary tweeted once, resentfully, perched on its bar and licking its wounds.

"It's fine," Andy puffed.

Tim barked at the door.

"Were those cages up there the last time?" Kerri asked.

"I don't know," Nate said, without looking. The open book on the workbench had caught his attention. It was a large, rigid volume whose pages had the colors, and possibly texture, of very thin slices of human bone.

"Nate, I warn you—" Andy began.

"I can't read it," he cut her off. "No one can. Except for the side notes. Deboën's translation."

Tim insisted once more, adding some growls for the door.

"Last time, this was the book on the lectern." He examined the floor: traces of red chalk pieced together the memory of a drawing on the boards, extending beneath the workbench and his feet. "Here it is, see? This is the circle. I was standing right here! And listen to this."

"Nate . . ."

"Tim!"

"It's okay, listen," he said, reading: "'Thus the Avatar shall exist only within the Circle of Light, and shall try to pour into a living Vessel, for only in a Vessel can it exist beyond the Circle, and shall only be revealed under the Spell of Zur . . .'"

"Tim, what's up?"

Andy coerced her mortified legs to stand up, cocked the shotgun, and cautiously approached the door.

"'. . . but each transference shall cost the Avatar dearly, for once it stains one Vessel it can never pour itself out completely, and every Vessel shall remain polluted after the Avatar reaches its Source.'"

Tim shut up as Andy yanked the door open and held the gun at the threshold.

No one. Still, Tim kept barking at the empty corridor.

"Uh. Andy . . ." Kerri called from her corner.

She noticed it a second later. A single sheet of paper hung taped on the outside of the open door, fluttering in the breeze. Albeit missing the envelope, the handwriting on the note was familiar.

And it simply read "GOOD-BYE."

There was uncertainty about which event happened next.

The first of the two disputing occurrences was the canary fluttering in its cage.

The second was the gentle clatter of some lids on their pots in the laboratory, followed by the jingling of glassware and the drumming of books, the marimbaing of brass and copper and iron birdcages, and then the deep, grave, intestinal grumble of Deboën Isle shrugging a murder of crows off its trees.

"We're leaving!" Andy announced.

Nate barely had time to grab the grimoire before the girls took him along with the birdcage and their bags and blundered down the last flight of stairs into the hallway. Books were lemminging off the shelves, portraits and furniture shuddering at the fury of the house stirring itself awake.

"The hole in the east wing!" Kerri commandeered the party, compass in hand, covering it from the dust raining from the roof beams. "That way!"

They ran to the end of a corridor, Andy's shoulder first, inspired by sheer faith to hit a door and not a solid wall. She crashed inside, landing onto a sun-kissed carpet.

White sky shone through the charred skeleton of the roof like a divine power through a rose window.

Kerri leaped over Andy and clambered up a pile of debris to peep through a gash on the wall.

"Through here! Tim, come! You come with me!"

The dog blissfully jumped into her arms, then reconsidered when he saw the almost vertical drop on the other side of the hole, but Kerri didn't give him a chance to cower: she hugged him tightly and plunged forward, and they avalanched down a steep pile of rubble to the ground, where they rolled to their feet and ran toward the sound of the approaching motorboat.

"A motorboat?!" Andy shouted in disbelief as she slid down with the cage and the bags. "Who the fuck—"

"Who cares?!" Nate cried, scurrying out himself, hugging the grimoire to his chest, trying to climb safely down and failing miserably, but happily, as he tumbled to safe ground.

The motorboat didn't even dock; Joey Krantz swerved at the shore and let Kerri jump from the pier to the front seat. Tim came right after, barking an introduction in midair and landing on Joey's lap.

"Quick, everybody on board!" Kerri called. "Nate! Move!"

Andy stopped by the pier, caught Nate once again frozen in front of the mansion, staring back at the dormer window to the attic they'd just escaped.

She followed his line of sight. She saw the magnificent mansion, long and boastfully tall, the ivy snaking up the façade and framing the round window on the central dormer. The tremor had passed. Nothing moved up there. Nothing shuddered. Not the ivy leaves, nor the window frame, nor the black-cloaked crow-figure standing in the attic they had just left not sixty seconds ago.

"No way," she muttered to herself.

A horn blared.

"Nate! Andrea! Come on board!" Joey shouted.

Andy popped out of the trance, grabbed Nate, glanced back at the figure she expected to have vanished in the lapse and saw it still standing there, as impertinent as only human-born things can be. Then they boarded the boat just as Joey was pumping the throttle and veering back to the mainland.

The house drifted away, hid back under the isle trees. The tectonic plates had settled. The waters were beginning to, disturbed only by the path knifed by the motorboat that ferried the detectives back to the mainland.

Andy shifted on the pile of backpacks and distressed animals and faced Joey. "What are you doing here?!"

"I called him!" Kerri explained. "I asked him to stand guard on the lakeshore in case we had to escape this way."

"Why didn't you tell me this?"

"Because I knew you wouldn't approve, Andy! We are going to need help—all we can get!"

"So what happened?" Joey pressed. "Was that an earthquake just now? Is it what tipped your boat last time?"

Kerri tried to remember every new clue they'd collected, but the pile of loose ends was too big to juggle with; they just fell out of her hands. She flipped her hair and stared at the horizon.

Andy suddenly noticed the canary expostulating in the most harmonious terms. She opened the cage, realizing they could have freed it ages ago, and the little bird hopped indecisively on the brim of the little door, then tried to flutter out against the wind and lost. It settled in the shelter of the backseat, where the leather was torn and cozy foam stuck out, and it cowered there, tweeting unambiguously angry messages at each team member on the boat: *Fuck you! And fuck you, fuck you, fuck you, and especially fuck you!*

And Tim yapped back with immense joy at the new friend he'd made.

Kerri swapped slides under the microscope, holding her breath at the abusive smell coming from the sample box. Andy was gargoyling over her shoulder, perched on a stool behind her at the front row of the classroom.

ANDY: So I'm not angry that you called Joey. I mean, I don't know how I would have reacted if you'd told me, but it's okay, 'cause I don't need to green-light every step; no one's in command. *(Pauses; sees Kerri taking notes.)* What's up?

KERRI: Oxidation of the marrow cells.

ANDY: Right. *(Beat.)* But anyway, the key to keeping it this way is being a team and sharing intel. Okay? I'm not pissed off; I'm saying that if we start *(treading carefully)* com-part-ment-al-iz-ing information, we're less efficient. *(Pause.)* What's up now?

KERRI: *(Leaves the pen on the notepad.)* Someone talking to me while I'm trying to concentrate.

Andy wisely repressed an unnecessary "okay" and shut

up. It had been Kerri's idea to hit the library, just like the old days, but the needs of the present case had vastly outgrown the once rich and always willing resources of the Blyton Hills Elementary book depository. She had now taken it upon herself to analyze the wheezer samples she and Copperseed had frozen using the best sixth-grade equipment available in the chemistry classroom.

The harsh population drop in Blyton Hills after the closure of the chemical plant was taking its toll on the public budget, and the school was expected to stop operating the following year and start busing the children off to Belden, as it did with high schoolers. Andy had never visited the building before, except for the library. She liked the classrooms better than those in the boarding schools she'd been sent to, but maybe it was just her grown-up eyes, distanced from the mean-looking periodic tables and plant taxonomy posters.

"Do you remember the Blooms' house?" Kerri asked, not raising her eyes from the lens.

She held on for an answer, which didn't arrive.

"You may speak now, Andy."

"Yeah, I remember," she answered promptly. "They had that swimming pool we were so jealous of."

"Do me a favor: go there and ask Mr. Bloom to let you borrow their pH test pen—that thingy to measure water acidity?"

"Okay."

"And take Tim; I can't keep him from putting stuff in his mouth all the time."

Tim caught the accusation, spat the tadpole back into

its aquarium, and came tail-nodding to Andy by the door.

"Uh . . . want something to eat?" Andy asked.

Somewhere behind a curtain of curly orange stalactites covering the microscope, Kerri microsmiled. "A Coke."

Andy left and closed the door behind her. Captain Al, Deputy Copperseed, and Joey Krantz were heading her way; she intercepted them.

"Don't disturb her; brief me," she ordered, walking on.

The three marched beside her, Captain Al reporting first: "Sentinel Hill's clear. The creatures you met must have sprung up the shaft there. After I heard them and I morsed you a warning, I stood guarding the adit mouth for a while, but nothing popped up."

"The air was too pure for them," Andy guessed, resentful.

"I just scouted the isle," Joey said. "I saw nobody."

"Why are you wearing a uniform?" she interrupted.

"Uh . . . I volunteer for the sheriff's office."

"Right. Did you enter the mansion?"

"No, the hole you jumped out of is impossible to climb back up without a ladder or any gear; there's no way in."

"Well, somebody was inside. What about the rowboat?"

"It's still there at the pier on the mainland; been there for over a decade. Andy, are you sure of what you saw? You guys were inhaling gases, running, climbing—maybe you saw a ghost."

"A ghost doesn't go around leaving notes," Andy argued. "Someone's been fucking with us since we arrived; find who he is. And check if RH lost an inspector in the gold mine."

"We checked that already—they didn't."

"Then who the fuck was Simon Jaffa?" Andy blurted,

drawing out the ID card and slapping it on Joey's uniform.

"Hang on." Copperseed pulled the party to a stop. He read the ID, then questioned Al. "That weasel lawyer who defended Wickley. Wasn't his name Jaffa?"

"Wickley?" Andy echoed. "Wickley was defended by a corporate lawyer?"

"That guy, a corporate lawyer?" sneered the deputy. "He was an ambulance chaser. He took the case after reading your story in the *Telegraph*."

Andy casually peeked through the door to the next classroom. It was time for the next meeting.

"Are the Blooms still living here?"

"He is; she left him," Joey said.

"Could you please go to their house and borrow the acidity test kit for their pool?" she asked Captain Al. "Kerri needs it for her lab work. And, Deputy, can you check your files, confirm it's the same Jaffa?"

"What can I do?" Joey offered.

"Get Kerri a Coke."

"Is that for the lab work too?"

"Yeah, I guess. Go."

She watched the three men march down the hallway, then she knocked on the classroom door, opened it, and ushered Tim inside.

"Hey, Nate."

Nate deminodded, eyes trapped on the half-fossilized book open on the teacher's table. The blackboard behind him and a second one on wheels he had placed to his right, forming a corner, were covered in mystic symbols and right-to-left script.

"Don't worry, I'm keeping my mouth shut," he said, flipping over a stiff, calcified page.

"What's that on the blackboard?"

"Protective spells. Just in case."

Rare evening light that only frequently detained pupils are familiar with seeped through the windows. Andy knew it well.

"We saw him, Andy," Nate muttered. "He was standing right there."

"It was a guy in a costume, Nate. Same as always."

She checked the page Nate was studying: scribbled pieces of younger yellow paper were clipped to the margins of the arcane parchment.

Andy had a rare inspiration. She delved into her pockets, retrieved the farewell note that the bad guy had left them inside the mansion, and laid it on the open book.

"Do you think it's the same handwriting?" she asked.

Nate examined the brief missive and compared it with the notations in the book. The latter were testimony of a time of valued penmanship, romantically slanted, embellished by experience rather than whim. The capitals in the farewell note were straight, high, and narrow, but overall ordinary.

"It's not the same," he ruled. "But that doesn't prove anything. The Deboën who wrote these notes is not the same that came back."

"One is Damian, one is Daniel?"

"Not exactly. One was alive; the other was brought back to life. From his essential salts. I'm not sure he can even get a real body."

"But we saw a man in the window."

"You called it 'a guy in a costume' before. I'd rather err on the side of caution and say 'something in a cloak.'"

The phrase was vague enough for the possibilities to make Andy's skin crawl.

"What does your friend in Arkham say?"

"I can't talk to him; they rescinded his phone privileges. Apparently he tried to reproduce the Seal of Zur and accidentally set fire to the curtains."

Andy nodded appreciatively, pondering that one of the areas the Blyton Summer Detective Club should try to improve in the future was its network of outside consultants.

"Okay. Get the book," she ordered, going for the door and fingersnapping the Weimaraner to attention.

"Why? Where are we going?"

"To see the second-best expert we have."

Nate gathered the book and his own notes and carried them out of the classroom and through the school doors, assured and somewhat satisfied that the big dark book was intimately annoyed by sunlight. The amber Chevy Vega glistened at them like a smiling Rock Hudson—the only four-wheeled vehicle parked in front of the elementary school. Tim jumped into the backseat and Nate rode shotgun. Andy started the engine, skidded onto the road, and turned north for Owl Hill.

"Hey, look there," Peter said, sticking his perfect face to the window. "Dr. Thewlis's clinic closed down."

Everyone in the car ignored him or pretended to ignore him.

"Dr. Thewlis? The dentist?" Peter insisted. "He was

nice. One of the best doctors I've been to."

"Simon Jaffa was not RH," Andy said to entertain on the trip, "He was Wickley's lawyer."

"Really?" Nate frowned, thinking what that implied, but his cache memory was too busy and waved him to leave the pending task on the tray. "Not a very good one, was he? In fact, I always wondered how he got thirteen years for—"

"Wickley just pleaded guilty," Andy said. "He told me."

Nate looked at her for the first time in this chapter.

"You talked to Wickley? When? Where?"

"Before going to New York for Kerri."

"Oh. So, how did he look?"

"Uh . . . fine, I guess," she summarized, swerving onto Klondike Street. "Until the moment when he started speaking in tongues while I was squeezing his neck."

Nate registered that, then loosened the grip on the grimoire a little as Andy pulled over in front of Mrs. Morris's house.

"That was interesting," Nate judged as they stepped out of the car. "Is there a way to know Wickley's whereabouts?"

"Yes. Copperseed can phone Wickley's parole officer and ask whether he's failed to touch base in the last forty-eight hours. Why? Do you think he might be the cloaked man?"

"No, I was just planning to mock your knowledge of the penitentiary system if you knew that."

Their pace was naturally slowed down by the narrow garden path and the untamed nature hindering the way. Andy rang the bell. A green light glowed in the bay window.

"She's going to love having us back," Nate predicted.

Steps approached, latches clacked, a door opened the whole four inches the chain allowed.

"You again?" Dunia greeted them through the crack.

"Mrs. Morris, we need your help," Andy said in her good-cop voice.

The woman unbolted the chain, let the door open just wide enough for Tim to parade in, his tail semaphoring, *Is that fresh tea I smell?* Dunia focused on blocking the other two. Andy noticed what she was wearing—something irrelevant, but Andy registered it nonetheless.

"Your friend Captain Urich's been asking questions about me," Dunia said resentfully. "Wanted to make sure I was in town all morning. What's happening?"

She referred to the captain by his real name, abstaining from his more widespread nickname, Crazy Al. *Honor among outcasts,* Andy thought.

"We've been to your old house again," Nate said.

"Not my house."

"Someone's living there."

Dunia waived her right of reply, ink-black cold-war eyes locked on him. Then she glanced down at the volume in his hands.

"I plan to return it," Nate explained, "but first I need to ask you a few questions."

"I don't want that thing in my house!" she exclaimed. "Do you know what happens to people who read this book?"

"I can't read it; I'm just going through your father's notes, and I need help."

He'd managed to carry the book inside at this point, with Dunia following. Andy closed the door behind them. As her pupils adjusted to the wallpapered gloom, she spotted something new in the cluttered foyer—a large package sitting next to the door. One torn half of a mailing label read "Banned Books, San Francisco." She flipped open the lid and pulled out a book with the word "Vampire" on the spine.

The cover featured a dark-haired temptress leaning over another woman on a canopied bed, red hair cascading over the mattress. *Undying Lust.* Seventh entry in the Vampire Sorority series.

Suddenly she noticed the ongoing conversation in the living room had halted. Dunia was watching her from the threshold, a fresh cigarette in her hand.

"Sorry, I …" Andy then noticed the author's name hiding in a corner under the displaced bedsheets: Dunia L. Morris. "Oh. This is your latest novel?"

"Uh-huh."

Andy flipped it in her hand. "Uh, can I keep it?"

"Sure," Dunia sighed.

(Offering it to her.) "Would you?"

Dunia put her on hold for a second, cigarette caught between her teeth. She lit it, puffed the first drag out through her nose, then took the book. She led her into the living room to her workstation by the bay window. A green-shaded lamp spotlighted a pile of books, a notepad, and a personal computer. Dunia wielded a black marker.

"Your name was?"

"Andy Rodriguez."

She scrawled a line on the title page and handed the book to her. Nate came next, carrying the Necronomicon under his arm.

"I need to talk to you about your father's arrangements."

"Once more: I didn't get along with my father," Dunia said resentfully, retreating to her beanbag couch.

(In a side paragraph, Andy put the anonymous farewell message under the lamp and compared it with the dedication in the paperback: *To Andy Rodriguez—remember to share*, heart, single-stroke signature. No match.)

"But you said he was able to raise the dead," Nate insisted. "Several books in Deboën Mansion expand on an alchemical process to distill the essential salts out of a person's remains, from which you can raise avatars—"

"I'm going to stop you there," Dunia cut in. "I've read those books." She noticed Nate's odd reaction, then clarified. "*The Dark Revenants*, by Bob Howard."

"You've read Bob Howard?"

"Yes! Wow, you read pulp horror too?" she said, pitch gliding off the sarcasm scale. "Finally someone sophisticated. I'm sick of this town of Milton hooligans!"

"Okay, Howard used the salts theme in a book, but you said your father could do it—he could bring back the dead!"

"No, I said he could talk to them. That's what the avatar is supposed to be: a ghost, the sublimation of a spirit from bodily remains."

"Yes, but only as long as you keep it inside the pentacle." Nate dropped the grimoire on the sequoia table.

"Don't—" She curled up her legs, grimacing at the tortured symbols on the page. "Don't fucking open that book in here!"

"Howard said what your father says here: that the avatar would try to 'pour itself into a living vessel.' Which is poetic phrasing for possession. What if your father prepared in advance his own essential salts, died, and waited for someone to raise his avatar so he could possess them?"

"And what meddling asshole would be stupid enough to do that?!"

Andy stepped in just then, in full eye-contact-luring mode. Nate registered it, swallowed back the line he had almost delivered.

"Let's say Wickley," he put forward.

"Who? The salamander klutz?"

"We know he'd been hanging out in the house for some time. He reads something he shouldn't, the avatar is raised, it possesses him."

"Wickley was not possessed," Dunia chuckled, a hair-thin crack in her voice. "I know that much. I know my father; he was nowhere inside that pathetic man."

"Okay. What about me? Could he be inside me?"

"No."

"How do you know?"

"*You* would know. You would fight it. You can't have another person's soul inside and not know—especially Deboën's. He would make . . . an impression."

"But he wouldn't be in me anymore; I'm telling you there's someone in the house already. What if I was just a vessel?"

"You'd still know. Because the vessel is soiled." Dunia smirked. "Same thing happened in Howard's story. Remember? The second astronaut?"

Nate stopped, flipped some pages in the grimoire until he found again the notes he had seen in the attic.

"'But each transference shall cost the Avatar dearly, for once it stains one Vessel it can never pour itself out completely, and every Vessel shall remain polluted after the Avatar reaches its Source,'" he read again.

"What's that supposed to mean?" Andy asked. "If someone had been a vessel for Deboën, how would they know?"

Dunia's eyes drifted away, imagining, the cigarette she'd been speed-smoking throughout the conversation almost out. "I don't know. You would feel . . . violated. Like . . . like there was a smear in your heart that you couldn't wipe clean, and it would stay there, always, darkening the world around you, making everything taste bitter. You would have nightmares every night. Hallucinations. Glimpses of his world. You would rely on alcohol or drugs to dull the pain, and even then, you would just wander through the motions. You'd feel . . . lost, bereft of purpose. At best, you'd become an underachiever, forget the goals you once had. At worst, I don't know. Jail. Mental institutions. Suicide."

She focused back on Andy. Andy looked across the table at Nate, and Nate at the sofa on his right where Peter sat listening.

PETER: Shit. Does that sound familiar, anyone?

"But it could be worse, of course," Dunia remarked through a bitter smile.

Andy wondered, genuinely astonished, "It could?"

"Yes, because . . . the problem is not that you carry a bad piece of soul with you. The problem is it doesn't belong to you. And eventually the owner might want it back."

She squished the cigarette, and for a while she seemed to just contemplate her own scenario, while Nate sat and

Andy stood staring at each other, both feeling their guts wither and die.

"Thank you," Andy managed to voice after a full minute, and she quickly grabbed the cumbersome book and gestured Nate to move on. A gag reflex had to hold on at her throat to let the following words squeeze through: "We'll be leaving now; you've been very kind."

Even Tim thought the visit had been awkwardly brief, but no one asked him. He trotted past their hostess apologetically, and Dunia barely had time to react and walk them to the door.

Not ten seconds later they were back in Mrs. Morris's garden and hurrying toward the amber Chevy, whose color for the first time didn't seem bright enough to Andy's eyes. The taste of lead was building up to her palate. She tried to spit, but her mouth was dry.

She started the engine, stepped on the gas, and heard Nate say, "Oh my God."

She checked on him after the first turn—his blue eyes like mere pilot lights, the grimoire dropped between his legs.

"This is impossible," she said, instantly surprised at how desperately wrong her voice sounded. "Nate, we're not possessed."

"We were. We were the living vessels," Nate mumbled.

"We were not! You said the avatar can't leave the pentacle!"

"I was inside the pentacle. Maybe. I can't remember where the lectern was. The salts were on the workbench to my left, inside the pentacle too. When I raised the avatar, it poured itself into me. It was set up that way."

"But what about us?! I never stepped inside the pentacle!"

"You didn't need to. It was in me already," Nate said, rubbing the distracting shadows off his face. "Just go through the events again. After I read the spell, I saw the smoke rising, I got really scared, and then . . . there was a tremor."

"We noticed that downstairs."

"The next thing I know, Peter is waking me up and pulling me by the arm." He rubbed his right shoulder. "That's when it transferred to him."

"I had found Kerri tied up when the tremor hit," Andy remembered. "I set her free, but then the creatures came up. We hid inside a dungeon—maybe it was a cellar, I don't know." Andy replayed the memory, and suddenly swerved to dodge a van that had been blaring at them for two blocks. "We could hear them, scratching the walls."

"We heard you two crying. When Peter and I got there, the creatures were gone. Peter opened the door."

"Kerri hugged Peter."

"And so it got into Kerri. And then somehow . . ."

"I took Kerri's hand." She bit her lip, the realization slapping her face with thirteen years' worth of stored potential energy. "But why? Why would it take us?"

"It didn't; we were just vessels. It was trying to get to its source."

"What source?"

"The body, Andy! Deboën's body! We were sharing an isle with it."

"But we never saw or touched Deboën's body," Andy argued, but the strength of her arguments, like her voice, had long ago begun to falter. A living vessel was too broad a definition; it only required imagination. A tree is a living vessel. Worms are living vessels. Suddenly every artery of ivy spidering up the front stairs and over the roof, every weed in the garden, gained meaning. Any blade of grass was a breeze away from the others, every bramble was connected to another bramble, every tree root was part of an underground network serving a single purpose.

And there, beneath an unmarked marble slab under the vault of a willow, the source just waited.

"We were just a transport," Nate summed up. "It went right through us." He swallowed, the skin on his neck bristling up at the sight of the ice-cold sweat drop that was coming down. "I did this to us."

Peter sat tranquilly in the backseat with his legs spread open, ignored by the dog.

PETER: It's okay to cry, Nate. Everyone here knows you're a pussy anyway.

NATE: Shut up! Just fucking shut up!

ANDY: Nate! *(Steers onto Main Street past a honking truck.)* What the fuck, man, who are you talking to?!

NATE: *(Diving into his palms.)* Shut up! Christ, shut up!

ANDY: Nate, c'mon, man! We can fix this!

(Tim sticks his head between the front seats, trying to soothe the boy.)

ANDY: We just wandered in. It was a trap, Nate. We just . . . fell for it. It could have happened to anyone. We . . . *(Her hand tries to grasp a word, fails, and falls back, slapping the wheel.)* We were the meddling kids.

(Nate reemerges from his hands, eyes inflamed.)

"Nate, please, pull yourself together, okay?" Andy begged. "We need you. Please."

"I killed Peter."

"No, you didn't."

"Let's just say thirty sleeping pills, a bottle of vodka, and Nate killed Peter," Peter suggested.

"Nate, you didn't!" Andy insisted. "Peter killed himself, okay? We were all used by—"

Right there the final piece fell into place, and the picture could not have been more disturbing.

"Then the guy in the cloak . . ."

"It's Deboën," said Nate. "In his old body. And he wants the rest of his soul back."

A car screeched two inches away from Andy's window as they drove past the school sign. She floored the brakes. The station wagon swung around, throwing Tim against the window as inertia made them U-turn, screeching to a stop right in front of the school.

Andy keyed the engine off. Her own heart boomed almost as loud.

Joey Krantz knocked on her window. Andy registered the can of Coke in his hand.

"Hey. You call that driving?"

Nate and Tim stumbled out of the car. Andy took the soda from Joey and led the troops up the front steps of Blyton Hills Elementary.

"So what are we doing now?" Joey inquired.

"I don't know," Andy responded.

"What are you gonna do about the lake creatures?"

"I don't know."

(The school doors crash open, the cast marching in.)

JOEY: I was thinking I could drive you back to the lake and—

NATE: We can never go back to the lake.

JOEY: Why not?

NATE: *(Ignoring him, paces up to Andy.)* He wants us. That's why he's sending us messages. He needs us there, in the house. We only got off the isle today because he didn't count on Joey.

ANDY: I didn't count on Joey!

JOEY: Who's after you?

(They stop in the middle of the hallway, Tim missing the cue and walking on before realizing.)

ANDY: *(To Joey.)* Daniel Deboën might be . . . *(She checks Nate, then rephrases.)* Daniel Deboën is alive.

JOEY: No way! *(Astounded.)* God. Did you guys know he descended from a witch that was burned in Salem?

NATE: FUCK SALEM!!

ANDY: *(Resuming the hike.)* What do you suggest we do?

NATE: We run. We should have never come back. All this time he's been gathering strength, and what's inside us are the only bits of him that he's missing. We must stay away. Peter did the right thing.

ANDY: Peter?! Peter did the right thing?! He killed himself!

NATE: And that's a bit of Deboën's soul that Deboën will never recover.

They had reached the chemistry lab, but Andy wasn't nearly ready to let Kerri join them at this point of the conversation.

NATE: Okay, maybe it's a little too drastic, but . . . In any case, we should stay as far from Deboën as possible. We should leave Blyton Hills tonight. And definitely never go back to the house.

(Door opens, Kerri steps out.)

KERRI: We have to go back to the house.

(All three stare admiringly at her timing. Andy shyly offers her the Coke.)

ANDY: Captain's gone for the pH test.

KERRI: I don't need it; there was one in there. I just had to give you something to do; you were driving me crazy.

(She takes the Coke and the lead, back down the hallway.)

JOEY: Nate just said we can't go back to the house.

ANDY: He said *we* can't go back.

KERRI: We have to. We gotta stop that guy.

NATE: You know who he is?

KERRI: It's irrelevant.

NATE: It's Deboën, Kerri!

KERRI: Irrelevant. We've got to stop him before he tries to raise Thookatoo again.

JOEY: Raise who?

NATE: Thtaggoa. A primeval entity that—

KERRI: Whatever, he's not the threat either.

NATE: Not a threat?!

ANDY: The creatures are the threat.

KERRI: No, they're not.

JOEY: Guys!

(They stop.)

JOEY: What the fuck is the threat?!

As an answer, Kerri shook the can of Coke, then opened

it right under his nose. Nate and Andy barely dodged the soda explosion that hit Joey straight in the face.

Tim ran to drink from the magic pool of caffeine forming at their feet while a drenched Joey swept the foam from his brow. Kerri stood glaring at him, unfazed.

"Why did that happen?" she pop-quizzed.

Joey considered the question, face dripping. "Because you're an asshole."

"No," Andy tried. "Because . . . uh . . . soda. Carbonated water. CO_2."

"There," Kerri pinpointed. "Coke is carbonated by injecting CO_2 into syrup and water, but CO_2 is a gas and water is liquid; in order for the gas to bind with the liquid it needs to be pressurized. When you open the can, you're depressurizing it: that's the *psst* it makes; then the gas molecules start slowly unbinding and floating to the surface. But if you shake the can before you open it, the bonds break and the gas separates from the liquid. If you depressurize the can right after, all the loose gas blows out." She pointed at Joey's perplexed face as evidence.

"Right," Andy digested. "So what does this have to do—"

"The water in the lake," Nate guessed. "It contains CO_2."

"It's carbonated," Kerri explained, "because it sits on a volcano. We saw the CO_2 leaking into the mines. Similar leaks at the bottom of the lake are injecting CO_2 into the water. I just analyzed it from the wheezer samples—the acidity is off the chart."

"So . . . Sleepy Lake is made of soda?" Joey speculated, puzzled.

"But the lake isn't pressurized," Nate argued.

"Yes, it is at the bottom, because of the weight of all that water above. In normal conditions, convection would make the water at the bottom come up and depressurize slowly, releasing the gas at safe levels, but if you shake it first . . ."

"How do you shake a lake?" Joey insisted.

"Earthquakes," Andy guessed.

"Which are somehow caused every time someone reads a spell out loud," Kerri concluded. "We've seen the effects already. We're on volcanic soil; small tremors are frequent. When it happens under the lake, it brings an unusually large volume of carbonated water up, releasing CO_2."

"CO_2 brings the wheezers up," Nate appended.

"CO_2 causes poisoning, makes you feel weaker," Andy added.

"It's probably why the Indians called it Sleepy Lake in the first place," Kerri went on. "It's what kills the animals on the shore and makes the birds scram. But if the quake is big enough, the whole lake will blow up like a can of Coke." She paused for air. "This is an astoundingly rare natural phenomenon called limnic eruption. Four years ago, it happened in Lake Nyos, Cameroon, and the resulting gas cloud drifted toward populated areas and killed seventeen hundred."

"And if it happens here . . ." Andy began.

"Provided there's no wind to blow away the cloud, which would be far greater than the one in Cameroon, it would naturally flow downhill, because it's denser than air, down the only logical path: the Zoinx River Valley, until it reached . . ."

"Blyton Hills," Andy finished. "That's almost a thousand casualties."

"Then it would continue past us until the Zoinx flows into the Willamette in Belden . . ."

"Three thousand casualties."

"And, if the wind's still forsaking us by that time and the cloud is large enough, I guess it could potentially follow down the Willamette into Portland." She cut off Andy. "I don't care how many people live there; there's a few of them I really like."

At the end of the hall, the main doors clacked open; Captain Al and Copperseed marched up to them, bearing news.

"Your Jaffa is the same Jaffa," Copperseed announced. "But his ID is fake—RH denies ever employing him. State police declared him missing in nineteen eighty; his car was found in the parking lot of the Saginaw Motel with a dead engine. Clerk says the driver was a mine inspector—used to flash his ID to anyone who cared. Last day he checked out, paid in cash, hitchhiked off saying he'd come back for the car, was never heard of again." He noticed his audience's sallow faces and the bubbling brown pool on the floor. "What?"

The Blyton Summer Detective Club rubbed their eyes, shifted on their feet, licked Coke off their noses.

"State also says they can send men to help in a hunting party," Captain Al appended. "All they need is a formal request."

"That issue has been . . . outprioritized," Nate said, diplomatically.

"Okay," the captain followed. "What do you want to do?"

Kerri faced Deputy Copperseed first. "We should

evacuate the town. Something big is going to happen, and we may be able to prevent it, but if we fail . . . Is there an evacuation plan?"

"There is," the policeman confirmed, in a tone that clearly implied that was the end of the good news, "but it was drafted when we were three to five stationed in Blyton Hills; now it's just me and a volunteer." He chin-pointed at Joey. "I can call the sheriff in Belden, but we'd still be undermanned."

"Quickest way would be to bring in the army," Kerri suggested, turning to Captain Al. "Maybe your friends at Umatilla?"

"I can't bring in the army, Kerri," the captain replied, overwhelmed. He seemed truly devastated to disappoint her. "I have friends at the airbase, but not that many friends."

"Look, there are people we can call in case of emergency," Copperseed assisted, "but they won't rush in unless the emergency is already happening, or we have staggering evidence it will happen. The dead thing in the freezer is not gonna cut it."

"It's not about the creatures anymore," Nate told him. "We're talking natural disaster." He underscored the word "natural."

The deputy paused, and the patent concern in his stern, furrowed guise intimately cheered Nate, a little. It was nice to have the tough cop's concern for once.

"Well, look, Joey and I might be able to convince people to leave everything and come with us," Copperseed said. "But we need to give them a tangible reason. What is the threat?"

"Okay, that's fair," Kerri started, flipping her hair and wishing she had an unopened can of Coke. "It's kind of a long story, but—"

ANDY: Wait.

(They all wait.)

ANDY: Would it be quicker to just give people an actual emergency?

PART FOUR

PANIC

Andy Humpty-Dumptied onto a steel girder, ripped a long strip of duct tape, and fixed the last four sticks of dynamite under the junction of the girder and the pillar, where the secondary explosion had the best odds to ignite it.

Below her, Deputy Copperseed, in charge of damage control, carted the last stack of flammable material out of the room while Captain Al finished fiddling with the power switchboard near the entrance, which when activated would send the triggering discharge into the fuse.

"I think we're set," he said through the pocket flashlight between his teeth, turning to inspect the mostly cleared blast area. "Should those barrels be there? I'd rather not cause a real ecological disaster if I can avoid it."

"They're all empty; I checked," Copperseed said, wiping his hands and joining Al in the middle of the vast cargo bay, under the long skylights. "And I thought we could use some shrapnel anyway."

Andy slid off the girder and squat-landed on the floor between them. The three reviewed the explosive charges they had placed strategically across the cargo bay to go off in chain reaction. They weren't handling that much explosive power, but each charge had been planted in key architectural joints to increase the damage and cover their tracks. It was like playing demolitionists, but without the years of study or the civil liability.

"You know," the captain began, "it's spooky how fast you came up with this idea, Andy."

"Yeah. Almost as spooky as how easily you can build a detonator out of junkyard material, Cap," she said, and then she spied a fraction of a smile on Copperseed's hair-thin lips. "And you were disturbingly quick to jump onto the *Let's blow up the chemical plant* wagon yourself, Deputy."

The policeman acknowledged the hit, but didn't avert his eyes from their opus.

"I always hated this place," he said. "Damn corporation, building their shit in town, shutting it down, and never cleaning up after themselves. And besides, they are kicking our asses in court."

"Oh." Andy frowned, mentally catching a loose end in the air. "Actually, if you're talking about the lawsuit for the death of the sheep, Kerri says it probably wasn't RH's fault after all. Chances are a small earthquake released a cloud of gas from the lake, and it traveled downriver to the grazing field and wiped them out."

All three fell silent for a second, admiring the seamless connection of that loose end.

"Huh," said Copperseed. "Still, they should've

dismantled this years ago. Maybe this will make them listen, if there's something left to dismantle afterward."

"Oh, there will be," Captain Al said with a downplaying grin. "It won't bring the whole thing down. Just a good bang."

Andy bit her lip on recalling. "Shit. Captain, I'm sorry, I . . . I lost your service pistol at the bottom of the Allen shaft. I'm so sorry."

Al scoffed, slapped her shoulder.

"Hey. Never cry about a gun. Sadly it's one of the easiest things to replace in this country. Shall we?"

They gave a final nod to their evening's work and then headed out, the captain laying the wire along the way. They were stepping out into the dregs of the day.

"You know what would actually happen if we were found responsible for this, right?" the captain polled as they marched across the flat, barren grounds around the chemical plant.

Andy smirked first at the loyalty implied in that first person plural, then answered. "Probably we'd get charged with . . . I don't know, arson?"

"More likely terrorism," Copperseed noted. "That's serious business. More serious than breaking out of a Texas prison, anyway."

The nonchalance of the remark didn't escape her. Still, she kept walking.

"How long have you known?"

"I looked you kids up as soon as you left the station," he said. "Don't worry; I didn't report you. The captain vouched for you, and that works for me."

Captain Al did not say a word. Ahead, they could already make out the silhouettes of the others waiting on top of the knoll against the last dying light. An orange flame sparkled among them.

"Do they know?" Al asked.

"Yeah," Andy said. "There are no secrets between us."

Kerri was sitting on the grass finishing off the detonator, with Joey spying over one shoulder, trying to offer advice, and Tim over her other shoulder, being even more annoying. Nate sat off on his own, chin propped on his knees, gazing at the early stars. Andy and the captain and Deputy Copperseed joined them shortly after, and the captain handed the end of the wire to Kerri, who connected it to the basic rocker switch upgraded to demolition detonator.

"Do we have enough firepower?" Nate asked, not sounding really involved. He could remember the names of at least three mental hospital patients he had met who had been committed for acts much less cinematic than the one he was about to be an accomplice in.

"Yup. It's gonna make some great fireworks," Andy said, helping Al complete the circuit by connecting the switch to an old car battery that would provide the minimal power needed. Bombs are efficient devices like that, she appreciated.

The hulking black silhouette of the chemical plant seemed suddenly unimpressive: overdressed with tortuous pipes and fire stairways, but also so ugly and forlorn and unsuspecting of what was coming, Andy couldn't help but feel like she was plotting to throw a firecracker at an old lady's feet.

"Right, let's go through this one more time," Captain Al prompted. "Once we hit the switch . . ."

"I go back to the police station," Copperseed picked up, "call the sheriff in Belden, report a massive explosion at the abandoned chemical plant. It's an environmental emergency. Everyone goes nuts. Sheriff calls the mayor, mayor calls EPA in Seattle, EPA notifies FEMA and orders evacuation. Which we will have already undertaken."

"Once the emergency is declared, my friends at Umatilla airbase are authorized to come and assist," Al followed. "I know two high-ranking officers, and they know already that the environmental emergency is a cover; what they come to fight is a biological threat. Pictures and notes from your autopsy helped there," he told Kerri. "But they can't leave the base until EPA has declared the emergency. Say . . . four, five hours."

"We'll be moving in at midnight," Andy said. "When your friends arrive, take them straight to the lake. Guard the shores; if you don't hear from us by dawn, or if you see flares, just take over the isle."

"I'll make sure they bring their swimsuits."

"By then," Copperseed resumed, "EPA will have set a perimeter, assisted with the sheltering, and sent in a damage assessment unit to this area. I reckon six to eight hours."

"One way or another, all four of us will be back by then," Andy said.

Joey reacted when he realized the number four included the dog. "You mean five of us."

"No, I mean four."

"Oh, come on! After all I— What more can I do to prove—"

"Joey!" Kerri said, so commandingly that Tim mistakenly stood to attention. "You don't need to prove anything, you already proved it. But we need you here. Blyton Hills needs you here. The people trust you; they'll listen to you. Their lives depend on you moving them to safety."

She waited for Joey to comprehend how literal her words were. He seemed to get it.

"If we fail tonight," she continued, "and there's a new tremor under the lake, everybody in Blyton Hills could go the way of the sheep. So it's vital everyone gets out of town and authorities be ready to carry out more evacuations if we fuck up. A chemical plant exploding will keep them on their toes." She held Joey's blue-eyed stare until he nodded, steel-resolved. "At dawn, find a way through the perimeter, drive your truck to the lake, and stand guard in our car; we might need you."

"Gotcha," he rogered. "Why your car, though? The truck will drive better up there."

"Because we're gonna rig our car," Andy one-lined, letting the science consultant expand on the premise.

"If a gas cloud rises, all combustion engines inside it will stop working. Fuel needs oxygen to burn," Kerri explained. "We'll attach one of the oxygen bottles we've got left to our carburetor, so we can switch to it if the worst happens. It might buy us just long enough to outrun the cloud." She checked Captain Al, with whom she had discussed the feasibility of that part of the plan. "We hope."

The captain nodded zenfully, and handed her the detonator. Kerri's hair proverbially shivered with anticipation when she touched the device, her mind considering the fabulous implications of a single click.

"Once we do this, there's no way back." She offered the device to Andy. "Do the honors?"

Andy didn't move. She was feeling like she had during the first day of their car trip together. She had never considered she and Kerri would ever be blowing up a chemical plant, but had she been able to foresee it, she would have expected the occasion to be more festive, not part of a life-or-death mission. That was a strange thought.

"Together," she said.

She took Kerri's hand, fingertips holding their breath on the contact, and hovered them over the switch, waiting for a third hand to join them.

"Nate?"

The boy was still camped a few feet away, just within earshot of the conversation, sunken in his thoughts more deeply than the girls had seen him ever since the loony bin.

"Nate," Andy repeated. "We will never split up. I promise."

Nate breathed in, then approached them, laid his hand on his cousin Kerri's, and swallowed the dry Rubicon pebble in his throat.

KERRI: On three. One.

NATE: Two.

ANDY: Three.

They flipped the switch.

Four seconds passed.

Then six.

Captain Al stood up, a frowning Andy followed suit, and then the flak of the first explosion blossomed, out of synchrony with the ground-shaking boom, until both the subsequent flashes and the sounds mashed together in a thunderous ball of fire rising into the starry sky.

Andy averted her eyes just a second to confirm that Copperseed was now fully smiling, the red glow of burning collateral damage expectedly suiting his sharp, rugged features.

They remained on the knoll for a while, under the magical spell of things going kablooey in the night.

Tim had grown tired of all the boat trips and he spent this last one nested on the driver's seat with Kerri, dismayed head draped over her thigh, hoping for some affection. The Pennaquick County Police had contributed to the Blyton Summer Detective Club's arsenal with a pair of pump-action assault rifles, a new two-way radio, and loads of extra ammo, which Andy was jamming into every available pocket, along with small boxes of strike-anywhere matches to perform flame tests. Kerri was still holding on to her knife. They all had flashlights and respirators around their necks.

A last familiar shape lay between the empty bags on the deck after Andy had finished gearing up: it was the pickax—the one she had retrieved from the mines and inadvertently left in Joey's boat the previous afternoon. She flipped it in the air, calibrating its weight, and decided to slip it through a belt loop in her pants.

"Can't be too prepared," she commented. "I'll trade you

Uncle Emmet's shotgun for a rifle, okay, Nate?"

Nate sat astern in the dark, careful not to lean his arm over the bulwark.

"Nate," Peter said beside him. "Lieutenant Ripley is talking to you."

"We're doing the same shit all over again," Nate muttered, to no one in particular.

Andy couldn't tell if she was supposed to overhear or just hear that, but she followed anyway.

"We're retracing our steps," she rephrased. "After the lake, after exploring the gold mines, we talked to witnesses, hit the library, connected the mines and the mansion, and we begged for someone to ferry us to the isle, until finally one evening exploring the lake we came across the rowboat, and here we are. This is the night we catch our guy."

"Yeah, 'cause it went so well for us last time," Nate snapped. "Remind me what's different?"

Andy simply opened her jacket an d let the weapons say hello. "We're prepared. We know who the bad guy is." A draft of ice-cold tailwind pushed a long-lost bang of black hair across her face. "And I, for one, am way angrier."

She left to help Kerri dock the boat, and Nate stayed sitting there, savoring her words.

"She was always angry," Peter sidenoted.

They were pulling over at the pier when Andy, rope in hand, noticed another line tied to the post. Kerri shut off the engine, and the hollow sound of the rowboat drunkenly nudging the pier became evident. The towering firs on Deboën Isle remained silent in expectation.

They debarked, and the girls moored the motorboat while Nate advanced inland and confronted the mansion.

Atop the building, in the round attic window, a soft yellow light pulsed.

The three kids and the dog stood in silence at the foot of the front stairs, in the hazy light-puddle from that one lit room. Thirteen years, and Deboën Mansion had not lost its arrogance.

Andy shoved a rifle into Nate's hands, flung another one at Kerri, and cocked Uncle Emmet's shotgun herself, single-handed.

Kerri, sight line pinned to the lit window, said, "We don't fire until we see his face."

Andy tried to make out the minutiae of her expression in the dark.

"You serious?"

"Yes. We faced guys in costumes before. And we always had the good sense not to kill them, but to expose them. Shoot first, ask later may be standard procedure for police in Compton, but it's not gonna be mine."

"You both talk like he can be killed," Nate challenged.

"He can be killed, Nate," Andy affirmed. "The wheezers killed him once. *(Points in the general direction of the mauled east wing.)* If that necrodouchebag thinks I'm any less nasty than those wiggly spider-armed motherfuckers, he's got a *Pennaquick Telegraph* Breaking News Edition coming."

"That was a good line," Peter admitted.

Andy stepped forward and rounded on them. From Tim's lower perspective, the smoldering yellow disk of the attic window shone around her head like the nimbus of a shotgun-and-pickax-wielding angel.

"Listen to me. This is nothing like the last time. *At all*," she spoke, challenging the team to argue it. "Last time we were kids. We came here scared, full of good intentions, trying to solve a mystery. And Daniel Deboën used us. He bullied us."

She blew the strand of hair off her face, then changed her mind and nodded it back on. This was a special night.

"We're not kids anymore. We're not taking shelter in the haunted house—we're going into the house to drag the haunter out on his sorry ass. Are you with me?"

Myriad tiny voices within Kerri's hair went *yeah* like a Rage Against the Machine chorus as Kerri cocked the rifle, lips pursed to keep the fury within.

Nate tautened up, gripped his weapon, and snorted his fear back in.

Tim barked as happily as a dog ever did.

The interior of Deboën Mansion blinked awake, startled at the first blast at the doors, and the portraits and sets of armory stared in disbelief at the front entrance as the pickax burst through the lightcrack, severing the lock, and Andy kicked her way in, moonlit and angerstruck, doors shattering the decoration behind as she shouted at the shocked furniture:

"Blyton Summer Fucking Detective Club! Anybody home?"

Kerri and Nate came to flank her right after, rifles aimed at the horrified haunted house.

Tim scurried between them, promenaded across the

hall, stopped by a decorative suit of armor, and peed on it.

KERRI: That's the spirit, boy.

Nate's flashlight surveyed the area while Andy struck a match. Fat, healthy-looking flame. The carpeted stairs to the second floor stared down at them like Old West bank clerks would at very loud, untidy robbers.

"Does anyone else think it's strange that someone lives here, yet the door is still locked from the outside?" Nate polled.

"I don't know." Andy shrugged. "Does it matter?"

"It kind of appeals to the detective bit in 'Blyton Summer Fucking Detective Club,' doesn't it?"

"Right." She nodded. "Well, we'll make sure he fills us in during his hog-tied villain exposition. Up we go."

"Wait!"

Andy froze halfway to the first step.

KERRI: This guy wants us to come upstairs and find him.

ANDY: Yup. Pretty much my plan, coincidentally.

KERRI: We shouldn't be doing his bidding. He knows we're here; he's got the light on to entice us. He's expecting us. We should do something different, throw him off-balance.

ANDY: Good point. Nate?

NATE: *(Shrugs, points distractedly at Kerri.)* Brains.

ANDY: Right. *(Gazing around.)* Okay, got it.

She stepped back from the stairs and led them through the double doors on the left, into the living room. Dead hanging curtains and embarrassed furniture squinted at their light beams.

Andy lit a match, okayed the flame, then stumbled upon an oil lamp on the mantelpiece and chose not to let the match waste. The colors of the room (bright hues, even conservatively joyful) stirred back to life in the tottering light.

"Nice," Kerri sarcasm evaulated. "Good to be home."

Even though the house had been officially abandoned in 1949 (except for a bout of illegal squatting from Wickley in '77), it had obviously fallen behind with decorating trends back in the early 1920s. The present tenant was clearly uninterested in catching up. In fact, the whole room was uncannily identical to their memory of it. Kerri could have sworn that no one had stood below the breeze-rocked chandelier since their own terrified teenage selves—and the impression it made on her was exactly the same. That bone-ringing familiarity was more unsettling than every haunted house cliché.

Nate even jolted when he peeked over his shoulder and recognized the face over the mantelpiece. Above the dead fireplace hung the somber oil portrait of Damian Deboën, the founding father. The man posed in flamboyant 1860s fashion, leaning on a crescent-bladed sword, like an ambiguous yet proud symbol of a previous career that had granted him the present status. He was the only thing in the room not to seem intimidated by their intrusion. Still, Nate could detect the scandal in his black eyes: the hateful, cryogenic look a Reconstruction-era gentleman would reserve for punks and lesbians.

The likeness, however, wasn't nearly as frightening to Nate as it had been to his eleven-year-old self—not even in the dim light of the oil lamp and the candelabra that Andy had just kindled. It was just brushstrokes on canvas. And the room, he noticed, wasn't that big. Rediscovery shrinkage.

Kerri checked the painting, then looked across the room at an ornamental shield on the wall. Visual memory or imagination placed two swords crossed on top of that shield, not dissimilar to the one in the portrait, but there was only one now. She spotlighted it, and she could outline the ghost of its twin in the dust.

She was about to point this out when she saw Andy sliding a vinyl record from its sleeve. She delicately alighted it on the gramophone (one of those with an external horn like something a Tolkien character would blow into and expect horsemen to rush in), wound up the device, tampered with some switches, and carefully landed the needle on the first track.

It seemed miraculous enough that the old contraption sputtered any sound at all—that of dust and scratches and the tungsten needle coughing. When the music came, it could hardly compete with the noise, but it came nonetheless, in the shape of a forgotten soprano's rendition of *Tessera*.

"What the fuck are we doing?" Kerri inquired in the name of pretty much every living and inert thing in the house.

"I bet you he wasn't expecting this," Andy answered confidently.

She propped the shotgun next to a sofa and sat down, spraying disgruntled dust into the cosmos. Tim did not hesitate to follow suit.

It was dark, and hostile, and downright frightening, but they had camped in worse places. Even lived in worse places. And the broken opera was starting to get comfortable in the room, and Andy loved camping anyway.

Nate browsed the bookshelves, picked something that seemed both ancient and innocuous, and took it to his newly assigned armchair.

Andy had pulled out a book too. Kerri, sitting across, pointed her flashlight at the back cover.

"Why are you reading 'another inspiring entry in our favorite pop-Gothic series,' according to *Sapphic Readers Quarterly*?"

"It was a gift," Andy said.

Then Tim raised his head.

The soprano quivered.

The books convulsed in their shelves, windowpanes rattled, paintings clopped, furniture neighed and furiously stamped the ground.

And then it all ceased.

The gramophone needle had drifted off the disc. Four pair of eyes checked one another.

"Okay. That's our vacation done," Andy gathered.

"Is this it?" Nate asked Kerri. "The limnic eruption?"

"I don't know," she said. "I was expecting something more dramatic."

She pulled a curtain back to reveal a window and peered through the shutters. The isle's lush plant life blocked her view of the lake. Andy had better luck with the window she chose. She could see gentle ripples surfing across the waters.

"It looks calm enough. It should explode like a Coke, right?"

"I've never seen it happen," Kerri argued. "I don't think anyone's seen it happen."

"'Should explode like a Coke,'" Peter quoted, from the armchair opposite Nate. "Really, man, why is she replacing me?"

"What was that noise?" Kerri wondered.

"I mean, Kerri is the logical choice. She's got the looks and the brains, no arguing that."

"What noise?" Nate asked, fighting to ignore him.

"God, I would even understand you taking over," Peter went on. "But Andy? I won't deny she's got initiative, but—"

Tim snarled at the window; Kerri instantly knelt beside him and tugged his neck.

"Shh. Quiet, Tim. Quiet."

PETER: See? Even the dog is smarter.

NATE: *(Rounding on him, hissing.)* Will you shut the fuck up!

SOMETHING: Ggguh.

Nate sprang to his feet. Kerri looked back at him, nodding, *That noise.*

Andy, spying through the shutters, muttered, "Oh fuck."

From the vaguely defined shoreline between vegetation and still water, half a Greek alphabet of gray, malformed figures was arduously and determinedly emerging. And then, staggering, undecided on which pair or pairs of extremities to stand on, they were approaching the mansion.

Andy tiptoed back from the window, readying her shotgun.

"Foyer," she whispered, luring them with a finger.

They retreated back to the entrance hall, and Andy picked up a chair and stealthily propped it to hold the door while Kerri and Nate aimed their rifles at it. The occasional shy wheezing had turned into a frank, raspy choir of a tortured, yet relentless anthem.

(All in whispers.)

ANDY: *(Side-glancing the room they just left.)* Shit. The lights.

KERRI: It's okay. They have no vision from living underground.

PETER: Really? Wonder Tomboy hadn't figured that out?

NATE: *(Appalled.)* I hadn't figured that out!

TIM: *(Stares at the door like an X-raying Superman, all muscles ready to jump forward and attack.)*

This standoff went on for longer than expected. Andy was able to count two full drops of sweat paragliding down her face while she stared at the door handle, daring it to budge.

It didn't. But the wheezing didn't cease either. Instead, it grew louder and lumpier and raspier than ever.

Andy couldn't tell where it was coming from anymore.

She backed away from the doors and signaled the others to follow, the floorboards squeaking treacherously under her feet.

"Where are they coming from?" she wondered.

"Below the lake," Kerri said. "They follow the CO_2."

"What about below the isle?"

That was the cue a wheezer was waiting for to slam

open the door under the stairs and grab Nate by the neck and try to bite his head off. It would have succeeded had Nate not managed to jab the rifle into its mouth. The wrong end.

Tim was faster than the girls and managed to grab hold of Nate's jeans, but the creature was already dragging him down to the basement. In a single second Nate screamed for help, his jeans ripped out of Tim's mouth, he was yanked down the stairs, and the door slammed shut.

It stayed closed for the quantum time length before Andy swung it open again, but in that unnamable lapse everything beyond the door was gone. Struggling shapes and screams. Light and sound. Kerri and Andy and Tim found themselves peering into a flat black rectangle of darkness and interplanetary silence.

"*FUCK THIS*," Andy spat at the intended end of the chapter, pulling out the flare gun from her pocket and shooting into the dark.

A wheezer at the bottom of the stairs opened its foul mouth to shout back, just in time to allow the flare to fly into its throat and burn inside its torso, the rubidium flames shining through its slimy translucent flesh like a bright red, black-smoking Halloween pumpkin of pain.

By the light of which Andy saw fit to jump downstairs, shoot a second wheezer charging for her, spot Nate's rifle on the floor, bat the skull halfway off a third wheezer, let the charging Weimaraner finish him off, and run for Nate as he was being dragged to the dark end of the room, the creature that had seized him preferring to secure a meal before the fight.

Had Nate not seen a pillar to grab on to by the light of that howling, sparking wheezer-lamp still spasming on the ground, he wouldn't have delayed the wheezer enough to let Andy jump on its back, sink her cannon into its spine where its four shoulders seemed to join, and pull the trigger, blowing up the concrete below.

Tim was latched on to the third wheezer's leg, just waiting for Kerri to come downstairs and take a swing at its head. A substantial part of the skull did come off this time.

The wheezer-lamp had stopped moving. A bright red light burned inside its abdomen, its skin blazing white and crawling with overexposed blood vessels.

Andy held Nate's head up. "Nate. Nate. Look at me."

His face was drained white, the way living people, or

even the recently deceased, never look. He had blood left inside him, though. It showed through his T-shirt, in groups of three parallel slashes at his chest and neck. Andy checked for arterial bleeding; there was none. Kerri was now trying to pry a word out of him.

"Nate. Can you walk?" she asked, propping him up. "Nate? Nate, speak!"

"CO_2," Nate fitted in one breath.

"What?"

(Facing Kerri, quivering.) "Flares . . . produce CO_2."

A change in the lighting marked the wheezer-lamp suddenly standing up, red light pouring out of the many holes in its torso and its mouth as it threw a ground-rippling, marrow-thirsty, pure carbon dioxide–fueled screech and crawl-ran on all six toward them.

Andy and Kerri both raised their weapons, aimed vaguely, and fired. The lamp exploded like any lamp would, throwing a wave of guts and severed limbs across the room to splatter off the wall.

"Upstairs," Andy ordered, helping Kerri with the wounded, her sneakers squishing on monster pulp.

The foyer was clear. The front door still held.

And yet the gurgling wheeze of the creatures surrounded them.

In the crowded penumbra, Andy struck a match. Yellow fleur-de-lis wallpaper ululated at the still-healthy flame. She cocked the rifle and gave a quiet military signal to head upstairs. Tim understood it perfectly and took the lead, while Andy helped Kerri help Nate upstairs.

The dog stopped on the sixth step, tail stiffening to

DEFCON 1. Two of the dozen wheezer-voices around them raised in tone and manifested, jumping onto the landing ahead, both on all sixes.

ANDY: Sheep smuggler rugsweep!

(Kerri swiftly grabs the carpet and yanks, causing the wheezers to slip off the landing and tumble down to Andy's feet, right in time for her to take the gun and blow the first one's head off, dodge three claws, step on the second wheezer's chest, and shove the cannon inside its gaping mouth and fire.)

PETER: Why didn't she just say "carpet"?! Like the fucking thing's gonna understand!

ANDY: Go! Get to high ground!

They rushed upstairs, crossed a hallway, flashlights sweeping the rooms frantically, trying to catch sight of the invisible wheezers that stood cheering around them, crawling all over the house, outside, beneath, above, a stereophonic choir crescendoing to homicidal ecstasy.

Andy gritted her teeth and swept the gore off her face to confront the inevitable conclusion: there was only one room to go.

She hurricaned up the third-floor staircase and hit the attic door. It wouldn't open.

"No way!"

The wheezer audio track around her grew into what sounded like sadistic laughter.

"NO WAY! *(Banging the door.)* Open up, motherfucker! We're here! Open up!"

"Andy! In here!"

She spun on her feet and ran back toward a second floor room, shutting the door behind her. Nate was there, and Tim, and Kerri, her flashlight pointing at the peculiar furniture.

Oxygen tanks. Tens of them in assorted sizes, the smallest ones as big as fire extinguishers, a couple of canisters looking like they'd barely fit through the doorway.

"What . . . ?" Andy stuttered. "These are the same kind we found under Sentinel Hill. He was smuggling oxygen here? Why?!"

"There." Kerri pointed for a close-up shot. One of the largest tanks was connected to a duct pipe that slithered into a vent in a corner. "He's oxygenating the attic. He holes up there while the whole lake is leaking gas!"

A high-pitched, overreaching shriek rose from the chorus; Andy and Kerri turned to face it. Their lightbeams hit a bare wall.

On the other end of the room, Nate slid down the flowery wallpaper, his anxious panting barely audible over the pandemonium.

PETER: *(Whispering.)* We're as good as dead here, Nate.

NATE: *(Really loud.)* You *are* fucking dead!

"What?!" Kerri shouted. "Nate, what are you saying?"

Tim growled at the door, claws ready to pry off the floorboards.

"They're right outside," Andy announced, aiming her gun.

"They're pouring in through the east wing," Kerri said.

"Nate." Peter was breathing hard too, like he actually had something to lose. "Listen to me. We're not gonna make it."

Nate could feel both icy sweat and lava blood dripping

down his spine. The wheezer-voices were accordingly dropping in volume, from warcry to drumroll.

"Look at this, man. This is her plan? Just walk into ground zero and fight? It's insane."

Andy pushed Kerri aside and let Tim take the middle of the room with her, both facing the entryway with gritted teeth and quivery trigger fingers, all eyes on the door handle.

It never moved. Wheezers couldn't handle handles.

So they blasted the door open.

Andy fired a welcome shot through the frontrunner of the horde, switched to the pickax, and jumped forward, her and Tim both roaring like face-painted warriors. The doorway was immediately taken over by a new creature digging its claws on the doorframe, and then another, and another, and another, and another.

Andy and Tim stopped halfway to the door, astonished, watching the five wheezers struggling to fit through at the same time. A ridiculous number of arms bashing at one another, mouths snapping in the air.

"Take note," Andy told Tim. "People wonder why bad guys charge at Jackie Chan in a single row. This is why."

In response to that, wheezers blasted two new doorways, one on each sidewall.

Drooling, hissing, claw-waving creatures poured inside like a tidal wave of sulfuric acid.

In amazement, Andy saw Tim jump at the first one and be flung across the room while she herself shotgunned one creature and pickaxed an eye socket into another one's face at the same time, all while watching Kerri move to defend

Nate and fight off the second wave with a stick.

"Kerri! It's a gun! *(Pickax through something's ribcage.)* Fire the gun!"

Kerri bashed the front wheezer, gaining room to aim the pump-action rifle and fire.

All action stopped for a fraction of a second, if only to admire how the blast went through no less than three screeching devils, silencing them instantly and making them fall to their knees and sideways like tux-clad dancers domino-diving in a swimming pool.

Nate staggered to his feet, cocked his rifle, and stepped forward into the three feet of ground Kerri had conquered against the quickly regrouping creatures, when something crashed through the dormer window on his right. Thorn-shaped teeth snapped an inch away from his cheek. He fired as he fell to the ground, and the gun blast knocked the wheezer out the window and off the roof.

Andy silently approved while she fired her shotgun at Lambda, felt Mu clutching her jacket and slipped out of it, nailed Nu onto the wall with her pickax, surprised Omicron with a butterfly kick while it complained that Xi go first, shot Xi's head off, ducked to dodge Mu again, grabbed one of its medial limbs in midair, and shoved it into the pickax point coming out of Nu, impaled four lines above.

KERRI: Nate! Ammo!

Andy's gun clicked empty. She threw it at somebody's eyeless head, grabbed an empty oxygen canister, dug in her heels, and spun. She swung the bottle around, knocked Pi and Rho off their feet, and kept spinning, off-balance and losing control, knowing she would fall eventually, but hopefully not before she'd broken at least one more neck, and indeed she heard a scream cut short by the sound of the canister striking one o'clock on Sigma's skull before crying out, "Duck!" and letting go of the bottle, which by sheer luck hit Tau right as Kerri was blasting a hole through its abdomen.

KERRI: Nate! Ammo, now!

Andy didn't wait to regain balance before she dove for the shotgun, a shell in her hand, and as she landed over the weapon, the nth shrieking monster leaped on her. She rolled aside to avoid being pierced by three claws at once, pried the pickax out of the wall, nailed the last wheezer's hand on the floor, and then finally chambered the shell and blew its head into goo.

KERRI: Nate! NATE!

Andy took a split second to reassess. Six wheezers were still stuck in the doorway, trying to chew one another's arms out of the way. The room was covered in two layers of writhing mutilated aliens and black gore. It took a while to make sure no human corpses lay among them. She skipped over the dead bodies toward the burst dormer window.

He wasn't down on the ground. Kerri spotted him first, at the end of the west wing, hanging off the roof.

Both girls called him.

"Don't listen!" Peter shouted into his ear. "Just go!"

Nate clung to the ivy on the walls, grabbed a thick trunk and slid down along it, the gnarls and severed twigs tearing the skin off his palms. The girls saw him crash-land on top of the conservatory roof, roll off it, and hit the ground somewhere in the shrubs.

Kerri stopped breathing for a second, clutching Andy's arm, until she saw him stand back up. Then there was an ephemeral relief, before her eyes convinced her brain that Nate was actually running toward the dock.

"Nate?! What are you doing?!"

They saw him jump into the motorboat, then stop by the controls and touch his pockets. Kerri had the ignition keys.

"Fuck it," Peter said, already aboard the rowboat. "Come on!"

"Nate, don't!" Kerri yelled from the window, watching Nate switching boats, untying the rope, and taking the oars. "Nate!"

Andy pulled Kerri inside a second before a wheezer that had crept up the façade onto the roof slashed her face off. It jumped into the room with them, jaws open at a thylacine angle, in the same second Kerri pulled her knife out and thrust it upward into its abdomen. It landed half dead, its guts lost in flight.

"Out!" cried Andy, pulling her away from the window and toward one of the new doorways the wheezers had been so kind to open for them.

A wheezer cut them off from the gap inside the hollow wall. Tim viciously pounced at it, throwing it down and biting at its neck as the thing tried to shake him off.

"This way!" said Andy, pulling Kerri to the opposite hole, loading shells into her rifle as she ran. They were relying on moonlight now, but Andy somehow recognized the next room.

A stampede of six-limbed monsters almost knocked the door off its hinges.

"We're trapped!"

"No," Andy replied. "This is where you disappeared."

"What?"

"This is the room where you fell into a trap! Where was it?"

"I . . . I was standing over there and I . . . pulled that lamp!"

Andy grabbed Kerri by the waist, stood on the corner, and pulled a candleholder on the wall. It came right off into her hand.

Right at that moment, the door came down, along with two wheezers stomped by the rest of the hollering pack.

ANDY: Aw, fuck this.

She shot at the floor. The trapdoor they were standing on crumbled under their feet, dropping them inside a hollow wall to land on a slide, Andy clutching Kerri all the way down and smothering a scream while orange hair went *weee* along the way, all through the first floor and down to the basement.

A single, bile-coughing wheezer was standing in the coal room where they arrived, its back turned to the end of the slide. It heard the girls crash-landing into the coal pile behind, scrambled to face them, and had its head blown into subatomic matter, thus starting and ending its overall contribution to the story in one paragraph.

Kerri clambered on the coal pile, tried to climb back up the ramp.

"We forgot Tim!"

"He's fine, come with me!"

"No! We need Tim!"

Andy had to pull her out of the ancient coal room and into the basement proper, frenzied screams of the besiegers booming all around them as they raced through the mansion's foundations. Under the paroxysm of their flashlights she caught broken glimpses of shadows scuttling around corners, passageways into blackness, a heavy door that seemed secure enough.

She opened it and yanked Kerri inside with her and pulled it shut behind them, and only when the door latched did she recognize the room. She whirled around and tried the door again: locked.

"Oh fuck."

"This is the dungeon!" Kerri cried, grabbing her own skull. "This is the same fucking dungeon!"

"I know," Andy panted, striking a match, about to gouge her eyes out for that mistake. "But they can't reach us here!"

"They can reach Nate! And Tim!"

"Nate's got a better chance out there, and Tim can hide!"

"Until when?! Who's gonna let us out this time?!"

"Kerri, please, calm down!"

"They're outside! They're scratching the walls!"

"I know!"

"We are going to die!"

"Kerri, keep it together, please!"

They were holding each other's wrists now, Andy's imploring hand feeling Kerri's frantic pulse and failing to calm it for what felt like a frozen minute, until she had to drop the match burned down to her fingertips. Darkness prevailed.

The ruckus outside was subsiding.

Andy searched her pockets. Ten minutes into the war, her once perfectly sorted equipment was in shambles. She found a couple of glowsticks somewhere, snapped one, and examined the wide, empty, preposterously jail-like cellar. A dungeon, for all intents.

Kerri had retreated to the back of the room. Her eyes were barren. Her hair had died.

"We should've never come here," she murmured.

"No, Kerri, you said we had to come, and you were right. We gotta stop him from gassing Blyton Hills, remember?"

"We should've never come to Blyton Hills."

"We had to come."

"We didn't! I was better out there!"

"None of us were better out there; we were a disaster!"

"I was safe!" Kerri yelled, yielding to tears. "I was better on my own, three thousand miles from here, and you dragged me here again to die!"

"What? That's not true!"

"This is your fucking fault!"

"Kerri, I would never put you in harm's way; I love you!"

"You don't love me! If you loved me so much, why did you fucking leave in the first place?!"

Andy stopped halfway to her, the shock wave of those words almost blasting her off her feet. The anger in Kerri's eyes hurt to watch.

"If you loved me so much, why were you just waiting till you turned sixteen to grab a backpack and leave?! Shit, you could've come to Portland with me! We could've been together! But you just hopped on a train to nowhere to be the lone rider and you left me alone! *(Voice shattering.)* I was terrified! My life was spiraling out of control! I needed you, for fuck's sake, I needed you then! And I had to wait for your fucking postcards from Alaska whenever you remembered I exist!"

She bent, exhausted, vocal cords burning, brushing her lifeless hair apart.

"You don't love me. You left me."

She sobbed like a gentle rain after the storm. She retreated back to her corner and slid down to the floor.

"You hate me," the rain said.

Unremarkably, the universe had once again vanished. Not outside that room, Andy realized, but including the room. A green glowstick, Kerri, and herself. That was the total inventory of the cosmos.

And it was disintegrating. She could feel it in her gut— her soul withering and crumbling into space dust.

Kerri was crying from the debris of her own cataclysm, stranded, light-years away, and she was trapped on her own planet, prehistorically overwhelmed, unable to reach. Andy looked into herself, fathoming the void, searching for something to hold on to. Something to evolve from. Something that could grow, one single seed.

"I was afraid."

She said.

"I was afraid to talk to you. To share what I felt. I thought that if you knew, if I poured my heart out for you, you wouldn't be able to handle it, it would scare you away. 'Cause it scared me."

She gazed up, into the lonely crying star.

"So I did the easy thing. I left because I would always know where to find you. I ran away to get my shit together, and I thought about you every single day. You were my last thought before I closed my eyes and your name was—is!—it's the first word on my mouth when I stir up, but I couldn't woman up and tell you. So I just kept it to myself, and whenever it hurt too much all I had to do was dial your number and hear your voice, and I'd feel better. And it never, ever crossed my mind that you would be needing me. *(Tearswipe.)* I was selfish. I was a coward. I am sorry."

She was kneeling down to Kerri now, her hand hovering near the orange planet by the neon-green light of Glowstick Nebula.

"Kerri, I'm so sorry I wasn't there for you. But I am here now."

Kerri's hair stirred, a once-fearful civilization gazing up to the sky with hope.

"And I'm getting you out of here."

Darkness dispelled.

Kerri looked around, smelled, listened.

"They're gone," she whispered.

Andy's sensors hummed back on. The room had returned. It was just dirt and bricks, but it was something to work with.

"The necromancer's got us, but he doesn't know yet," she said. "Don't speak up. We're nowhere we haven't been before."

"But last time Peter was here to get us out."

"I know."

"And Nate deserted us," Kerri sobbed.

"I know," Andy repeated through a grimace. That one hurt like someone fingering a fresh wound. "But Tim didn't."

"Oh, God, Tim," Kerri moaned, fighting the gloom off. "If something's happened to him . . ."

"Nah, he did pretty well up there. The monsters were within the walls, inside the brickwork, and Tim chased them back in. *(Points at a vent.)* He must still be inside."

"How is he going to find us?"

"He will," Andy said, as she fished out of her jeans the last treasure in her armory—the one thing she had found when the universe faded, the one thing she always held on to.

A plastic penguin.

She squeezed the little toy next to the vent, and the sound wave of a squeak rippled through the walls of the newly silent, carcass-ridden haunted house.

Parsecs away, under the Milky Way, firs watched the thin white scar of a rowboat in the middle of the lake.

PETER: Faster, Nate.

The lights on Deboën Isle were gone; the sighing of waves breaking onshore long lost.

"Don't think about it, just move. Fuck Andy and her stupid plan. *(Leaning forward, whispering.)* This was all a mistake, Nate. Their mistake. We should've never come back."

Nate canvassed the horizon. The jagged line of trees

could be made out against the sky in any direction, though in one direction stars were yielding ground to wind-riding rain clouds. No shore seemed nearer than any other. Nate realized he wasn't sure he'd been sailing in a straight line after all.

As soon as he'd started rowing, his arms had kindly pointed out that, in the last eighteen hours, they had descended a mineshaft, gone spelunking, climbed back up, trekked, run, and fought a horde of carnivorous underworld fiends. Rowing didn't seem so taxing when Andy was doing it, but that was two days ago and, as Nate's arms patiently reminded him, he was no Andy. The straw that breaks the camel's back always looks light enough, until it lands.

He squinted back at the isle, camouflaged against the storm. He checked the stars. Four or five of those stupid tiny glowworms should form Ursa Minor; he should know which. Kerri would know which.

"What, are you waiting for a signal or something?" Peter said. "Oh, wait. Here comes one."

Nate returned his attention to the surface. He didn't feel it, but the moonlight showed ripples on the still water. Coming from the storm's direction.

Damn high ripples under his watercraft.

The boat rocked gently once, violently twice, and then a wave nearly flipped it over, sending the sailor overboard.

Darkness, and then cold—in that order—stung every pore in his skin.

He frantically swam up to the surface, too scared to even stare into the depth of the second-deepest blackest lake in the Americas.

"Here, let me help."

He grabbed Peter's bloated white hand, and Peter smiled back from the boat, worms crawling out the corners of his smile.

Every fir in the county heard Nate's scream.

"Kidding!" Peter said, laughing, a beautiful punchable white grin across his face. "Sorry! Come on, Nate, it was a joke! Hurry up, or you're gonna die in there."

He smiled a rascally apology, offering a hand over the bulwark—a clean, strong hand that Nate refused to take.

"I'm sorry, man. I couldn't resist. Come on. We need to get out of here."

Nate, blood and gore washed from his face, stayed in the water, barely afloat, completely ignoring his body's cries of pain, staring at Peter from this new perspective.

When he finally climbed back on the boat and sat across from Peter, wet clothes stuck to his skin, wounds too cold to bleed any longer, something had changed.

Peter retrieved the oars that had fallen overboard and handed them to him. Nate didn't take those either. That had been the last straw indeed. As light as they come.

NATE: Why would you do that?

PETER: *(Confused.)* Do what?

NATE: Help me. Why would you even want me to escape?

PETER: *(Frowns, puzzled, then shrugs.)*

NATE: If you are a smear in my heart, if you are a piece of Deboën left inside me, haunting me in the shape of my dead friend . . . why would you let me go now? You wanted me in that house. You wrote messages inviting us.

PETER: *(Genuinely nonplussed.)* I don't follow you. *(Then challenging.)* I thought I was a manifestation of your subconscious.

NATE: Yes. Either you are my subconscious and you want me out of here because you're scared—which means I'm scared, but I should be braver than you—or you're truly an avatar of Deboën and you don't want us here anymore . . . because we can actually beat you.

PETER: *(Blank.)*

NATE: In either case, you're a coward, and I should go back.

A gentle thunder unexpectedly switched sides and rumbled triumphantly for Nate as he snatched the oars from Peter's hands and forced his arms to start rowing again—back to Deboën Isle.

Peter sat as powerless as an overwhelmed female character in a Victorian drama.

"How . . ." he began, amusingly astonished. "How the fuck did we go from me scaring you shitless to me being a coward?"

"Logic," Nate puffed. "You keep mocking Andy, but you were never that smart yourself, Pete."

"Oh, so I'm Pete now. Very logical. So one minute I'm Peter, the next I'm some evil spirit, the next I'm your subconscious voicing your inner mind, registering side details and bringing them to your att—ooh, what's that red thing over there?"

Nate turned, expecting literally anything. There was a red buoy dozing on the water, some sixty yards to starboard. It was probably the same one Andy had spotted two days ago; they'd seen it through Kerri's binoculars.

He could see the landmass of the isle now, much closer. The buoy was way off his path. He checked Peter.

PETER: *(Shrugging.)* What?

Nate nodded and forced himself to veer.

"What?" Peter cried. "We ain't going to the isle anymore?"

There was something about rowing for the buoy that reminded Nate of approaching that one mental patient even the other inmates avoided. The nearer one got, the crazier he seemed, just like a weather buoy standing under the rain in the middle of the Atlantic, determined to announce to the world that there was something worth signaling there, although logic dictated that most likely there wasn't. Nonetheless, in his experience, Nate had noticed crazy people have a way of being right.

Some grueling minutes later, the boat bumped gently into the buoy and Nate put his hand on the hard plastic surface. He felt strangely good upon thinking he was the first person to touch it in years, to give it that level of attention.

When it bobbed, he noticed the marking spray-painted on the side.

He searched his pockets for the flashlight he'd lost long ago. He couldn't make out any rocks or reefs in the water anyway. He moved the boat around and saw the complete monogram. He knew the book it had come from.

A rope hung from the upper tip of the buoy, sinking underwater. Nate took it in his hands—it felt viscous and sticky—and fished out a lidded jar.

"Want me to open that for you?" Peter offered.

Nate opened it himself. The inside was perfectly dry.

An interested moon seemed to peek over his shoulder, lighting the scene; and yet, it had just begun to drizzle.

He tipped the jar over. Rice poured onto his left palm, padding for the soft, prickly object that fell right after.

He'd seen one like this before—a nest made of twigs and straws, pressed into a rough ball. He unwrapped the nest and moonlight shone on what was hiding inside. Fortunately, its color almost blazed in the dark.

It always used to do that.

It was a flock of orange hair.

Two blank lines later, they were still sitting there.

Peter shook the daze out of his head.

"Okay, I think I speak on behalf of at least fifty percent of the people on this boat when I ask, What the fuck is going on?!"

Nate looked up at him, red herrings scampering away from his mind.

"How come you know Dr. Thewlis?"

"Who?"

"The dentist. This afternoon, in the car, you pointed out the town's dental clinic. When did you ever visit Dr. Thewlis?"

"I had a cavity. The last summer, before Andy arrived. He pulled my last baby tooth out."

"Did you keep it?"

"And leave it under my pillow—are you kidding? I was thirteen, Nate. Who knows where it is right now."

"I fucking know! It's wrapped in another nest, inside a

dying tree on that isle! We saw it—it was your baby tooth, Pete!"

(Frowning, touches his jaw.) "No shit! But why would Dr. Thewlis—"

"Dr. Thewlis threw it away! Someone took it. The same person who collected this from the barbershop where Uncle Emmet took Kerri every June to have her ends cut!"

(Meditating.) "Hmm. Yeah, that makes . . . no sense at all."

(Manning the oars.) "It will in a minute. Even to you."

The penguin called out once more, its squeak echoing through the hollow walls of Deboën Mansion.

"What if he's hurt?" Kerri wondered.

"He may be hurt, but he'll still come," Andy said. "Besides, the wheezers fear him more than they fear us. I guess they respect teeth and claws more than guns."

Kerri's hair suddenly inched off the wall. She stepped away and stared back at the bricks behind her. Andy pointed a fresh glowstick toward it.

She heard it clearly. Something scratching behind the bricks.

And yet she couldn't feel less afraid.

"Speak!" Kerri ordered.

The thing on the other side woofed.

"Out of the way," Andy bid, wielding the pickax.

It took her only a couple of minutes to dig a hole large enough for Tim to scurry through into Kerri's arms. A trifingered claw had carved a wound across his right flank, reaching from the ribcage to his hip. This was only the biggest of several over his whole body; blood trickled out of different spots where his fur had been bitten off. He was missing a large portion of his right ear. And he was sporting the proudest, bloodiest, happiest smile a dog could pull.

"Tim!" Kerri cried, trying to assess the damage as he clambered over and drooled on her, panting joyfully. "God, you're so brave! You are the bravest, smartest, toughest son of a bitch in the family! *(Kissing him back.)* Yeah, you are! You're such a good boy! Great, great boy!"

"Going back up this way is gonna be tricky," Andy ventured, inspecting the inside of the wall. "We should keep digging our way into the next room."

Tim scurried out of Kerri's grasp for a second to catch the plastic penguin in his mouth and allowed her to praise him some more. The next battle could come along whenever it pleased.

The isle was deserted. The motorboat was still moored as expected, but Nate had lost the rope when he fell off the rowboat, so he beached the dingy watercraft on the shore where they had landed two days ago. The mud there now showed a bedlam of fresh, webbed footprints.

"Why are we here again?" Peter whispered.

"You don't need to whisper, Pete, I'm the only one listening to you."

He walked inland, but not toward the house, apparently asleep and nonchalant like it hadn't just hosted a skirmish of three and a dog against the army of an underworld evil god. Instead, he knelt in the underbrush and searched for the patch of land where Tim had first detected the line of sulfur. The moonlight was kindly cooperating. He soon noticed the dead weeds signaling the presence of chemicals. The line stretched to the cancerous tree they had seen two days ago, the one with the first monogram and the nest with the tooth inside. Peter. In the other direction, it seemed to lead toward the old willow with the second monogram and the marble grave at its foot. Deboën. The third monogram they had discovered between those two, farther south, on a tree stump. The fourth was on the buoy. Kerri.

By that time he had reckoned there would be a fifth on one of the rocks off the west shore, between the cancerous tree and the buoy, but he didn't need to take the boat again. He checked the stump first.

It had been a fir, taken down by lightning or wind decades ago. The trunk section remaining was some four feet tall, laureate with a crown of promising, tender green sprouts. Moss was blotching out half the red monogram. There were no cracks or folds in the bark big enough to hide any treasure.

Nate knelt down, delved his hands in the moist earth, and started digging.

He scratched solid rock pretty soon, but a familiar prickly sensation came first. He felt aware of both Peter and the moon around him holding their breaths as he unearthed a new spherical nest.

He unwrapped it, trying to make out the elongated, soft object that at first he failed to identify.

It helped when Peter yucked away; then he understood.

It was a used tampon.

"Mother—" *(Stands up, facing the house.)* "—fucker!"

"What?" Peter begged, at a loss.

"He played us, again!" Nate yelled, battling fear and anger and humiliation. "It wasn't the pentacle in the attic that counted, the pentacle is the whole island! This is the pentacle!" he said, pointing at the monogram and the lines of sulfur that stretched across the fir-plagued landspit. "We formed the pentacle!" He showed the open nest in his hand. "He set us up!"

"Okay . . ." Peter began, sure to imply how little okay everything was. "But . . . I mean, how did he do it? He died in 'forty-nine; this stuff had to be laid before we came to the island and brought him back. Who collected all this trash in 'seventy-seven and put it here?"

Nate gazed up at the attic, then at the woods, around the spot where he'd landed from the second floor.

"Help me find my rifle and we'll find out in a minute," he grunted, his inner battle almost decided in favor of anger.

Andy kicked away the last of the crumbling brickwork and stepped over the debris into the thick, gossamer darkness, panting, ready to switch her pickax from tool mode to impaling device in a second. Tim followed, his bigger slash wound patched up with Kerri's shirt wrapped around his body, proudly bearing a glowstick in his mouth.

"Clear," she reported back at the dungeon.

Kerri crawled out, loaded rifle in hand, calling the torchbearer not to stray off. The new room was low, deep,

352 | EDGAR CANTERO

yet broken into narrow corridors by shelves or racks ranked across. A twisted intuition told her it wasn't wine bottles in those racks.

She stepped back, disturbing a rotten casket, and its contents rattled inside.

"Jesus. These are . . ."

"Catacombs," Andy completed. And she watched Tim gleefully pacing by, oblivious to his neon-green halo panning over the sordid rows of stacked coffins piled together, bloated by dampness, cracked open, occasionally toppled onto each other, offering glimpses of leg bones jutting from under unfitting lids and skeletons poured onto their neighbors, smiling in embarrassment.

"But catacombs . . . how?" Andy reasoned. "The house was built by the Deboëns, and for all we know it was always one guy for a hundred years. Who are these people?"

"These are no catacombs," Kerri answered. "It's a warehouse. This is a necromancer's storage room."

She knelt down, with Tim dutifully approaching to assist her, torn cobwebs dangling from his nose. Small labels were glued to the niches and the caskets, handwritten. The first one she checked read "Hutchinson," followed by a numerical reference. Another one read "S. Orne." A third one read "Hyppachias."

Andy located a candelabrum and scratched a match to light it, then remembered she had forgotten to check the oxygen levels. They seemed passable.

"So Nate was right," she said. "Deboën stole these bodies from their burial sites, distilled the salts from them, raised the avatars from the salts, and tortured them for knowledge. And this is where he kept the bodies."

"His personal library," Kerri capped. "This is where the dead end up."

Andy winced at the snap of two ideas clicking together like a fractured bone being set. "Where the dead end," she revised.

She rummaged her pockets, fingers ignoring the ton of annoyingly useful things like ammunition and matches, until she touched the bundle of papers crumpled in the deepest strata of her inventory, then fished out and unfolded an almost forgotten piece of paper. Kerri fingersnapped for the light to approach.

"This is what we found on the dead guy in the mines."

"Simon Jaffa. Who happened to be Mr. Wickley's lawyer."

"And who was carrying a fake ID from RH Corp."

"And also this map, which looks hand-copied from the blueprints at the city hall. And look at the words here: 'Deboën shaft,' 'Where,' 'Dead end.' This is a single sentence. This room is where the dead end. This is a map to this room; Jaffa was trying to come here through the mines."

"But what was he hoping to find?"

"'Deboën Shaft Where Dead End. From W, S-5, E-2, bottom.'" She scoped out the area, then laid out a hand to Kerri. "Compass?"

Kerri pulled out her Colonel Mustard instrument, consulted it, needle wobbling giddily at first in a *Did I hear some heavy action sequences earlier?* fashion, and pointed west.

All three strode to that end of the room, then turned on their feet and clacked their heels.

"Now from here, south five," Andy instructed.

They walked to the right, counting the gaps between the shelves, up to the fifth. Blind rats scuttled away from the torchbearer.

"East two."

They walked to the second rack of coffins on the right. "Bottom."

They crouched and dragged an unbelievably heavy stone coffin into view. The label on its side came loose and fluttered to the floor. It read "Capt. D. Deboën, 1849."

"That's the year Deboën arrived in Blyton Hills," Kerri recalled.

Andy pushed the lid off the casket, convinced that there was no skeleton to disturb. For one thing, bones couldn't possibly be that heavy. Tim hovered the neon-green light over some neatly piled bricks. Then he checked with Andy, equally disappointed.

"Okay, that was anticlimactic," she said.

"Not really," Kerri pointed out, hovering the candelabrum over the coffin. Without the green tinge of the glowstick, the bricks showed their true color. "These are gold ingots."

Andy picked one up. Her second hand came swiftly in assistance of the first, surprised at its density.

"These are . . . ? How much is this worth?"

"What you're holding in your hands right now?" Kerri said, fighting a chortle. "About the GDP per capita of Monaco."

"What?! Holy shit!"

She went through her pockets again, excited, this time planning to do some rearrangements.

"I can carry one; can you carry another?"

"Are you for real?" Kerri smiled. "I thought we were

here to stop an apocalypse."

"Yeah, but shit, look!" She didn't even need the lights; her smile was blazing, daring the dark. "We found pirate treasure! And it's real! I mean, it's not like that Redbeard's plunder of stolen jewelry we found! This is the real thing!"

"Shh! Keep your voice down!" Kerri giggled.

"I know, but come on! Oh, shit! I told you! I told you this is the only thing I'm good at!" She shook her head, tried to curse the adrenaline out of her system. Tim attempted to fit one of the bars into his mouth, but it immediately proved too much for his jaw. "This is . . ."

She turned, searching for an adjective, but got distracted by the way Kerri was looking at her.

"It's awesome," she settled with.

"Yeah."

TIM: *(Gazes queryingly at the girls in a close shot for padding.)*

"I really liked your postcards from Alaska," Kerri said. "And the late-night calls."

"Good," Andy puffed, tossing the ingot back into the coffin. "I really wanted to write more; I just . . . I never knew how to say things. I can't write to save my life."

"They were very nice postcards."

"Right. Well, I promise I'll write you something better one day. A great love letter like—"

Floorboards squeaked once more as shoes stepped over the mangled dead creature at the foot of the stairs where the carpet lay coiled up in a gored mess. The haunted house foyer gazed down at the cloaked figure coming downstairs to inspect the collateral damage.

Nate and Peter, crouching in a dark spot behind a sofa, waited for him to step into the living room.

NATE: Shh.

PETER: *(Surprised.)* Why the fuck do you tell me to *shh* for, asshole?!

"Andy?" Kerri tipped her shoulder. "Andy, you just stopped in midsentence."

Andy blinked back to reality. She checked Kerri's legs. "You were wearing those pants yesterday."

"Uh . . . yeah. I only brought two pairs, and I've kinda outgrown my old bell-bottoms."

"Peter's love letter. You put it in your back pocket yesterday when Nate barged in on us."

Kerri frowned, checked her derriere. "Damn. It must be all crumpled."

"Show me," Andy ordered, while she checked her own pockets once more.

PETER: Brilliant plan, Nate.

Nate gripped his rifle, ears ignoring the voice beside him and waiting for incoming footsteps, knees ready to catapult him out into the light at the right moment.

PETER: I mean, yeah, let's just shoot the guy. He's lived for like a hundred and fifty years, but surely no one thought of this before.

Floorboards sulkily greeted the host into the living room. Nate risked leaning out and taking a peek.

The cloaked figure stood by the phonograph, inspecting the lounge area where the kids had been chilling out. The candles were still burning, the area unscathed from the battle.

Nate observed him bending near the sofa and picking up a book. The Vampire Sorority series.

The necromancer flipped it open, his impressions mercifully concealed.

Nate jumped in frame and pointed the rifle at him.

"Freeze!"

The figure obeyed. In fact, he didn't even bother to flinch. He just stood still, book in hand, awaiting further orders.

Nate was standing five feet from him. Good thing, because he wouldn't miss the shot, regardless of how spectacularly the gun was trembling in his hands.

"Take off your hood!" he ordered, not caring about sounding scared. It felt good. He felt scarier when scared. "Show your face!"

The villain dropped the book and slowly turned to face him. Nate gritted his teeth, trying to make out the visage under the cloak.

"What's wrong?"

"I just have a bad feeling," Andy explained, laying the letter on the floor, and then, on the right side, flattening the last thing she'd fished out of her pockets.

Kerri leaned closer, and so did Tim.

"Hood!" Nate cried, the tip of his weapon inches away from the necromancer's head.

The necromancer raised his hands, letting Nate notice his big, bone-white fingers, and grabbed the rim of his hood.

The neon-green light in Tim's mouth adumbrated the long, beautifully penned letter headed by the words "Dear Kerri" on one side and the short missive "Good-bye" on the other.

Andy was about to ask, "Do you see any similarities?" but she needed only to read the transformation in Kerri's eyes.

All the Dixie cup skin, Sahara lips, *Titanic* eyes, despair look in the world could not begin to masquerade his face. *Peter Manner, 26 (24 of which alive), his tall, powerful frame clad in shapeless black, stares back at Nate from the wrong end of an assault rifle.*

Nate's hands stopped trembling. His muscles stopped aching. His mind stopped working.

All he could do was turn to his right for an answer.

And his own Peter—the one with perfect hair, in a letter jacket and jeans, standing right next to him, seemingly as amazed as he was—simply stood jaw-dropped for a minute and then acknowledged:

"Okay, this is awkward."

Andy pickaxed the lock off the necrotheque door. It didn't resist.

She checked Tim for approval: he seemed perfectly ready to leave their stronghold. She pushed the door, and the dog, glowstick in mouth, beaconed the way along an arched gallery.

"It can't be," Kerri objected, joining her as she stepped into the new tunnel, which curved off constantly to the right and climbed a step upward every few yards. "It can't be him, Andy; Peter is dead."

"Really? How do you know?"

"Because I know. Fuck, everybody knows; it was on the news!"

"Teen sleuths unmasking the Sleepy Lake creature was in the news too," she mumbled resentfully, hurrying up the steps with the candelabrum in hand, like a distressed countess from a Walpole novel.

"But he died! He overdosed in his house in Hollywood; he was buried in L.A."

"And you were at the funeral?" Andy challenged her.

"No, but . . . Christ, he was a celebrity! It's like discussing whether Elvis is dead!"

"I'm beginning to question that too," she said as they walked into the glowstick's light-pool again. Tim was waiting for them to open the next closed door. Andy raised her pickax, then hesitated and tried the handle.

Tim led the troops in once more, highlighting the terra incognita. The chamber he mapped was circular, without any furniture. Candle stubs were wax-welded to the rock floor, arranged in a circle and connected by broken lines of bright red. Andy checked the candlewicks: cold as fossils.

"This kind of scene is getting old," she said, crossing the room for the next door ahead. "Don't waste your time—I doubt we'll work out the details of a death in Hollywood while trapped under a house on an isle in a lake in Oregon."

The next cave seemed to be drilled through solid rock. There was no masonry or beams; the door they had stepped through was the only man-made feature in the long gallery, which extended both to the left and right. Tim unilaterally chose the path to the right, which incidentally went uphill. Andy just shrugged and followed.

"For the record, I think you're right," she told Kerri. "Peter is dead. But that doesn't change anything."

"What do you mean?" Kerri panted behind her.

"Well, we've learned there are gray areas between life and death. Maybe it isn't Peter writing the notes. It could be an avatar."

The cavern seemed to follow a symbolically spiraling

path. Water dripped from invisible crannies. Thick, bulbous tree roots now poked through and slithered down the walls.

The final stretch of the slope met the ceiling. The stone above was suspiciously flat.

"I think I know where we are," Andy said.

"Who would raise Peter's avatar, and why?" Kerri insisted, watching Andy trace the edges of the slab above them. "Deboën wants us dead; why would he go and resurrect the one of us who died?"

"Yeah, you're right," Andy said, pausing for a second before going on to inspect the carved rock columns that seemed to support the ceiling. "Unless it's Deboën's avatar using Peter's body." The candlelight was now outlining the links of a heavy chain and gears fixed to the rock. "Maybe that's what happens if we die—the part of Deboën inside us would take control."

"Yeah, sure," Kerri said, defeated. "It's magic, so who cares how it works."

(Touching every part of the mechanics.) "Gee, Kerri, I wish this were closer to your area of expertise too, but we're fighting lake creatures and a necromancer, so common science is not going to help us much and *how the fuck does this secret door open?!*"

Kerri snatched the pickax from Andy and struck a brick jutting out from under a column in a corner. The brick smashed to dust, the column descended, gears rattled, and the marble slab above them slid back before Andy's eyes.

Kerri pointed at the different pieces of the puzzle.

"Door, rails, cogs, counterweight, wedge. *(Embracing all with a gesture.)* Physics."

ANDY: *(Smirking, foolproven.)* You enjoy this, don't you?

KERRI: Being trapped with you in dark miserable caves? I can think of worse things.

They climbed out of Deboën's grave to cold, clean air inside the vault of the willow tree.

Andy pushed aside the curtain of drooping branches and met a full moon and gentle rain. Kerri took the glowstick from Tim before allowing him to explore the isle again.

"Okay, so this answers the question of how they sneak in and out of the house with the front door chained," Kerri explained, glancing at the open tomb and the spiral cavern they had just ascended. "I bet you the other end of this cave flows into the basement. Or even the mines."

Andy shushed her, then pointed up. The mansion slept peacefully, a round cat eye shining yellow atop.

"He's still bunkered up there," Andy said, glaring at the attic window, and then she checked herself. She had lost much of her gear, considerable ammo, one man of the team, their two-way radio (which Nate happened to carry), and about 40 percent off her health bar, judging by the bleeding cuts all over her arms. And she was back at square one, standing in front of the mansion, armed with a shotgun and a pickax.

An icy lake breeze took the opportunity to remind her she'd also lost her jacket somewhere during the skirmish, raising goose bumps on her neck.

"Okay, look . . . uh . . . maybe . . ."

She had no trouble finding the words—they weren't

difficult ones. It was just that they caused her physical pain to utter.

"Maybe . . . we should just wait for someone else to take care of this. I . . . I mean, we barely got out of there alive, and we're right back where we started. *(Checks her Coca-Cola watch.)* Copperseed and Joey must've evacked the town by now. Maybe Al and the cavalry are on their way. We can just take the motorboat, find Nate, and wait on the mainland. Right?" Her own ears couldn't believe what her mouth was babbling. "I mean . . . it's not our fight. We're just a summer detective club. Let's go home."

Kerri, rain-freckled, replied, "I don't think that's an option anymore."

Andy followed her line of sight to the nearest shore. For a second she feared (and felt her heart clenching, anticipating the blow) that Joey's motorboat would be gone. It was still there. But not far from it, the rowboat was beached there too. The rowboat Nate was supposed to have escaped in.

Tim came back from reconnaissance, looked expectantly at the team leader.

"Nate's inside," Andy muttered.

All three gazed up at the house, black and huge and pointy like the back of a sleeping dragon.

ANDY: Okay, listen, new plan. We go in, bust the attic door, take Nate—

KERRI: That's exactly what he's expecting us to do, and we can't be sure that Nate's up there anyway.

ANDY: Right. Okay, so we cut his oxygen supply. We connect the duct pipes there to the motorboat's exhaust and we gas the fucker!

KERRI: Not enough pipe, and if Nate is in there, we just killed him.

ANDY: Right. What if we lure him out and set a trap like last time? We build a Lake Creature Phony Express!

KERRI: You expect a hundred-fifty-year-old necromancer to pull open a fake door in his own house, roll down two flights of stairs on a serving cart, and land in a fishing net? Also, no cart and no net.

ANDY: True. *(Thinks, then to Tim.)* Feel free to jump in any time.

TIM: *(Tilts his head, resenting the pressure.)*

ANDY: Okay, wait, I got it. We go in the way Tim came to us in the dungeon—inside the walls. We can just follow the duct pipes to the attic and reassess. If Nate's there, we rescue him; if the necromancer is, we catch him by surprise.

Kerri figuratively sat on it for a minute.

ANDY: I don't need to hear it's a good plan, just tell me it ain't the worst thing you heard me say.

KERRI: Actually, "ain't" is the worst thing I heard you say.

ANDY: Good enough. But first, let's plan our escape route. And we need to pack.

The packing bit was arduous but relatively quick: it involved taking a gold ingot each and hiding it inside the glove compartment in Joey's motorboat. Andy decided to take a second one, for Nate's sake, and then Kerri pushed herself to carry two as well, for Tim's. In the end, they had carried up the spiral cavern about 1,800 ounces, but as Andy put it, any man could carry that.

They inventoried their equipment next. Considerable ammo had vanished along with Andy's jacket. She kept a pocketful of loose matches, a couple glowsticks, a dozen shells, Uncle Emmet's shotgun, a plastic penguin, and Pierce. Pierce was the name she had just given to the pickax, the tool-slash-accessory-slash–slasher weapon that had become her dearest item in their arsenal. Kerri carried her assault rifle and her knife. Tim held a dying glowstick and looked fairly concerned about the amount of wound-licking he had pending.

After that, they charted out the rest of the underground tunnel system, going back through Deboën's grave and following the rest of the spiral cavern, past the door to the circular chamber and the necrotheque. As expected, it ended at another door opening into the lower basement, next to the hatch through which they had emerged from the mines the previous afternoon. The bookcases they had dumped over the hatch had been bashed away from the inside. Tim, chest wrapped in Kerri's blood-smeared checkered shirt, inspected the area and seemed to corroborate that wheezers had surged up that way, and retreated down later.

From that point, Kerri had no trouble finding their way back upstairs, as they did before. Some sixty seconds later, the three of them resurfaced through the door under the main stairs, inside Deboën Mansion.

The house, at that point, shuddered lightly—not an earthquake so much as a passing subway, a slow double-bass note that hardly rocked the frames on the wall. Tim raised his one whole ear and let go a most embarrassed whine.

"I missed you too," Andy told the mansion when the tremor subsided.

From there on, Kerri had to tut Tim away from the decomposing carcasses, starting with the pair at the foot of the stairs. The smell, as they stealth-walked up to the second floor, was something not even the language of the mole people under Manhattan would have words for.

The ruinscape in the corridor upstairs was worthy of post-Godzilla Tokyo. By then, even Tim avoided lowering his snout as they squelched through the trapdoor room and into the oxygen tank storage. The battlefield there was literally flooded in a quarter inch of black jelly, polka-dotted with islands of scaly bodies shining like rotten fish under the moonlight.

Go dark now, Andy mimed to the team, switching off her flashlight. Kerri nodded and clutched her rifle firmly. Tim led the way toward one of the gaping holes and into the narrow passageway between the walls.

Even he had trouble negotiating the corners; the girls were forced to sidestep. They didn't take any wrong turns before Tim spotted the flex-duct conducting the oxygen that was to be their white rabbit. They encountered further challenges climbing up to the third floor, especially with Tim, but the Weimaraner didn't even whimper when Andy had to pull him up by the collar. Even the dog had a gut feeling that some very old open business was about to be closed.

Around the final corner, some light sifted through a few accidental peepholes in the woodwork. Kerri was surprised to realize it was electric light. Which, together with a new, peculiar smell in the air, made her raise a suspicious eyebrow.

"I can see Nate," Andy whispered.

The sound of footsteps hushed them down. Slow, heavy, alert footsteps.

Kerri needed only to touch an atom on Tim's head to make him repress a growl. Andy peeked through the smallest woodworm hole in the wall.

A cloaked figure was roaming around the attic. He had stopped idly by the alchemist workbench, gazing over the pots and urns out the southward window, where night was inappreciably beginning to dissipate: a teaspoon of predawn dissolved in a black ocean.

He walked another three steps to his left and fronted Nate. Their faces were obscured; Andy could make out that Nate was standing against a wooden beam and he neither moved nor uttered a sound. The necromancer had his hood up. He contemplated Nate, hands behind his back, with the curiosity of a visitor in a museum.

He then turned around and looked at her.

He stayed in that spot, for almost a minute, contemplating the blank wall in front of him like it was a mural.

He walked closer, examining a detail, stopping one step short of the woodwork.

He raised an inquisitive hand.

He breathed out.

He staggered back as Andy crashed through the wall, pickax in her left hand, shotgun in her right, a Mongolian city-raider cry out of her mouth summoning her redheaded and gray-furred sidekicks to battle. The entrance was so spectacularly off the Rodriguez scale, the necromancer literally fell on his ass.

When he started to rise, his hood cast back, the face beneath made the space-time continuum glitch.

Kerri lowered or dropped her gun, stunned, her heart dried up and crumbling to ashes at the sight of the lunar pallor, the Death Valley skin, the absolute surrender in Peter Manner's eyes.

"Oh my God."

Andy had barely a tenth of a second to acknowledge Nate in the middle of the room, comprehending he was not standing against a beam, but tied to it and gagged.

Then time resumed and Peter, disrespecting the dramatic pause he had conjured himself, sprang forward and slapped the shotgun barrel away from his face. Andy swung the shotgun back at him, but Peter hit her arm and she lost her grip on the weapon.

Kerri could do nothing but watch as Tim barked himself sore and Andy and Peter engaged in hand-to-hand combat, his hands vipering to clutch her wrists, her arms fending off six hits a second before she remembered her other limbs and kicked Peter's knee, snapping the bone and gaining a microwindow to grip the pickax and try to drive it into the enemy's heart.

KERRI: No, Andy, NO!!

On his knees, Peter raised his arms, caught her wrists and twisted them sharply, and Andy spun in the air and landed on her feet and took Peter for a spin to the floor and rose a second before he did. She juggled the pickax to her left hand and stepped on his thigh and swung it in an uppercut, and Peter blocked her left with his right and his left on the handle, stopping the point of the pickax an inch from his liver.

And the next second had them still locked in that position, forces equal, contenders' arms trembling under the torque in their muscles.

"Andy, stop!" Kerri begged, barely keeping Tim from jumping onto the cloaked man and tearing him apart. "It's him! It's Peter!"

ANDY: Peter died in Hollywood! He wouldn't be doing this!

KERRI: Andy, don't kill him!

Peter's eyes shifted to Kerri. Despite the strenuous tension and the gritted teeth, despite putting everything he had into that fight, his countenance had been that of total defeat from the very beginning.

KERRI: Peter, what did you want to tell me on the phone?

ANDY: Kerri, it's not him!

KERRI: Pete, tell me, please!

ANDY: I gotta kill him!

KERRI: Don't kill him!!

Tim was barking beyond his pain threshold. Andy sought the tiebreak vote.

ANDY: Nate!

NATE: *(Muffled shout.)*

ANDY: Do I kill him or not?!

KERRI: No! Pete, what did you wanna tell me on the phone?!

ANDY: Nate! One stomp he lives, two stomps he dies!

KERRI: Pete, speak! Say something!

Peter, with all of his strength channeled to deadlock Andy's, but his hazel eyes anchored to Kerri's, mouthed only two words.

Nate stomped the floor once.

I'm. Sorry.

And twice.

Then Andy headbutted Peter, kicked his arm out of the way, and embedded Pierce under his sternum.

The body entangled in black robes fell to the floor, on the faded lines of the ancient pentacle.

Kerri covered her mouth to block a sob so brutal it would have destroyed her throat on its way out.

Andy exhaled, and so much of her was lost in that breath that her legs quivered and she fell to the floor and her left hand dropped the pickax and her eyes burned with the pain of what she had done.

Tim, the only one trying to understand what had actually happened, trotted out to sniff the body.

A minute of silence was cut short by Nate's muffled screams.

Andy tried to pull herself up and failed. She tried again, tears blurring at the sight of Peter Manner dead on the floor. She staggered across the room and tore the gag off Nate's mouth.

Nate gulped in some air and returned it with his first words: "It wasn't him."

Andy was just realizing they had overlooked something big when Tim, his nose to the floor, homed in on the cupboard. The cupboard opened. Tim looked up and wagged his tail.

Dunia stepped out and stroked the dog's bloodied head, a curved sword in her other hand and the most peaceful expression on her face.

She scoped the room, checking the body on the floor, then Andy, then Kerri, then Nate, and she shrugged.

"Well. I won't say everything went exactly as I planned, but . . . close enough."

"Who are you?" Kerri asked.

"Dunia Morris?!" Andy answered.

"Oh, Deboën's fine," Dunia dismissed with a wave. "Whatever."

"It was her!" Nate shouted from his corner, still tied to the beam, red with anger and possibly near-suffocation, but mostly anger at the woman strutting around the room. "She brought us here! She needed us to come!"

"Yup. Guilty," she said, resting gracefully on the workbench.

"We are the pentacle! Not this one, the whole island— the four of us and her, we made the pentacle! She took our blood signatures thirteen years ago! The tooth was Peter's," he told Kerri. "And she had your hair too, from the barbershop! And Andy's blood! And I haven't been to the rocks, but I bet there's something of mine too!"

"Used gum and saliva," Dunia clarified. "Good thing you're good little campers and dispose of your trash properly. Mother Earth thanks you."

"But . . . What did she . . . Fuck, why?" Andy settled on.

Dunia drew her cigarette case from her leather pants, opened it, and produced a cherry lollipop. She put it in her mouth and shrugged coquettishly, grin-biting the stick.

"Because the ritual requires five," Nate narrated for her. "Like the glyphs at the bottom of the mines said: five priests to open the gate and release Thtaggoa. Only we weren't priests. She just stole samples from the four of us to form the pentacle and then she lured us to the isle! We weren't meddling kids; we were pawns. She probably caused the tremor that made our boat capsize, so we would be trapped here and be part of the ritual without us knowing."

Dunia leisurely paced the room, entertained by his rancor.

"You were bound to come," she said. "How could Blyton Hills' teen sleuths fail to visit the local haunted house?"

"And she would've gotten away with it," Nate resumed, "if I hadn't resurrected her father by mistake!"

Dunia stopped on her feet, wincing like the record had scratched.

"What?"

She eyed the gang as if trying to identify the smart one and despairing.

"God, okay. Sorry. My fault. Sometimes I forget I'm dealing with the Blyton Summer Detective Club, not the FBI."

"I read your spell book," Nate told her. "I raised his avatar and it used us!"

"No, you didn't," Dunia said with a scowl, at the same time that Tim began growling at the door.

"I did! I resurrected Deboën," Nate cried.

"Deboën wasn't dead!" she snarled. *"I am Damian Deboën!"*

Tim burst into riotous barks, oblivious to the mainstream focus of attention—the little owl-eyed woman parading among them.

"You . . . what?!" Kerri half-phrased.

"That's impossible," moaned Nate. "I brought Deboën back!"

"Please," Dunia droned. "Avatars and resurrection—not the same thing. Resurrection is impossible. Believe me. *(Pointing at Peter's corpse wrapped in black on the floor.)* That's the closest I ever got, and he was little more than a puppet."

NATE: But I saw your book. I read the spell!

DUNIA: Don't flatter yourself. You read my notes.

NATE: I saw smoke rising from an urn on that bench!

DUNIA: Said the kids who spent their childhood running from losers in costumes.

NATE: We have all the symptoms you listed: the nightmares, the bitterness, the feeling of being lost!

DUNIA: I just described any twenty-five-year-old ever, you self-centered twit! *(Gracefully turning, leaving Nate to shatter behind her back.)* I'm afraid the only evil that possessed you was Generation X. It's a shame, really, what youth has come to. When I was your age . . . *(Pause. She pops the candy out of her mouth, tastes her own lips, then retreats.)* Bah, forget it. You wouldn't even believe where I was when I was your age."

She drifted toward Andy, stroking the Weimaraner's

back en passant. He was still growling threats at the door. And the worse part was something was threatening back from the other side.

Nate, Kerri, and Andy stood wordless. Night was falling apart.

"The world has changed a lot," Dunia went on through a deep sigh. "But people are the same. A few keep pulling the wagon of progress while the rest just truck along. Always the same ignorant, pitchfork-wielding mob. Easily scared. Easily cheated. They started growing suspicious once, so I chose to leave and come back as my son. Oh, nothing noteworthy—it's been done before. But two decades later, they start harboring suspicions again—you'd almost think they're getting wiser. So I try the same trick with a flourish: I die and come back as my daughter, and voilà! Cheated again! They don't even know how easily you can do the switch today!"

She stopped in front of Andy, scanned her from bottom to top.

"You might be interested—ask your doctor."

Andy unexpectedly brought the shotgun between them, hardly restraining her trigger finger.

"I'm gonna give you something to ask your doctor about, bitch."

KERRI: NO! Andy, don't shoot!

Dunia put the lollipop back in her mouth and smiled, watching Andy scourging her brain for a valid reason not to open fire.

"Oxygen," Kerri cued. "The air in this room is saturated with oxygen. If you light a spark it could blow up."

Dunia yielded to a chortle.

ANDY: You're kidding.

KERRI: No. Oxygen is flammable. We can't shoot in here.

The chortle paved the way to frank, disrespectful laughter.

"Weee! Look how everything falls into place!" Dunia said, delighted at the infinite hatred under Andy's brow. "C'mon, you gotta see the humor in this!"

On a side note, the door came off its hinges and slammed on the floor.

Andy immediately switched targets and Kerri ran to pull Tim out of the horde's reach at the sight of an imprecise number of wheezers staggering in from the staircase.

But to everyone's surprise, they stopped. The lead one dropped onto four limbs right outside the doorway, its third pair writhing in the air like the forearms of a praying mantis. It hissed at Tim, the dog barking his heart out in hard-learned hate.

"There they are." Dunia smirked, swaying with her pirate cutlass. She walked idly toward the door as if to greet them, and the first one took a step forward and shrieked at her. Dunia looked on like she would at a yapping poodle.

"Interesting vermin, aren't they?" she remarked. "They'll try to eat you, but they don't actually need to eat. In fact, they don't even need to breathe. They've got these gas bladders or something they can fill with air and waltz in here. You'll see; they'll come in in a minute. *(To Kerri.)* You should write a paper on them."

Kerri was busy enough holding Tim back, just as Tim was holding the most daring of the creatures at bay.

"The first time I tried the ritual, in nineteen forty-nine," Dunia once-upon-a-timed, back to her easy-minded ambling, "I was young and reckless. I'd just found the way to the underground city after searching for it for like a hundred years; I had performed the proper steps down there, knocked on the door like the book says; everything was ready to wake up that sleepyhead from his millennial slumber. I knew the ritual called for five officiants, but I reckoned a well-versed expert like myself would be worth five amateurs, so I thought I could pull it off by myself." She scoffed, inviting some sympathy. "Boy, was I wrong! I failed to wake the big one up, but these pesky little buggers took over the house and nearly smothered me."

The amphibian section of her audience raised a liquid hiss at the mention.

"I lived, all right, but they'd almost destroyed my house; I would have to face some tough questions and it wasn't like I had many allies in town. So I decided it was time to change generations again and faked my own death in the fire."

"But they buried you," Kerri objected.

"They buried some charred corpse," Dunia brushed off. "If you nosed about my basement, you'll have perceived human samples is not something we suffer a scarcity of in this house. I had left the instructions in my will and dug my grave in advance. You've been inside; all I did was seal the entrance into the caverns: they dumped the body, threw a marble slab over it, and moved on—hurtfully swiftly, I must say. But whatever; dying is easy. The tricky part was to return as my daughter."

"You . . . killed your own daughter?" Andy asked.

Dunia stopped again in front of her and gave a disappointed moue.

"No," Kerri second-guessed. "You never had a daughter."

"Thank you," Dunia approved. "It was all a strategy to solve my image problem in town when I first became Daniel. My wife was a concession, and my daughter was a ruse."

"But someone must have seen the child," Nate complained.

"Oh, of course they saw an infant. My wife's daughter born out of wedlock, her oh-so-shameful scarlet letter. But hey, I had no trouble calling her mine! I pretended to mail her off to a boarding school as if she were my own blood! Luckily she actually died in infancy—those places are expensive."

"You supplanted a teenager?" Kerri asked, trying to navigate through all the other objections arising.

"Yes. I mean, you're what? Twenty-five? You could still look twenty-one with the right makeup. Considering my real age, taking thirty years off your skin is basic magic. So, yes: new gender, new age . . . People still detested the family name, but I needed my claim on my old property. Luckily, my gutless wife/mother had offed herself already. I had to live in the house on Owl Hill and the townsfolk were as friendly as ever, but at least they stayed away from here. And I could come and go as I pleased through the gold mine. So I just had to sit and find a way to circumvent that stupid five-officiant thing. And then in 'seventy-seven, because I'd been such a good girl for so many years, you came along"—she grinned, spreading her arms to kindly embrace them all—"the Blyton Summer Detective Club."

Andy awkwardly acknowledged the reference as she

finally untied Nate, side-eyeing the creatures that were gathering inside the doorway.

"Use the gun," she told Nate, giving him his rifle and switching to Pierce herself. "Just don't fire it."

"'Blyton Hills' heroes'!" Dunia quoted happily. "When you started building a name for yourselves, I knew you'd eventually visit my mansion. All I needed to do was start a rumor in the right circles. Rumors lure gold diggers like Wickley, and Wickley lured you. As soon as you arrived that summer I started arranging things. I got the jock's tooth from the dental clinic, your pretty red hair from the barbershop. *(Re: Andy and Nate.)* You two were a little more difficult, until you came to the lake and I swept your campsite while you were away. That was enough to build the isle-wide pentacle. All I had to do now was wait for you all to enter into it, which you did some days later . . . although I rocked your boat a little to persuade you."

"And so we became the other four officiants," Nate summed up, his knuckles white around a rifle gripped like a baseball bat.

"Nobody said that the participants had to be willing," Dunia argued through a shrug. "I mean, when the rules call for pentacles and incantations, you know they are going to be pretty flexible, don't you think?"

Andy swung the pickax at a skulking wheezer, making it recoil and sneer at her in a vicious teeth display.

"Wait, so . . . you were here in the mansion that night?" Kerri asked Dunia.

"Of course. I've got my safe room underground; maybe you've seen it. Oh, I didn't mean to harm you, really! It just happens that as soon as you go through the first motions in the ritual, Thtaggoa stirs in his sleep, the ground shakes, and these buffed-up gremlins crawl up and go all *Night of the Living Dead* on your posterior. So while you lot were yelling and running all over my house, and incidentally causing a hell of a mess, I was down there going through the ritual, and I would have gotten away with it if it weren't for that meddling kid Thomas Wickley!"

Andy and Kerri and Nate turned at the name, ignoring the knife-clawed needle-teethed hordes of hell.

"Who?!"

"Yes!" she said, feeling her indignation supported. "Can you believe it? That sad old jerk-off finally found the way to my treasury and walked right into the ritual while I was in the middle of the aklo—the most glorious moment! Of course he got scared—I've been told before I'm on the theatrical side when I summon. So he ran away upstairs and fell right into that Wile E. Coyote contraption you call a trap, but by then he had led the vermin to my safe room, and I had to escape through the mine, thus stepping out of the pentacle, and ... Basically that asshole ruined everything!"

A wheezer chose that exact moment to step forward and hiss in a particularly nasty way at the hostess, to which Dunia responded by swinging her sword at the provoker and decapitating it as cleanly as such a thing can be done. The severed head rolled to Kerri's feet, who instinctively kicked it away.

The headless body was still writhing on the floor as Dunia continued, now pointing the black-stained blade at the kids. "You'd think I could just start again, but noooo! Turns out once the ritual has started, it can only be finished or undone by the same five officiants! *(Falsetto.)* 'Ooh, look at me, I'm the Necronomicon, you must follow my rules!'" she mocked. "And by the time the creatures wormed back into their holes, your army friend and the sheriff were poking around on the isle, reporters were knocking on my door in Owl Hill, and soon after that summer was over. You kids left and didn't come back."

The next line she delivered in a serious, almost sympathetic smirk—the closest thing to respect the kids would get from her.

"Oh, but I knew you would come back. You'd seen too much to just turn your back on it. You couldn't just smile it off and pretend forever. You were broken. You had to come back."

Her eyes strayed for a moment to the dead human body on the floor.

"Of course I began to worry when this one killed himself, so I went to California and got him. I pulled him out of the grave. Did my best to make him pass for living. Fortunately, his death was the triggering event that set the rest of you in motion. Now, you are all here. I had him posing as the villain just to keep you off my back. He wrote the messages; I dictated them. Maybe I misjudged you there; you would have obeyed the messages like idiots thirteen years ago; not now. But whatever. You're here now. All four of you."

She saber-pointed at Nate, a wicked smile on her white face. "You scampered off a little too early." Then, at the girls: "Oh, but don't be hard on him. He came back. He tampered a little with my pentacle too, so I had Dead Pete apprehend him and fix the damage. All systems are go!"

Kerri, munching through the lengthy villain monologue, was only left to ask: "But . . . why? Why do you want some alien god to rise and end the world?"

Dunia paused, surprised, and carefully observed the question.

"Oh. Well, I don't know. Same reason you want to open a frog or split an atom. I just . . . *(Shrugging.)* Fuck, I just want to see it!"

She paced around them once more, intimately proud of the unskimped attention.

"There's not that many things I've got left to see in this world, you know? Shit, when you're writing fantasy erotica for a living, you're really scraping the bottom of the bucket list!"

"Well," Andy intervened, stepping forward, "let me help you put an end to your boredom."

In a lightning-fast movement she drove the pickax right at Dunia's neck, stopping it just short of puncturing the jugular. Dunia stood still, the cold steel point perched on her shoulder like a skeleton sparrow.

"For thirteen years I've been hiding from this," Andy uttered through gritted teeth, an opportune slash of hair darkening her face. "For thirteen years you haunted me. You ruined the better half of my life. But that's over. I'm going to beat you. I'm going to feed you to these goddamn things. And I'm going to see you dead once and for all before you have time to complete the fucking ritual."

Even the bad guys fell silent.

Dunia stayed in position, head held high, neck tendons inching away from the sharp instrument pointed at them, mouth closed tight, struggling to placate a mischievous smile.

ANDY: *(Understanding.)* You finished it already, didn't you?

DUNIA: *(Giving up, chuckling.)* Please! Why would I even be telling you all this otherwise?

A wheezer ruled that enough time had been wasted on uneventful dialogue and charged at Andy from behind. A shout from Kerri warned her to spin and duck, dodging an eviscerating slash, and then she blocked the other claw with her left as she dug her knee on the floor and struck upward with the pickax, nailing the point through the creature's chin and into the palate.

Two more jumped into the ring, Tim immediately catching one in midair and pounding it to the floor, Nate delaying the second's attack by batting its head with a Browning nine iron while Kerri jumped to the forefront to fend off the hissing peanut gallery still sitting it out and Andy rolled back onto her feet, struggled to yank the pickax out of the dead creature, finally pried it out, along with its head, just in time to swing at a fourth one coming out of nowhere.

The wheezer took the hit, staggered for a second, unharmed from the torn-off head corking the point of the tool, then shrieked into Andy's face. It was its last action before Kerri and Nate clubbed it at the same time, Tim going for its legs a second later to keep it occupied while Andy stepped on its shoulders, gripped the edges of its lower upper jaw, and twisted its neck.

"Whoa, look at that!" Dunia cheered, along with the rest of the wheezers still waiting by the door. "See? I told you they would get used to the atmosphere in no time! They can hold their breath long enough to disembowel you!"

"We need to get out of here!" Kerri urgently suggested.

"Good luck with that," Dunia intervened, inviting the kids to peer through the circular windows.

The night had dissolved into white. An Endeish Nothing had erased the lake and the firs and the sky.

"How long can you hold your breath?" Dunia challenged them. "Long enough to reach your car from here?"

"But you will die here too," Andy told her spitefully.

"Me? I already survived this situation once."

"I wasn't talking about the situation, bitch!" she retorted, as she swung the uncapped pickax at her face and Dunia leaped back, amused by the surprise attack. She raised her saber to block the pickax's comeback, tried to yank it from Andy's hand, failed, and then took advantage of her rival's weapon's unwieldy shortness to hack at her arm. Andy pulled back an inch shy of amputation, the pirate blade missing the bone and slashing cleanly through skin and muscle.

Andy threw out a cry of pain, and in the next breath she retaliated by jumping forward, swinging back vertically then horizontally one, two, three times, forcing Dunia to bend backward and spread her legs for balance, and then, suddenly channeling all of her pain-born energy into her right foot, Andy launched the Tsar Bomba of nutkicks into Dunia's leather-wrapped groin.

The hit lifted Dunia two feet off the ground.

She landed on all fours, saber still in hand, eyes wide open at the shock, then wider once the pain hit her neuroreceptors.

The room held its breath for a long while, all through that unconfirmed knockout, even after Dunia coughed out her surprise.

And then she scoffed.

"Aw, ffffuck!" she puffed through an astonished, astonishing laughter, her hand still shielding the offended area. "God, that was literally below the belt, you stupid cow! What the fuck was that about?!"

The kids remained silent while she caught her breath. Then they turned to Andy for the reply.

"Uh . . . I was hoping you'd still have your birth genitals."

Dunia laughed again while she brought herself back on her feet, color flushing back to her cheeks.

"Girl, you're so adorable," she said, having more difficulty speaking due to hilarity than fatigue or pain. "I do keep them. Remember the rumor about me being the son of a witch that was supposedly burned at Salem?"

She burst into laughter while the kids queried one another, the realization etching a new age line around their eyes.

"I told you it's been done before!" she hollered. "Boy, you should see your faces! Gets you every time!"

She laughed for another two seconds before Andy charged at her and she had to parry her off, then lunge back.

Andy stepped back to defend, at the same time checking her six o'clock to find several wheezers ready to jump in, and she rolled out of the way of the first one to let Dunia deal with it while she started to dig for gold on the second and Nate swung his rifle at the third and Kerri lost her rifle to the fourth and Tim dashed to her assistance while the rifle slid across the floor into Andy's hand, who stood up, flipped it in the air, butt-bashed the wheezer ahead and barrel-stabbed the one behind, and threw the firearm back to Kerri, shouting, "Catch!"

A new throng of slimy, eyeless maniacs avalanched onto the battlefield as Andy gripped Pierce, dove to the ground with a hand anchored on some writhing creature's face, and merry-go-rounded, slashing wheezers at three o'clock, twelve o'clock, nine o'clock, and finally Dunia at six, who blocked the pickax with her blade down, smiling with joy at the sight of an actual spark from the clashing metal that Andy and Dunia paused to follow throughout its microseconds life span, witnessing how it failed to set the room on fire, and then forgot about it as they engaged again, Andy striking blindly with Pierce, trying to knock Dunia off-balance, Dunia repelling the hits coming faster and faster and hoping for the gliding steel to trigger a new spark until she got tired of waiting and connected a surprise kick at Andy's nose, time dropping to slo-mo to appreciate the beautifully arcing wake of blood as she backflipped, then speeding up again as Nate dented the butt of his rifle against Dunia's face and took the opportunity to swing it back at the wheezer charging from behind, and in the same circular motion try to finish off Dunia by hammering the base of her neck, a blow Dunia dodged by rolling away and then using her sword to attempt a twirling moulinet counterattack to the heart that Nate's ribs barely shielded, forcing him to trip backward over a dead wheezer and allow the actually-not-so-dead body to clamber on him and try to bite his face off, which Tim forbade by leaping onto the creature's neck while Dunia somersaulted back to her feet in time to deflect Kerri's rifle swinging her way, only noticing too late that the rifle was a distraction for the knife slicing toward her jugular, forcing her to jump back and lose a heartbeat to recover her balance before ducking under the next blow as she directed her momentum to strike back at Kerri with an angry, vertical hack that the redhead parried with the stock of her rifle, then a slash from left to right that hewed the scalp off a passing wheezer, then finally a kick below the belt at which Kerri's outraged hair hollered in shame as she crashed into the workbench, her center of gravity on tilt for the crucial instant where Dunia advance-lunged to impale her through her stomach, their eyes locking in midair, Kerri's suddenly catching the alarm in Dunia's as she glanced down to notice she had planted her left foot too far ahead and that Andy, lying on the roadkill carpet, was driving Pierce right through Dunia's leather boot and the floorboards and into the second floor where Dunia's vintage blood dripped on the heads of the wheezers below turning their eyeless heads up and hallelujahing the red rain in a pitch that could not possibly eclipse Dunia's bestial, gut-born cry of pain threatening to blow off the ceiling.

Andy grabbed Kerri and kicked a wheezer off Tim and snatched Nate from a one-on-three skirmish, ordering retreat.

"To the walls! Quick!"

They clustered into the hole, Andy shoving the others first as she looked back at the melee in the center of the room. The last sight she ever caught of Dunia Deboën was a terrified black eye trapped in the middle of a nest of slashing, friendly-firing gray limbs, her voice muffled under the dozen creatures fighting for a bite of her flesh.

"You . . ." her little voice gasped. "It won't end like this! I swear, Andy Rodriguez, this has just begun!"

Andy slithered into the passageway after the others and tried not to listen to the bone-snapping sounds coming from the attic.

They emerged into the room with the oxygen tanks on the second floor, surprising a single stray creature that faced them and threw the proverbial massacre-promising hiss.

Andy and Nate backswung their firearms like hockey sticks before Kerri mentioned, "It's okay to shoot now."

The wheezer grunted a question mark as both flipped the weapons in their hands. The next second, two-thirds of its obliterated body were flying through the broken window in convenient snack-sized chunks for vultures.

Andy led the way through the hole to the next room and down the trapdoor slide. This allowed her to blast away two wheezers that were crawling up the ramp.

They landed softly onto the pile of coal and spine-dangling bodies in the basement.

ANDY: To the mines! We're going under the lake!

Buried alive under a living mass of sleazy, cold-skinned, frenzy-feeding hellspawn, suffocating under the corrupted air out of their dripping mouths, Dunia lay squirming on the floor, one leg and a torn, bleeding arm defending her vital organs while her other hand, lost amid the pandemonium, scurried blindly among webbed feet and dead bodies in the viscous dark, desperate for a last resource.

And then a brave fingertip reported back to the brain: the touch of ivory.

The scouting hand clutched the pommel of her cutlass and Dunia summoned from her heart, her gut, the house, the isle, and the unnameable powers the final burst of strength necessary to bring the sword home, slashing through every minion in the way. The pile exploded from its core, catapulting mauled, severed, intestine-kiting wheezers through the air as Dunia rose with an ecstatic, life-bearing scream, her sword swaying at lightning speed and splitting the very atoms of oxygen in front of her.

The ridiculously high number of wheezers still able for combat watched mutely and then shrieked in senseless, suicidal joy as Dunia knelt down to yank the pickax from her foot with an appetizing crunch of ground bones, raised her head, eyes devoid of pupils and glowing white, and snarled.

The handles of the pickax and the sword gasped in pain under her grip while she said through a psychotic shark smile: "Come and get it."

Andy and Kerri and Nate and Tim had stampeded through the lower basement and dove through the hatch to the mines when, as they were reaching the lower end of the winding staircase and facing the tunnel to the Allen stairs,

Kerri, carrying the only working flashlight, noticed the relatively improved lighting of the cavern.

And once facing the stairs, she needed only to formally peek down the crevice to find out the reason: what the last time had been a far, picturesque stream of red magma glowing at the bottom of the rift had grown into a river of yellow lava, flowing at whitewater speed not ninety feet below the lower ledge of the crack.

Tim leaned over the edge, saw the fire, unintentionally trod on the first blazing metal step, and yelped.

"Whoever is down there, I think Dunia really pissed him off," Kerri said.

The stair bridge, temperature aside, looked just like they had left it: no rails, no second-to-top step, quivering, clattering, dying of old age.

"You two first, over the sides," Andy instructed.

Nate took a deep sulfurous breath and placed his foot on the top step. Every bolt in the structure moaned for euthanasia as he transferred his weight. The thin sheet of iron under his feet and the beams supporting it were the only things separating him from a dip into the three-thousand-degree caldera. The idea that lingering up there for too long might roast him alive prompted him to leap across the gap onto the third step, and then hurry down the middle ones and skip over the last five. Kerri followed his steps, to the letter.

Andy lifted the dog in the air, careful to avoid putting pressure on the green-checkered bandages. Sixty-two pounds.

Tim whimpered increasingly on every other step that Andy leaped on, but fell silent as she just jumped off the middle of the stairs, too scared to even vocalize his impressions for the second it took them to land on solid rock.

"Nice!" Nate said admiringly while Kerri hurried to take the dog into her arms.

As another token of appreciation, a tiny nutcracker noise announced the secession of a large slab of volcanic rock from right under Andy's feet. Andy leaped from the falling rock and grabbed the ledge, but her fingers slipped in the dust. Gravity claimed her full weight just as Nate miraculously clasped his hand around her outstretched forearm and Kerri dove to catch Nate's leg and Tim ran to grab Kerri's foot.

At the other end of that line, Andy hung a few meters above evaporation, sweat sizzling down her back as she looked up and Nate gave her back a smile.

"We're not splitting up, are we?"

A plethora of besieging Thtaggoalites gathered in the attic and clogged the stairway, eyelessly and brainlessly listening to Dunia Deboën in the center of the floor wasting perfectly good lines on them.

"Come on, you ungrateful bastards! I freed you from hell, I can send you back!"

A wheezer finally replied with a multipurpose, nuance-rich shriek as it ran forward to meet her, leading the final charge.

The foremost one was neatly dodged, a single clean slash through the throat; then followed numbers two and three, who shared a single Zorro cut, but Dunia noticed with surprise that even as the dead piled up, the high morale among the fiends did dwindle not but rather thrived, and soon the eyeless screaming things weren't coming forth in ones or twos but bumrushing the barricades and climbing over bodies too, and Dunia's strikes became much wider, splashing black gore right and left, tornadoing on a single foot, her saber ever bringing death, severing arms and legs and necks in whirling, dazzling pirouettes, and stabbing one only to get her pickax stuck inside its chest—she had to use him as a shield to bump her way out of the press, all this while slashing through more wheezers not expecting to be next, prancing impishly on their corpses toward higher ground ahead, leather boot heels squeezing brains out of the skulls of mangled wrecks—and wheezers welcome it and shriek in glee to join the slaughterfest—forcing Dunia to dive into a jungle of claws out to gut her alive and she's fallen, yet still she just lobs off their legs and they fall to their knees and she rises again and keeps slashing away, and they keep coming roaring clambering piling up, smothering her, reaching her, scratching her, making her bleed, and she knows it, she feels it, lungs wolfing down oxygen, heart pumping at drill speed, muscles overdosing, brain ordering a dash to the left, stab to the right, kick to the stomach, elbow at four o'clock, comeback through the jugular, triple gut combo ahead bonus 10K for style, slice the neck, bash the head, nail the hand, twist inside, eviscerate decapitate mutilate amputate cut it hack it stab it kill it die motherfucker die motherfucker die die die die die die—

* * *

The two-way radio on Nate's belt was beeping.

"Al!" Nate shouted into the microphone, breath rasping its way through the vocal cords as they all sprinted along the tunnels below the lake. "Al, do you hear me?"

Andy paced down to take the radio from him, pushed him forward. "Cap! We're underground and heading back to Sentinel Hill! Do you copy, over?"

The radio cracked, but Captain Al's voice still pushed some words between the noise: ". . . Andy . . . and clear . . . on our way, over."

"Cap, the isle is infested! Dunia Deboën is there—she's the necromancer! Repeat, don't go to the house! Over!"

". . . understood . . . worry . . . bringing a ship . . . soon, over."

"Al, you're breaking up! Did you just say you're bringing a boat, over?"

The last message came loud and clear:

"No. I said a ship. Over and out."

Dunia rolled down from the last mountain of corpses, sinking the pickax into something that gasped, and she found herself unable to take it back. She was beyond extenuation. Beyond ecstasy. Beyond death. But she kept moving.

The penultimate monster still clambered on top of her, missing four out of six limbs, digging its nails into her right arm, snapping its teeth at her turned cheek. She kicked it aside; it bounced back. She ordered her arm to swing the sword at him, and the arm came up empty-handed. The saber was lost.

The torn monster shrieked, tongue whipping her face, while her hand felt through the corpsescape for anything not viscous. She touched wood.

The air, despite the insane smell of quick-rotting viscera, still felt cool and zingy with oxygen, tense like a gas explosion waiting to happen. But it was unavoidable: she had to use a firearm.

She breathed in the last feast of oxygen before death and injected it into her right arm, then clutched Uncle Emmet's shotgun, brought it home, and rammed the barrel into the creature's mouth. Deep down into its gullet where oxygen is unknown.

The definitively ultimate wheezer charged at her at that exact moment, and she rounded on it, a legless hellroach dangling off the point of her gun. The muffled blast liquefied both targets at the same time and sprayed them to the far end of the battlefield, loose chunks of monstermatter pluffing into the gore pool.

Dunia staggered to find a spot of flat wooden floor between the many strata of dead wheezers, panting, waiting for someone else in the room to dispute her point.

Nothing did.

She breathed, dropping the shotgun and sweeping six ounces of blood off her gracious white face.

"And not a single spark was produced."

She pulled her cigarette box from her pocket, chose a lollipop and put it in her mouth. The cherry taste of victory.

And then she turned at the sudden roaring noise coming from the round window.

USAF veteran Captain Al Urich cordially saluted her,

a close-lipped smile on his face, from the right seat of an airborne UH-1C Iroquois helicopter gunship, while with his left hand he popped open the lid of the fire button and thumbed it down.

An AIM-9 Sidewinder missile flashed to life and launched from the chopper, screaming on its brief trajectory to the mathematical center of the circular window.

DUNIA: *(Mostly annoyed.)* Oh, fuck off.

The missile crashed through the glass and into her chest, exploding on contact with the opposite wall.

And thus Deboën Mansion and all of its contents were vaporized from the Western Hemisphere.

The station under Sentinel Hill was still lit from the previous visit, just as the detectives had left it, down to the far echoes of wheezing laughter as they rushed in— one of them incidentally falling to the floor after tripping on the rails.

"Nate, come on!" Andy puffed, picking him up. "Just a little more!" Her own arms could barely help him.

Nate peeped into the adit, caught the wink of one white dot of daylight glowing at the very far end, like a minor star in an obscure constellation.

"I can't do it," he puffed. "Please. Let's take a mine cart."

"The carts are too slow, Nate, it's quicker to run!"

"Not necessarily," Kerri mentioned. Andy saw her kneeling by one of the six-feet-tall oxygen tanks, still loaded onto one of the carts, reading the specs on the side. "Quick, push this onto these rails."

Tim ran behind them, desperate to help as the three pushed a heavy cart along the rails, aiming it toward the adit, until they felt the almost unnoticeable slope was starting to take over. Then Kerri lifted the dog up and dropped him inside.

The whole party clambered on board, struggling for the scarce foot space the oxygen tank left. It rested at the rear of the cart, with Nate and Kerri and Andy and even Tim forced to lean on it and against themselves, Andy caught somewhat off guard by surprisingly happy orange hair on her face.

"We're riding a mine cart," she realized.

"Even better," Kerri said, reaching for a rifle. "I give you the Lake Creature Rocket Wagon."

"Uh . . . I don't remember that move."

"I know," Kerri said, suddenly pulling her by the waist and hugging her tight. "I just invented it."

And then, as the first wheezers poured from the drift into the station, Kerri shot the nozzle off the oxygen tank.

As first experiments go, it didn't turn out bad, even if not completely according to Kerri's calculations. Some aspects exceeded expectations, some didn't. The opening wasn't spectacular, though the sound was deafening from the very start. And even the combined weight of all four passengers on the tank did not prevent it from rattling like a caged mad robot, threatening to rocket off or blow them all up well before the cart wheels reacted to the jet force. But when they finally did, much to Kerri's teeth-gritting satisfaction, the car went in record time from 0 to 5 mph, and on to 20, and on to 80, and on to roller-coaster-on-

Mars velocity, with Tim as the ecstasied figurehead at the prow, wind baring his eyeballs and gums and threatening to rip his flapping tongue off, and the humans' voices rivaling the roar of the gas-belching rocket in a continuous scream while they zoomed through the concrete tunnel, approaching the bewildered light of day.

The cart flew out of the adit mouth, far over the debris slope at the end, hurling the passengers out to free-fall ouching and whoaing and F-word-yelling all the way into the Zoinx River. The freezing water straight from the Cascades was the last but not least of the shocks the ride offered.

Kerri was the first to swim up and locate the rest of the team's heads bobbing up, coughing water, paddling to the rocks.

"Everyone okay?" she polled, aware of how stupid the question was. "This way"—she pointed—"we gotta get back to the lake!"

It was Nate who, as they were climbing back up the slope, dripping icicles, first noticed the trees around.

"I don't hear any birds."

The sky was blank. The world looked like an unfinished oil painting—every rock and reed on the dilapidated banks of the Zoinx neatly detailed, the trees sketched lifeless against an empty canvas. There was no sun nor clouds nor space.

The party ran, or let gravity pull them downriver along the shore, legs slowly awakening from the cold into the agonizing weariness of the last twenty-four hours. Andy viewed the sharp line of the horizon against the white sky and feared they would reach it and simply meet the void beyond the rim of the paper.

What they reached instead was the vast mirror surface of Sleepy Lake, and the fogged-out hills on the other side, and black smoke.

The kids caught sight of the majestic pyre burning where Deboën Mansion used to be, just as the helicopter gunship flew into view.

Captain Al greeted them through the two-way radio. "Morning, detectives. Over."

"Cap!" Nate responded above the deafening cheering of the girls and Tim, in celebration of the one violent deed that they had not been involved in. "Al, I love you, man! You're my hero! Over!"

"Thank you, thank you," the captain said, and Nate was able to spot him among the crew by his grandiose saluting as the helicopter veered their way. "Let us find a landing spot so I can congratulate you in person, over."

"Copy, Al. There's a clearing over there. We'll meet you in—"

The communication was cut exactly then.

On the radio, it was just a spittle of static. But Nate and Kerri and Andy and Tim didn't need the radio: they saw it happen in front of their eyes. They didn't understand it; reason rejected it. But they saw it anyway.

What they saw, altogether spanning no longer than three seconds, was something—a sequoia, an oil derrick, perhaps a colossal snake—darting out of the water, piercing the gunship's sides, curling around it, and bringing it crashing down. In spite of common intuition, the fall was so violent that the helicopter just broke apart against the water. A spinning rotor snapped like a twig and the spark ignited a short-lived fire whose flames swam and choked over the sudden frantic waves while the rest of the helicopter was dragged to the bottom.

It had long disappeared from sight before Andy and Kerri succeeded in boiling down all the impossible interpretations of the thing they'd just glimpsed into some sort of tentacle. And by then, Nate had almost convinced his own confounded brain that the disproportionate, insane, blatantly wrong-sized-for-earth leviathan that had just swatted a four-ton gunship like a fruit fly in front of his eyes was, most likely, one of Thtaggoa's fingers.

PART FIVE

ANNIHILATION

The hills began to rumble. A booming, vibrating, quadruple-bass murmur shook the continent under their feet and the bones in their bodies.

Tim paced in circles, whining at the inconvenience of earth-crust displacement, begging for some comfort. Not that Kerri could give him any: her mind was stuck on the spot on the lake were she had last seen Captain Al, gone in a whiplash—the spot now disturbed by a new, ominously regular pattern of ripples expanding in every direction, to the farthest, tiniest confines of Sleepy Lake, announcing to the world that the dimension of whatever came next would be unprecedented.

Suddenly the earth struck an impossibly low note. It was a single descending pound, so grave the kids felt it in their guts, not their ears, and it had Tim digging his nails into the mud, fur bristled up, and suddenly at some point in the middle of the lake, far from the devastated Deboën Isle, the water dropped.

And then the vortex turned white. Like a massive cloud swimming up to the surface.

Which was exactly what was happening, Kerri thought. A limnic eruption.

The lake was boiling. Microscopic bubbles rose to surface from the black depth, covering the lake with froth, building on it, growing, spreading to the shore, and the fizzing tide began to crawl up, inches first, then feet, suddenly yards, and before the kids could even step back they found the ground flooded up to their ankles, except for Tim, who ran all the way to the trees to escape it, and from there he demanded the lake to go back.

And it did. The waters quickly retreated, yielding half of their conquered territory, while the vortex in the middle only grew.

And then everything stopped.

And then there was the blast, an invisible explosion that knocked the kids from their feet and blew askew all the trees around the shore, all along the perimeter of the lake, for miles.

And when Andy sat up and breathed, her body returned a single, positively unbelievable message: *Breathe what?*

The eruption had swept away every molecule of useful air in a two-mile radius. And the fall had slammed the last lungful of oxygen out of her body.

She suddenly understood that this mental connection was the first of about ten she'd be able to make before passing out.

And that one just now was the second. A genuine waste.

She checked her clothes. She'd been carrying a

respirator around her neck all this time, or so she believed; she'd lost it amid the butchery. She turned to see Kerri and Nate, whom the blast had pushed farther behind. Kerri was clutching her neck. Nate just lay in a pool of lather, gasping like a goldfish.

Tim, farther away, had already lost consciousness. At least.

She staggered up, only to fall back on her knees two steps closer to Kerri, trying not to think how much precious oxygen she'd just wasted to be next to her when she knew there was nothing she could possibly do to help. She couldn't conjure air for her. She couldn't speak. She could hardly move. Her vision fogged up, and her fingers twitched. Kerri registered that, her eyes surrendered to terror; worse, to the assimilation of terror. *Hypercapnia*, the girls lipped to each other. They were flying express through the symptoms. They'd be dead before they knew it.

Kerri's hair became an orange blur. Andy's head dropped down on the mud. It was cold, but she didn't care. She could have sworn her right arm was around Kerri's waist last time she could see that far. She would die hugging her.

That idea became almost tolerable.

A shape inside the orange blob in front of her split from the main cloud.

Not completely orange.

It had black racing stripes.

The 1978 Chevrolet Vega Kammback station wagon, its rigged engine keenly chugging on pure bottled O_2, honked gloriously like a choir of Rapture-announcing seraphim as Joey Krantz behind the wheel banged the windshield and shouted, "Andrea!"

It was a good thing he didn't say Andy. She might not have reacted to her name at that point. But someone who knew her preference insisting on calling her Andrea—that was the trigger she needed; there was a special reserve of energy in her body to deal with that. It was enough to pump some oxygen into her limbs and make her speed-crawl the ten feet separating her from the car, reach inside through the open driver's door, and greedily inhale the biggest, loudest dose of cigarette-stained, dog-smelling, pine-deodorizer-blessed lifesaving air she would ever take.

That one intake was enough to run back to the others, signal Joey to get the Weimaraner, drag both Nate and Kerri across the mud and stuff them on the backseat. Joey tossed Tim on top of them and closed the doors to preserve the oxygen inside. Half a station-wagonful of air was all they had left.

Tim was, amazingly, the first to regain consciousness. Nate needed only to be shaken, but his restitution was much slower; he was hardly moving when Tim started barking madly into Kerri's ear. She still wasn't responding.

Andy pinched her nose and blew air into her lungs, so angrily no observer would ever call it a kiss of life.

ANDY: *(Massaging her heart.)* Kay, come on. Breathe.

JOEY: Andrea . . .

ANDY: *(Still.)* Kerri, don't do this, baby, breathe! *(Dives*

into her mouth, continues to massage.) Come on, baby, breathe.
Breathe.

JOEY: An, you gotta see this . . .

ANDY: *(Crying, bangs fists on her chest.)* Motherfucker breathe!!

Kerri bent up under the punch, eyes open, gasping deafeningly.

ANDY: Yes! *(Hugs her, smothered in bright orange hair charging up, every strand of every curl in high definition.)* Yes!

JOEY: Andrea, we've got a fucking problem!

Andy turned toward the front seat to slap Joey in the head and froze halfway as she caught the landscape. Sleepy Lake had become a maelstrom. But the most remarkable thing was that that wasn't even remarkable. The water mass had unleashed its own storm, but that was happening in the background, behind the line of creatures. At least three rows of them, walking side by side, all along the shoreline. Marching inland.

And they didn't seem to have any trouble breathing at all.

"Move," Andy cued, nudging Joey to the passenger seat. "Now."

"Where the fuck did those things come from?"

"Hang on!"

She clutched, shifted, refused to even make a guess at how much oxygen would be left in the Chevy's rigged carburetor and how many seconds the engine had to live on that before they reached useful air again, and gunned the car backward toward the waterline, wheels spraying mud into orbit, knocking off at least ten wheezers by the sound of their useless skulls cracking open on the station wagon rear while the others joined in a bloodcurdling cry and clung on to the bodywork, claws squealing on the glass, teeth snapping at the side mirror showing Andy's frown as she changed to first and floored the gas, swerving south toward the road.

That offered her the first full view of the eastern shoreline, plagued with an overlimbed gray swarm of wheezers. Only that had already ceased being remarkable too.

The remarkable thing now was emerging from the vortex, a thing for which no one had words and Nate was only able to punctuate with "Holy Satan's crotch."

The wheezers, jumping into the Chevy's path and being bashed away like bowling pins, were kind enough to block the sight of what would have likely rendered the witnesses completely mad. As Andy sharply steered the station wagon to the left and bounced onto a path through the woods, she could afford only the corner of her eye to see it in the mirror, and all she could say was that a mountain, a slithering mountain, had risen from the lake. Nate and Kerri peeped through the back window and still didn't see it fully. They caught some tentacles, or at least one freight-train-long swirling limb, lined with feelers like a giant centipede; and bright red lava flowing through a highway of veins; and Nate even counted five giant trees like baobabs waving on its top, each the rough size of a blue whale, though red in color, and before the woods blocked it out he caught one of them blossoming into a five-jawed mouth, suggesting the notion that all the giant trees were heads. But they didn't really see it, the same way one can be in New York and not see New York. Because you can only see New York in satellite pictures.

Then a wheezer jumped into frame, clinging to the back window like an incredibly grotesque parody of a suction-cup toy, and tried to smash the glass with its head.

The Vega was doing eighty through a meandering, rippling path about six feet wide, and wheezers were raining from the trees, banging on the car, shrieking through the windows. Andy saw one in the mirror running behind them and taking a leap, and felt it landing on the roof.

JOEY: What the fuck?!

KERRI: It's the carbon dioxide; this is their medium!

ANDY: Bump ahead!

The Vega flew off a slope, letting a fir branch swipe off the wheezer on the roof, and landed as gracefully as a buffalo on a quadbike. Another wheezer had clung to the side in the few confused seconds before regaining terminal velocity, shrieking into Kerri's window.

KERRI: Where are our guns?!

ANDY: We lost them!

JOEY: I carry one. (Draws a revolver, greeted with sudden silence.) I wasn't sure if it was gonna help.

ANDY: Well, it can't hurt!

A wheezer's fist suddenly smashed in Joey's window in a new demonstration of peak strength and perfect timing. Joey stopped the alien claw an inch from dissecting him alive, stuck the cannon out, and blasted the creature away.

KERRI: Keep going south! We need fresh air!

ANDY: I'll take the shortcut!

JOEY: That's no shortcut—it's a mountain bike trail!

ANDY: Close enough!

Andy bypassed a turn and swerved south, and the car was flung off the road and into the woods, losing the rear license plate and two yodeling wheezers on the first bump. She kept the gas floored all the way downhill, Attilaing every single bush and bramble and sapling not tough-looking enough to be worth dodging, and landed the station wagon back on track at the other side of the meander, wheels peeling off three geological strata as she steered it back in the right direction and fishtailed on, watching three wheezers stampeding down the same slope after them, landing on the road.

She ran over the one ahead; Joey leaned out to gun down the one in the rear. The one in the middle stuck itself to the left side of the zigzagging car, punching through Nate's window. Tim jumped over Nate to bite the slimy arm, making it lose its grip; the hand clung to the broken glass, the rest of the creature dragging along.

"I need a gun!" Nate shouted.

"I'm out of ammo!"

Tim growled as a fourth unforeseen creature almost jumped through Joey's window, too close for Joey to try to push it out. Andy shouted to use the door; Joey opened it, the creature tried to sneak a second or third arm through the opening, and then Joey pulled it closed again, and once again, and again, and again, until a vicious, slushy crunch and a bump signaled that most of the wheezer had fallen under the wheels.

Nate grabbed the severed limb and used it to bat the wheezer on his side off the car. "Out!"

On the third strike it fell tumbling on the road, splashing black blood over the whitened tarmac. The road was improving.

JOEY: We're clear! *(Frantically seeking confirmation.)* We're clear! *(To the others.)* Jesus fuck, this is what you normally do?

KERRI: Tim, stop it! It's over! Tim! Quiet!

TIM: *(Keeps yapping and pinballing around the backseat.)*

ANDY: We're fine! We're fine, let's try to reach . . .

WHEEZER: *(Leans in from the roof through the driver's window, grabs Andy's face, spreads its jaws attempting to swallow her whole skull.)*

SOMETHING ELSE: *(Crashes against the same side of the car, splicing the wheezer in half.)*

The Chevrolet Vega spun out twice before coming to a full stop, twenty yards from the police cruiser. The creature caught in between lay scattered all along that distance.

Kerri was the first to exit the car and circle it to check on Andy. Blood ran down her head and neck, but she was conscious. Barely sane after the close-up into a wheezer's mouth, but conscious.

"Are you okay?" Kerri inquired. "Andy. Andy, look in my eyes. Are you okay?"

Nate and Joey, the latter toting his revolver, were already limping for the police cruiser. No one had come out of it.

"Gonna need help here!" Nate called.

"I'm okay," Andy said, sighing and swiping the blood off her eyes. "Go check on Copperseed."

Kerri approached the Pennaquick County police vehicle to find the officer conscious as well, despite everything else. The air bag had spared his head. His leg didn't look that good.

"Deputy?" Joey ventured.

Copperseed raised a hand, petitioning for a few seconds to pull himself together. He breathed a couple of times, glanced at his leg, stiffed up his upper lip, and then spoke. "Boy, I'm glad we evacked the town."

"Me too," Kerri panted. "We couldn't stop the eruption; the cloud will hit us soon. We need to go."

"Al and his friends . . ."

"We lost them." She willed a long-due sob back down her throat with a hurried promise of real mourning later.

Joey pointed at the horizon behind them: "Uh . . . guys . . ."

Kerri looked over the cruiser. Over the fir-spiked hills, beyond a swarm of thousands of panicking birds fleeing away, a grayed-out, never-mapped hill had risen. An extraterrestrial karst; a tower wobbling in the wind; a parasitic polyp attached to the planet.

Tim, badly patched up and limping, burst into a desperate howl at the naked sky.

Copperseed intoned, "The undergod's returned."

Andy, in the Chevrolet, squinted at the front mirror.

JOEY: Guys?! What the fuck is that?!

Nate, eyes mutinying and refusing to look away, simply replied, "Apocalypse."

Copperseed turned the key in the ignition. Wasted car parts clattered back to steadiness and the engine roared a groggy *Yessir!*

Andy popped out of the Chevy and raised the dislodged

hood. The oxygen bottle she and Captain Al had attached to the carburetor earlier came off easily in her hand. She tossed it away and tried the ignition. There was plenty of air for the car to run now; it was a matter of determining how much car was left.

The discombobulated Chevy Vega revved once. Twice. At the third call, the engine resuscitated.

"I'm calling in the army," Copperseed told Kerri. "You go south as far as you can get. And don't stop. *(Blocking an interruption.)* Now."

"Wait!" Andy had reversed to level with him. "Deputy, we've got a better chance to stop this if we stay."

"We what?!" Joey yelled.

Andy ignored him. "Deputy, trust us."

Copperseed seemed to disagree, but somehow stetted the suggestion. "You will need a distraction," he said.

"No, Copperseed, you leave town! You hear me?"

Copperseed chuckled as he shifted into reverse and switched on the sirens. "Like I'm taking orders from a teenage detective club."

And with that he U-turned the car and then floored the gas, speeding past any possible reply and back into town. The rest all squeezed themselves back into the station wagon and followed the patrol car ahead blaring toward the empty streets of Blyton Hills.

The police cruiser continued downtown, sirens hollering, while Andy steered the Chevy left and sped down the last stretch on Kerri's street. The gardens were deserted.

A little girl's bicycle lay abandoned on the curb under the blank sky.

Blyton Hills was a ghost town.

The little house with the pink shutters stiffened up like an old hen at the amber Vega screeching onto the sidewalk, discharging a crowd of bleeding, mud-soaked misfits into the garden, all jumping over the gate and running indoors, not one of them bothering to wipe their feet on the doormat.

"Seal and block every door and window!" Andy commanded as she stormed into the living room. "We're barricading in Kerri's room!"

"Are you nuts?" Joey replied. "You expect to lock out that?"

"Them," she corrected from upstairs already. "And they don't know we're here. Yet."

Nate was following her to the second floor and Kerri was taking care of the ground floor. Tim took the penguin Andy had dropped and ran to secure it. Everybody but Joey had something to do.

"Andy, this is crazy! We have a better chance driving out of town!" he shouted, running upstairs and spotting the girls' room at the end of the hallway. "Even if we weather out the cloud, you can't hold back that . . . *(Stops inside the empty room, then spots Andy carrying the mummy of a book, walking past him.)* . . . that fucking mountain, for God's sake—it will crush us!"

Andy rounded on him, nearly shoving him into the wall.

"Nothing bad ever reaches this room! You hear me?! *Nothing!*"

She turned to Nate, who had just stepped in, and threw the Necronomicon at him.

"You! Look for the way to put that thing back to sleep!"

"What?! No, wait, I can't; I'm not a wizard!"

Andy stabbed him with her index finger, shouting at the top of her lungs: "If the town whore from ass-raping Salem put two and two together with the help of that book, so can you! Get rid of that monster! Now!"

Nate digested the line, refused to let it make an impact, and turned to Kerri as she walked in.

"I can't do this."

"Nate, I can't even pronounce its name," she said, grabbing his shoulders. "You've been preparing for this for thirteen years."

Nate fell silent. His body took the pause to remind him how dangerously far behind in medication, food, and sleep he was, while his mind just wandered around Kerri's room.

"Clear everything away," he said. "We need a pentacle."

Andy rolled up the carpet and instructed Kerri and Joey to push the furniture out of the way, while Nate went through the pencil jars on the girly desk and chose a red crayon to start tracing a wide circle on the floorboards. After that he offered another crayon to Kerri and showed her a grimoire page for reference.

"Draw this one here, facing that wall, then this one with the horns in that corner. Andy, I'll need candles."

"First drawer," Kerri assisted as she started drawing a monogram.

"I know," Andy said, going for the aromatic candles Kerri kept in her desk and a match in her pocket.

The whole thing took some three minutes to set up.

"We need a signature now, from all of us," Nate panted, standing up. "Choose a point of the star each; use your blood!"

He needed only to squeeze one of the many fresh gashes across his arms to produce some drops of thick, bright blood on the floor; Kerri and Andy did the same.

Joey stood awkwardly over his own point of the star.

JOEY: Uh . . . I am not bleeding.

Andy jumped across the pentacle to punch his face, Kerri stopping her fist an inch from connecting.

KERRI: Ah ah ah! Hair will do, I think.

Andy drew back grumbling while Joey made a big deal of Kerri plucking a pinch of hair from behind his ear.

"That's four," Nate said. "We need five."

"We don't have five," Andy objected.

"Dunia needed five to wake it up; we'll need five to put it down!" Nate insisted.

Andy turned to Kerri. Kerri to Joey. Joey to Nate. Nate to Kerri. Kerri to Andy. Andy to Joey.

Then all four glanced down.

Tim, sitting on the last corner of the pentacle, dropped the plastic penguin over the red line and smiled broadly at them, thankful for the attention.

Kerri raised a brow at the wet, tattered toy and concluded: "Saliva counts too, I guess."

"But he's a dog!" Nate complained. "I'm pretty sure the specs call for five *human* summoners!"

"It's the best next thing! Adapt!" Andy ordered.

Nate flipped through several dry, stiff pages in the book,

looking for the annotations he'd noticed while examining it the previous evening.

"Just so you know," he mentioned, "I know a college professor who ended up in the loony bin for just staring at this book too long."

"Well, you fucking came out of the loony bin a week ago, so that's work done in advance!"

"I doubt the professor would have done very well in the creature-splattering bit, Nate," Kerri told him. "Give yourself some credit."

Pencils rattled in their jars. Tim barked.

Joey popped out of the circle to lean toward the window. "God, it's getting closer. *(Turning.)* Nate! It's getting closer!"

"Yes, I fucking heard!" He flipped back a couple pages, then read across a note. "Okay, what we're trying here may not put it to sleep again, but it's said to push it back where it came from."

"The lake," Kerri guessed.

"No, where it first came from. But remember, the second I start reading these spells, the wheezers will spot us."

"They've got no way in," Andy said after dragging the dresser in front of the door. She returned to the circle, between Kerri and Joey. "Read."

KERRI: *(Pocketing the lighter.)* Read.

JOEY: *(Firmly.)* Read.

TIM: *(Pants encouragingly.)*

Nate, kneeling over, made sure the candles were properly arranged and started reciting: "'Ngaïah Adolon, Ngaïah Metraton, Ngaïah Zariatnatmik, Kheïa 'nthropapena,

Kniga Necronomnkon, Thtaggoa ishta nukflarr suk'lzark'ui methragamnon!'"

Tim barked a loud four-letter word at the sudden thunder that made the butterfly displays flutter on the walls. Kerri, Andy, and Joey turned to the dormer window to see the booming sound reverberating away, the shock wave fading down the trees on their street.

And then, from the silent aftermath of that thunder, rose the distant, ultrasonic, hypermassified shriek of a hive-minded, saw-larynxed Doomsday army zeroing in on the enemy.

"Tim, stay in the circle!" Kerri ordered. "Tim! Shut up and sit! Sit!"

"'Ia Melekemnis, Geïadhar laïak sekh zfr'khack'ui . . .'"

"Tim, sit! Joey, hold him!"

Thunder boomed in the north, perhaps a mile closer by Andy's reckoning. She wanted to block her ears, not at the sound of a mountain moving, not at the wheezers, but at the words that Nate was reading. She couldn't understand them, but she could read in Kerri's eyes the confirmation that she wasn't imagining it: the words sounded forbidden; they poisoned the air around them; they gave her nausea. They didn't talk to her, but something buried deep in her genetic memory was eavesdropping and was extremely shocked.

"'Ganna sabakhhazk'ui, mlif nglk'ui, Ia Melekemnis gizranabakhhaztuk! Ngaïah Adolon, Ngaïah Metraton . . .'"

KERRI: You read that already!

NATE: I gotta do it three times!

ANDY: Shut up and go on!

Joey, wincing at the sound of the spells, struggled to hold Tim in place.

"Come on, boy, here, stay. Look, you like the penguin?"

He squeezed a peep out of the doll. Tim nearly bit his hand off upon recovering it and curled up around it in the pentacle, shielding it from another clap of thunder shaking the house.

Nate speed-read through the verses, returning to the first line for the third time just as Kerri peeked through the window.

"They're here!"

Andy made out three or four creatures racing down the street. The speed they were able to reach scared her, but the impunity with which they dared run through the streets of Blyton Hills, how they skipped over the fences, how they trod on the amber station wagon parked in front, which in the last few days had so seamlessly fitted in the neighborhood—that had her clenching her fists until the bones cracked.

"Are we sure the doors are blocked?"

"'Ia Melekemnis'—don't leave the circle now—'Geïadhar Thtaggoa . . .'"

"How do they know where we are?!" Joey cried.

"The spells attract them," Andy explained.

"'Ia Melekemnis, gizranabakhhaztuk!'" Nate flipped the page. Andy gaped at the amount of lettering contained on the next.

"All that?! Are you fucking kidding me?!"

"What did you expect?! It took Dunia like a whole night!"

A thunderbolt crashed, literally, not far away from the

town. They could make out the sound of crushed trees in the echo.

"Wait!" Kerri yelled. "It took Dunia all that time because she was the only willing participant. We can read too, right?!"

Nate glanced over the notes, tore them out of the book and distributed them.

"You read this, you this, you this. Pronounce like it's badass Italian; *kh* is Jalisco, *zh* is Jean-Jacques." Something banged the door downstairs. "Go!"

Kerri and Joey joined him immediately, their own words pronounced too quick to even let someone notice the difference; Andy checked the first word and almost panicked.

"'Nara . . . Nyara . . .'"

KERRI: Just read, I'm sure whoever's listening won't complain about your diction!

"'Nyarlathotep nemumfur, sum jag'rwi kjagadar uzuzwi nekrogradin . . .'"

Something made of glass just ceased to be in the living room downstairs.

"They're inside!"

"Read!"

Tim started barking again—the only thing that wasn't causing noise at that point was the plastic penguin he was protecting. Everybody was reciting verses that thickened the air and condensed on the walls; creatures berzerked through the first floor; thunder multiplied, splitting timber and rock, destroying the world outside, creeping up the Richter scale, blocking the light. Andy noticed the shadow cast over the paper she was reading.

Nate finished his verse and flipped the page, the others hurrying down their lines to keep up. Kerri finished first, then Joey; Andy sped through a couple consonant clusters and tossed her paper on the floor just as something started slamming on the bedroom door.

"Nate?"

The dresser blocking the entrance signaled it would come apart at the next blow!

"'Lamakomn ngufli charkflk'ui, ngaïah, ZHRO!'"

The house instantly quieted. Tim, embarrassed by the silence, lay down.

Kerri and Andy locked eyes, recognizing the jagged breathing sound coming from the other side of the wall.

"Nate?" Kerri whispered.

"All that's missing is the aklo backward," he said. "It's gotta be here somewhere."

"What the fuck is an aklo?" Joey asked while Nate turned over the page, devoid of side notes.

Something bony and sharp began scratching the door.

KERRI: Well?

NATE: It's not here.

KERRI: What?!

NATE: The aklo is missing! Dunia must have known it by heart; she summoned the thing while the book was here!

The new hill two blocks from there howlretched, for lack of a real word. The solid, blazing, ear-shattering noise blew the curtains in the room and knocked the butterfly displays off the wall.

"Wait! Wait!"

Every human, canine, and plastic eye focused on Andy, who was staring back at the dog.

"The aklo . . . it's the part of the ritual that Dunia was reciting when Wickley interrupted her thirteen years ago, right? So it's what Wickley heard! It's what got stuck in his head and he repeated it to me when I put him under pressure!"

Everybody held their breath, lest their respiration distract her.

"Which . . . backward would be something like . . . 'Zhro . . . ng'ngah'hai . . . nekrosunai mwlgn iä Thtaggoa fhtagn iä!'"

The words puffed out the flames on the candles.

Silence conquered the room. Andy stared at Tim, Kerri and Nate at the broken display cases on the floor, Joey at the door that had fallen silent.

Then it rattled softly, but the breathing of the creature outside increased.

Outside their window, Thtaggoa groaned.

Faraway, scattered wheezer squeaks began to pop up here and there, some fading into distant screams, different from the crazed, cannibal rage that the kids and the dog had learned to respect. It was a new kind of wheezer vocalization they had never heard.

It was their fear.

Andy queried Nate, stepped out of the circle, and looked out the window.

The street was empty.

Then her heart jumped to her mouth when a wheezer

appeared in the window, shrieking, not at her, but past her, flying against its will from over the house's roof.

She opened the window and leaned out as Kerri and Joey and Nate joined her. Two more six-limbed creatures rolled out of the first floor and into the garden, bouncing off the walkway, as though a silent, invisible hurricane were dragging them through the neighbor's yard, heading northwest, in the general direction of something that glimmered green on the horizon. A star that had never been there before.

The crying from the wheezers increased in volume and pitch, rising too high to hear for everyone except Tim, who was too interested to even turn his ears away. And their cries were accompanied by the ebbing, throbbing, rock-splitting howl of the cyclopean undergod standing behind the house, mercifully out of sight, its poisonous shadow cast over Blyton Hills now dissolving.

Kerri and Joey and Nate turned suddenly as the banging on the door increased, in time to see it blow off its hinges, toppling the dresser, and they ducked to dodge the wheezer that was fired overhead across the room, out the window, pulling Andy with it.

Kerri barely gripped Andy's waist in time as she was lifted off the floor, with Nate and Joey and Tim grabbing her in turn, and then they all felt the hurricane blowing around them, deafening, devastating, trying to snatch them from Earth's gravity and drag them toward a star beyond the explored universe.

Andy, half her body out the window, stared into the gaping, eyeless, terrified face of the creature flapping out in the vortex like a kite in a tornado, digging a claw into her arm, boring into her bones, having decided to carry her along to its exile off this galaxy cluster simply because fuck you, Andy Rodriguez.

She glanced back, and she saw Kerri, and she read *Hold on* in the lips she'd kissed only once, her own lips crying *Please no* as one of Kerri's hands let go.

And then it returned. Carrying a knife.

Kerri stabbed the wheezer's paw so hard that Andy felt the blade prick her own arm beneath and uttered an ouch of pure joy as the wheezer lost its grip and fell away, spinning, through the enormous worm body of Thtaggoa, now corrupted into subatomic particles carried like dust by the cyclone surrounding the shrieking miserable wheezer and its blasphemous brethren as they crashed through the garden and the town and Pennaquick County and Oregon and over the ionosphere in Canada and out of Earth's gravitational pull, cruising at lightspeed past the moon and Mars and the asteroid belt and the orbits of Jupiter, Saturn, Uranus, Neptune, and Yuggoth, ripping wormholes through space and being spat out at the far end of the solar system, their agonizing cries heard for the last time as they passed through a gas nebula in the constellation of Virgo before squeezing through a physical paradox leading to a barren dead region of outer space.

The green star appeared to blink and disappear from the horizon several seconds after the portal outside Mars's orbit had actually closed, having swallowed the very last piece of Thtaggoa's spawn and Thtaggoa itself.

The Blyton Summer Detective Club stumbled up from the floor in Kerri's bedroom. The firmament was filling up again. The white veil was lifting, painting a blue sky grazed by fat smuggled-sheep clouds.

All four, plus a dog, stood in their sloped-ceiling bunker, wordless, contemplating the end of war.

Then Andy clutched Kerri's waist and shot into her mouth the most violently soft, bloodily sweet, furiously rainbow-waving kiss either had given or received, flooding her tongue with summer rain and lime dew and tropical tidal waves.

She pried herself apart, a string of saliva unbroken between their lips, orange hair gasping in awe, and pointed her index finger at Kerri's nose.

ANDY: *And* you and I are gonna try skydiving this summer. All right?!

Tim smugly trotted off the scene to tell his penguin everything was fine.

They walked out into the first morning after the apocalypse—a day that had just barged in sweaty and unkempt like a late commuter, asking, *Anything happen while I was out?*

A lazy rain began to wash out the defiled streets, all casual and gleeful like a late authority figure at the end of a teen detective story.

They roamed into the middle of the road strewn with tree debris, overall not worse than your average rock star's hotel room. That mild impression lasted until Joey pointed out the hillside in the north, at the beginning of Kerri's house row. The last time they had seen that hillside, luscious dark green woods covered it completely. Now it was a great expanse of exposed earth, salted with the stumps and corpses of a razed forest. Thtaggoa's path of destruction came from beyond the hill, where the sky was still sore and veiled by frayed clouds of smoke, and stopped two yards short of Kerri's backyard. Its width was too much to measure from the ground.

"Holy shit," Andy appreciated. "That was cutting it close, Nate."

Tim called their attention from the other end of the road, where a white car had pulled over to the sidewalk and crashed into the side of a parked Chrysler. They recognized it immediately, even though it had lost the sirens. Several sets of claw marks, fingers two inches apart from each other, were etched all across the roof and the sides, striking out the county seal. Smoke poured from under the warped hood.

Andy jogged toward it and leaned through a shattered window.

"I'm fine," Deputy Copperseed said before she could lay a finger on his wrist. He was barely sitting up, drenched in reddened sweat. "I tried to lure them away, but they really liked your house. And then, while they were flying back, they got attached to my car too. Dragged me all the way from Main Street."

Andy nodded, turned to signal to Kerri and the boys that the cop was all right, and then she glanced at his left leg. Operating the pedals with that broken kneecap must have been tricky, she thought.

Coincidentally, that was the last clear idea in her mind before her own legs began to ring and suddenly yielded. She fell on the asphalt, back against the car door, and an insane number of overdue injury reports from all over her body finally flooded the complaint department.

"Oh fuck," she gasped, overwhelmed by fatigue.

Tim approached her, a sympathetic look in his own bloodied, ear-torn face. She lifted a bruised, blood-streamed hand and caressed his nose.

"Good job, soldier."

"What are you doing sitting down there?" the policeman mocked her, peering through the window. "Get in. I'll drive you and your friends to camp."

"No. No thanks," she pushed out between puffs. "We'll just stay here."

"Are you sure? The army will be here any minute," he said. It might have been sarcasm, Andy thought; it was hard to tell with Dirty Harry types.

"It's okay," she murmured, gazing at the rest of the team standing near Kerri's house. "We've got a bunker here."

The others stood under the gentle drizzle and fresh morning sun, eyes still lost on the desolation road on the hillside.

NATE: You know what would be a brilliant twist now? If everything turned out to be just a guy in a mask.

Kerri laughed first; it was the kind of humor that ran in the family. Joey came to it a little later. About to surrender to her own fatigue, Kerri rounded on Nate and hugged him tightly.

"I am so proud of you," she whispered. "Peter would be so proud of you."

Nate said nothing. Instead, he looked past Kerri's hair, at the jock standing by them. He leaned out a hand for him.

Joey inspected it first, smudged with human blood and alien blood and who knows what else, and checked that his own did not look much better, and they shook.

"We okay now?" Joey asked.

"We okay. Thank you, man."

Joey gazed back at the scarred hillside. Beyond it, far away, black smoke billowed up.

"You think the lake is still there?" he wondered. "My father's gonna kill me if something happened to the motorboat."

"He'll be fine when you show him what's in the glove compartment," Kerri commented.

The boat was not afloat, as a matter of fact: the tidal wave caused by the undergod rising had hurled it to the shore, actually into the woods, unmolested by everything that came later. The glove compartment was still locked, four gold ingots safe inside, guarded by the vigilant firs.

Across the waters, Deboën Isle was now a pile of ruins, the trees there conspiring for the best way to bury the ton of bricks and mortar under their roots and pretend that the last two centuries had never happened.

A brave little bird was the first to descend to the isle and check the air quality for itself, only hours after the cataclysm. It was used to this dangerous task. It had worked as a mining canary for a whole day.

First, it perched atop one of the firs on the isle, rocked by the breeze, then fluttered farther down, chirping for animal life, to alight on a little mount of blue shingles. From there it hopped onto a jutting split beam, still warm from the recent fire the waves had extinguished, and then it skipped along the scattered bricks of what had been a chimney onto a leather boot, from which it could survey the eastern and southern shores. The water level was a little lower, although the scouting canary did not consider asking for an official calculation that might have stripped the lake of the title as the second deepest in the Americas.

Suddenly the leather watchtower collapsed under the canary's feet, and the poor scared thing barely held itself in the air, heart skipping a beat out of 200 per minute, as it scurried out of the way of the awoken mammal jacking up from the grave, spraying stone and timber.

Tarantula fingers, burned down to their phalanxes, caressed the bricks around their burial site as she scanned the landscape, the black eye in the whole half of her face taking in the glorious cobalt-blue sky, a rainbow, a panicking yellow bird fluttering by in the immaculate morning quiet.

DUNIA: Shit. Did I miss it?!

Summer came early and yellow and mint-flavored. Nate grabbed a two-liter Diet Coke from the fridge while he skimmed through the *Pennaquick Telegraph* and observed that the accustomed reports on roadworks around Belden had finally bumped the Blyton Hills incident off the front page. An item dealing with the outraged defense statement from RH Corporation, entrenched on defending the safety of its lost chemical plant, had been moved to page four. Poor smeared ecovillains.

Nate paid for the newspaper and the groceries, jumped on his bicycle parked on the sidewalk, and headed home, with Tim scouting ahead and deviating from course every now and then to dissolve suspicious groups of pigeons. The detectives didn't make it into the papers this time. Kerri and Deputy Copperseed agreed that it was better to wait for the authorities to string their own interpretation of the events. Once Kerri tipped the words "limnic eruption" to FEMA personnel, the official version clung to that rare but not unprecedented phenomenon and pointed at the frequent seismic activity in the area as the probable cause behind both the explosion in the abandoned chemical plant and the violent gas leak from Sleepy Lake, which in turn had poisoned the pilot of a rescue helicopter assisting the evacuation, crashing it against Deboën Mansion. Scientific tests performed around the area confirmed its affinity with the incident in Cameroon, and the media agreed that the prompt evacuation of Blyton Hills had saved hundreds of lives.

As for public opinion in Blyton Hills, the proverbial hostility toward RH Corporation and Dunia Deboën, who had mysteriously disappeared before the town evacuation, kept suspicions from attaching to the Blyton Summer Detective Club.

Military funerals were held for the whole crew on the helicopter: USAF Captain W. B. Ainslie, First Lieutenant B. C. Grand, and veteran Captain Al D. Urich, with full honors. Deputy Sheriff Copperseed of the Pennaquick County Sheriff's Office and the Blyton Summer Detective Club attended. Andy Rodriguez was presented with the flag from Urich's coffin. She kept it folded on top of all the trinkets inside his cookie tin of BSDC case mementos.

The way everybody, including the media, had embraced the official explanation and neglected loose ends that clearly deserved further inquiry (such as the hardly random distribution of squashed trees in a twenty-mile-long straight path from Sleepy Lake to Blyton Hills) had kept Nate wondering for some time—particularly after reported sightings of a colossal disturbance among the hills, coming from as far as Brish Quarry, forty miles north, were so quickly dismissed as hallucinations caused by mild hypercapnia. It was as if authorities, or some authorities, had been too swift to provide explanations for a story that seemed not to have caught them completely by surprise. Maybe, Nate thought, the Necronomicon and its mythos were known outside scientific circles and sci-fi aficionados by people in relevant positions who did not take them as a mere historic curiosity. Or maybe Nate was missing the comforting Saturday morning harangues of conspiracy theorists in the low-security floor of Arkham.

His train of thought was derailed by Joey Krantz knocking on the window of Ben's Corner as he rode by. He stopped by the curb and waited for him to scoot out, in apron and hat.

"Hey. Have you seen the *Telegraph*?"

"Barely. Got it right here."

Joey stole his copy from the basket, flipped to page four. The one column not part of the item led by "RH Speaker Digs Company Deeper into Disrepute" dealt with some mysterious occurrences in the abandoned amusement park in Sossamon Valley. Nate didn't read past the first paragraph.

"So what?"

"So what? One guard's gone missing, the other talks about an evil clown sabotaging the rides. Sounds like our next case."

"Sounds like two assholes stealing aluminum," Nate retorted.

"Probably, but not every case's gonna be all car chases and creatures from the underworld," Joey said, with an interesting mix of relief and resignation. "You should tell the girls about this."

"They're very busy," Nate lied.

"Oh, come on. I'm taking two weeks off in July; we should look into this."

"Okay, okay, I'll pass it on to them."

"Do it!"

"I will, promise. See you, Joey."

"Okay, bye. Bye, Tim!"

He hurried back into the restaurant as Nate pedaled back onto Main Street. On the other hand, in a country where the words "evil clown" still made it into the local paper, how could "limnic eruption" not sound convincing?

He raced Tim for the last blocks, the dog kiting ten inches of tongue happiness behind him and a single tattered ear flapping in the air. Fur had grown back over his flanks, concealing his scars as much as they ever would. Still, he wore them with pride.

They came into view of Aunt Margo's house, windowsills brimming with orange helenium flowers. Rivaling them, the freshly waxed Chevrolet Vega Kammback wagon shone boastfully on the driveway, black racing stripes darkening its brow like the memory of past battles. Nate had to shield his eyes from the glint as he closed the little gate door behind him and entered the house.

They parted ways inside, Tim running upstairs while Nate popped into the kitchen to unpack the groceries and get a knife. Then he crossed the living room to the new screen door to the backyard. Aunt Margo was bound to freak out when she saw this part, but they had asked for her permission. And she would have to admit the white stone pavement outside helped lighten up the living room.

Kerri and Andy were just where he'd left them and where they'd spent the afternoon and most of May: lounging on the deck chairs by the lustful blue swimming pool, water glistening like an Oscar nominee's sequined dress under the Tom Jones of suns; Andy's dark skin indifferent to ultraviolet rays, Kerri's impervious to them, a childish smile on both their faces that not even a month of pool enjoyment had managed to wear off.

Nate unbagged the Coke while Kerri talked on the (also brand new) cordless phone.

NATE: You two are the most spoiled heroines I ever worked with.

ANDY: Shh. *(Re: the phone in Kerri's hand.)* University.

NATE: *(Loud, into the phone.)* She's so spoiled! Give her a job, for God's sake!

KERRI: *(Laughing, shielding.)* Ah, you prick. *(On the phone.)* Sorry. Mad cousin. We're mailing him back to Arkham first thing tomorrow.

ANDY: *(Serving the refreshments.)* Where's Tim?

NATE: Upstairs, with me. I told you, he doesn't like the new lake.

(He goes back inside.)

ANDY: *(Gazing over the pool.)* Can't figure out why.

KERRI: *(On phone.)* Okay, I'll come for a tour then. No, no, thank *you*. Sure. Thanks. Good-bye.

She hung up, sipped on her soda, and for a while basked in the recent praise, pretending nothing happened. Andy watched her, spying smugness behind Kerri's sunglasses.

"Well? Which was it this time?"

Kerri flipped her hair, waited for her own ego to ebb down a little. "Berkeley."

"Ooh. You really like Berkeley."

"Yup. Amazing how many doors a spec paper on carbon dioxide–breathing cells will open."

Andy noticed her smile fading out.

"What's up?"

"Berkeley is a little far, isn't it?"

"Nah. Must be a . . . six-, seven-hour drive?"

"I thought Copperseed was supposed to help you with your criminal record—when are you gonna be able to get on a plane?"

"I don't know; when are we gonna jump off one?" She sat up, pointing at the imaginary scoreboard. "Boom! In your face, Kerri Hollis!"

(Laughing.) "Shit, I don't even know whether this is literal or not anymore and I'm afraid to ask at this point; it's so embarrassing. *(Beat.)* No, but seriously. It's a little too far from . . . this."

Andy understood what "this" implied. The house and the swimming pool could wait; one had waited for thirteen years, the other they had waited for even longer. "This," however, was beautifully delicate.

"I could come along," she said.

"You would?"

"Why not? I could find a job in San Francisco. We'd rent a studio. Drive here on weekends."

"A one-bed studio?" Kerri smirked.

"Would you rather have two beds?"

"No."

"Then one it is."

Andy closed her eyes and pointed her face to the sun, declaring the subject settled.

Kerri instead faced her, raising her sunglasses. "I feel a little bad for you."

Andy turned again, a twenty-five-year-old woman in a bright saffron bikini, lying on a deck chair two feet from a paid-in-cash swimming pool: "Kerri, tell me how anyone can feel bad for me right now."

"Andy, I know this is not what a normal girl-girl relationship is like."

"This is not any girl-girl relationship; it's a you-me relationship. There has never been a precedent; there has never been a normal. There has never been a better either."

"But I feel like you're waiting until I allow something to happen."

Andy sighed, stretched out a hand across their chairs.

"Baby, I'm not waiting until you allow anything."

Kerri's fingers reached to latch on. They held hands for a few seconds, like they would often do, and said nothing.

Then Andy dissolved the handshake, took a sip of Coke, and added: "I'm waiting until you beg."

And the imaginary scoreboard went up another point, while Kerri stared in awe and orange curls went simply mad.

"You . . . you bitch and your one-liners. Where did you . . . ?" she argued, while the camera drifted away from them. "Don't give me smiles; how am I supposed to leave you alone in San Francisco eight hours a day?"

"*V.*"

"No, stop it with the word games. *V,* what? It's probably . . . 'vagina,' I bet!"

"What?! No, it was 'voluptuous'!"

"Fuck off!"

"Honestly, Kay, you're obsessed!"

"Shut up, Andy Rodriguez."

Their voices faded away as Nate closed the window to the backyard and returned to the half-drawn diagram on the boys' room floor.

He took one of the eggs he'd just bought, cracked it, poured it in a bowl, and placed it in the center of the circle, left of the Sign of Clairvoyance. Then he went on to his signature: with the kitchen knife, he drilled a wound on his fingertip and smudged his own blood on the south edge.

The Seal of Zur was ready, if he had correctly interpreted the notes in the grimoire and Old Acker's advice. All that was left to do was light the candle (one was enough for a small seal) and burn the parsley leaves.

"Okay. Tim. Come here, boy."

Tim, cuddling with his penguin in a corner of the room, looked up, scarcely interested, but decided to see what the fuss was about. He sat down where Nate indicated, in the middle of the drawing, and awaited the next command.

Nate, on his knees, drew back from the circle, dragged the Necronomicon closer, and read aloud:

"'Per Anemai, per Ngovalis, Ab Vrna Driadha quaeso spiritua dh'flui Zur vsathla uthurragathik.'"

He paused for a reaction from the earth's tectonic plates. They refused to comment.

He set aside the grimoire and faced the Weimaraner, his own eyes slightly above the dog's ghostly blue ones.

"I am very sure that the ritual to summon or expel Thtaggoa required five human souls," he told the dog. "Not animals. Otherwise, Dunia could have just tossed a hedgehog, a dung beetle, a toad, and a smuggled sheep inside the pentacle and gotten it over with. So, if the ritual worked with you . . . if there is an avatar inside this vessel, then show yourself," Nate concluded.

A thin slice of summer afternoon flew by. Tim's attention drifted over the ceiling, then over Nate's jeans, then at some scar on his hip that still itched from time to time.

Nate insisted: "Just tell me who you are."

Tim looked at him, eye to eye, his Byronian visage peacefully sliding into a solemn acknowledgment.

Nate clenched a fist when he saw the Weimaraner's loose lips stiffening up, then deliberately moving.

"I am Ashen Fox," the dog said. And like in the aftermath of a nightmare, in a split second Nate captured the unfakability of the event, all the meticulous details that made it real: the slim tongue cooperating with the tiny front teeth, the droopy lips helping, the voice not essentially different in pitch from Tim's barks, the pale blue eyes unequivocally addressing Nate as an equal. "Third Moon Shaman of the Walla Walla, from the Sky City in the Warm Snows."

Nate tried to swallow that revelation, forced it down his throat, then spoke again.

"You helped us with the ritual. You told Andy about the

aklo. No way she could remember that on her own."

"I simply helped her recall the words she had heard. You are a powerful sorcerer, Nate Rogers."

Nate made sure to record that compliment.

"How long have you been here?"

Tim answered, words blown gently out of his mouth like the whisper sound of a summer breeze on firs. "You did raise an avatar from a jar of salts that night when you were a child. They were my salts, prepared by Deboën from the remains he stole from my burial site. They were still on his workbench when you wandered in, read the spell, and brought me back."

Tim licked his leg. The itch must have been too much.

"Your dog was kind enough to serve as my vessel," Ashen Fox added. "Please do not feel deceived: he has been your dog all this time. I just ride along."

"But that was Sean," Nate argued, fearing the next answer. "Sean was the dog we took to the house thirteen years ago; not Tim. Tim is his great-grandson."

"Well, as Deboën told you, aging forth and back is not difficult. Switching ourselves with one of the younger cubs is. It became easier once Kerri left for college and went months without seeing us." Tim shrugged, a bittersweet smile in his mouth. "You know. It's all been done before."

ABOUT THE AUTHOR

Edgar Cantero is a writer and cartoonist who was born in Barcelona in 1981. Once a promising author in the local scene with his awarded 2007 debut *Dormir amb Winona Ryder*, the highbrow Catalan literary tradition soon lost influence on him in favor of Hollywood blockbusters, videogames and mass-market paperbacks. *Meddling Kids* is his second novel in English; his first was *The Supernatural Enhancements*. His material, ranging from short stories to screenplays, often features women kissing, stuff exploding, and ill-timed jokes.

John Dies at the End

BY DAVID WONG

My name is David Wong. My best friend is John. Those names are fake. You might want to change yours.

You may not want to know about the things you'll read on these pages, about the sauce, about Korrock, about the invasion, and the future. But it's too late. You touched the book. You're in the game. You're under the eye.

The only defence is knowledge. You need to read this book, to the end. Even the part about the bratwurst. Why? You'll just have to trust me.

Unfortunately for us, if you make the right choice, we'll have a much harder time explaining how to fight off the otherwordly invasion currently threatening to enslave humanity.

I'm sorry to have involved you in this, I really am. But as you read about these terrible events and the very dark epoch the world is about to enter as a result, it is crucial you keep one thing in mind:

NONE OF THIS IS MY FAULT.

This Book is Full of Spiders
BY DAVID WONG

WARNING: YOU MAY HAVE A HUGE, INVISIBLE SPIDER LIVING IN YOUR SKULL. THIS IS NOT A METAPHOR.

You will dismiss this as ridiculous fearmongering. Dismissing things as ridiculous fearmongering is, in fact, the first symptom of parasitic spider infection—the creature secretes a chemical into the brain to stimulate scepticism, in order to prevent you from seeking a cure. That's just as well, since the "cure" involves learning what a chain saw tastes like.

You can't feel the spider, because it controls your nerve endings. You can't see it, because it decides what you see. You won't even feel it when it breeds. And it will breed. So what happens when your family, friends, and neighbours get mind-controlling skull spiders? We're all about to find out.

Just stay calm, and remember that telling you about the spider situation is not the same as having caused it. I'm just the messenger. Even if I did sort of cause it.

Either way, I won't hold it against you if you're upset. I know that's just the spider talking.

What the Hell Did I Just Read?

BY DAVID WONG

From the writer of the cult sensation John Dies at the End comes another terrifying and hilarious tale of almost Armageddon at the hands of two hopeless heroes.

It's the story "They" don't want you to read. Though, to be fair, "They" are probably right about this one. No, don't put the book back on the shelf – it is now your duty to purchase it to prevent others from reading it. Yes, it works with ebooks, too; I don't have time to explain how.

While investigating a fairly straightforward case of a shape-shifting interdimensional child predator, Dave, John, and Amy realized there might actually be something weird going on. Together, they navigate a diabolically convoluted maze of illusions, lies, and their own incompetence in an attempt to uncover a terrible truth that they – like you – would be better off not knowing.

Your first impulse will be to think that a story this gruesome – and, to be frank, stupid – cannot possibly be true. That is precisely the reaction "They" are hoping for.

Futuristic Violence and Fancy Suits

BY DAVID WONG

- **NIGHTMARISH VILLAINS WITH SUPERHUMAN ENHANCEMENTS.**

- **AN ALL-SEEING SOCIAL NETWORK THAT TRACKS YOUR EVERY MOVE.**

- **MYSTERIOUS, SMOOTH-TALKING POWER PLAYERS WHO LURK BEHIND THE SCENES.**

- **A YOUNG WOMAN FROM THE TRAILER PARK. AND HER VERY SMELLY CAT.**

- **TOGETHER, THEY WILL DECIDE THE FUTURE OF MANKIND.**

Get ready for a world in which anyone can have the powers of a god or the fame of a pop star, in which human achievement soars to new heights while its depravity plunges to the blackest depths. A world in which at least one cat smells like a seafood shop's dumpster on a hot summer day.

This is the world in which Zoey Ashe finds herself, navigating a futuristic city in which one can find elements of the fantastic, nightmarish and ridiculous on any street corner. Her only trusted advisor is the aforementioned cat, but even in the future, cats cannot give advice. At least not any that you'd want to follow.

Will Zoey figure it all out in time? Or maybe the better question is, will you? After all, the future is coming sooner than you think.

The Anno Dracula series

BY KIM NEWMAN

ANNO DRACULA

It is 1888 and Queen Victoria has remarried, taking as her new consort the Wallachian Prince infamously known as Count Dracula.

ANNO DRACULA: THE BLOODY RED BARON

It is 1918 and Dracula is commander-in-chief of the armies of Germany and Austria-Hungary. The war of the great powers in Europe is also a war between the living and the dead.

ANNO DRACULA: DRACULA CHA CHA CHA

Rome 1959 and journalist Kate Reed finds herself caught up in the mystery of the Crimson Executioner, who is bloodily dispatching vampire elders in the city.

ANNO DRACULA: JOHNNY ALUCARD

1980s America. Dracula has fallen from grace. A young vampire outcast makes a new life for himself in America, but it seems the past might not be dead after all…

ANNO DRACULA: ONE THOUSAND MONSTERS

Japan, 1899. Vampires exiled from Britain seek refuge in Tokyo and are confined to a ghetto. But what secret lies under the Temple of One Thousand Monsters?

For more fantastic fiction, author events, competitions,
limited editions and more

VISIT OUR WEBSITE
titanbooks.com

LIKE US ON FACEBOOK
facebook.com/titanbooks

FOLLOW US ON TWITTER
@TitanBooks

EMAIL US
readerfeedback@titanemail.com